MICHAEL JECKS

The Malice of Unnatural Death

headline

First published in Great Britain in 2006
by HEADLINE BOOK PUBLISHING GROUP

An imprint of Headline Book Publishing

1

Cataloguing in Publication Data is available from the British Library

0 7553 3276 8 (ISBN-10)
9 780 7553 3276 2 (ISBN-13)

Typeset in Times by Avon DataSet Ltd,
Bidford-on-Avon, Warwickshire

Printed and bound in Great Britain by
Clays Ltd, St Ives plc

Headline's policy is to use papers that are natural, renewable and recyclable
products and made from wood grown in sustainable forests. The logging and
manufacturing processes are expected to conform to the environmental
regulations of the country of origin.

HEADLINE PUBLISHING GROUP
A division of Hachette Livre UK Ltd
338 Euston Road
London NW1 3BH

www.headline.co.uk
www.hodderheadline.com

This is for the men of Tinners' Morris . . .

Especially for
Mike and Shelagh Palmer

With many thanks for all the laughs
– and your patience
with us!

Cast of Characters

Sir Baldwin de Furnshill – once a Knight Templar, Sir Baldwin de Furnshill has become respected as a shrewd investigator of crimes

Simon Puttock – formerly a stannary bailiff, Simon has recently been made responsible for the Customs of the port of Dartmouth

Sir Richard de Welles – the coroner for the king at Lifton

Rob – Simon's servant at Dartmouth, Rob is a young lad who has grown up in the company of sailors

Brother Robert Busse – a monk from Tavistock, and contender for the vacant abbacy

Brother John de Courtenay – another monk from Tavistock, and son of Baron Hugh, John is determined to win the abbacy

Robert le Mareschal – a student of the magical arts in Coventry, Robert studies under John of Nottingham

John of Nottingham – known as a necromancer, John is feared even by the most powerful in the country

Walter Stapledon – Bishop of Exeter

Sir Matthew de Crowethorne – Sheriff of Exeter

Maurice Berkeley – the son of Lord Maurice Berkeley and brother to Alice, Maurice has been on the run after ill-advisedly ransacking Despenser properties

Madam Alice	– Sir Matthew's wife, daughter of Lord Maurice Berkeley
Sarra	– a servant girl from the country north of Exeter
Jen	– Sarra's friend, Jen has recently joined her at Sir Matthew's house
Norman Mucheton	– a worker of bone and antlers in the city
Madam Mucheton	– wife to Norman
Elias	– a beadle
Ivo Trempole	– a watchman, who lives with his mother Edie
Michael Tanner	– a moderately successful tradesman, Michael rents properties to those such as his friend Richard de Langatre
Richard de Langatre	– familiar to many in the city, Richard is a fortune-teller famous enough to have even monks from Tavistock come to consult him
James of Wanetynch	– a king's messenger, James has recently arrived in the city with messages for the bishop
Robinet of Newington	– also known as Newt, and once a king's messenger, Robinet has retired now, and is visiting his friend Walter in Exeter
Walter of Hanlegh	– once a king's man, Walter has retired to obscurity in Exeter
Will Skinner	– the watchman down at the southern gate
Madam Skinner	– Will's wife
Sir Richard de Sowe	– a knight in the king's household who was murdered by witchcraft on 28 April 1324
Sir Simon Croyser	– Sheriff of Warwick, and the main official responsible for the arrest of the men involved in the attempted assassination in Coventry

Glossary

Cokini	literally, 'kitchen knaves', the early term for the king's messengers. Later this was replaced by
Cursores	'runner', which must have seemed more suitable!
Maleficium	harm done to another by the use of magic, whether *necromancy*, *sorcery*, *witchcraft*, or *wizardry*
Necromancy	communicating with the dead to tell fortunes or work magic
Nuncii regis	the term for mounted king's messengers
Salsarius	Purveyor of salted meats and fish within Tavistock Abbey
Schiltrom	an enhancement of the Saxon shield-wall, this Scottish development involved the warriors lining up behind a solid wall of shields, bristling with long spears, which could withstand even a cavalry charge
Sorcery	performing magic – usually to do harm – by the use of substances or objects which are believed to be imbued with supernatural powers, often involving certain gestures or spells spoken aloud
Witchcraft	performing magic – again to harm another – by making use of powers which exist within the practitioner. Occasionally may involve the use of objects or spells, but not necessarily
Wizardry	see '*necromancy*'

Author's Note

When I try to think what actually led to a story's forming in my mind, it is often remarkably easy. Usually the court records or coroners' rolls lead me to a basic plot, and then the format of the story, the characters, and sometimes the location, can be conjured up.

This story was a little different. I had been hunting about for some little while for a decent concept for book 22 in the series, because I felt very satisfied with its predecessor, *The Death Ship of Dartmouth*. That book seemed to me to have a strong story, with some excellent action and fresh characters, and I wanted something as strong – but different.

My problem was that the next important piece of history would not be until early 1325, which was some months after the last story. I needed something to fill in the gap. By sheer good fortune, as so often happens, a strange little snippet led me straight to a new plot and the book.

I happened to read in Alison Weir's book *Isabella, Queen of England, She-Wolf of France* a paragraph in which she mentioned a curious assassination attempt. The Despenser was alarmed in late 1324 and early 1325 to learn that Lord Mortimer was paying a necromancer to try to murder him with magic. This, apparently, put the fear of God into him, and he even went so far as to write to the Pope to apply for special protection – to which the pontiff somewhat testily responded that if the man would confess his sins, behave better and stop making enemies, he'd find he felt more at ease with himself. I paraphrase, but the letter's meaning was clear.

It put me in mind of a short paper produced by that marvellous historian, H.P.R. Finberg, called *The Tragi-Comedy of Abbot Bonus*, in *West Country Historical Studies* (David & Charles, 1969), which described the dispute between John de Courtenay and Robert Busse, two monks who contested the abbacy of Tavistock in 1325. In that case, Courtenay complained about Busse's election to the top job for a number of reasons, but one was that he had been visiting a necromancer in Exeter to make sure that he won the post.

That was enough to give me my starting-point. I began to look up necromancers in other books, and soon gained a lot of useful material, especially from Norman Cohn's brilliant study *Europe's Inner Demons*, published by Heinemann Educational and Sussex University. From that I learned much about how magicians would conjure spirits. However, it was a visit to the library and a quick look at the Selden Society books, Volume 74: *Select Cases in the Court of the King's Bench part IV*, that fleshed out the story of the Despenser murder attempt.

The case was exactly as set out in my story here, so I won't perform the tedious act of repetition. Suffice it to say that John of Nottingham never, to my knowledge, escaped from Coventry and Warwick, and I have taken the unforgivable step of suggesting that poor Sheriff Sir Simon Croyser was guilty of trying to free a felon in order to fulfil his ambition of killing the king. Oddly enough, though, other aspects of the story are correct, such as the mysterious illness and subsequent death of Sir Richard de Sowe. His death would appear to have been enough to make Despenser tremble.

As well it might.

From my point of view, only one thing was important here, though, and that was the fact that there was a story begging to be told. I just had to sit down and let the characters tell it their own way.

The subplot of the poor servant girl is one that has been in my mind for quite a while now. I first came across the sad story of Jen when I was reading Elliot O'Donnell's *A Casebook of Ghosts* many years ago.

This fascinating book is the record of a ghosthunter, or purports to be. He came from a long line of illustrious Irishmen, and asserted, I seem to recall, that being the seventh son of a mother who was herself the seventh in her brood he was more than usually prey to ghostly visits. Whether or not this was so, it is certainly true that he was a keen researcher of strange phenomena, and an avid collector of stories from eye-witnesses.

Many of the stories are pleasantly gruesome, as one would hope. However, the story of the young maidservant was peculiarly sad.

He told (so I remember) of a young servant who became infatuated with a guest at the country house in which she worked. All too often in those days, visitors would come to spend a significant time with the family: you need only read Wodehouse to get a feel for the relaxed atmosphere of such places. The young visitor, so O'Donnell wrote, was probably entirely unaware of the effect he had on the young, malleable heart of the servant girl. Without doubt, he was moderately courteous to her, as a public school educated young man would have been to the servants in his host's house, but that was almost certainly all there was to it.

But she convinced herself over a matter of weeks that he was utterly enraptured by her. She began to dream of the day that he would leave, how he would take her away from the drudgery of her miserable working life, and elope with her. They would marry in splendour, honeymoon in Europe, and return to a small house of their own, where they would raise their little family. All this was in her mind.

And when he left? He thanked her, along with all the other staff, and gave her as he gave all of them, a small gratuity. A coin.

She, apparently, was appalled, and stood rooted to the spot, staring at the coin, but then, as the coach door shut behind him and the horses were whipped up, she was heard to shriek. The coach moved off, and she launched herself after it, to the surprise of the others standing by to wave off the young gentleman. No one had any idea of the fixation she had with the man, and to see her fling herself down the driveway after the carriage must have had a terrifying impact. In those days, madness was viewed with horror.

So the upshot of the story was that the girl spent the whole of the rest of her life bemoaning the fact of his departure, predicting his imminent return, and keening to herself in the local lunatic asylum. And in all that time, she never once let his coin leave her hand. Such asylums in those days were not pleasant, and it is sad to consider this poor young woman walking amongst the insane, between those who stood screaming in shackles and the others who lay in their own mess, with no possibility of a cure. It would be many centuries before anyone began to think of psychotherapy.

It was said (which is why Elliot O'Donnell heard of it) that when she died she still had that coin in her hand, and an unscrupulous pair of gravediggers saw it and tugged it from her clenched, dead fist. But they were then hounded by her wraith, which sought her coin all over the asylum and in their homes, and made their lives a misery. The two returned it to her grave at the earliest opportunity, and the ghastly visitations ceased.

I can treat the story slightly flippantly now, but when I was eleven years old, reading that while listening to Neil Young's *After the Goldrush*, it had a significant impact on my impressionable little mind. Neil Young's voice and tracks from that album still have a nostalgic effect upon me.

The story may or may not be true, but I do believe that young girls, young women, call them what you will, can occasionally form these intense bonds with the *concept* of a man or a future. This is something which I have never seen in a male of a similar age. Perhaps it's a gender thing.

So the idea of a young girl who formed an entirely mistaken view of how a social superior regarded her was something that stayed with me for a long while – and I am glad to have exorcised it at last!

I should also apologise to certain other people in this story.

Not only have I unfairly slandered Sir Simon Croyser, who, for all I know, was a perfectly honourable man who served his king with diligence (although from the sheriff's records, that would make him unique), but I have taken liberties with the movements of Sir Maurice Berkeley. He was most certainly on the run at this stage, although whether he ever approached Exeter is pure speculation on my part. The fact that he had a sister and she was married to Sir Matthew de Crowethorne, however, is not speculation. That is the purest fiction!

Finally, by way of an acknowledgement, I should mention the marvellous Jonny Crockett and his team at Survival School in Devon. Without Jonny and his lads, I would never have learned the pleasures of camping without a tent at minus four degrees, of shelter-building, fire-making, and, of course, pulling two pigeons inside out with my bare hands.

Sadly I missed the delights of toasted woodlice, but no doubt that experience is yet to come.

If you would like to experience a genuine survival experience, you can contact Jonny at *www.survivalschool.co.uk*. I can highly recommend them.

And that is enough on how this story came together. As usual I am enormously indebted to my agent, Jane Conway-Gordon, and all those at Headline who helped make this book reach the shelves, and as always any errors are entirely my responsibility – unless they were caused by faulty typesetting, poor editing, over-zealous copy-editing, inefficient proof-checking or other failures by other people.

Michael Jecks
Northern Dartmoor
May 2006

Map of Exeter in Early 1300s

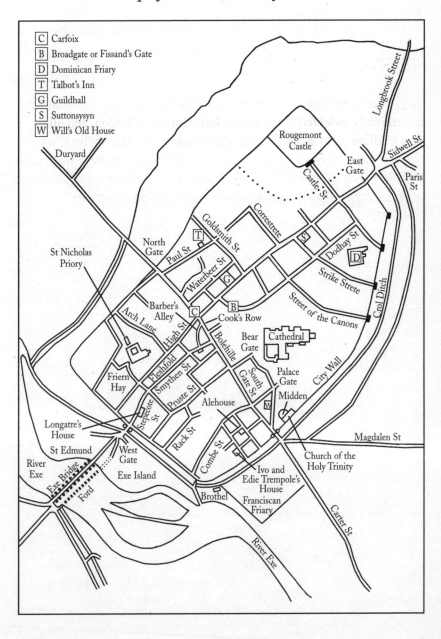

C | Carfoix
B | Broadgate or Fissand's Gate
D | Dominican Friary
T | Talbot's Inn
G | Guildhall
S | Suttonsysyn
W | Will's Old House

Longbrook Street

Duryard

Rougemont Castle

East Gate

Sidwell St

Paris St

Castle St

Correstrete

Goldsmith St

North Gate

Paul St

Dodhay St

D F

St Nicholas Priory

Waterbeer St

Strike Strete

G

Col Ditch

Barber's Alley

Arch Lane

High St

C

B

Cook's Row

Street of the Canons

Bolehille

Bear Gate

Cathedral

City Wall

Fleshfold

Smythen St

Pruste St

South Gate St

Palace Gate

Friern Hay

Stepcote St

Midden

W

Alehouse

Rack St

Magdalen St

Longatre's House

St Edmund

West Gate

Combe St

Church of the Holy Trinity

River Exe

Exe Bridge

Ford

Exe Island

Brothel

Ivo and Edie Trempole's House

Franciscan Friary

Carter St

River Exe

Detail of South Eastern Exeter

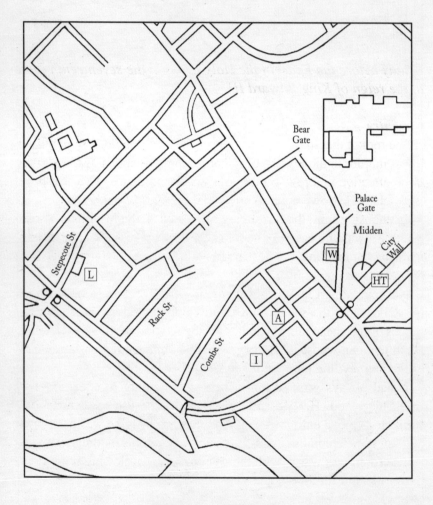

HT	Church of the Holy Trinity
L	Longatre's House
I	Ivo and Edie Trempole's House
A	Alehouse
W	Will's Old House

Prologue

Friday before the Feast of the Holy Cross in the seventeenth year of the reign of King Edward II [1]

Coventry

At the root of that murder there was no jealousy or hatred. If anything, it was murder in the interest of science. A new weapon must be shown to be effective before it can be used with confidence. That was why Sir Richard de Sowe died: to prove that they *could* kill him.

In choosing him, the necromancer had selected a local man whose health it would be easy to ascertain. Sir Richard was a secular knight in the pay of the king, but he had not harmed John of Nottingham. No, *his* death was due to his proximity.

Not that Robert le Mareschal cared about that. No, as he stood in the dark room, the seven little figures illuminated by the flickering flames of the cheap tallow candles all about them, he didn't even think about the man whose death they were planning. He felt only the thrill of the journey: the journey of *knowledge*.

It had always gripped him. There was nothing like learning for firing his blood. He had early heard about the use of demons and spirits to achieve enlightenment, and that was why he was here now, to learn how to conjure them, and have them do his bidding.

The room was warm, with the charcoal brazier glowing brightly in the corner, but for all that, he suddenly felt a chill.

It was as he was holding the figure of de Sowe that it happened. He was thrilled with the experiment and aware of little else, but as his master told him to take the lead pin there was a sudden icy chill in the room. It almost made him drop the doll, but fortunately he didn't. John

---

[1] 27 April 1324

was a daunting man, tall, thin, with cadaverous cheeks and glittering small eyes that looked quite malevolent in the candlelight, and Robert had no wish to appear incompetent in front of him.

'Thrust it into his head,' John said in that quiet, hissing voice of his.

Robert le Mareschal held the pin in his hand and stared at the figure. Glancing at John, for the first time he realised what he was about to do: kill a man. Until that moment his thoughts had been on the power of magic, but now he was faced with the truth. The pin was a three-inch length of soft lead. No danger to anyone, that. Press it against a man's breast and the lead would deform and bend.

'I showed you what to do. Warm it in the candle, then thrust it into his head.'

The necromancer was wearing a simple black tunic with the hood thrown back, and Robert could see the lines about his neck. In this light, his ancient flesh was like that of a plucked chicken, and Robert felt repelled. But the penetrating eyes were fixed upon him, and the gash of his mouth above his beard was uncompromising.

Robert warmed the pin and then, as quickly as he could, he pressed it into the head of the wax model.

When he had been young and attempted something dangerous for the first time, Robert had found that his heart began pounding and his throat seemed to contract; then, as soon as the trial was over, he returned to his usual humour.

Not tonight. It was after midnight when he pushed that cursed pin into the model's head, and the moment he did so the horror of what he was doing struck home. His heart felt as if it would burst from his breast, and he shivered and almost fell.

John of Nottingham took the doll from him and observed it, smiling to himself, holding it gently in both hands almost as a father might study his first son. 'Now, now: you mustn't drop it, Robert. You could hurt him!'

Exeter Castle

Jen finished her work with a feeling of anxiety lest she might have failed in her duties, but when she was done beating the bed's pillows into submission, ensuring that they were plumped nicely, and making them as soft and appealing as she knew how, and had almost finished tying back the beautiful, woven drapery about the bed, she heard the door open, and gaily called, 'Nearly done, Sarra. Leave me a moment, and I'll be out.'

'I am glad to hear it.'

Spinning, her mouth agape, Jen saw that the woman there in the doorway was not her friend Sarra, but the lady of the house. 'Oh! Oh, my lady, I am sorry, I . . .'

'Do not have eyes in the back of your head. I know that.'

Madam Alice looked at her with that emptiness in her eyes that Jen had already come to recognise. In her opinion, a servant was little better than a beetle. Jen curtsied, then hurriedly made her way from the room, all the while under the woman's silent gaze. She felt she was some unappealing, if necessary, feature of the woman's household.

'I didn't see her coming, Jen; I couldn't warn you,' Sarra said in a whisper as Jen closed the door behind her. 'Are you all right?'

'Of course I am – what do you think?'

'No need to snap! I was only making sure that you weren't upset by her turning up like that.'

Jen looked at her. 'I don't know why you all get so upset by her. She's the lady of the house, but she seems perfectly all right to me. She's just a bit too self-absorbed, that's all. She isn't airy-fairy like some, but that's no bad thing.'

'She doesn't talk to us at all.'

'She's spoken to me. She did just then.'

'What did she say? She always ignores me,' Sarra said.

'Nothing. Just that she didn't expect me to know it was her. She was fine. I don't know what you're so worried about.'

'Wait till you've been here a bit longer, then you'll understand.'

'Perhaps I will,' Jen agreed, but she couldn't see why. The mistress was not friendly, but no one expected a great lady to be friendly, not really. Better to be ignored for most of the day, because while you were ignored you weren't looked upon as a pest. The servants who lasted were the ones who could seemingly move among the family of the house without disturbing them. Jen intended being the best of all the servants here.

'Sarra! Sarra, come here. *Now*, you stupid draggle-tail!'

'Oh, saints preserve me! Coming, Steward,' Sarra called. With a sidelong glance at her friend, she hurried into the hall.

Jen continued on her way. She was new to this place, whereas Sarra had been here for at least a year already. But the girl who had helped Sarra had suddenly fallen prey to a disease, and wilted away in a matter of days until she could no longer do her work. She'd been sent home to rest, and in the meantime another girl had to be found. Sarra had recommended her friend Jen, and after a brief interview with the cold-eyed steward of the household, she had been employed.

That was two days ago, and now she was here, living in unfamiliar surroundings with all these new people. It was enough to make any girl of only seventeen years anxious, especially as she was determined to please her new master and mistress.

'Jen, come and help me,' Sarra called, and as Jen walked to help collect up cups and dishes from the table, she almost bumped into her new master. She looked up at him for the first time, and as she met his laughing dark eyes she felt a curious stirring in her heart. It was only with an effort that she managed to pull her eyes away from him, and hurry to help Sarra at the table.

Coventry

Robert le Mareschal slept fitfully. When they had put away the dolls and packed up the potions carefully, he had waited until his master had returned to his chamber before falling on his own cot. He was exhausted, the weariness more than the mere tiredness of muscles or eyes that he was accustomed to. No, this was something much deeper. It was almost as though all the energy in his body had been sucked from him.

As the night wore on, he found himself waking regularly, each time drenched in sweat and fearful, as though he had just had a nightmare. And yet if a mare did visit him, it left no memory of his dreaming. In the morning he felt drained, and yet in his mind he was perfectly clear about his actions and the potential results. If the dolls worked, there would be an end to a dreadful tyranny, and that was surely better than leaving matters as they were.

John of Nottingham had explained that the religious teaching about the devil and his demons was based on a lack of understanding and the

Church's own bigoted animosity towards any kind of learning that was not founded in their own limited understandings. For his part, John asserted that he was as Christian as any man in Coventry. 'Look to the world outside the church, Robert, and you find that there are more truths in this world than priests could ever comprehend.'

However, in the morning, as Robert walked the last few steps to Richard de Sowe's house, his courage began to fail him. From the street outside he could hear the hoarse screams from the shuttered window.

Robert tried to boost his quailing spirit by reminding himself that there was a splendid irony about de Sowe's fate. John of Nottingham had a dry, acerbic wit, and Robert attempted to emulate it now. He reminded himself that throughout his life this man Richard de Sowe had been content to take what he could at every opportunity, willingly using force to steal from those weaker or poorer than he. So now the irony was, that his life was being ripped from him without the motivation even of theft. There was no revenge in this – *nothing*. The assassination of Richard de Sowe was nothing more than an experiment. If John and Robert achieved his death, it would be the proof of the process and other victims could be worked upon.

But this first, slow death *was* hideous. Even as he listened to the demented screaming from the solar, he felt appalled to think of what he had achieved.

'Please, in God's name, help us!' a servant blurted, and Robert jumped. 'Are you all right, Master Robert?'

'I am fine! Don't interrupt my considerations!' Robert snapped, and saw the man's eyes drop as though cowed; but even as le Mareschal turned away, the thick black gown swirling about his feet, his cloak flapping, he was sure that he could feel the man's eyes on him weighted with loathing, as though he knew what Robert had done. It made his heart shrivel. The penalty would be fierce if he was discovered.

At first it had been the thought of what he might learn from his master that had prompted him. To take up a position with a necromancer was daunting only for a man who was not determined to learn all he might. For a man like Robert le Mareschal, the fact that Master John plainly knew much about succeeding through his use of magic was enough to lure him. With the knowledge he would glean here, he would be able to follow his own ambition. Only after that came the desire for money.

Fifteen pounds! That was Robert's payment, all in silver, simply for helping his master as he may. At the time it had seemed an enormous amount of money, and all of it just to help him to learn his master's arts. The men were paying John of Nottingham to assassinate some other men, that was all. Many of the foul churls from about the priory here at Coventry, those who scraped a living by their skills at begging from the doorman, would have accepted far less to overtake the knight and slip a knife between his ribs, but that was not the point. Any man might kill another in a brash and bloodthirsty manner: the art here was to do so *without* anyone's realising. To kill a man without touching him; to kill him while murderer and victim remained miles apart – therein lay the skill.

The payment had been made in part, along with the seven pounds of wax and two ells of cloth, and soon afterwards Master John began instructing Robert in how to form the bodies. One was larger than the others, and wore a small crown encircling his head. A second was shorter, a more corpulent fellow; the third taller, more slender, with a hawkish, cruel set to his features; another squat and fat . . . seven in all. Each wonderfully, if simply, fashioned to indicate whom they represented . . .

There was a lengthy shriek from the solar, and Robert crossed himself. The man was enduring the torments of the devil in there.

'Come with me! You have to help us! He doesn't recognise any of us – no one! Please!' Robert recognised the shouting figure: Henry, Richard de Sowe's steward, a short, thickset man with an almost bald head and gaunt, anxious features. Henry grabbed Robert's arm and all but dragged him indoors, turning into the little hall, and striding through it to the stairway beyond. He mounted the stairs two at a time, gripping the rope to heave himself upwards, all the while clutching Robert's sleeve, while the apprentice panted reluctantly behind him, and then they came into the room.

It was a spare chamber lit by clusters of guttering candles and a large charcoal brazier. Over the burning tallow Robert could smell the sourness of urine: the knight had lost all bodily control. The windows were fastened and shuttered to keep unhealthy odours from the sick man, but within the place there was an overwhelming, unpleasant stench. Robert had smelled enough dead and rotting flesh to recognise the foulness of decay.

When he had discussed the commission with Master John, it had seemed almost a game. The idea of killing a man from half a mile distant had seemed – well, almost laughable. It was ridiculous. Even when they had taken the down payment, Robert felt more like a mischievous student than the accomplice to a murder. Now he was being confronted with the fruits of his labours.

Steeling his heart, he took two paces into the room.

Sir Richard was straining, every muscle taut, as though the bed was drenched in a burning acid. He was a man in agony, bound to the posts of his bed with thongs, and gripped by four of his strongest servants, who tried to prevent his thrashing too vigorously and hurting himself still more. They gazed at Robert pleadingly, hoping that he might procure a swift release from Sir Richard's anguish. Which indeed he would.

'How is he?' Robert asked now, and Henry looked at him as though he was mad.

Sir Richard de Sowe's teeth were bared. Every sinew showed, from his neck to his skinny calves, and his red-rimmed eyes darted from one to another of his retainers like a torture victim surveying his tormentors. There was blood at his mouth, at his wrists, at his ankles. It had sprayed from his lips to spatter the breast of his stained linen shirt. With every jerk and twitch of his body came a relentless moaning, like a dog's whining anguish when its back was broken. Richard de Sowe knew, in that small space where rational thought still survived, that he was dying. Yet when his servants glanced at him, he flinched as though not recognising any of them.

Robert recoiled as Sir Richard's gaze flicked towards him. 'My Christ!'

With the shutters firmly closed, the only light came from the tallow candles, but their fumes were those of animal pyres. It made the chamber a charnel house.

'He was fine yesterday,' the man who held Richard de Sowe's head mumbled. 'What could do this to him?'

'Perhaps his humours are disturbed,' Robert blurted. 'Let me go to . . . I can ask Master John of Nottingham. He will know . . .'

Henry released Robert's sleeve, as though recognising at last that the fellow before him was as unable to help his master as he himself. He held Robert's eyes for a long moment, before a gasp and shriek from the bed drew his attention once more. 'You ask him. Me, I'd think it more likely that only the devil himself could answer for this.'

Tavistock Abbey

As soon as he heard of the death, John de Courtenay knew that at last he would receive the reward he had craved. There was no sorrow, no sadness at the ending of a life which had been so full of generosity and goodness, only a boundless relief. At last that God-bothering, cretinous obstacle to his advancement had been withdrawn.

For the rest of his life he would recall this moment: where he sat, how he felt, what the weather was like. Abbot Robert Champeaux was *dead*!

He was in his chamber, feeling the somnolence that came from a well-filled belly and a seat positioned comfortably close to the fire, while in his mind he contemplated the days to come. There was the promise of good hunting. Since the abbot had been warned to keep his hounds away from the king's deer, he had enforced a strict code of abstinence among his brethren, but not even a forceful nature such as old Abbot Champeaux's could effectively command obedience while he was confined to his own bedchamber. While he had been laid up with this last illness, his face grey-green in the thin light from his window, shaking like a man with the ague, it was clear that he could not enforce his rules.

Some had been fearful, and had thought that the abbot might recover at any time. They had drawn up terrifying pictures of him in their minds, a grim-faced old man leaning on a heavy staff as he always had, with great white eyebrows that scowled so a man might be frozen from thirty paces. Many a newly tonsured brother had cause to dread his chastisement; they had all experienced the rough edge of his tongue when they had fallen short of his high expectation. The abbot was a strong-willed man, and punished any transgression that might affect *his* monastery with ruthless determination.

John de Courtenay had held no such terror of Abbot Robert. The man was, when all was said and done, only a monk; while he, John de Courtenay, was the son of Baron Hugh of Okehampton and Tiverton. Yes, he owed the abbot his obedience and respect, but that was all.

And with any fortune, the election for the next abbot would be uncontested. Who could hope to stand in the path of the son of Baron Hugh de Courtenay?

Evesham Abbey

And in the guest room of the great abbey devoted to St Ecgwine, the man who slept on the floor as far from the door as possible turned over and was still, listening raptly to the heavy breathing and snoring of the others in the room. He closed his eyes, his breast rising and falling gently, but even as he teetered on the brink of sleep his fist remained clenched firmly about the dagger's hilt.

There were too many men who wanted him dead for him to dare to give himself up entirely to the sleep he so desperately craved.

It was the problem he had been trying to avoid, but he couldn't any longer. The abbot here knew his secret and wouldn't betray him, but unless he was prepared to take the tonsure he could not stay. And he was not going to become a celibate.

There was only one place in the country where he could be safe. Perhaps he ought to go there . . .

To Exeter.

Chapter One

Thursday before St Edmund's Day in the eighteenth year of the reign of King Edward II[2]

Exeter City

Some months after John de Courtenay and Robert le Mareschal contemplated deaths which must affect them dramatically, the former glad to hear of one demise and the latter actively pursuing another, a man whom both knew was himself contemplating murder.

Standing in the gloom of the alleyway, close to the Fissand Gate to the cathedral close in Exeter, he smiled to himself without humour as he watched his quarry. Leaning against the dark walls, he was just a blur in the twilight. There was no torch or brazier here to touch his hooded face with flickering beams. Positioned in the angle of a projection in the wall, even his outline was concealed.

When the object of his attention moved farther away and joined the crowds in the main street, he pushed himself away from his place of concealment and followed on his long legs, his thick woollen cloak snapping at his shins.

Over the years Robinet of Newington, known as Newt by his friends, had covered many leagues with that determined lope, his narrow features squinting into the middle distance as he strode over the old greenways. The smaller paths of this area, the great roads that led over downs, the pilgrim routes over to Canterbury – he had seen them all. His cloak showed the effects of a hundred rainstorms and had faded in the sun; his boots were made of good Cordovan leather, but their paint was scratched and worn away from great use, and

---

although when new they had been identical, neither designed for left nor right, over time they had moulded themselves to fit his feet. Once he would have bought new ones sooner. Once, aye, he could have replaced all his clothing twice a year at the expense of his master.

Reaching the top of the street, he peered round the corner. The crowds were thinning now as the sun sank in the west and the cold of the November evening persuaded all those with a room to go to it and huddle by the fire.

Newington pulled his cloak tighter about his shoulders and gazed after the man. If Newt knew him at all, he should be entering the stables. Yes, even as Newt gazed frowningly, he saw the man dart in.

After so much time there was a desire to hurry after him and shove his knife into the faithless bastard's throat, but Newt was too wily a man to do so, he told himself. Others would have impetuously followed their enemy, but Newt knew he was craftier. He hadn't survived so many years in the royal household by being unaware of the dangers of precipitate action. No, he waited, running through all the tasks his quarry would have to see to. It was possible, of course, that he was returning to collect his horse to ride from the city and continue on his urgent round – but Newt knew in his heart that it was deeply unlikely. When night fell it was hazardous to travel. He knew that. James of Wanetynch was no fool, whatever else he was, and he also knew it made no sense to travel in the dark.

Of course he did. Robinet had taught the godless whoreson everything he knew.

Monday, Vigil of St Edmund's Day[3]

Dartmouth

When the summons came, Simon Puttock, bailiff and representative of the Keeper of the Port of Dartmouth, was first aware only of a huge relief.

The port was a pleasant little town stuck out on the western shore

---

[3] 19 November 1324

of the River Dart, with a large natural haven for shipping. Simon could not complain about his position there, or the goodwill of his abbot, who had installed him here as a proof of his trust, but nonetheless Simon had not enjoyed his time here. He had left his moors behind, the lands where he had been happiest in his life, and, worse, he had been forced to leave his family too. Now, if he was being called back to Tavistock, at least he would have a chance to see them again. It had been too long.

When Abbot Robert had given him this job, that kind-hearted gentleman had been attempting to reward Simon's years of loyal service to the abbey. Since the famine years, Simon had been working on Dartmoor as one of the stannary bailiffs responsible for protecting the king's tin-mining ventures and trying to negotiate between the landowners and the miners, never an easy task. At the time he had thought that he would never have another position, so he had brought his wife and young family to Lydford, where they had made their home, and he had never asked more than to be left to his job.

But he had been too successful at the work for his own good, and the abbot had sought to reward him, and ensure the success of his new investments in Dartmouth, by giving him this post. It was intended as recognition of Simon's efforts, but it felt like a punishment.

He eyed the man who had brought the summons, trying to contain the thrill of relief that was washing through him. This fellow was no ordinary messenger: he had the look about him of a man who felt himself superior to the recipient. He was a full three inches taller than Simon, and he had an arrogant air about him. Clearly one of the newer men who was less enamoured than his older colleagues with Abbot Robert and had allied himself with one of the monks who wanted to take over the abbot's responsibilities. There were enough of them, God Himself knew.

'You say this is urgent?'

'You should leave today.'

Simon shrugged. 'I will go in the morning. It'll make little enough difference in time. If I leave now I'll scarcely quit the vill's boundaries before seeking an inn.'

'You should leave at dawn, then.'

'What can be so urgent?'

'No doubt you will be told when you reach Tavistock,' the man said in a haughty tone.

'If I go tomorrow, I'll have time to clear up some business.'

'You needn't worry about that. It can be sorted later.'

'You will pay my debts with the baker and butcher, will you?' A thought struck Simon. 'Do you mean to say that I am not coming back here?'

'I don't think so.'

'If that is so, who is to take my place? Ah, I see!'

The stranger languidly reached out to touch the limewashed wall with a lip curled in disdain. 'I have been asked to assume responsibilities during your absence.'

Simon frowned at the parchment in his hands. Looking away from the insufferable man was the only way to keep his temper under control. The tiny writing was little help. It was difficult to read in the gloom of his chamber. 'Stephen? You are Stephen of Chard?'

'Yes.'

'So you are to be in charge here when I am gone. Have I been accused of something?'

'I am sure you will already know that, won't you? After all, if you are guilty, you will know what you have done. And if you are not, you have nothing to fear, do you?' Stephen didn't bother to smile at Simon. Plainly, to his mind, Simon was an irrelevance already, and the sooner he was gone and Stephen could take over his duties the better.

Simon was torn: there was a sense of enormous delight at the thought that he might soon be able to get home to Lydford and see his family, but that was presently being swamped by his rising anger at this insignificant little puppy's manner. 'I will leave in the morning. If you want me to let you know . . .'

'Oh, I don't think I need trouble you. More important that you get off, Master Puttock. That message does require your urgent attention.'

Simon smiled, and this time his pleasure was unfeigned. 'And I am sure that you will be able to cope with the job admirably, Master Stephen.'

'I shall need to look through all your records, naturally. You will instruct your clerk to assist me.'

'It will be a pleasure,' Simon said, and stood to leave.

'Wait! First, if you please, I would like any keys you have to this place.'

Simon smiled thinly. 'You want to take my house? I fear not. Until I know what the affair is that demands my presence at Tavistock, you will have to find your own accommodation.'

'I do not think that the new abbot would be pleased to hear that you slighted me in this manner.'

Simon's smile broadened at the sly note in his voice. 'My friend, I don't know who you are or what you think you'll be doing here, but you've no right to anything of mine. And just now I'm not in the mood to help you at all. So I should find another place to stay. There's an inn along the roadway here. I'm sure they can help you there.'

'It is a quiet enough place?' Stephen of Chard looked mildly concerned at the thought of staying in a rowdy hostelry.

'Why, of course,' Simon assured him with his enthusiasm driving any note of dishonesty from his voice.

Exeter Castle

There was *no* mistaking it! Holy Mother Mary, but she couldn't have mistaken that. There was a look in his eye that showed her he loved her, and the way that he held on to the bowl when passing it to her, keeping hold just for that moment too long, as though worried she might drop it, but really only trying to keep her close . . . it was a miracle others didn't see it as well!

Jen placed the bowl gently on the tray with the other bits and pieces from the meal, and walked carefully from the hall.

This was the best thing that could ever have happened to her. She had been raised, like Sarra, on a small farm at Silverton, and she'd never thought she'd ever have a job like this one. The opportunity to come and work in the city, when Sarra's message came to her, was exciting, but only because it was such a wonderful place to live and work. She'd never dreamed that she might fall in love as well.

He was so handsome, so tall and straight, and he had that wonderful confidence that came from his position in the world. It was marvellous to see him sitting there so languidly, as though he hadn't a care in the world. Whereas after seven months, now Jen knew he suffered, really. It was that poisonous bitch of a wife of his. Everyone knew it: the woman tried to do all she might to ruin his self-esteem, carping on about this or that, making his life a misery. He'd be quite within his rights to bind her to a post and beat her unmercifully. If Jen was his wife, she'd just want to sit and gaze at him adoringly all day long . . . and make his life a pleasure by being on hand to fetch his drinks or foods. She would make him sweetmeats and bring them to him at his table so he could enjoy them without rising. She would make his bed such a place of joy as he could never have imagined. She would adore him.

And now, now she knew that he loved her too. It was in his eyes.

Sir Matthew de Crowethorne sat back in his chair and looked about him with that sense of satisfaction mingled with fear that was so much a part of his life recently.

His climb to success had hardly been meteoric, but if all went poorly his fall would be infinitely swifter.

When he had been made sheriff, this hall had been like the rest of the castle, dilapidated, decaying rapidly, the paint fallen off the walls, the ceiling rotten . . . he had been forced to spend much of his treasure to put it into some sort of order. Now that it was complete, he was forced to contemplate losing all.

Sir Matthew had been a loyal supporter of Despenser for many years. Their fathers had known each other, and as the Despenser star rose after the death of Gaveston, so too had Sir Matthew's. Despenser had looked after those whom he trusted – for so long as they had nothing of value which he coveted, anyway. Those who had trinkets or lands he desired could all too easily discover that their possession was fleeting. Whether they chose to give them away, or waited until Despenser had contrived to force them to give them up, was all one. Despenser was the most powerful man in the realm after the king. Some thought he was more powerful even than the king himself.

His greed had become known to all. Even the peasants spoke of him in hushed tones. It was no surprise that men wished to remove him. The writs spoke of a necromancer who had intended to kill the king, Despenser and five others. James of Wanetynch, the messenger, had brought them together with the other notes, including those from his peers. At first Matthew had been appalled, but then, as he began to consider the idea, it became apparent that he should act.

In Exeter, as he knew, there was one man who had the experience and expertise to help with matters of this kind. Walter had been used before, when the king had needed to clip the wings of a merchant, and he had succeeded so magnificently that a threatened mutiny between the city and the king had been averted. The agent was still here, and Matthew wondered whether he could be used again.

He had a fertile brain for planning. Now he sat back in his chair and bent his mind to the question of how he might best use the killer for the greater good, and by degrees a scheme occurred to him, one in which he could protect himself from risk while also ensuring that others would receive the full weight of any danger.

And he began to smile to himself – until there came a crash of metal from outside.

'What the devil . . .?'

A red-faced man-at-arms peered in apologetically from the screens passage. 'Sorry, Sir Matthew – I dropped my bill.'

'Be more careful!' Matthew snapped, and then returned to his contemplation. Gradually his annoyance dissipated, to be replaced by a certainty that his plan was not only workable, it was perfect.

Chapter Two

Exeter City

It was late afternoon when John of Nottingham at last reached the city. From the wide flood plain, he could see it from far away as a smudge in the sky. He had to stop and rest, his sore feet aching and blistered from his hastening march.

His had been an arduous journey. Thanks to Christ that he had learned of his danger and escaped quickly, because otherwise he'd be dead already. It was only the speed with which he had made his escape that had saved him.

In part it was the example of his master that had given him the spur. When Lord Mortimer of Wigmore had been captured, he had little opportunity to resist; to have defended himself would have meant instant conviction for treachery to his liege-lord, the king. All through the war, Mortimer had been careful to avoid raising his own standard against the king's, but instead he'd held up the king's standard while razing the Despenser lands so that when he explained himself later as only having the king's interests at heart, none would find it easy to reject his assertion.

He had been forced to surrender when the long hoped for support from Thomas of Lancaster never arrived. That cowardly son of a diseased sow stayed in his castle and refused to make the leap to defend his own comrades – with the result that the king destroyed Mortimer's armies, and then turned on Lancaster himself. And when Lancaster was caught, he was condemned out of hand with no opportunity to defend himself against the charges, and executed – the first of hundreds to be slaughtered by that vengeful, vicious king. The man didn't deserve his throne. He didn't deserve his life.

To remove him had been the most precious desire of so many, and yet only so few could have achieved it. And it had been so close. But when the assassination plot had been discovered, all were taken. All but John of Nottingham.

He eased the staff over his shoulder, his pack an almost unbearable weight. Few enough possessions: mostly it was his one heavy book. That was all, wrapped up together with some clothes in his blanket, but they had rubbed the flesh in a broad swathe, and now he spent much of his time trying to forget the pain. Still, better to be foot and shoulder-sore than dead, or held and tortured.

Exeter was a new town to him. He had never been here before, which was itself an advantage, but it had the additional merit of being far enough away from all central sources of power in the realm for him to be perfectly secure. And there was a port, which meant that if he needed, he could escape over the water, too. For now, though, all he sought was a warm fire, a bed, and some hot wine to ease his chilled bones.

The smudge in the distance began to acquire definition as he followed the old roadway and found himself skirting a high plateau. Now he could see that it was composed of many fires throwing their fumes up into the air. And then, as he continued, he found himself face to face with a broad city wall, all red stone, with ditches raised before it as additional defences. There were houses lining the route now, some well built with little garden plots before them where straggling plants grew in the chill: spindly stems of rocket with the last few tiny leaves, and some harsh-looking cabbages. Not much still grew at this time of year.

From close to, the gates were enormous, and he stood before them with relief to know that here at last he would be able to sleep indoors. He marched in, and soon found where he could take a drink or two. After asking advice, he chose a place called the Suttonsysyn, which was only a very short distance from where he stood. And it was while he was there, looking about himself, that he saw *him* again.

It was a shock. He had been ready to relax, take a drink, and then retire to his cot, but now here was this fellow, one of those guaranteed to remember him – the king's messenger from Coventry. There was nothing for it: he must leave the city, escape, run away again. Perhaps head straight for the coast, take a ship to Guyenne . . . Lord Mortimer had done just that, after all: he'd fled the land, and was now living with the French king, so they said.

But to run now might mean he could never achieve the destruction of the king and his favourites. The thought was unbearable. He had to stay.

It had taken him four days to march here. Four days of walking without halt except at night, avoiding people as far as possible, and now he had arrived here and already his safety was at risk. He sank onto a low wall, thinking desperately about his mission. It was enough to make a man weep, seeing an agent of his destruction so soon after arriving in a town where he had thought himself secure. Perhaps there was nowhere which was entirely safe. This, maybe, was to be the tenor of his life from this moment forth: to wander the lands, ever seeking safety, only to discover at every vill yet another familiar, and dangerous, face.

But he was not the man to accept defeat. Other churls might whine and complain at the way that fate would play hazard with their lives, but that was not for *him*! He was stronger than that: he made others change their situation to suit *him*! It was he who was in control. Events were so constructed by him that they guided others to obey his whims.

He would not be thwarted. Standing, wincing, he watched the man disappear down the street ahead of him, and squaring his shoulders he set off after him, his hand pulling at the little weighted cord under his tunic. With that, he could defend himself.

And then, as he stepped out, he saw another man follow him, a short, dark man who watched him closely with wide-set, dark and serious eyes.

John took a closer grip on his cord.

Tuesday, Feast Day of St Edmund[4]

Exeter City

It was Will Skinner, the watchman at the South Gate, who first noticed the body slumped just inside the alley on that Tuesday morning.

Will was one of the older night watchmen. When he first took over duties down here near the gate, he had been middle-aged, but that was six years ago now. Felt like a lot longer. At the time he had only recently lost his house and everything he loved.

---

[4] 20 November 1324

Poor Margie had never recovered from that fire. Badly burned, seeing their bodies drawn from the house, she'd lost her mind. They'd both doted on the little mites, all three of them. They'd had seven children born, but they'd had to bury the other four only a short while after their births. Not many children lived to four years old.

Bob had been twelve, Joan eight, and Peg six when they died. That damned fire had rushed through the house like . . . like anything. Will had been speaking at a small meeting, telling his audience they should fight to reject the latest demands for extra taxes, when the woman came to get him. She was herself distraught, and he gaped at her, not really comprehending what she was saying. It was like a dreadful nightmare, hearing her talking about his children, his wife badly burned . . .

He had run to the house, but by the time he got there there was nothing. Just a smoking wreck.

It was a friend who had managed to get him this job. Others had told him not to take it, because his house had been around here, not far from the gate itself. That was why he liked it, though. He walked down there at every opportunity, past the alley where his children had died, where his wife had lived with him happily, before that dread evening. It was his daily pilgrimage.

The gap where his house had once stood remained, shut away behind a wooden paling fence. Now, as he wandered down the alley, he saw the emptiness where his family had once lived. It made him feel – not *sadness* exactly, more a sort of broad space. He had long ago grown accustomed to the fact of their deaths; that was something any man must learn to cope with. But passing the space he was reminded again that it seemed out of place, as though he still almost expected his house to reappear.

This month was always hardest. It was at this time of year that his children had died, and the chill in the air, the naked trees denuded of leaves, the ice in the lanes, all reminded him of them.

He couldn't help but stop and stare at where the house had been. Leaning on his staff, he gazed hungrily, as though the intensity of his regard could bring them back to life. But nothing could. Turning to continue on his way, he stumbled, and nearly fell headlong.

Over the body in the alley.

* * *

When the keeper of the gatehouse heard the pounding on his door, his immediate thought was that his blasted son had been on the sauce again, and he threw off his bedclothes with an angry curse at the thought of what the damned fool could have been up to this time.

Old Hal was not a particularly ill-tempered fellow. Certainly, many would agree that he tended towards a melancholy humour at the best of times, but more often than not he could be amusing, and good company when a group got together in the tavern. His jokes were risqué, his songs filthy, his mind invariably lewd, so men got along with him enormously well – provided that they never mentioned his good-for-nothing son Art.

Art. It was ironic that he and Mabel had named the little devil after Hal's grandsire, for if ever a man was unlike his namesake, it was Art. Where old Art had been reliable, responsible, honourable and dedicated, young Art was the opposite. He wouldn't wake on time, he was always late and blaming others for his failings, and when he did turn up of a morning, it was invariably with a headache and a pathetic, shaking demeanour. Twice in the last month Hal had been called to have him released from the gaol after drinking too much and fighting. He hated to think what else the little bastard had got up to without being discovered.

'Why do you fight?' Hal had demanded after the last escapade.

'It's not that I want to . . . when I've had too much ale, it just happens.'

'You'd best stop now, before someone stands on your head too hard,' Hal had said unsympathetically, looking at the wreckage that had been his son's face. Now it was a mass of bruises and scabs. The trouble was, Art was born with more sense than he now had. He couldn't assess odds, apparently. If he was drunk and his dander was up, he'd pick a fight with a man in armour.

Reaching the door, Hal threw aside the bar and pulled it wide. 'What's he done this . . . oh, Will? What is it? Christ alive, man, it's hardly daylight yet!'

Will entered hurriedly, and from the look on his face Hal knew it wasn't good news.

'Murder – there's been a murder!'

South Dartmoor

Simon Puttock's journey to Tavistock was eased considerably by the memory of Stephen of Chard's face the night before when he realised that Simon's recommended inn was a place frequented by gamblers, sailors and whores.

Even this early, a little after dawn, his mood was sunny because he would soon be seeing his children and his lovely Meg. It seemed such a long time since he had last been with her. That was when he had first heard of the death of his friend and mentor, Abbot Robert. Even now the memory was depressing. Strange to think how close a man could grow to his master.

With uncanny timing, his own servant's whining voice intruded on his thoughts. 'Is it much farther, Bailiff?'

'Yes.'

'Many miles?'

'Boy, be quiet! It is a long way, and the more you chatter, the longer it feels. Enjoy the views and the air, and hold your tongue.'

If it weren't for Rob trailing along with him, he would have been enjoying this perfect morning. As it was, he was constantly aware of the lad behind him, muttering and complaining under his breath as he stumbled along after Simon, the reins of the packhorse in his hands. Rob was little more than a lad, only some thirteen summers or so, but as hard and devious as only the illegitimate son of a sailor could be. He was sharp-eyed, with dark eyes set close together in a narrow, weaselly face. His accustomed expression of suspicious distrust reminded Simon of a small ferret who was forever seeking the next rabbit. He was clad in a simple tunic, a leather jerkin and a cowl, and bare-footed like so many who live near the ships. Boots cost money, and when sailors disdained such wastefulness, many of their children had to learn to do without too.

In the middle of the summer the journey was an easy one. In winter even a man like the obnoxious Stephen could make the distance safely by keeping to the larger roads, but only slowly. Stephen had apparently taken two days to cover the thirty or more miles between Tavistock and Dartmouth. Simon was disinclined to take his time. He was keen to learn the reason for being called back, and still more so to see his wife. That was why he avoided the lower roads that encircled the moorland, and in preference made his way along the muddied trackways until he reached the open heights, and then took his way north and west until he met up with the Abbots' Way, the great path marked by enormous stone crosses that guided a man safely across some of the most treacherous parts of the moors.

This was land where a man could breathe, Simon thought as he stopped his mount to wait for Rob to catch up and gazed about him. From this hill, he could see nothing but rolling countryside on all sides. He had joined the Abbots' Way near Ter Hill, and westwards he could see the first of the three crosses that showed the safe route past the Aune Head's mire. The path here wandered north of that, then curved to avoid the Fox Tor mire a short distance farther on. The bogs were deadly, and all too often the ghostly shrieks and wails of animals who had blundered into a mire would be heard as the terrible muddy waters gradually enfolded them and smothered them. No matter how often Simon crossed and recrossed the moors, he would never get used to those cries. They sounded like tortured souls screaming out from hell.

But Simon adored this landscape just as much as any lord would love his deer park. For Simon it was the picture of a modern working environment, with the smoke rising from the miners' camps, great trenches dug to show where the peat was being harvested, and rubble all about where great hunks of moorstone had been dug up and roughly cut to size. All over the moors people worked the land. It might not be so fertile as some of the valleys nearby, but to Simon these open, rolling hills were as near perfection as anywhere in the country.

Not that he would ever admit to such thoughts in front of his old friend Sir Baldwin Furnshill, of course. Baldwin would merely scoff at such views.

'Where's the nearest inn?' Rob demanded, gazing about him with unconcealed disgust.

'Probably about ten miles west.'

'Christ's ballocks, what a privy!'

Simon clenched his jaw and dismounted. He would lead his old horse for a while to rest him.

They had left Dartmouth as the sun rose. The night before, Simon had introduced his clerk to the new Keeper of the Port, and told Rob about his impending departure, and to his considerable surprise Rob had insisted on leaving with him. There was little chance of refusing him. The mere thought of trying to persuade Rob's mother that it would be a good idea for her to keep him with her at Dartmouth was enough to persuade Simon that he might as well accept the lad's company. She was not a greatly maternal woman, and as soon as she heard that her firstborn was leaving her she'd be out of her house and into the nearest tavern to meet another man. She had only ever looked on Rob as an unwelcome nuisance at the best of times. He got in the way of her search for a husband.

Besides, having an additional servant was always a good idea. Simon had no idea how his household was faring just now. It was always possible that one of the other servants had been taken ill or died. Yes, bringing Rob was almost certainly a good idea.

He had brought a skin of wine, some cheese and a loaf of bread for the journey. Others might look upon a ride of ten leagues across the moors as dangerous at best, and more probably near suicidal, but Simon had covered these moors regularly in the last eight or nine years, and he knew the different parts better than he knew his garden at Lydford.

They stopped in the lee of a hill and lunched together, drinking the wine and chewing lumps of cheese with the loaf, a harsh brown one which proved to have more fragments of grit from the millwheel than actual grain, judging from the foul crunching. Several times Simon had to search out shards of moorstone and discard them. Still, it was enough to fill their bellies, and once the horses were watered they set off once more, Rob muttering under his breath all the while.

'Why did you ask to join me, if you are so bitter?' Simon demanded at last, exasperated.

'I didn't know you were bringing me up here. Thought we'd be going on a real road, stopping off at a tavern for the night. Thought it would be a laugh.'

'Now you know the truth,' Simon said unkindly. 'So shut up, or take yourself to the main road south of here and meet me in Tavistock tomorrow.'

'I can't go alone! I'll get lost!'

'Let me dream,' Simon muttered.

Chapter Three

Exeter City

Master Richard de Langatre was a comfortably-off man. In his early thirties, he had the paunch of a man considerably older, and his cheery smile won the attentive gazes of many mothers of unmarried daughters who saw in him a potential son-in-law. After all, the man from Lincoln was fortunate enough to have a good business and a near-monopoly in Exeter.

He was not the most handsome man in the world. The round features and fleshy jowls showed his financial position, but did not add to his charm. However, the shock of mousy-coloured hair and his grey eyes offset the appearance of unbending probity and financial expertise. The eyes were too prone to laughter, and the hair would never submit to a comb or brush, always ending up unruly and discreditable no matter what the barber did to it. The first impression was that this man would be pleasant company for an evening in the tavern.

Today he had been shopping, a task which he viewed as essential not only to the efficacy of his mixtures, but also to his reputation. There were some hideous concoctions he had made in the past which now he recalled with fondness. The more foul the medicine, the more the patient valued it, he believed, and provided that he didn't kill too many with his potions – and none had died as a direct result of taking his medicines, so far as he knew – he should find his reputation improving and his purse growing heavier.

This year, ah, this year had been a good one. First the consultation with the sheriff over the little matter with his woman, then some woman who had been nervous about her husband's learning of her infidelity – she had paid well for the correct answer! – and finally the man who wanted to be abbot. He had been willing to pay well, thank the Lord! Yes, this year had been good to Master Richard. A good necromancer was always in demand, he reflected happily.

He was back at his room as the sun began to dip towards the west. After shopping he had betaken himself to Suttonsysyn near the Guildhall. In there, near the great fire, he had warmed his hands and feet from the chill outside, and partaken of a quart of good strong ale warmed and spiced and sweetened as he liked it with honey. Afterwards he bought himself a few honeyed thrushes from a stall, and chewed them standing at the street corner, watching the passers-by.

You could tell much by watching and observing how people walked and talked, he always thought. And just now, people were wary.

It was no surprise. He had been discussing it this morning at the inn. Michael Tanner had been there, and the two had sat together as they drank, as was their wont. Michael had a friend who was working in the cathedral close, and he was often one of the first to get news, but today everyone was alert to the latest gossip.

'It is true, then?' Richard had asked.

Michael nodded grimly and set his pot aside. He was a short, dark man with a square face and a thin salt and pepper beard. His eyes were sharp and grey, always darting about, watching to see if anyone was listening to them. 'Absolutely. I heard it from the steward himself. He was there in the room when the king's messenger arrived, and heard every word he spoke. The queen has had her household broken apart, her income is slashed, and even her dower has been taken from her. They leave her nothing. It is hard to believe, but my friend tells me that the messenger spoke of the king's children.'

'What of them?'

'All taken from the queen. All being looked after by trusted maids – those trusted by the king, I mean.'

Master Richard whistled low. 'He must *hate* her. Do you think he could suspect her of treason?'

It was a proof of their closeness that such a word could be used. Michael and Richard had grown to know each other because the latter rented his house from Michael, but they had soon developed a mutual regard. Richard appreciated that. It was not often that others would respect a man who was a dabbler in magic.

Michael pulled a face. 'How could a man trust a woman like her? She has French blood, my friend. Her loyalties are split. It's hardly fair to blame her – but if you were the king, how could you trust a woman who was sister to the French king just at the time that the French are threatening to steal King Edward's remaining lands?'

Master Richard shook his head at the thought. Since the fight over the French attempt to build a fort at Saint Sardos, the French and the English had been at loggerheads. A truce had been agreed, but that would only last a number of months. And once it had expired, the French king Charles IV could all too easily take over all the remaining English lands in France. 'It is a terrible thing when a man and a woman fall apart. The marriage vows should hold them together.'

'You can't expect an Englishman to cleave to a flighty French wench,' Michael said harshly. He finished his drink and bade Master Richard farewell. Then he leaned down quickly and whispered in Master Richard's ear. 'You know, there's talk that she paid a man like you to remove her enemy and her husband. That would make a husband think carefully about her, wouldn't it?' He winked and was gone, leaving Master Richard with a full pint remaining in his pot, and a delicious rumour to absorb.

The uppermost thought in his mind as he walked homewards was that he would dearly love to meet the queen and see what he could learn from her . . . it was never likely to happen, but she must be a fascinating woman. Especially when she was being dispossessed like this. Could she really have hired someone to kill off her own husband? If she had been involved in an act like that, it was no surprise that she should be considered a malign influence on her children. A woman who plotted her husband's murder was surely inadequate as a mother. She might raise them to hate her husband as much as she did herself.

It said much about her, though, if she was prepared to hire a necromancer like him to remove a king, he thought. Then, as he opened his door to enter, he was shocked from his reflections by the hand at his shoulder.

'Master? Are you Master Richard of Langatre?'

Stilling his anger, he smiled. 'Yes, mistress. Can I be of service?' After all, it wasn't so often that the sheriff's wife came to see him.

Tavistock Abbey

Simon reached the abbey in good time, with at least an hour of daylight remaining. Overall, a pleasing journey, apart from the whining behind him. The only cure for that was to ride on a little faster, so that the lad's legs couldn't keep up.

'Are we there now?' Rob was staring at the great moorstone walls with trepidation, eyes wide like a rabbit watching a hunter.

'Yes. This is it.'

'Oh, thank Christ for . . .'

Simon winced. Rob had been raised in Dartmouth, and his language was designed more for the tavern than an abbey. 'Try to be careful with your words, Rob. The monks in here expect respect. If you use language like that, you could be thrown into their gaol and left there for a week. I won't pay to get you out if you are guilty of embarrassing a monk.'

'God's teeth.'

'That's enough!'

There was a lay brother at the gate who volunteered to take Rob and the horses to the stable. Simon was happy to pass over the reins, taking his pair of bags from the saddle before he bade the beast farewell. It was not his own, but one of those rounseys which the abbey purchased and kept for the use of its workers. When Simon left tomorrow to see his wife, he hoped to be able to borrow another horse and packhorse for the journey. For now, though, there was more urgent business, if Stephen of Chard was to be believed.

Rob was somewhat pathetic, staring at Simon like a boy bidding farewell to his father before going to sea. Simon waved him off irritably, then turned on his heel and made his way across the main court to a door which had been pointed out to him. A novice opened it for him, beckoning him to enter.

Over the years Simon had come here many times to meet his abbot, but those encounters had always been held in the abbot's own house overlooking the gardens and the river. Many were the pleasant meals and drinks Simon had enjoyed there while supposedly briefing the abbot on matters pertaining to troubles on the moors, or more recently the affairs of Dartmouth. However, the last few meetings they had had were more sombre. It was clear to Simon that the abbot had known he was dying. The death was long and slow, but the good man endured it with equanimity. He was glad to be leaving the world, Simon was convinced. Abbot Robert had done all he could to serve God and the abbey, and he knew he deserved his final rest.

'Bailiff. Good. Come in here.' It was John de Courtenay, the son of Baron Hugh de Courtenay. He was standing in a narrow passage, and he opened a door as Simon approached, motioning him inside. Seeing the novice, he jerked his head. 'You! Fetch us wine, and be quick!'

The room had clearly been used for some while as a working area. It was not large, but there were two tables set up inside, with a series of rolls of parchment set out on them. A few were weighted flat with stones, and it looked as though John de Courtenay had been studying them. He walked in behind Simon and stared down at the nearest parchment with distaste, before removing some of the stones and allowing the skin to roll itself up again gently as he seated himself on a stool beside it.

Between the tables stood a large brazier half filled with glowing coals. Simon walked to it and held his hands to it while he wondered why he had been called here to see the baron's son. It was only after a short period that he suddenly felt a sinking sensation in his bowels.

There were many in the abbey whom Simon would have been delighted to see take over: the cellarer was a kindly, well-intentioned man; the sacristan was astute, worldly wise and effective; even the salsarius was more than capable – but this man was the very last whom Simon would wish to see in charge of the place.

John was no fool, it was true, but that only added to Simon's concern now as he turned and warmed his backside. Once, while he was discussing fathers and sons with his friend Sir Baldwin, the knight had observed that it was a general rule that if a strong-willed man sired a son, the son would be as feckless as his father was brilliant. Not always, of course, but there were many examples of weakly sons who followed potent parents. At the time, Simon recalled, they had been alluding to the king himself. No man would have thought that so jealous, foolish and incompetent a man could have followed Edward I.

No, he didn't think that this John de Courtenay was a fool, but that did not make Simon feel any better. When Simon was a boy, his father had been steward to the de Courtenays, and Simon had grown to know John moderately well. Where his father was cautious and aware of the machinations necessary to protect his estates and treasure in the confusing modern world of politics, John was devious to a fault, determined, frivolous, vain and a spendthrift. It was no surprise that Hugh had supported his eldest son in his ambition to go into the church rather than take over the vast family estates. God forbid that he should ever grab the reins of power of the abbey.

'Where is that wine?' de Courtenay grumbled. He was a powerfully built man, with a square face and thinning fair hair about his tonsure. That he kept himself moderately fit was entirely due to his passion for hunting, which was not actually permitted, although he didn't allow that to stop him. Recently, though, his belly had started to grow, and Simon noticed that since he had last seen him his posture had changed. Whereas before he had always stood dignified and erect, now he was beginning to bend his back to support his growing paunch, and he sat with his neck thrust forward in a vain attempt to conceal the growing pouch of flesh beneath his chin.

Simon waited silently. He was anxious. Whatever had occasioned his recall to Tavistock, he felt sure it would not be to his benefit.

At last the novice returned with a thin, old monk who entered, nodded kindly to Simon, and then glowered at his brother. 'Perhaps you forget, John, that you should not command the novices to fetch and carry for you? You may do that if you ever win the abbot's seat, but until then you should leave the boys alone. And if you want wine, come and ask me to provide it for you. Since we are lucky enough to have a guest in our midst, I suppose this once it will be all right.'

'We have matters to discuss here, Reginald,' de Courtenay said sharply. 'You may leave us.'

'Oho!' Reginald said, and passed Simon a jug of wine, winking as he did so. He handed a second to de Courtenay, who took it suspiciously. Then the old monk gave them both goblets, and Simon tasted his wine with pleasure. An excellent vintage, strong and fruity; meanwhile de Courtenay peered into his own goblet with an expression of doubt.

As soon as they were alone again, de Courtenay shook his head. 'I am sorry about that old fool. The churl has little in his head any more. I am sure the vindictive old brute watered this wine. It's like piss!'

Simon hurriedly agreed, pulling a face, before de Courtenay could think of taking a taste of his own jug. 'Why did you ask me to come here?'

De Courtenay looked at him for a long period without speaking. Then he set his goblet on the table beside him and leaned forward, his elbows on his knees. Motioning towards another stool, he waited until Simon was seated.

'Since poor Abbot Robert has gone to a happier place, it will be up to the brothers here to elect a new abbot. There must be a vote early in the new year. Now when that happens, naturally I shall be selected. There is no one else who can lead our little community. And yet there are one or two misguided fellows here who might seek to prevent my taking my proper place in the abbey. They could try to put another in my stead, if you can believe it!'

Simon could very easily believe it. 'That has nothing to do with me, though.'

'Not directly, no. But I remember you from when we were lads. You always followed your father, and he was a good, loyal servant. How is he?'

'Dead these last nine years,' Simon said shortly.

'Amazing. Still, you'd want to continue in his footsteps, wouldn't you?'

'How exactly do you expect me to do that?' Simon asked warily.

'There is one brother here who could be a threat to me . . . the fool Busse. Robert Busse. He is not a serious contender, of course. I mean, I'm the son of a baron, and he?' He gave a dismissive shrug and wave of his hand. 'No. No one in their right mind would vote for him. And yet he's a crafty old devil. Perhaps he might threaten some, or bribe others. You never can be sure with that devious old . . . anyway, I want someone to keep an eye on him.'

'Wait! You are asking me to spy on a brother of yours? I cannot wander about the abbey trailing after this fellow. I am no brother.'

'Calm yourself. I merely want you to go with him when he leaves to visit Bishop Stapledon. All it will involve is travelling with him to protect him on his way, and then ensuring that no danger comes to him – or *me* – when he reaches the city.'

'No. Now, if you do not object, I shall leave and visit my wife. I haven't seen her in some weeks.'

'Wait one moment, Bailiff.' John de Courtenay's voice was as smooth as a moleskin. 'Before you decide to rush off in a sanguine humour because I have requested that you help me in this matter, you should be aware of something.'

'What?'

'You do not like me, Master Bailiff. I know that. You and I have never been particularly close. Do not protest! Please, we are both sensible men. I am frivolous and enjoy the trivial. Yes. However, I do serve Our Lord, and I am determined to do all I may to succour the souls of the people who live here. Not all monks are like that. I know some who would be happy to leave their paths of service and instead follow the path of knowledge. Some are so determined to learn as much as they may that they have left the sensible courses of learning and sought out more . . . curious routes to knowledge.'

Simon stood. 'I have no part in the election of the next abbot, and want nothing to do with it.'

'What? Money wouldn't tempt you?'

'I shall take my leave,' Simon said coldly. He had never been open to bribery.

'Simon, I was only teasing. It is my habit, when I am anxious, to be light about my concerns. Look: sit a moment and listen. Please?'

He waited until Simon was seated once more, and then turned to the parchment on the table baside him. His eyes were floating over the words, and Simon had the impression that he was reading from it as he spoke.

'I know some little of Busse. He is a man of lowly birth. Did you know that? I have learned that he was the son of a priest, a man called Master Robert de Yoldeland. That was how he acquired his Christian name. His surname came from his mother, a concubine of his father's called Joan Busse. He is not the sort of man we want as abbot here, Simon.'

'I have always found him to be a fair and sensible man,' Simon said coldly.

'Would you say that if you thought that he had made use of a magician? That he was asking someone to use *maleficia* to help him become abbot?'

Simon shivered. Everyone knew of sorcerers and witches – *maleficus* and *malefica* – who could use their evil spells to harm others or cause benefits to accrue. Some would use a witch to win a woman's love, while others would seek a sorcerer to help enhance their prospects.

'I see from your expression that you have as much liking for such people as I do, Simon. Aye, well, Busse has been using a necromancer. He has already made enquiry of Master Richard de Langatre. You know of him? He is the chief fortune-teller in Exeter. Busse came here from Lincoln. They say he consulted unclean and malignant spirits while he was there. Do you really think he would make a better abbot than me? Even the most biased fellow must wonder whether he would be a safe and sensible master of a place such as this ... a place constructed to save souls and protect the people of the area. Simon, you must follow him. I need a man who is responsible, and I can think of no better man than the son of my father's own best and most faithful steward.'

Chapter Four

Exeter City

The traveller had reached a tavern early on to try to get some heat into his bones. He had a simple requirement, now he was here: to find as many as possible of the materials he would need to continue with his experiments.

Here he was, a master of the secret arts, and he was constrained by the lack of simple tools. It was infuriating. He had money, he had the knowledge, and yet he still lacked those basic requisites. Even a piss-swilling brewer had them, but not he. Not just now.

He had the one, of course. Cautiously, from beneath his robe he brought out the small bone needle. It was perfect: smooth, thin, elegant and ideal. There were other items he needed, though: sickle, wax and linen would be easy to find . . . but the daggers, the hat, the other bits and pieces, would be harder to procure. And of course he would need peace in which to pray and fast and prepare mentally for the task. Ideally he ought to have a servant, but that was too much to hope for. That had been made clear.

It was as he reached this conclusion that he saw the two lurching inside. Plainly the pair of them had already enjoyed a good evening, and they were ready to continue a little longer, until they fell down in a drunken stupor. Well, so much the better. If only he weren't staying here, he would be happy to go to them and slip his dagger between the ribs of the younger one. One good turn deserves another, he mused as he turned to his drink.

Their conversation was loud, as such conversations often are, and he could hear snatches.

'You ought to come back to my place, Jamie. It's not far from here. Walter would like to see you again.'

'I wouldn't want to see *him*, though . . .'

There was some quieter murmuring, then: 'Come on, Jamie, let him be. He's no worse than me.'

'I remember what he used to do.'

'That's a long while ago.'

'Not long enough.'

For all the brashness of the younger man, this Jamie could plainly hold his ale better than his companion.

'And besides, I must be off in the morning. I have urgent messages for my master,' he said with a significant tap at the pouch on his belt.

And at that moment, John of Nottingham glanced up and saw Jamie's eye on him, and he felt a lurch in his belly to think that he could be discovered so easily.

Wednesday, Morrow of St Edmund's Day[5]

Exeter City

It was cold, a freezing night, and thoroughly miserable for a watchman.

Of those who spent their nights pacing the territory trying to ensure that, so far as was possible, draw-latches and robbers were prevented from plying their trade and the rest of the population could sleep easily in their beds, all had their own lists of the worst kind of weather. For Will, his list had once been topped by the autumnal showers that drifted over the city every so often. They would appear from nowhere, and in moments he would be drenched. There was something almost unnatural about them, the way that with just a mild breeze behind them they could seep through even a leather jack and leave a man sodden and uncomfortable. Yes, in the past he had hated those nights more than any other. The cold hadn't bothered him.

Now, though, as the years went by, he had learned to detest the ice that came with weather like this. He was that little bit older, and whereas in the past he had been able to avoid slipping on frozen cobbles, now he was wary of anything that could unbalance him. He was not so secure on his feet as once he had been.

[5] 21 November 1324

'Evening, Thomas.'

'Will.'

Thomas atte Moor had a brazier going to keep him from joining the puddles all about here and becoming iced. He was a younger man, perhaps only four-and-thirty, so but half Will's age, but even so young he could be chilled to the core in this weather. Set to guard the body Will had found yesterday, the last thing he wanted was to be stuck outside in this weather, but when the coroner commanded, only a fool would disobey. Especially this coroner!

Leaving Thomas, Will went on to the end of the alley. Here he was almost at the South Gate. The alley opened out to show the pile of rubbish which was waiting to be cleared just in front of the Church of Holy Trinity, the mound lying almost against the wall.

A hog had been rootling in the heap, and as Will watched it shoved with its short, stubby snout at the pile, hauling at something. Will was just eyeing it speculatively, wondering whether, if he killed it, he could persuade a butcher at the shambles to help him joint and sell it for a share of the profit, when he caught sight of a flash of blue. It was strange to see a piece of material in among all the rubbish left out there, most of it ancient food and rubble. After all, cloth was expensive. A watchman could hardly afford to see it thrown away.

He thrust with his staff at the hog, who eyed him angrily at being pushed from his feast, and Will was anxious for a moment that the beast might attack him, but then the animal snorted and backed away, looking about for other morsels. Not before he had snatched another quick mouthful, though.

And Will saw that behind it, under the blue material, was the remains of a chewed hand. A human hand.

Furnshill, near Cadbury

Sir Baldwin de Furnshill was a man of certain habits, and as the light breached his shutters he was already awake.

After so many years of soldiering, he was used to being up with the dawn. In the past it was because his order, the Poor Fellow Soldiers of Christ and the Temple of Solomon, the Knights Templar, demanded rigorous training. Woe betide the knight who remained in his bed when his horse needed grooming or his weapons sharpening. For

Baldwin, all his life this period after dawn had been a time of intense effort. There were masses to be celebrated, equipment to be checked, and, of course, his exercises.

A Templar who sought to serve the order must spend many hours each day in training, and Baldwin was a keen exponent of the most stringent efforts possible. It was only by striving for perfection that a knight might achieve the degree of excellence which was sought for by all. He used to rise early from his bed and stand outside in the chill morning air, often bare-chested, sword in hand, practising defensive manoeuvres, retreating on his feet, stamping flat-footed as he gripped the hilt with both fists, then suddenly moving to the offence, his sword stabbing forward to strike an imaginary foe, then rising to block a sudden hack, before swirling round smoothly to strike another.

Yes, every day of his life for thirty years or more he had been a devout exponent of practice, and now . . . well, it was cold outside, and he was growing older. An experimental hand reached out to stroke his wife's flank, and he listened to her muffled groans as she protested against his advances, but then he found the junction of her thighs, and her complaints became less urgent. She straightened a leg so his hand could be more easily accommodated, and as his other hand found her breast she rolled over, one arm over her head, eyes still closed, lips parted. She turned to him, her head thrusting forward slightly, her naked body tensing luxuriously under his hands. She arched her back and spoke breathily into his ear.

'Isn't it time you were up? You haven't forgotten today you have to go to the bishop?'

There were words he could have used about the bishop that morning, but instead he gripped her a little more urgently. 'Not until later.'

And it was much later that he managed to leave the warmth and comfort of his bed and make his way down the stairs of his solar, and out to his hall, all the while rehearsing in his mind how he might be able to refuse the offer which the bishop had made to him.

'Offer? Hah!'

No, it was no offer. It was an ultimatum. Bishop Walter wanted Baldwin to go to London for his own reasons. Baldwin had no idea what those reasons were, but Walter Stapledon had decided that he wanted Baldwin to attend parliament, and the good bishop was determined. It was rare that he was ever thwarted in his aims. As Baldwin knew only too well, Stapledon, once a close and trusted friend of his, was at the very centre of power in the realm, and as one of the king's key advisers, the Lord High Treasurer. That was enough, in Baldwin's eyes, to make him less trustworthy.

Since the destruction of his order by an avaricious and unscrupulous French king and his lackey the Pope, Baldwin had been less prepared to place his trust in the hands of such men. His faith in politics and the Church itself had been ruined by his experiences as a Templar. Recently, since his friend Simon had introduced him to Bishop Stapledon, he had begun to change his opinion, but then he had been forced to accept that the bishop had misled him intentionally, and now he was unable to trust the king's closest adviser.

The bishop wished him to become a knight of the shire in London's parliament, and Baldwin was determined that he would avoid that fate. The idea of being sent away from his wife and child for weeks or months was unbearable. Only last year had he been off on pilgrimage with Simon, and the sense of loneliness and desolation at being cut off from his wife was still a weight on his soul when he thought of it. Better by far that he should not leave her again. Remain here in Devon, where he was content. He had no interest in or need of politics and its practitioners.

Unusually for him, he demanded a warmed and spiced wine as he sat at his table, and sipped it slowly as he chewed on a slab of meat, listening to the thundering of small feet from the solar behind him as his daughter woke and ran about the place. It was inconceivable that he could be tempted away from this house and his little girl again, he thought, and grinned to himself as she burst through the door, her accustomed smile leaping to her face as she caught sight of him.

He took her up in his arms and cuddled her closely. The two year old always enjoyed being hugged, and she threw her arms about his neck, shoving her face into the point of his jaw.

There was nothing, Baldwin told himself, nothing that could tempt him to volunteer for a parliamentary career. And fortunately there was little likelihood that the freemen of Exeter would be willing to help the bishop in his ambitions anyway. No, Baldwin reckoned himself safe enough.

Exeter City

Robinet woke with a head that felt as though a man had taken to driving a hole through his skull by the simple expedient of using a small awl and twisting it with determination, slowly.

He cautiously opened his eyes and stared about him. The room was unfamiliar: a high ceiling, bare, white wooden beams, a smell of fresh hay. It was no room in which he had slept before, clearly. The place was too new.

Sitting up quickly, he winced at the pain at his temples, and reached up with a hand. As he felt his skull, he was aware of a soreness and swelling above his ear, but then a rolling wave of nausea overwhelmed him, and he retched without release for a few moments.

There was nothing new about this. Someone had cracked his skull last night. Quickly he reached for his essentials: his little wallet, in which he had stored his spoon and the pewter badge of St Christopher from when he went on pilgrimage long ago. His knife was still at his belt, and his few coins were not stolen. All seemed in their place. And there was this place, too. *Where*, in God's good name, was he?

Shaking his head gently, he walked to the doorway. From here he could gaze out into a small yard. It was entirely unfamiliar, and he wondered whether he might have been brought here by James last night.

The fellow had a sound heart. He had explained all about how his uncautious words had come to the ear of the king, and how his guilt had assailed him immediately he heard what had happened to Robinet, but by that stage there was nothing he could do. The harm was done, and Robinet was after all the architect of his own downfall. He should have kept his trap locked shut instead of shooting his mouth off like some idiot with word diarrhoea.

Bearing in mind how fearful James had been on meeting him again, the lad had proved stout-hearted. He'd insisted on buying Robinet, his 'old mentor', as he would repeat over and over, more ale until Newt had been quite cheerful. And then, for some reason, the pair of them had decided that they needed to go out for a walk in the middle of the night. A God-cursed miracle they hadn't been seen by the watch and arrested.

Why, though? Was it just to clear their heads? To his shame, Newt couldn't remember. It was an affliction he'd noticed before, this loss of memory after a few ales. It never used to happen to him when he was young, but now he was into his fiftieth year, whenever he drank more than usual, it led to this forgetfulness.

The light was bright in the doorway, and, feeling still rather fragile, he walked slowly to the bed where he had slept last night, letting himself fall into the hay. Eyes closed, he groaned gently to himself. James must have brought him here rather than deposit him with Walter. James had always been scared of Walter – natural enough, but Robinet had long ago lost any terror he had of Walter. The man was retired now, anyway, and it was plain silly to be scared of him. Still, it had been kind of James to find him a safe, warm stable to sleep in. If he'd been left out in the cold and ice, he could have frozen to the cobbles.

It was strange to think how he had hated James for all those years. The lad had been the focus of all his bile and loathing, and yet now James had protected him from the miserable weather.

Curious to think how they had changed. When they had first met, it was before the famine. Christ Jesus, Robinet was still too used to the miserable weather of the last years. It would never leave him, no, nor any of the others who had experienced it. The famine had touched every household in the realm with the kiss of death. Barons, the rich, the poor, all were affected. And as people died, the cost of food had risen until many like Robinet could no longer afford feed for their horses.

Robinet had already decided to end his career in 1320, but when his corrody had been granted at Ospringe, he had taken leave to travel a little more. For a man like him, to be tied to one religious house was a torment. Better by far to be permitted to wander still as the urge took him. There was little of the country which he had not already seen, admittedly, but he still had a desire to see some other aspects of it. He had come to Exeter, and then he had seen the man whom he loathed above all others. The man who had reported him and destroyed his career. Young James.

It was peculiar to see him there in broad daylight as though there was nothing for him to be fearful about. The fool. There was always someone to fear, no matter how strong or courageous you might be. Even the king himself . . . but that was a separate story.

A cry in the street startled him out of his mild torpor. He put his hands on the hay and pushed himself upright. There was a liquid mess on the hay under his left hand, and without wanting to look at it or discover what it might be, he averted his head, still queasy, and wiped his hand dry on the stems before walking to the door and peering out into the sunlight.

Shielding his eyes from the brightness, he was relieved when a cloud drifted lazily overhead and shut out the light. He crossed the yard, aware at every step of the looseness in his belly. It felt deeply unpleasant. At the gate to the yard, he found himself looking out into an ancient alley which smelled rank with the odour of faeces and rotten meats.

From here, the alley ran southwards down to the southern gate. It lay a distance below him, down the hill. His eyes were not as strong as they once had been, even before the ale last night, yet he could make out a group of people standing in a ragged line at the bottom of the hill. One was a great, bearded fellow, and Robinet wondered who he could be. Certainly, the fellow was haranguing his audience with vigour, from what Robinet could see. And then he saw the body being drawn from the rubbish, and he withdrew from the doorway in alarm, his hand on his knife. Quickly, he snatched it free and stared in horror at the blackening stains on the metal of the forged blade. Filled with a rising horror, he noticed his hand – the mess that he had rested his palm on was blood . . .

His common sense rose swiftly now, and he strode across, back into the stable. Yes, the mess in the hay beside the flattened area where he had slept was indeed beslobbered with blood. He quickly grabbed a handful of straw and wiped his hand again, then rubbed at his dagger's blade until it was clean.

'Must leave the town,' he said to himself. His pack must be here somewhere, and he cast about for it. The room appeared to be a storage house for a rich man or someone, and was filled with hay and barrels of salted fish among other items. Nothing good for him just now, certainly. He must find his few belongings and be gone, that was all that mattered to him now: to get to Walter's house, collect his belongings and make good his escape.

And then he heard voices approaching the place, and he must

retreat into the shadows, his eyes as wide as a felon's as the rope tightened about his neck.

'Sweet Jesus, what have I done?'

As soon as the voices had passed by up the alleyway, he kicked the hay about to conceal where he had lain and cover over the blood, and then slipped out into the alley himself.

Chapter Five

Exeter City

'COME, NOW! WHO FOUND THIS BENIGHTED SOUL?'

Will was fretting enough already, without this giant bellowing at him. He tentatively put up his hand and confessed that he had discovered the corpse.

'You again, eh? You found the poor devil up that alley as well, didn't you? Don't be so damned nervous, man. You make me twitchy! Come along, come along! What happened, hey?'

Not only was Will a watchman, he had also been involved in several juries over the years, and the thought of a coroner's inquest held no fears for him. He knew the coroners of the city, and they were not scary. Yet this man . . .

Sir Richard de Welles was a large man – not over-tall, perhaps a little more than six feet, nor grossly fat, but in some way the bearded knight appeared to take up more space than an ordinary mortal. He stood with his legs set widely apart and gazed about him with an expression of benign approval on his cherubic face. Much was concealed by the thick bush of beard that overhung his chest like a heavy gorget. His eyes were dark brown and shrewd, and criss-crossed with wrinkles, making him appear older than his true age of some fifty summers.

And just now those keen, narrowed eyes were studying Will.

'WELL, MAN?' he suddenly barked, and Will all but dropped his staff.

'Sir, if it pleases your honour, I found him here. A hog was at him already, sir, and I had to beat it away, but the man was down here under the rubbish and I had to clear away a little of it to see him. Then the gatekeeper here came to help me when I raised the hue and cry, and . . .'

'Enough! God's pain, but you'd witter here while the city burned about your ears, wouldn't you, man? No doubt you're a fine fellow when it comes to maintaining the peace at night after curfew, but you just leave matters to me when it comes to dead men, eh?'

For all his bluster, the coroner was a kindly man. He could see perfectly well that the watchman was petrified at being questioned by him, and, to be fair, Sir Richard de Welles was not concerned with the fellow anyway. He was much more interested in the men who should be here as witnesses. He wasn't holding a formal inquest yet, but he did want to see who the neighbours were so that tomorrow, when he did hold the full inquest, he would know whom he was dealing with.

'Two murders in as many days, hey? Suppose that's what you get when you live in a city. Damned unhealthful places, cities. Give me a good vill in the country. Somewhere with dogs and a park to hunt the deer. You can keep your alleys and winding streets,' he said conversationally. 'That other fellow,' he said, jerking his head up the alley where he had already inspected the body from the previous morning, 'he'll be safe to leave exactly where he is. This one, though, I suppose we ought to pull him free. Can't have him lying in the middle of this rubbish heap, eh? Someone might decide to tidy him up . . .' He stopped and took a long, considering view of the neighbourhood. Then, shaking his head sadly, he confessed, 'Although I can't see it meself. No one ever cleans up around here, do they? Damned mess.' He glanced back at Will, who had started to relax, feeling the coroner's attention moving on. 'Tell me: did you knock up the neighbours?'

'Aye, all four nearest.'

'And are those excellent fellows here now?' Sir Richard asked, gazing about him amiably.

'Three of them are, your honour.'

'Three, you say? That is good. It is almost very good. What sort of man is the fourth, who failed to come here today?'

'He is a tradesman, sir. He is working. We didn't think you'd hold an inquest today, because it'll take a day to gather the jury . . . sir . . .'

The smile on Sir Richard de Welles's face grew brittle. 'He is working, is he? And a fine thing to be doing, too. Is there any here who knows this man? What is he called? John Currier? Excellent. Excellent. Now, my fine friend Will . . .' Sir Richard placed his hands on his hips and smiled, leaning down to the petrified watchman. 'Will, I would like you to go to this marvellous man, right now, if you don't mind, and when you see him, you *tell that benighted excretion of a minor demon that whether or not I hold the inquest here today, I am working too, and if he doesn't want his balls separated from his body and spread over my roasted bread before the full inquest tomorrow morning, he had best get his arse over here* RIGHT NOW!'

'I'll bring him,' Will bleated anxiously, all but tripping over his staff in his hurry to escape that fearful face with the blazing eyes. He stumbled once on the rough cobbles, and then hared off as fast as his ancient legs would carry him.

The coroner, satisfied that the man had an appreciation of his need for urgency, turned away from him and studied his audience. All male, their ages ranging from some twelve or thirteen years, the jury ringed him, their faces registering their own displeasure. None was happy to be there, especially when a body had been found so near to them. A corpse meant one thing: punishment. They all knew that if this man had been murdered, they would all be amerced.

Sir Richard allowed his eyes to range over the jury, and then he selected two to pull the man from the pile, his eyes going to the body as the men grabbed a wrist and an arm and tugged.

The man at the wrist was a younger fellow, and the churl was as ineffectual as a damned maiden in the way that he pulled at the hand which had been all but chewed away by the hog, but Sir Richard's attention was not focused on him, or on the hand with the missing fingers. Rather, his serious gaze was fixed on the uniform of the dead man. Particoloured: half blue, half blue striped.

'Sweet mother of Christ,' he muttered. 'The man's a king's messenger.'

Watching from a short distance away, the man sucked his teeth as the messenger's body was tugged from the garbage heap, and then, having seen enough, he turned away and crossed the street towards the tavern at the top of the Cooks' Row. From there he could watch the streets east and west, which gave him some comfort. He didn't want to be arrested without seeing her.

Maurice had spent too much time running. His boots were almost worn through, his hosen frayed and ripped from crossing too much wild land through bracken and bramble, and his cloak was scarcely any use as protection from the weather. Although he still carried a small riding sword, it was concealed beneath his cloak where men would not see it so easily. A man of his condition should not carry a noble weapon like that. It attracted too much attention.

He bit into a loaf of bread and ate it ravenously, his eyes going about all the men in the room. No one appeared to be taking too much notice of him, and he felt moderately sure that his sudden departure from Evesham had gone unnoticed. In any case, he had covered the distance quickly, and even mounted men would have taken longer. Riders had to bear in mind the condition of their horses.

Finishing his meal, he rested his left hand at his thigh, feeling the comforting weight of the sword beneath. He had one thing to do here, and he would do it, no matter what.

In the alley, Robinet was marching at a rapid pace. First thing was, to get out of the city. There were plenty of places where a man like him could hide, but the first thing was protection. While he remained here in the city, there was the danger that someone might have seen him with the dead man and report him. In his shabby clothing, he was scarcely conspicuous, but with his luck the man who saw him would be a fellow with a perfect memory for detail. Better by far to leave the city and put as many miles between it and him as possible.

How could he have been so *stupid*! It was insane to kill the man. Yes, he had been a complete bastard to Robinet, and betrayed his trust entirely, but that was no excuse for such a mad act. He must have been beastly drunk to have done something like that. Anyway, he thought they'd been getting on fine by the third quart of strong ale. Had they argued late in the night?

The memory of the blade at his belt, smothered in a slick coating of gore, was enough to make his belly clench, and he was close to heaving as he reached the end of the alley. His pack was made of his cloak, rolled and tied with thongs to keep everything inside, and now he slipped his arm through one and threw the parcel over his shoulder, gripped his staff, and let his head hang as he walked towards the southern gate.

As always the way here was blocked with the crowds coming into the city. Exeter was so busy now, the four key gates were always hectic. Today the southern gate was blocked by what looked like a solid mass of people marching towards him, all carrying wares on their heads or yokes about their necks. A woman with a bucket of fish had dropped it and was wailing as she tried to gather up her merchandise; a short distance behind her a tranter on his cart was hurling abuse at her for holding up everyone else, and when she remained there in the road the man swore loudly, whipped up his old nag, and tried to ride around her. His wheel caught between a pair of loose cobbles, and although the horse tugged for all it was worth, the cart rocked but wouldn't rise from the small gulley. In a fury, the carter jerked the reins, and the poor brute, trying to obey, twisted to pass across the road. One hoof caught the woman a slashing blow on her arm, and she screamed as the sharpened metal of the shoe tore down her upper arm and opened the flesh for six inches. The horse, panicked by her scream, reared and plunged, and terrified people screamed as they saw those metal-shod feet flailing.

People were shouting and pushing, and the man's hoarse bellowing helped little. Robinet stood gaping as the people hurried past him. Two barged into him, but he scarcely noticed. There was no point in joining the confusion. Rather, he fell back with the people, gradually slipping to the edge of them, so that he could gain the protection of a house's wall, and wait there.

By good fortune, from where he now stood, he could see the figure of the dead messenger in the roadway. A guard stood watchfully over the corpse, and Robinet could not help himself. He walked over to the body and stood peering at it while the guard leaned against the wall and watched the people running past. The urgency and terror was already abating, and there were already more people laughing than screaming. Children had arrived to see what was the cause of the uproar, and the watchman was chuckling at the antics of the tranter as he clambered down from his cart and tried to pull his nag forward, out of the little gulley.

'This man. Has the coroner given his verdict on the death?' Robinet asked.

'Yes. He was throttled some time recently. Didn't want us to take him away yet, said someone else had to see him. God knows why. Clear enough what happened.'

'What, a robbery?'

'Yeah. Course. Someone found him here drunk, and pulled him out from the road with a cord round his neck. Wouldn't take long to kill him like that.'

Robinet nodded, but his mind was far away. He wasn't even looking at the body now. Instead he stared down towards his belly, at the knife that dangled there.

So if he had been strangled, *whose* blood was it on his knife?

Coroner Richard was loud, bullying and ferocious when he thought it necessary, but he was not a fool, and now, as he walked away from his brief investigation of the body, he wore a frown.

The man had been murdered, that was plain. As had the other fellow. But the first had been robbed after having his throat cut – a simple theft by some scrote who happened by the dead man while hard up for money. It was a common enough event. The other was very different: he was a king's messenger, and as such should have been safe from any kind of attack. The fact that someone dared to assault him was worrying.

He entered a tavern and bawled for ale while he considered the matter. One thing was clear – he must report it as soon as he could. He would go to the sheriff and advise him of the messenger's death.

Chapter Six

The Bishop's Palace

'Sir Baldwin, I am glad to see you once more. You are well, I hope?'

The Bishop of Exeter sat coolly as Baldwin entered his chamber. Bishop Walter II was a tall man, with peering eyes, a stooped back, and all too often a frown on his face. Just now his expression was welcoming, but as Baldwin bent to kiss the episcopal ring, he was quite sure that before long that cheerful smile would fade.

Their greetings over, the bishop sat back and toyed with his spectacles. Baldwin knew that Walter was very short-sighted. It was the natural effect of so many years studying religious books, and more recently keeping a close eye on the detailed reports of the nation's finances. He was Lord High Treasurer, close adviser to the king, and recently he had become friend and ally of the Despenser family.

'Sir Baldwin, I was very sad to hear that you were unhappy with the idea of becoming a member of the king's parliament. No!' He held up a hand as Baldwin tried to interrupt him. 'Please let me finish. My feeling was, and is, that you would be a perfect foil for some of the more foolish people who presently advise the king. There are many who would be better employed elsewhere. A man such as yourself would bring more experience and sense to many of the discussions.'

'My Lord Bishop, I am very mindful of the honour you do me by suggesting me for this,' Baldwin said with a smile, 'but I am afraid I think that it is a step too far for me. I am at bottom a simple knight who is happy with my quiet life here in the country. I have no interest in lengthy journeys to London or York to attend great meetings with other knights, barons and lords. And the help I could give would be minimal. Look at me! I'm a rural knight with an interest in rural affairs, not those of great moment in the nation's politics.'

'That is precisely the point,' the bishop said, pouring a goblet of strong red wine and passing it to Baldwin. 'The parliament is there to bring to the fore all the views of all the king's subjects. He is as interested in the affairs of the lowliest churl steeping a hedge as in the doings of a great lord.'

Baldwin said nothing as to the peasant steeping a hedge. There were strong rumours that the king enjoyed such activities far too much. It was hardly the occupation of a man who would lead barons into battle. 'You mean a great lord such as Thomas of Lancaster?'

Bishop Walter looked at him coldly. 'Earl Thomas was a traitor. He spoke treason, and supported those who would have destroyed the king's honour and dignity. If it were not for his influence, I doubt that the Lords Marcher would have dared to rise in rebellion.'

In his heart Baldwin disagreed. The Lords Marcher had risen against the Despensers, the acquisitive and ruthless father and son who had enriched themselves by robbing others up and down the country, depriving widows of their estates, bearing false witness against those whom they considered their enemies, and preventing any from petitioning the king without paying them bribes. There was none who dared stand against them, not since the king had brutally executed his own cousin, Earl Thomas of Lancaster, in their support. Their hold on his affection was so strong that to murmur against the Despensers could be viewed as treason. And Baldwin hated himself for not saying as much to the bishop.

'There has never been more need of cool, calm advice than now,' the bishop continued. 'The threat from the French king . . . if we were to lose Guyenne, the crown would be greatly damaged. We have to protect the king's lands over there, but how? You are a man experienced in war. Your advice could be invaluable.'

'My fighting days are long past,' Baldwin said shortly.

'I did not say you should fight, Sir Baldwin, but that you ought at least to be prepared to share your knowledge of battle. You were involved in the last great battle of Acre, I recall?'

'It was a long time ago, my lord.'

'Perhaps. Much has happened since then, naturally.'

Baldwin felt his blood thicken. There was a sudden emptiness in his belly as he absorbed the bishop's words. He had told Stapledon many years ago about his experiences in Acre, but surely he had never mentioned the fact that he used to be a Knight Templar? Yet there seemed to be an edge to Bishop Walter's voice that implied he knew – and more, that if Baldwin didn't acquiesce to being elected, the bishop might tell others of his position. To be a known as a renegade Templar could cost him his life. Those who were found after escaping the original arrests were still potentially at risk of a pyre.

His mind flashed with scenes of his life today: his daughter and wife at their home near Cadbury. Then came the memory of bodies burned and unrecognisable lying in the smouldering ashes of a large fire, and the sight of Jacques de Molay standing proudly before the Cathedral at Notre Dame and declaring that the accusations were baseless, unfounded, and malicious ... He could see himself in a burst, his clothes on fire, his mouth wide in a scream of agony so intense it curdled the fluid in his veins just to think of it.

And then the anger flooded him. 'You say I should go to advise? And what good would that achieve when there are so many near the king who enjoy his trust and whose words he will accept over all others?'

'We have a truce with France, but there is no guarantee that this time next month, or even next week, we shall not be at war again.'

'The king is fortunate enough to have a ready-made ambassador. He married her,' Baldwin said sarcastically. 'Perhaps he ought to enquire of her what the best action would be?'

'Come, now, sir knight!' Bishop Stapledon snapped. 'You think that the sister of the French king would be an impartial counsellor? She may well seek to return to her mother land. What better ally could the French hope for than a spy within the king's own household? She is too dangerous.'

'Who made her so?' Baldwin demanded sharply. 'Is it not true that her husband left her for others?'

The Bishop stared at him for a long moment, and Baldwin wondered whether he had overstepped the bounds of his patience, but then Stapledon closed his eyes and held them shut for a few minutes. At last he opened them, and now his tone was simply weary.

'In God's name, Baldwin, I swear, I believe that the woman could be inimical to the security of the realm. I have myself argued for the sequestration of her lands and the reduction of her household so that the threat is reduced, but I did not enjoy it. Nor the other measures taken. But whatever the reasons for her behaviour, they are not justified. The king is king, and master of the whole kingdom, and whatever she feels about his actions, she should not be provoked.'

'You think she has been?'

'I know her. She is a woman of intelligence and spirit,' the bishop answered. 'And while the French challenge us at Guyenne, she must remain here – safe.'

'You see, though, Bishop, that we do not agree on the issues here,' Baldwin said. 'What useful purpose could I serve in parliament? Leave me here to remain as a contented rural knight, raising my family in peace and without the interruptions of national affairs.'

'I wish I could,' the bishop replied. 'But, Baldwin, I believe your intellect could help save the country from disaster. I am being frank with you, old friend.'

'It is neither to my taste nor to my interest,' Baldwin said with conviction.

The bishop leaned forward and fixed Baldwin with a serious gaze before speaking both urgently and quietly, as though trying to conceal his words from any who may be listening. 'Think of your duty, then, Sir Baldwin . . . if you do not go, will it not be only those who seek to flatter and promote the king who will be granted positions in the parliament?'

There was a soft knocking at the door, and Baldwin saw the bishop's expression alter, just slightly. It was a fleeting thing, a sudden sharpness in the eyes, as though this interruption was expected, but not anticipated quite so soon, and then the bishop was calling to the visitor to enter.

'Oh, Sheriff. It is good to see you,' he said.

The tall, urbane figure who had just entered walked across the room and stood before the bishop, bending to kiss the episcopal ring. Only then did he acknowledge Baldwin. 'Sir Baldwin – it is good to see you again.'

'And you, Sir Matthew. All must say it is always a pleasure to see you.'

Sir Matthew de Crowethorne smiled at that as he moved over the floor to a chair. Once seated, with a goblet of wine from the bishop's steward, he shot a look at the bishop as though questioning whether he should begin. He was clad in rich velvet, a shimmering green with particoloured green and red hosen, and the cloak which he so carelessly tossed over a bench was trimmed with warm squirrel fur. He was, like so many sheriffs, keen on ostentation, and glanced at Baldwin's faded and worn red tunic with amused contempt.

Bishop Walter did not see his look. 'The good sheriff has many duties here in Exeter, Sir Baldwin, as you know. But just now he is seeking to find the best knight to send to the next parliament. I have suggested to him that we need someone with some intellect, a man of honour. I have, in short, suggested you.'

'It is very kind of you, but I would be most reluctant to accept any such position.'

'Even though it would be for the good of the shire? And the state?' Sheriff Matthew pressed.

Baldwin opened his mouth to respond, but before he could there was a loud knocking at the door of the palace, and the sheriff and the bishop were both quiet, listening intently. For once, Baldwin felt relief at the interruption of that familiar voice.

'*Didn't you hear me, you cretinous little scrote? I asked if Sir Baldwin de Furnshill was here, man. Don't hop from foot to foot, damn your arse. Just fetch him here, or tell me where to find him. Oh . . . and my compliments to your lord bishop, too.*'

Exeter City

The morning in the city was less bright already. The sun was concealed behind clouds, and to add to the dimness, as soon as dawn reached the town people were already gathering their faggots of twigs and thrusting them onto their fires. In less than a couple of hours after the sun's light had first licked the tops of the cathedral's towers, already there was a thick fume rising from the city: the proof of civilisation anywhere.

It was a delightful sight and smell, Robinet thought to himself. Others might have different feelings, but to him as an experienced traveller there was little better than the view through a group of trees which showed a rising plume of smoke. That held the promise of warm, dry beds and rooms with a fire inside for the weary. It was like a place he had seen many years before – at least fourteen – when he was in France. He had been sent by the king to visit Vienne, and he could well remember the feeling of relief to see that after so many miles on unfamiliar roads in a strange, hot land, there was a set of gibbets with fly-blown corpses hanging in chains. Those parcels of decaying flesh meant that at last there was a place nearby where law held sway. Outlaws were no more to be feared.

Exeter was different, though. He knew how dangerous a city like this could be, and Robinet had no intention of being harmed. He needed to escape the place if he could. Walter would be able to help him as soon as he had got his belongings back.

But if he did grab his things and run, he might never find out what had happened. James's death might never be solved – a dreadful thought. The two men had been estranged for so long, and now he was thinking of bolting only the morning after they had sealed their renewed friendship. That was sad. No: worse than that: it was *sick*.

The swelling over his ear was slightly crusted with blood, but the pain was reducing, thanks to Christ. He was sure now that someone had struck him down. He really should leave. Others were here to learn what had happened to the dead messenger. It was a city, it had its coroners and keepers. He could scarcely do anything that they couldn't.

Except he hated to leave the affair like this. James deserved a little loyalty. Was it James who had knocked him down? The whole of the evening after they had left the tavern was a haze . . . there were some images, but all indistinct, unclear . . . no matter how he tried to concentrate, he couldn't bring anything back. Someone had struck him at some point, someone had helped him to the hay. And then James had been thrown into a rubbish heap, the foul stuff hauled over him to hide him. It was demeaning, disgraceful, to treat a man so.

Suddenly Robinet felt a flash of anger. His belly roiled, but his eyes narrowed and he began to think more quickly as he started to walk.

Chapter Seven

Tavistock Abbey

Simon had not been in a good mood the next morning when he had woken up. All too soon he had remembered the half-grin on de Courtenay's face as he delivered the final blow: bad enough that he should want Simon to follow a man who might well be consulting a *maleficus* – someone who might take offence at being followed even to the extent of having Simon murdered. And by supernatural powers, not even the normal, everyday risks of a knife in an alley.

Anyone who knew Simon knew of his . . . *caution* when it came to matters of superstition. There were some, like Baldwin, who thought that his attitude bordered on the fringes of credulousness – or worse. Simon didn't care. So far as he was concerned, the idea of magic was nothing new, and he had personally seen people who had used it to cure cattle of various diseases. They would incant a phrase or mumble some weird words, and in the time it took the farmer to get back to his house, the animal would be cured. And there were evil spirits who could be used to attack people who stood in the path of their human patrons. Simon had heard of plenty of examples of that kind of evil: where people were harmed, or their libido destroyed, or their energy sapped, and all because of an evil-doer.

The idea of chasing after someone of that kind was enough to make his flesh creep.

He rose and dressed slowly in the old guesthouse above the main gate, kicking Rob as he passed the lad snoring gently in the corner of the room on a thin palliasse. Rob muttered a comment concerning Simon's parentage, but today Simon was not of a mood to listen, and instead strode downstairs to fetch himself some food to break his fast.

It was a cold day, with white and grey clouds hanging in the air as though plastered to the sky. Simon sniffed: there was a metallic edge to the air, and he was unhappy with the thin, insubstantial sunlight that filtered through the clouds. Although their edges gleamed silver, the sun kept herself behind them, and Simon had a horrible suspicion that this was to be the rule for the day. At best they would be chilled by the icy breeze as they rode, and at worst they would be drenched in freezing rain. It was not a prospect to thrill.

He found a warm loaf in the bakery, and sat on a bench nearby with a slab of cold sausage. An amiable monk made an offer of warmed ale, which Simon accepted with alacrity, and when he was feeling a little more normal he went to seek Robert Busse.

A helpful monk pointed him in the direction of the cloister, and Simon soon found the man who sought to grasp the abbacy before de Courtenay could. Busse nodded to Simon, and then led the way down a short corridor to a chamber.

Busse was a genial man, a little taller than the old abbot had been, but considerably shorter than the younger de Courtenay. He had pleasantly rounded features, twinkling blue eyes, a high brow and, when he spoke, a soft tenor voice. More than that, though, Simon was aware of a chuckle that was always nearby. He appeared to be on the brink of laughter all the while.

'So you are the bailiff? Aha! Good. Just what I need to make sure that I get to Exeter in one piece.'

'With the weather the way it is now, I doubt we'll be there in less than a day and a half at least,' Simon said grimly.

'That soon? I had hoped for a pause at a tavern or two, Bailiff. Especially if this inclement weather continues. It's too chill for a body to sit a horse for too long – and woe betide the man who tries to sit out in this stuff.'

'I cannot argue with that,' Simon said.

Busse tilted his head and studied Simon. 'Are you quite all right?'

'Yes. I am fine.'

'I know that this must be a rather sore and tedious task for you, Bailiff, but I will try to make it as pleasant as possible. You must have covered the journey many times in your term of office as a stannary bailiff.'

'Oh, yes.' Simon smiled without humour. 'I've certainly made the journey many times.'

'Well, it is a long way to go. Perhaps we should fetch our belongings and meet down in the court?'

Simon left him and strode ill-temperedly to the guest house again, where he found that Rob had disappeared. 'God's fist! The little sodomite is going to hold us up,' he muttered as he returned down the stairs with his pack in his hand, and gazed about him. On a hunch, he paced across the cobbled yard to the stables, and peered inside.

'Go on, another ha'penny.'

'I'll lay on.'

'And me.'

'I'll pay later . . .'

'No, you don't,' Rob said, and then caught sight of his master in the doorway.

'What is this?' Simon demanded, entering the gloomy interior. There were four youths inside, three grooms, and, Simon saw with a sharp pang of guilt, a novice too. 'Rob, tell me you aren't tempting these fellows into gambling?'

'Gambling? Hardly that, Bailiff. No, it's more a sort of trial, that's all.'

The others were hurriedly gathering up coins and thrusting them into their purses. If any were discovered here gambling during Abbot Robert's tenure, they'd have been given short shrift – or maybe not. The good abbot was no hypocrite, and he was a man of contrasting interests himself. Perhaps if he had found the lads there, he would have pretended anger, and then insisted that they joined him in a game too, so that he could fleece them and thereby give them a clear and unforgettable demonstration of the evils of gambling.

'What sort of trial?'

Rob shamefacedly held up a number of dice. 'Just a game,' he amended. 'Hazard.'

'Put the things away, Rob. And don't let me see you trying to take money from others like that. In God's name, taking cash from a novice!'

'It's what we all do in Dartmouth to while away the time. If they aren't so practised, it's hardly my fault,' Rob said heatedly.

'Enough. You'll have time to reflect on your actions later as we ride. You're too late for breakfast now. You will just have to make do.'

'Oh, I've had my breakfast, master. And I've got some vittles for the journey, too. Enough for three meals.'

Simon blinked. 'How did you do that?'

'Well, I played them for it. The novice was taking all this food from the kitchen to the servants somewhere, so I played him at dice for it, and then the others wanted to join in too, so I took their money. It would have been daft not to.'

'What of the horses?'

'They're already tethered to the rail by the gate. I had the grooms promise to do them before I'd play them at any games in here.'

Simon took three paces back and peered across the yard. True enough, there were three horses, two riding beasts and one packhorse, ready loaded, out near the gate. And as he stood staring, he caught sight of Busse standing and gazing up at the sun.

'Oh. Right. Yes. Well, come on! We're late,' Simon said.

The Bishop's Palace

'Coroner, it is good to see you again!' Baldwin said, smiling broadly as Richard de Welles entered.

'Keeper!' de Welles boomed as he saw the knight. 'Good to see you too. Ha!' He glanced about the room, nodding to the sheriff. 'This reminds me of a story about a young whore and a . . .' He suddenly recalled whose room he was in and cast an apologetic glance towards the bishop. 'Ah, a good day to you, my Lord Bishop . . . Sir Matthew. But that's not why I'm here. No, I was going to ask you for your assistance, Keeper. I heard the sheriff was here, and the man at the castle said you would be here with him.'

'I am here to be commanded,' Baldwin replied. 'What is it you wish from me?'

'Is it a matter for the keeper, or for me?' the sheriff demanded, somewhat petulantly.

'A man has been murdered out near the South Gate, and I fear it's a matter which will affect the whole city if something is not done about it, and that swiftly. A king's messenger . . .'

The bishop's head snapped up. 'What was that?'

'Yes, Bishop. A youngish lad, with a shock of chestnut hair, green eyes and a kind of oval face. His cheek is marked with a ragged scar, as though someone has stabbed at him with a blunt or jagged blade, and . . .'

'I know him,' Sheriff Matthew declared.

'Ah, good,' the coroner said with satisfaction. 'I knew this matter could soon be cleared up. What was his name?'

'His name? I have no idea! He was just a messenger, not someone I would chat with.'

'My lord?' Baldwin asked.

'I am afraid he was quite new to me. I did not know his name.'

Baldwin's eyebrows rose. Messengers trusted by the king tended to be insiders at court, and he would have expected a wily politician like the bishop to have a great interest in speaking to them and showing himself to be courteous and friendly. After all, whether he liked the messenger or not, the messenger would have the ear of the king.

Stapledon had turned to face him. 'Sir Baldwin, this is most important. You must go with the good coroner and investigate this killing. Is that clear? I want to know if he was murdered for his money, or whether it was something more serious.'

Baldwin exchanged a look with the coroner. 'Bishop, this man – he was a messenger, so had he come here to give you a message?'

'Yes. And I sent him away with a response. It is a most important document. You have to seek it.'

'It may well still be on him. What sort of document is it?'

The bishop glanced away from Baldwin, and appeared to be staring out through the window. 'Sir Baldwin, if he has it still, it is a small parchment some four inches long, with my own personal seal at the top, and the seal of the Lord High Treasurer in the middle to secure it. I cannot emphasise strongly enough how important it is that the document is found. The thing is incredibly sensitive. You have to find it.'

Baldwin sighed with some exasperation. 'Very well. Coroner, you will have searched the man's clothing. What was in his pouch?'

'There were messages there, but I did not feel free to rifle about in the king's business. I didn't look.'

'What is in the document?' Baldwin asked the bishop. 'If you want me to find it, you have to tell me what I am looking for.'

'Sir Baldwin, I cannot. You will know it if you find it. Just search the man and see if it is there. I must press you – it is enormously important to me!'

Chapter Eight

Warwick Gaol

The warder was back again. The crash of the great oaken door with the iron furniture was so loud, the noise of it echoed along the corridor. Even at the farthest end of it, Robert le Mareschal was stirred. He only prayed that the man wasn't coming to question him again.

He had lost track of time. It was certainly a long while since he had gone to the sheriff and insisted on telling his story, how the figures had been made, whom they represented, how he and John of Nottingham had taken the figurine of de Sowe and pulled out the pin, then waited a moment and thrust it deep into the waxen figure's breast. God, but Robert had been so scared by then. He had almost fainted away with the fear. And then, when he heard of de Sowe's death, there had been only an all-encompassing terror of what his master had achieved, and, together with that, a dread of his own fate.

The money was nothing. Money could buy nothing that mattered to him now. The whole affair had started with money, it was true, and then he had realised that it also gave him a chance to win his revenge on the faithless devils who had so ruined his father, but that was not enough, no, not by a long measure, to justify his own destruction.

It was when he heard that de Sowe was dead that he truly realised his peril, and only then did he take that terrible step, and go to see the sheriff. And soon after he and all the others were taken and held in gaol. All twenty-five of the men who had asked them to make the figures and kill the king and his favourites, as well as Robert and John of Nottingham. And John had stared at him, and then smiled, as though he knew full well that the betrayal came from him, and Robert feared that more than anything: the knowledge that his master knew his guilt.

Because Robert knew – *Christ Jesus, he knew!* – that John of Nottingham was a truly evil man.

Exeter City

'What do you think of this, Coroner?' Baldwin said quietly as they made their way from the bishop's palace, out through the palace gate, and thence down to the southern gate of the city.

'Me? I'd reckon he's either lost a large part of his senses, or he has reason to know that there's a dangerous document in the messenger's purse.' Normally a man who would have a hundred filthy jokes to hand, the coroner was unusually quiet today. The seriousness of the matter had eradicated his sense of humour.

'Is it likely that the messenger could have been killed for any other reason than the theft of his purse?' Baldwin wondered. King's messengers were almost never attacked or harmed. They were known by their small pouches with the king's own arms on them as much as by their uniforms.

'A man might have seen him and desired to know what was held in his purse, I suppose. An off-the-cuff decision. A chance encounter. Man saw him, thought: "Nice little purse, wonder how much money's in it," ' Coroner Richard proposed. He looked at Baldwin. 'No. You're right. He was murdered for this document, whatever it was.'

'Which puts us in a very difficult position, old friend.'

'Why?'

'Because whoever killed that messenger must have known what was in his pouch, and desired it for his own reasons. And that man therefore must be known to the bishop. He is probably in the bishop's own household, because how else could a man have come to know what was in the pouch?'

'There was the messenger himself.'

Baldwin shook his head. 'The messenger would be the last to know what was held in his pouch. He would only know the destination of the message, not the content. No, it must have been someone in the bishop's household who heard what was in it, and sought to take it.'

'Why?'

'We cannot tell that until we have it in our hands. Perhaps blackmail, perhaps information that could be easily sold to someone?'

Such as the French king, he told himself. If Bishop Stapledon had written something defamatory of the queen, the information could be enormously useful to the king of England's leading enemy.

'Well, let's go and check, then,' the coroner said easily. They were already at the gate, and he motioned to their left, to where the body lay, a beadle standing alert nearby.

Baldwin nodded, and crouched at the corpse's side. The pouch was a small leather purse with the king's arms painted carefully on the side. It was well constructed, with a waxen coating to protect the contents against wind and rain, and the fastening was tight, so Baldwin found he had some difficulty in opening it at first. Inside were some small message rolls, each some four inches long, and two in diameter. He glanced over at the coroner, who stood now leaning against a wall, picking at his teeth with a small stick he had sharpened. He eyed Baldwin with a contented, untroubled look.

Sighing to himself, Baldwin carefully studied each seal before removing the pouch from the dead man's belt and reinstalling all the messages in it.

'Well?' Coroner Richard demanded. 'Was it there?'

'No,' said Baldwin, and he couldn't help but glance over his shoulder towards the bishop's palace. This would not be a surprise to the bishop, he felt sure, but no matter whether it was or not, the fact was that Baldwin was being asked now to seek out a roll even though he knew nothing about the contents.

Looking away from the palace, he found himself wondering how many people within the city walls could be carrying a roll just like the one which had been stolen.

Dartmoor

'I hope you do not mind my observing,' Busse said, 'that you seem to be rather reserved today, Bailiff. In the past you have always struck me as a happy fellow, but today you are reluctant to speak to me.'

'No, no. I am just thinking about my wife,' Simon lied. 'I had been hoping to go straight to her when I was called back to Tavistock. Being sent on this journey was not in my mind.'

'I am sorry, Bailiff. I had no idea. I did not want company myself. It was only the insistence of others that led to my accepting your escort. I would much rather you returned home, if you wish to, than continued with me to a meeting you have no desire to witness.'

'I am sure that it is best that you have company on such a long journey,' Simon said shortly.

They had left the abbey and crossed the river by the old bridge, then taken the steep lane that rose from Tavistock heading east and north up to the moors themselves. It was Simon's intention to cross Dartmoor towards Chagford, and then head east towards Exeter. They would probably have to take it relatively slowly because the monk was unused to such journeying, but Simon was hopeful that no matter what happened he should be able to return to his home within the week.

'But why? Because I am elderly and infirm? I have been living here on the moors for more than twenty years, Bailiff,' the monk declared with a look of bafflement.

Simon could have snarled with annoyance. The sole reason for his being here was the one which he could not admit: that he was spying. 'The moors can be dangerous. You know that.'

'There are many dangers in the world,' Busse commented, looking about him. There was a furze bush nearby, and he trotted to it, reaching down and picking some of the brilliant yellow flowers and popping them into his mouth.

Simon agreed with that, glancing at Busse from the corner of his eye. He had no intention of admitting that he was afraid of no earthly dangers quite so much as the supernatural, but even as he watched the amiable monk at the gorse bush he was aware of the spirit of the moors, the spirit of old Crockern. If a man treated the moors disrespectfully, Crockern would take his revenge. There were many stories of how farmers would seek to change the moorland to suit them, but the moors would always revert, and the farmers would be ruined. No man could beat Crockern.

But for all that, the day was clearing nicely, with the grim clouds floating away, and the sun appearing every so often. Hills in the distance flashed bright in the light, then darkened as clouds drifted past, and from this higher point Simon could see the shadows washing over the hills like an ink poured over them. It was a thrilling sight, and one that made his heart leap for joy. No more sea and arguing sailors, no more John Hawley complaining about the amount of customs due on his imports, no more bickering between his neighbour and his servant . . .

'How far is it, then?'

Simon glanced down at the urchin at his stirrup. 'I will tell you when we are nearly there,' he grated. Rob was limping. Simon had insisted on buying boots for Rob before they tried to cross the moor, but the lad's feet were unused to them, and Simon had a feeling that he would take them off before long. He saw no need for such things, when he had never worn them before.

'But how much longer is it?'

Rob was peering ahead, eyes narrowed as the sun came out again, and suddenly Simon appreciated his interest: this was a lad who had never before travelled more than perhaps three miles from the house in which he had been born. He was a mere child when it came to experience of the world, and here he was, anticipating a visit to the largest city for hundreds of miles. He might never see such a place ever again. Although he had no comprehension of the distance to Exeter, he was as excited as a puppy with its first stick at the thought of it – and probably petrified in equal measure.

'We should be there tomorrow,' Simon said. 'It's a long walk from here. Perhaps forty or fifty miles? And the ground is not so easy as most of the way from Dartmouth to Tavistock. How are your feet?'

'This ground's fine,' Rob said. 'But God's ballocks, that's a long way to go.'

'Sooner we get on the sooner we'll arrive,' Simon said more curtly, nervously shooting a look at the man who wished to be abbot.

As if feeling his eye on him, Busse winked at Simon. 'I can see that a prayer for the easing of profane comments from the mouths of children could be a good idea.'

Rob frowned, then pulled a face that seemed to indicate that his respect for the monk was not increasing. Not that Simon reckoned it was because Rob was concerned that he might have offended the monk with his language; it was more that Rob hated being described as a child.

Exeter City

The messenger had been pulled free of the pile of rubbish and lay face down on the packed earth beside the roadway. When Baldwin enquired, Coroner de Welles confirmed that he had given the body a cursory inspection. The inquest would be in a day or so as usual, and the body would be stripped naked and rolled over and over in front of the jury so that they could see and witness all the wounds. So far, the coroner had merely watched the body being pulled from the rubbish, and briefly glanced at it before seeking Baldwin, who was kneeling at its side now, examining it carefully.

He looked up at de Welles. 'Your conclusion?'

'You can see for yourself. The man had a thong pulled about his throat. Dead fairly quickly, I should think, although it wouldn't have been pleasant. He struggled. Look at the marks on his neck, eh?'

Baldwin peered frowningly at the thin line about the pale, slightly bluish flesh. 'Yes. But not a simple leather thong. If you look closely, you can see that there is a weave in the bruise. I should think that this was either a woven leather cord, or a hempen one. But very fine. Perhaps it could have been either, although if I were the assassin I should aim for leather as being stronger and safer. I see what you mean about the marks, though.'

'Yes, he fought back as he might, poor devil.'

Baldwin nodded. All along the thin line of the bruise left by the ligature there were scratches and scrapes. He had seen them often enough, as had the coroner: when men were hanged with their hands unbound, they would often struggle to release the cord in this way, scrabbling with their fingers at the cord, desperate to tug it free and give themselves some air. This man had tried in his desperation to hook his fingers under the cord and pull it away; his nails had made these sad little futile scratches. The blood had run heavily to the right side of the neck.

'Look here – this is strange. It is as though blood had been smeared over his throat, for none of the scratches under the cord could have bled enough for all this.'

'Aye, so perhaps the killer was himself wounded. I wondered whether the poor fellow managed to get a knife out and mark his assailant. Perhaps he stabbed the man's hand?'

'Indeed. Yet if he succeeded in that, surely he would have cut the thong that throttled him? A man would not fear a scratch from a knife compared with strangling, would he? But there is blood.' His gaze moved over the rest of the body. 'What else?'

'If you open his tunic, you will see he was stabbed, but only when he was already dead. Once he was on the ground, the killer thrust a dagger into his breast – I suppose he wanted to make sure, hey? No other reason for it. The knife was long and thin. I reckon at least nine inches long, because that's how far into his body the hole goes, and about an inch at the hilt, from the look of the wound.'

'And he was stabbed after death because the wound did not bleed.'

'Not at all. The man opened his tunic and stabbed him through the heart.'

A good job for someone, Baldwin told himself. Somebody would win these clothes, and at least this way they were undamaged. 'The body was in the rubbish there?'

'Yes. Well concealed, too. If it wasn't for the hog finding him, he'd still be there now. Might have been there for a year or more, the way the lazy bastards about this town leave their trash all over the place. Look at the stuff here! Blasted disgrace! Wouldn't let it happen at Lifton, I can tell you.'

'I think that a hundred like Lifton could be easier to maintain and police than a city the size of Exeter,' Baldwin murmured patiently. 'So you say he was fully covered in the stuff?'

'Apart from his hand and the forearm. The hand was pretty badly chewed, as you can see.'

Baldwin nodded and peered closely at the hand. It made him frown. Certainly it looked as though it had been mangled by the teeth of a hog – the forefinger and middle finger were gone, and there were deep lacerations in between the bones where the hog's teeth had sunk through the man's flesh ... but then Baldwin stared again at the stumps where the man's fingers had been removed. 'What do you make of this, Coroner?'

'Hey? Hmm. Didn't look so closely at the thing. It didn't kill him, and the hog had been chewing pretty well at his hand. Why?'

He leaned over Baldwin's shoulder as he spoke and then his brows rose and he tutted to himself. 'I think I am perhaps the most stupid rural coroner whom the king has ever had elected to post. Who could have done that, then?'

Baldwin was still studying the clean cuts where two fingers had been snipped from the hand. 'Anyone. Someone who is used to butchery, or a man who is used to skinning, or a cook . . . the number of men who could be practised in this kind of neat work are too numerous to count. More interesting is why someone would have wanted to do such a thing to him.'

'Torture, you think?' Coroner de Welles guessed. 'Punishment, for something the fellow had written?'

'Those are both perhaps possible,' Baldwin said. But in the back of his mind he was recalling a story he had once heard of another case, when a man's finger was removed. It had been carefully cut from a living man's hand for use in *maleficium*.

Baldwin was not superstitious, and he often laughed at Simon Puttock's credulity, but even in broad daylight, with the noise of people pushing and shoving their way past him on the road only yards away, he suddenly felt a sharp chill at the thought that there could be a sorcerer working here in the city.

Chapter Nine

Exeter City

John was exhausted after all his efforts the previous day and night. He had many of the implements, but he still needed some more. Only a complete fool would try to conjure a demon without adequate protection, after all, and he had desperate need of all the requisite tools of his trade. Sadly, almost everything had been left behind in his flight.

It was enough to make a man spit with fury. To know that all his tools, gathered carefully over the years, were sitting probably in that idiot sheriff's chamber in Coventry was infuriating. But complaining over that which could not be altered was at best futile. Better that he should forget it and find something similar.

There must be somewhere he could get hold of the things he needed.

Baldwin shook his head. There was something unpleasant – he would not use the word 'evil' – about this affair. He stood by the messenger's body, studying the area all about.

Once, when he had been at Acre, he had seen a man hit by a crossbow bolt, and he had been transfixed with panic and fear. The man was a burly fellow, clad in mail for the most part, with a shining helm which he had taken from another man who had died in an earlier attack. Somehow, Baldwin had felt that the fellow radiated invincibility, and he had edged nearer and nearer to him, hoping that if there was an attack this man's aura of authority and power might give Baldwin too some protection. And then, suddenly, the man had gasped as though punched in the chest.

Baldwin had turned in time to see him flung backwards, arms flailing, under the impact of a massive bolt. It passed almost all the way through his body, and hurled him back to be slammed against a wall some yards behind and pinned to it.

Such a large bolt must have been fired from an enormous crossbow. Yet there was no sign of the man who had fired it, no sign of the weapon's presence.

Time, for a while, seemed to stand still for Baldwin. Struck mindless with terror, he was paralysed, and all he could do was stare about him with his mouth agape, as though waiting to be executed. And then a Welshman behind him gave him a shove, and as he stumbled forward he heard a swift thrumming, and saw three, no four, arrows fly up over the castle's wall at a window in a tower. And he heard the scream, saw the fresh bolt fly from the window, and thump harmlessly into the wall above the Welshman, some yards over the dead man's body.

He had the same impression of danger here as he had felt that day. Something was not right here. It was almost as though he was being watched, and someone was lining up a great siege crossbow bolt with his chest even as he stood here.

To distract himself from these unpleasant reflections, he pointed up another alley. 'What is that man doing there?'

The coroner followed his pointing finger. 'Him? He's a watchman. There's another dead man up there. He can't be anything to do with this fellow, though. He was dead the day before.'

Baldwin's brow furrowed, and he glanced down at the body at his feet, then back at the alley again. It was a strange coincidence that on consecutive evenings men should have been murdered in this area. 'Were the neighbours all asleep for both deaths? Was nothing heard?'

'Both late at night. I've found men and women who walked past that spot, for example, quite late at night, and no one appears to have seen him lying there.'

'Nor this messenger?'

'No, not him either. They were attacked by thieves who wandered about late at night.'

'One of them was a man who enthusiastically robbed a messenger of an important letter,' Baldwin pointed out. 'Let us go and view the other body as well.'

'Hah! You don't care that the bishop has commanded us to find his roll?'

'If we are to find it, we'll need some hints as to who took it, and why, and if the bishop won't help us, maybe that man will.'

The coroner nodded amiably. 'You know, there are times I think you must be soft in the head, old chap. The fellow's *dead*.'

Langatre was a serious practitioner of the mysterious arts, and when there was a knock at his door he would always insist that his servant Hick should go and answer it. It was not dignified for a man of Langatre's status to perform such a menial task. Far better that he should have his boy go. Apart from anything else, it enhanced his position in the mind of many of his clients if they could see that he was able to afford his own staff.

This afternoon he was trying to brew some potions. When the door was struck, he was in the middle of straining the fluid from a concoction made from roots and yew berries. It stank, and he was not keen to handle anything made from yew, because all was poisonous, whether the bark, the sap, or the leaves. Still, the mixture smelled very potent, and he had often found that the efficacy of his spells was aided by the odours of the mixtures he sold with them.

They were worthless, of course. He knew that perfectly well. The real benefit to those who paid him was in the chanting that he alone understood. When a woman came to him and begged for help in keeping her man's love, or winning it, he would use a sweet-smelling fluid; when it was a farmer who wanted a neighbour's herd to suffer, the odour was not so pleasant. Either way, it was not the liquor that achieved the result: it was his intellectual efforts later. His prayers would work adequately without hoaxes designed to fool people, but some didn't believe in his efforts unless they had concrete proof in the way of a small bottle of foul-smelling and probably poisonous juice to go with it. He sometimes despaired of people, he really did.

'It's a man to see you, master,' Hick called from the front door.

Langatre grunted and shook his head. There was always an interruption of one sort or another. He had an alembic bubbling nicely, and he eyed it doubtfully, wondering whether he could afford to leave it alone for a consultation, but then shrugged. He didn't dare to leave an expensive piece of equipment lying about here to boil dry and break. Instead, he bent and blew at the flames, putting them out.

As he did so, there was a rattling knock at his door. 'Yes, yes,' he called testily. 'I am coming, in God's good time. Wait a moment, Hick.'

The knocking stopped on the instant, and Langatre picked up a cloth. He doubled it quickly, and used it to pick up the alembic by the snout. As he did so, to his surprise, he heard a step behind him. Someone had entered his chamber without permission!

'What do you . . .'

His voice was cut off as a fine leather cord whipped round his throat and was yanked tight, cutting off all air. With his left hand, he grabbed for it, his fingers trying to prise their way behind it to loosen it, but there was nothing he could do. He tried to grab his attacker, poke at his eyes, *anything*, but the man was out of his reach. At last, desperate, as he felt a rising mist begin to smother him, he swung the alembic over his shoulder.

There was a crack as the alembic smashed. The shards, fresh from the flames, were extraordinarily hot, and he heard a muffled shriek as the pieces of clay scorched his assailant, and then a piercing scream as the boiling, poisonous liquid sprayed.

The cord was dropped, and Langatre fell to the floor gasping, grabbing for a knife on his table. There was no time to use it. As his fingers fell on the hilt, his belly was kicked with main force, and his back arched as he felt the air gush from his breast in a great moan of pain. It was so intense, he could not breathe for some moments, and all he could do was roll into a ball to evade any further punishment. When at last he was able to take notice of his surroundings once more, he heard his door slam, and then there was silence.

'Who are you?' Baldwin asked as they reached the watchman.

'Thomas atte Moor, sir,' the man responded, but not quickly, and when Baldwin glanced at him he saw that the fellow was chilled through. His teeth chattered slightly as he spoke, and he had to grip his staff tightly with his blue-grey hands.

'How long have you been here, Thomas?'

'I was sent here yesterday to guard this fellow. I thought someone would relieve me last night, but no one came by, so . . .'

The coroner glowered at him. 'Is that our concern, man? Come, pull yourself together! Do you know who this man is?'

'Yes, he was well known. He carved antlers and bone to make fine combs and other decorative pieces. His name was Norman Mucheton.'

The body was in a terrible state. Plainly he had been drunk when he came here, for there was a thick, acrid patch of vomit nearby. Baldwin could smell it even though it was frozen. He could see peas and carrot, and smell malt – a man who had drunk several ales and eaten a good meal, and then thrown up on his way home.

'Where did he live?' Baldwin asked, studying the man's throat.

'Down there, over west of the gate, quite near to Westgate Street.'

'Does anyone know what he was doing up here?' the coroner asked.

Baldwin peered closely at the body as Thomas spoke of someone who had been drinking with the man until the early hours, a friend who had left Norman near the lane to the bishop's palace. Many others had seen them, and there was no suggestion of an evil word, let alone a fight.

'He would have turned west from there to go home?' de Welles confirmed.

'Yes, sir. His friend went home – he lives a little way down South Gate Street. He thought Norman had gone home. It never occurred to him that Norman might have come down here. It's the wrong direction.'

'Well?' The coroner sucked at his teeth as Baldwin leaned over the body and gazed down at a pool of blackened, icy blood.

'As you can see for yourself, he's had his throat cut, and cut so violently that his head has been all but severed. His purse is gone, so I assume it could have been a simple robbery.'

'I've only ever witnessed wounds like that on men who were attacked by those who had grudges. It's the sort of cut that a man who is serious about murder would inflict. No doubt about his intention, eh?'

Baldwin shook his head. He hunkered down again and studied the body carefully. 'Did you know him yourself?' he asked the watchman.

'Quite well.'

'Is there anything about him that strikes you as odd? Anything at all – his clothes, his flesh – anything?'

The guard drew down the corners of his mouth and stared at Baldwin a moment, then gazed down at Mucheton. 'Well, there is one thing. All the years I've known him, he's always had a pin in his cloak. A big one, you know, like a brooch. He said it was his good luck pin. He made it when he was an apprentice.'

'And it's not here.'

'No, sir.'

Rising, Baldwin stared down at the ground, at the pool of vomit, the man's body, the blood, and once again he had that unpleasant feeling that he was exposed here, and in danger.

John of Nottingham walked erect, if stiffly, from that fool of a tanner's house to the small cellar which had been loaned to him.

It was a pathetic little cell, in reality. Probably only half the size of his last place in Coventry, but adequate for all that. He looked about him as he entered. Illumination came from a shaft in the ceiling, over near the road, and because there was a wide space before this building there was a fair amount of light entering. It was unnecessary for him to have candles down here until dusk came, and then he must shut up the space under the shaft as he lit them so that anyone walking past wouldn't notice him down here.

Damp walls; two rotten tables, their tops scrubbed and salted to clean them of the filth of the years; a single stool for him; a low truckle bed in the corner, with a palliasse set atop; a box full of the essentials.

He sighed, shoved over the bolt on the door for his privacy, and set out the tools carefully before gingerly sitting on the stool, wincing and drawing in his breath as he did so, shivering with the pain. There was nothing to be done about it, but he gently teased his robes away, pulling his shirt from the wound, and peered down at the terrible scalded mess of his shoulder.

The fierce heat of the shards of pottery had scorched his clothing, and then the foul concoction within had soaked into the material, burning his flesh. It was red and weeping already. There would be a terrible soreness there, he knew. Without medications, he must simply endure it, though.

He could sit here all day staring at his wound, or he could get on with his work. There was much to be done: the wax must be shaped and moulded, and then he would have to begin his period of fasting and prayer before taking the necessary steps to ensure the success of this venture. It would be difficult, strenuous even, but he was sure that it would be worth it. After all, his new patrons had offered the same money as that which he had been promised in Coventry – another twenty pounds to add to the deposit given by the men up there.

Grunting to himself, he rubbed his stomach. The fasting would begin today. There was no point in delaying matters. He had to get on with the job.

Chapter Ten

Exeter Castle

The sheriff's wife, Madam Alice, was a willowy blond woman, with the body of a girl hardly out of her teens. All who saw her were impressed by her gentle, soft demeanour, her excellent manners, her flawless pale complexion, the eyes of clear grey with little flecks of hazel, and her steadiness. There was a stillness about her as she listened to others, as she spoke to them – as she did anything – that was almost unworldly.

Women would mutter grimly about her, saying that there was something 'not right' about her. For a woman who was nearly into her thirty-first year, such calmness and cool beauty, such an unmarred figure, seemed frankly *wrong*. She looked as though she had made use of spells to keep herself young.

Their husbands would agree with their wives. They would look at Madam Alice sternly, eyeing her perfect oval face with the little rounded chin, her soft, slightly pouting lips that somehow always contrived to look moist, and they would turn back to their own women with gestures of concern. But in their minds they had all undressed that youthful figure, they had weighed her heavy breasts in their hands and kissed her flat stomach.

Alice knew that she was the source of jealousy amongst the women of the city, and she knew that their menfolk desired her. It was nothing to her. She was content with her man, and if none of the women wished for her friendship, that was no matter. There were plenty of others who enjoyed her company. The difference was, they were not the rather tatty women from this little provincial city, but the wives of noblemen. She had even been introduced to Queen Isabella herself on two occasions. No, she had no interest in other men.

The castle was a hotbed of intrigue. She rather supposed it was like the household of the king himself, if a copy in miniature. There were other places which might have been the same size, with similar enormous expenditure in food and drink and cloth – the household of Sir Hugh Despenser sprang immediately to mind – but few could rival Exeter for the sheer enthusiasm of her disputes. Arguments ran on between the city and the cathedral, between the cathedral and the friars, between the friars and the monks, between the friars and the city . . . there was no aspect of city life which was not constantly running contrary to another.

It was a source of amusement to her that so many people strove so hard to make their little marks on the world. Surely any one of them could see that it was pointless. Great people carved out great lives, and little people from a place like this were correspondingly dull and little in comparison. She was born to greatness because she had come from a great family. Her father was the famous Lord Maurice Berkeley.

From her earliest years she had been highly aware of her position. It was impossible not to be. Her father ranked amongst the most powerful in the realm, and his army was one of those which was most often called upon to support the king. Every year, so it seemed, while she grew up, the family had a ritual sending off of the young men, the knights, esquires, men-at-arms and all their servants, as they answered the call to help the king defend his realm or attack his enemies. Each year the army would gather, and then drift off, more commonly than not heading northwards, the sprawling mass of men and horses consuming hundreds of yards of roadway, churning the surface into a foul mixture of mud, discarded bones and broken pots, dung and human faeces. Once, when she was very young, she had overheard her mother exclaim that it was a relief to see them all go: there had been scarcely enough food to keep the men fed at the castle and estates, and now that they were gone they could steal provisions from the vills through which they passed and leave the household's stores alone.

It had been a militaristic upbringing. She had known how to wield a sword and dagger from an early age; she learned both at the same time as her brother. Although her father had no sympathy for women who sought to equal the prowess of their brothers, he was content to see his child learn how to protect herself. There were few enough defences for a woman in this rough world. Teaching her skill with arms was one of the best methods of seeing his child safe.

Not that there was much safety these days even for her family. Poor Father! He was in his castle much of the time now. Once, only four years ago, he had been so trusted that he had been given the post of seneschal of Gascony and the duchy of Aquitaine – the king's own representative and commander-in-chief of the king's forces there in his absence. It had been a wonderful time for the whole family. Ah! She had been so proud.

Not now. Since the king appeared to have lost his mind – not a happy thought, and not one which could safely be repeated to anyone now that his spies were everywhere, but true, nonetheless – and had provoked the war against the Lords Marcher, her father's fall from grace had been inevitable. The only source of consolation was the fact that her father had surrendered and avoided involvement in the battle of Boroughbridge. So many of his friends and their sons had perished either at the battle itself, or in the reprisals that occurred up and down the country afterwards. Even here at Exeter there were the remains of one or two knights who were thought to have been involved, still hanging from a post outside the South Gate. Almost all the cities in the land had their own reminders of the king's brutal retaliation.

She had known King Edward II. The man had never struck her as particularly cruel. It seemed strange to think that he could have so changed. Unless it was those devils in human guise, the Despensers. It was much easier to think of them as being responsible for the killings. They, father and son, were so avaricious, they would take a widow and torture her to have her sign away her rightful possessions to them. Like poor Madam Baret.

But no matter who was responsible for it, the fact remained that her father stayed in his castle. He was under suspicion because a few of his knights *had* gone to Boroughbridge: Sir Thomas Gournay and Sir John Maltravers, to mention only two, had been forced to fly the realm and find new lives abroad as free-lances. At least there were always places for a man to fight and earn a living, thanks be to God.

What was less pleasant was to reflect on the fate of her brother, also called Maurice. He had been implicated in the looting of Despenser lands and estates, and as soon as the Despensers had survived the last wars they had returned filled with wrath to avenge themselves on those who had taken their plate and plundered their treasure-houses. Maurice had simply disappeared, and although it was rumoured that he was hiding somewhere in the country, no one could find him.

She walked into the main hall of the castle, where her husband sat working with his steward, the undersheriff, and his keeper and returner of writs. Madam Alice nodded to her husband, but paid no attention to the scribblers with him. They were only servants of one kind or another, when all was said and done.

'Wife.'

She smiled at him. 'I shall be walking about the town shortly, husband. Do you wish for anything from the market?'

He waved a hand in bland denial. 'No, I have all I need, my love.'

'Then I shall see you later.'

She turned and left the hall, and behind her heard the sound of the men talking again, the gruff tone of the keeper and returner of writs, the laugh of the undersheriff, but there was nothing in her mind, as she walked from the hall down to the courtyard and out into the open, grassed area between the castle and the city, other than her coming meeting.

If she had seen the expression of black distrust on her husband's face, she would have paused to wonder what might have caused it.

Exeter City

Before they left, Baldwin sucked at his bottom lip and took one last look at the body of Mucheton.

'Was he married? A sweetheart?'

'I think he was married, yes, but I don't know the woman myself.'

'Send someone to find her, and bring news of her to me at the Talbot's Inn.'

'I can't leave my place here, though'.

'I will send a man to replace you here,' Baldwin said. 'You need to be rested.'

He walked slowly after the coroner. Sir Richard took him down the alley towards the South Gate. As they reached the messenger's body once more, Baldwin shook his head, eyes narrowed.

'I find it very peculiar that the bishop could not tell us his name. And it is more strange still that the fellow should die within a short while of being in receipt of a message from the bishop. But for now, what we need to do is speak to all those who have had anything to do with his fellow's death. As soon as you have held the inquest, I should have him carried away to the nearest church ready for his burial, poor soul.'

'Hoi!' the coroner boomed back at Thomas. 'You! What is the name of the man who found this fellow? Older man, looked like a hare that's been chased by the hounds too long?'

'It was Will Skinner, the watchman from the gate.'

'Does he live there?' Baldwin glanced at the gatehouse and again felt like a man about to enter an ambush. It made a chill wash through his frame, and he had to wrap his arms about his breast to calm the shiver that threatened. And then he saw something. In a low window to the left of the main gate, he was sure that he caught a fleeting glimpse of a pale face. He kept his eyes on that little gap as he listened to the response.

'Next to it, in that small cottage, aye. But he'll be asleep by now, I reckon.'

'Really?' the coroner said. 'How quaint.'

His manner was one of simple amusement, but Baldwin did not feel the same lightness of spirit. The sun was being smothered by some grey, unwholesome-looking clouds as they made their way to the gate, and Baldwin kept his eyes on the window all the way until the opening was out of sight, wondering who had been watching. It didn't matter: surely it was only a child watching the two king's officers at work, or perhaps a servant.

No, he must put the thing from his mind. Feeling a pattering on his head, he looked up to see a fine spattering of hail falling from the leaden clouds. It didn't bode well for the rest of the day, he thought as they reached the door. The keeper of the gate lived in the rooms built into the gateway itself, but the watchman had directed them to a small building to the right of the roadway, a ramshackle affair that was almost a lean-to shed with a thick roof of thatch sorely in need of patching or renewal.

Baldwin shot a look about them, and then rapped smartly on the timbers of the door. They were all mis-sized, fitted together inexpertly, and would provide little defence against the elements. Just standing outside here, Baldwin was aware of the wind that whipped along the line of the wall from the quay over to the east, and straight over as though using the wall as its own roadway.

'Piss off!'

The coroner turned and looked at Baldwin. There was an expression of mild pain on his face. Then he closed his eyes for a moment, and Baldwin was about to knock again and call out his title, when the sound of the Coroner's deep intake of breath warned him, and he took a quick pace backwards.

'*Hoi! You festering piece of dog's turd, OPEN THIS DOOR IN THE NAME OF THE KING!*'

In what was for him a whisper, the coroner added for Baldwin's benefit, 'I tend to find that voice works with reluctant witnesses.'

Baldwin was not surprised. Nor was he surprised when a few moments later he saw an eye appear in one of the cracks, an anxious eye that stared at him for a short while. Shortly thereafter there was the sound of a wooden beam being lifted from its rests, and the door was opened, scraping over the dirt and making an arc in the soil of the floor.

Entering behind the coroner, Baldwin found himself in a small, noisome dwelling, with a mess of dirt on the floor, a single small table and stool, and a filthy palliasse. The smell was a mix of damp dog, urine, and sweat, all mingled in an unwholesome fug. There being no window, the only light came from the doorway through which they had just entered, and in it Baldwin could see that the whole of the rear wall was red sandstone like the rest of the city wall, although here it was streaked with green where water was leaking at the junction of the roof and the wall itself. The water puddled at the base of the wall, making the floor perpetually damp through the winter. Perhaps in consequence, because it would have been difficult to light a fire and keep it going, instead the watchman made use of a charcoal brazier for his heating. There was one small cauldron for heating water and perhaps making a pottage, but apart from that Baldwin assumed that Will Skinner ate at a pie shop or bought an occasional loaf of bread. There was no sign of any cooking.

'You remember me from this morning?' the coroner said, and in the small room it sounded like a bellow.

'You are the coroner,' the small man said, and he almost shivered as he spoke. It was plain to Baldwin that the fellow was entirely unused to being questioned by men of such standing, and he didn't enjoy it. He had been asleep, from the look of his bleary eyes.

'What do you want with my man, then, eh? You going to try to have him arrested?'

Baldwin and the coroner spun about to find themselves confronted by a woman. In age, she could have been anything from forty to seventy. Her face was dreadfully scarred, and she was bent like an old crone, but Baldwin had seen a woman like that before – the survivor of a siege who had been engulfed by flames in a final assault.

'Mistress, you are this man's wife?' he asked.

She peered up at him, turning her head sideways to accommodate her bent spine. 'You guess well, master.'

From nearer, he could feel sympathy for her. Lank hair straggled at either side of a long, thin face pinched with the grief that was reflected in the eyes. Intelligent, they were red-raw with weeping, and Baldwin had the impression of paleness, as though all the crying had washed the colour from them. She was an aged peasant woman in shabby clothing, and clearly pain and she were long-standing companions.

'Woman, I am the coroner, and I would speak to him. Pray sit and don't interrupt,' Sir Richard said.

To Baldwin's surprise she made no protest, but walked over and sat down on the stool, one arm on the table while she turned and listened to the men talking.

'Now, fellow. This friend of mine here is the Keeper of the King's Peace, and he has some questions for you. So listen and answer honestly. Is that clear?'

'Yes, sir.'

Baldwin was tempted to suggest that they leave the hovel and speak outside, but even as he considered the suggestion there was a rattling, like gravel thrown at a wall, and when he glanced out he saw that there was a sudden shower of hail. Steeling himself, he faced Will Skinner.

'The man you found out there. You found him because there was a hog there?'

'Yes, it was chewing at something, and I saw the blue and thought to myself that it looked like cloth. So I chased the brute away, and saw this fellow's arm. I thought, "That's not right," and pulled at it, and there was the man. So I raised the hue and cry.'

'Very good. Did you recognise the man? Have you ever seen him before?'

'Not likely, sir. I'm the night watchman for this area. He's not the sort of man I'd expect to see down here at night. It's drunks or men wanting the stews I tend to see. During the day, I try to sleep,' he added with a sidelong glance at the coroner.

'So do I, my man!' Coroner de Welles said, and laughed long and hard.

'In the time while you were raising the hue and cry, did you leave the body alone? Could someone have got to it and searched it?' Baldwin wondered.

'You mean, have a look in his pouch? No, I don't think so. When I found him, I pulled his arm free, and tugged hard enough to know that the whole body was there. Soon as I felt that, I stopped pulling, and left him instead. If anyone had tried to get into his pouch, they'd have had to clear all the muck away from him. No one had, though. When I got back, he was still just as covered in stuff as when I left him.'

'Was he absolutely cold when you found him?'

'Yes. Stone cold. But it gets cold here at night.'

Baldwin nodded, his eyes going to the brazier. 'Do you keep that going all night, then? Somewhere you know you can come to get a warm-up when you need it through the dark hours?'

'Well, yes. There's nothing to say that a watchman has to freeze,' Will said truculently.

'No, I was merely wondering how long you have to spend on your patrol, and how long back here indoors to warm up again. It could have a bearing on when the man was killed.'

'I . . .'

'Because it is mightily unlikely that he was murdered and dumped in that pile of rubbish during the day, isn't it, Will?' the coroner added.

'Why?'

'Because, my fellow, the *damn roadway is full of people during the day*, isn't it?' the coroner explained testily. 'How could someone walk round there and happily throttle a man in broad daylight?'

'Oh.'

'Yes, "Oh", as you say. So how much time do you spend outside compared with inside?'

Baldwin was struck by the man's evident nervousness as the questioning continued. He was not the kind of man to impress as a reliable witness.

'I don't spend much time indoors – I would lose my position if the city's receiver thought I wasn't doing my job.'

Baldwin wondered if that might be a cause of his nervousness: the simple fear of being thrown out from a job like this. It might not be lucrative – judging from how the man lived it could scarcely be less so! – but nor was it strenuous, and the man had an easy enough time of it. 'We will not discuss your strengths or otherwise with the mayor or his men,' he said briefly.

'Well, perhaps I do take some breaks when the weather really is bad. Last night it was so cold, I had to keep warming myself at the brazier. Few nights ago, some men had lit a fire in the street near the bishop's palace gate, but there was nothing yesterday, and by the time I'd walked up there I was perished.'

'What area do you cover from here?' Baldwin asked.

'Oh, I'm supposed to walk from here up South Gate Street, then up along the lane towards the Bear Gate, before turning back towards here again, coming down to the Palace Gate, straight on south to the wall, then up the alleys between the Bear and Palace gates. Sometimes I go the other way about, for the variety.'

'So, you would occasionally have to come back here after walking the circuit. I suppose when it was that cold, other people would hardly be about much anyway, would they?' Baldwin said. It was clear enough what the man was up to. He'd walk around the perimeter of his patch, then stop back at his hovel to warm himself and forget about criss-crossing the smaller alleys and lanes.

'No one in his right mind would be out on a night like last! It was terrible. All the puddles had frozen. God's teeth! This morning when I tried to break the ice in my bucket, I couldn't: the water was frozen right to the bottom!'

'So a sensible man would have spent much more time indoors, then,' Baldwin said. 'I suppose that you saw absolutely no one while you were supposed to be walking your rounds.'

It was there: a not-so-subtle shift in the man's stance, and then his head dropped a little, and his eyes moved away.

'In the night, you sometimes see shadows and imagine a man, I suppose.'

'That doesn't answer the keeper's question,' Coroner Richard pointed out forcefully.

'Did you see someone?' Baldwin pressed him.

The watchman shook his head hopelessly, and Baldwin suddenly realised that this was the aspect that had made the man so nervous: it was nothing to do with the fact of being indoors when he should have been walking his territory, it was something else – a man he had seen while out on his walks.

'Who was it, man?' Coroner Richard demanded. 'It'll all come out in the end, but the fact that you forgot to mention it before won't look good unless you make up for your forgetfulness now, and *quickly*!'

'When you're out, you can imagine things, yes? I wasn't sure if I saw anyone at all. It was a shadow, that's all. Just a moving shadow in the moonlight. There was only a brief glimpse . . .'

'Where was this "brief glimpse"?' Baldwin asked patiently, but with a hint of steel in his voice.

The man sighed and closed his eyes for a long moment. 'I was up past Palace Gate, walking down this way again, and it was towards the middle of the night. I know because of the cathedral bells. They were tolling for Matins when I saw it, so it must have been . . .'

'Get on with it,' the coroner growled.

'Well, I was past the entrance to the little alley, the second after South Gate Street, when I saw something down in the alley. I looked down it, because I wasn't sure I'd seen anything, holding my torch up high, and I was almost sure that there was a flash of paleness.'

'What does that mean?' Coroner Richard snapped. 'Be precise, man!'

'I thought it meant that there was man down there, that I'd seen his face,' the fearful watchman explained. 'My torch could light quite some few yards well enough, especially with the moon's light falling down in the alley too. I thought it was a man in dark clothing.'

'But you didn't go down the lane to check?' the coroner said accusingly.

'That was it: I did! I was really scared, sir, but I did go in. And I thought I saw a man, but then he disappeared, and when I got there, there was nothing. Only . . .'

'*Spit it out*, man, in God's name!' de Welles blurted.

'There was a cat. A black cat. It yowled at me as I approached, and I almost stained my hosen at the sudden noise. Christ alive! If you could have heard that sound down that alley!'

'I have heard cats before,' Baldwin said wearily. 'In many alleys. Even, occasionally, in houses. You were startled, then?'

'Startled? I was terrified, sir! I had seen a man, and now he'd gone and here was this cat! I tell you, I turned and fled the place!'

'Because of a cat?' Baldwin asked scathingly.

'There are some say . . .'

'Yes, yes,' Baldwin said impatiently, 'sorcerers!'

Will didn't meet his eye. 'Necromancers can change themselves into cats,' he agreed.

Chapter Eleven

Exeter City

He had seen her. God in heaven, but she was beautiful! Her face was like the Madonna's, and her gentle gait was enough to make a man sigh for jealousy that another could possess such perfection.

She hadn't seen *him*, of course. He couldn't let her. Not yet. Better that he wait around here and observe. With a caution that was entirely unnatural, and yet he was learning to use most cunningly and quickly, he set off after her, his long legs covering the ground easily.

Her path was leading straight along the High Street towards the Carfoix. He allowed her to move on a little, and then he gave her some moments to continue while he apparently lounged idly, all the while watching the people hurrying about. He looked at faces, wondering whether here there was someone who was taking too much interest in him or not.

No. All appeared safe. He quickly set off again.

It would be easy to overtake her whenever he wanted. All he needed was for the streets to become a little quieter and then he'd have her.

Warwick Gaol

It was enough to make him weep with despair when they came to tell him that his master was dead.

Robert le Mareschal had taken his life in his hands when he finally submitted to the voice in his head that told him to confess his crimes, praying to be treated leniently for attempting to rectify his earlier errors.

He had gone to the Sheriff of Warwick, Simon Croyser, and told the whole story. How he and his master had been approached by twenty-five men of Coventry, how they had offered John of Nottingham twenty whole pounds sterling, offered Robert himself another fifteen.

A fortune! And for it, they were to use their skills to assassinate the king, his friends Sir Hugh le Despenser, Earl of Winchester, Sir Hugh le Despenser his son, Henry Irreys, the Prior of Coventry, the prior's cellarer, and Nicholas Crumpe, the prior's steward. And they had chosen the poor Sir Richard de Sowe as well, for a trial of their skills.

It was the sight of de Sowe's petrified expression that had persuaded him in the end. The man had done nothing to harm John of Nottingham or Robert, but John and the others had picked him to be the test of their abilities. If they could kill Sir Richard de Sowe, they would have a proof of their strength. That was their reasoning.

But when he saw de Sowe dead, the reality of what he was doing was suddenly brought home to him. This was not some abstract scientific experiment, it was murder.

Croyser acted immediately. Robert le Mareschal was held and kept in a dungeon below the castle, and news of his capture and the events which he said had led up to the death of Sir Richard de Sowe were sent to London. And within a matter of days, the king's men were back, and the arrests began.

That was all some while ago. He didn't know how long. Long enough for his hair to grow rank and greasy; long enough for his clothes to rot in the dank chamber; long enough for his muscles to cramp and shiver. His teeth ached; his flesh crawled with creatures that nipped at him.

He could weep to think that all was thrown away. The death of de Sowe had been dreadful, but the man had been a liar. He deserved some sort of punishment. Dear Christ, though, the man had suffered . . .

Robert stood and made a slow perambulation, going as far as his leg-iron permitted him. It wasn't far; the chain secured to the ring in the wall only allowed a short walk. As he went, his arms wrapped about his torso, he kept his head huddled down in his shoulders.

There was a rattle of locks, and he turned slowly to face the door, his flesh creeping at the sound. The arrival of a man here was invariably the precursor to pain. The keeper of the gaol was a brutal man with no sympathy, only a hatred for all those who lived under his power. And he had an especial loathing for traitors.

In here there was almost no light, for the only pale imitation of the sun had to curl and twist about many passages before it reached these depths, but as Robert le Mareschal peered at the door he was sure that he could see a glimmering orange light. The glow appeared to grow nearer, and Robert was tortured with conflicting emotions: an urgent, sensual desire to see that torch or candle, whatever it might be – to see it and hear it crackle, imagining that he could warm himself by its flames – that would be so good! And then there was the opposing terror that whoever it might be, he was coming here to inflict some torture on Robert's weakened frame.

There were steps now. Loud, confident paces that marched along the flagged corridor, until they had grown so loud, their echoes were a torment to his ears. They must pass . . . they *must* pass . . . they would go to another cell . . .

But they stopped outside his door, and looking up at the barred hole in the door Robert saw the glittering of the sheriff's eyes. Croyser spoke.

'All taken. John of Nottingham was first, but the others are all secure now.'

'Thanks to God!'

Croyser looked at him with contempt in his eyes. 'You pray to God after what you've done? You summoned the devil and sold your soul to kill a man. And would have killed your own king, no doubt, if fear of your punishment hadn't stopped you.'

'No! I summoned no demons! And I did tell you of the plot!'

'Yes, you did, didn't you? And all, I suppose, because you'd rather risk being hanged than suffering the death that the king might plan for you.'

'What will happen to them now?'

'The others? They'll all try to plead innocence and ask for sureties to help them escape from prison. They'll only be here a short while, I expect.'

'And my master? How is he?'

'I thought . . .'

There was a sudden doubt in the sheriff's voice. Robert le Mareschal felt a griping in his belly that was not due to the thin pottage he had eaten that morning. 'He hasn't escaped? If he has escaped, he can make an image of *me* and kill me!'

'Well, he has escaped in a way, I suppose.' The sheriff grinned nastily. 'His body's here, but his spirit's escaped, I suppose you could say. More than you will do.'

'All I did was make mommets and obey my master,' Robert declared.

'You made the figures very realistic, too, didn't you? So realistic even I could recognise my king when I saw it. No, you only came forward because you thought you'd make a safer pact by selling your companions to the king than by killing him. What was it, did someone else hint that they'd give you up?'

'I've already told you . . .'

'Yes, you've told me what you want me to hear. You haven't told me everything, though. Not by a long shot. But you will, you will. I'll have you shrieking in agony and begging to tell me all. We are skilled in the use of our devices here, and the king is upset to hear that you helped make the imitation of him so that you could kill him by your *maleficium*.'

'I wouldn't have done anything to him! I couldn't!' Robert pleaded. He had surrendered himself as soon as he could when he realised that the attempt must be discovered: the thought of the punishment that would come to a man who had dared to make an attempt on the life of the king had petrified him with fear.

'You'll have to convince him, not me. And not only him. You know, I don't think that the good king's friends are happy either. From what I've heard, the Despensers are also distressed to think that you and your master could have taken money from these malcontents and traitors to kill them. I don't know, but I rather think that Sir Hugh le Despenser will want to be involved in your punishment personally. And God help you if he does!'

Exeter City

It took Baldwin and the coroner only a short while to walk up South Gate Street towards the area in which the watchman had seen the shadow, but it took considerably more time for Baldwin to persuade the coroner to enter the lane with him.

'You are seriously suggesting that there could have been a man in here who had the skill to change himself into a blasted cat to escape that poor excuse for a guard?'

'Of course not! Yet he may have seen something which was out of place, even if he did succumb to superstitious nonsense shortly afterwards.'

'I think we'd be better served fetching ourselves a pie for our dinner.'

'Come, it will take little enough time,' Baldwin said.

With a bad grace the coroner gave in, and Baldwin was grateful for his company as they walked along the busy lane towards the Bear Gate.

'He did say the second alley after the main street?' Baldwin confirmed, his nose wrinkled at the stench. 'I can understand why he would be reluctant to enter this noisome little trail.'

It was a narrow gap between houses like so many others, and yet here the width was much reduced. As Baldwin took a first tentative step in, he felt as though the houses were all leaning in towards him, their upper storeys bending down and blocking out the sky.

Oddly enough, once the two men had walked about ten paces, the whole area brightened. Here there was a curve in the alley, and now it ran straight towards the south. The sun was up in the clouds there, brightening a thinner layer of cloud, and the alley appeared less repellent than it had at first because once they were away from the entrance, it widened somewhat. However, the odours of excrement and urine were all-pervasive. A scuttling ahead showed where a rat was scavenging, and the sounds stopped as the two drew nearer.

'I cannot imagine why any man would want to come down here.'

'For a fellow making good his escape, it would be as good as any,' Baldwin considered. 'Look at this place! No one is here during the day, so it must be guaranteed to be deserted at night. Say you had killed a king's messenger, and you had to escape. The South Gate would be shut, so where else could you go? This would be the ideal route to take, I should say.'

The coroner lifted his boot with an expression of distaste and stared at the sole. 'So long as he didn't mind being covered in the ordure of the centuries, damn it! Look at that!' He began to scrape the muck from his boot on a step.

'The rat would explain why there would be a cat up here,' Baldwin continued, walking on a short distance and peering about him. 'I dare say this would be a cheerful hunting ground for any feline. And the appearance of a man suddenly coming up the alley from the gate might startle a cat so that it decided to bolt for it, and that was how it met with the fearful watchman.'

'Perfectly logical,' the coroner agreed.

'And the watchman said he thought the man looked like a sorcerer. Let us go and visit the fellow, eh?'

Lady Alice reached the house late in the afternoon, with Sarra as chaperon, only to find it encircled by a small group of gawping men and women. There was a beadle she recognised outside, a scruffy little fellow whom her husband had once said he suspected of half the crimes in the city, except he'd never managed to catch him.

'What is all this?' she asked a woman nearby.

'Mistress, the man here was attacked and almost killed.'

Lady Alice's eyes widened. 'You are sure of this?'

There was no need to respond. The only reason for a crowd this size was an attempted murder, or, better, an actual one.

'My lady, we ought to get back,' Sarra said nervously.

'Yes, of course,' Lady Alice said with some irritation. It was so hard to get time away from the castle just now, and she was desperate for any help she could get.

Matthew had never said as much, but she knew that he felt the lack of children as sorely as she herself. They had tried – God knew all too well how hard! – but she could not conceive for some reason. And then she had had the idea of enlisting the help of this man Langatre.

It meant lots of foul potions, which she did her best to apply as he suggested, rubbing them in about her body, but, as he explained, the trouble with these kinds of problem was the womb itself. It was a strange organ, which could move about the body. Only when it was positioned firmly could a man pierce her with hopes of success. And in her case, it was rarely fixed.

She would have to pray that he made a swift recovery so that she might see him again soon.

And just then she felt her heart seem to stop. Time ceased as she stared at the man with the black eyes, the scruffy stubble at his chin, the deep creases like knife-slashes at either side of his mouth, and there was a moment's confusion in her mind as she felt her belly roil.

'Mary Mother of God!'

Sarra saw her confusion and paleness. 'Mistress? My lady? What is it?'

'Sarra, go to the tavern up on the corner and fetch me a pint of strong ale. Go! Now! I shall wait here.'

And as soon as her maid had left her, she sank down onto a moorstone trough that sat nearby and waited, not daring to look as he approached her grimly, his hand ready on his knife.

Chapter Twelve

North-East Dartmoor

Simon was growing concerned. He had been out on the moors of an evening often enough, but today the weather was rapidly growing chillier, and the clouds looked threatening. It might rain, but more likely they were going to be attacked by a blizzard.

'Rob, can't you hurry a little faster?' he called over his shoulder. The boy was a nuisance at the best of times, but today he had excelled himself, whining about crossing a small area of boggy land when he had already seen the horses walk through easily enough, and then falling flat on his face and refusing to get up for some little while, complaining that he had broken his toe on a rock. Now he was some yards behind them again, his face set in a lowering black mask of fury at the indignity of hurrying after the others.

'I'm the one who's not on a horse, master Bailiff,' Rob responded with some asperity. 'What do you expect me to do? Run the whole way?'

Simon grunted his answer. It was only the truth. The worst delays had been caused by Busse. He had insisted on regular halts, supposedly to pray at the requisite hours of the day, and also to rest his horse, but Simon felt sure that it was more to do with his own sore buttocks. The last time, he had begged Simon to light a fire to warm his hands. True enough, Simon could see that Busse's face was turning a little blue with the cold, but that was no excuse to use up their meagre supply of firewood and tinder. Simon was painfully aware that they would need both tonight, and he was not going to risk the main supply of good tinder to light a fire when they might have need of it all later.

His attention was on the clouds forming to the north. It was plain enough that the weather was settling in for a cold blow. Simon was deeply unhappy to think that they could all be stuck out here on the moors for an extended period, but if the snow fell hard, that was exactly the risk.

It was growing dark as he stared about him, and he cursed the short winter days. 'Right. We won't make it off the moor before nightfall. We have to find a shelter. I won't continue in the dark, not with the moon hidden. It would be too dangerous.'

'Surely we are almost at the end of the moors, Bailiff,' Busse said, hearing his words. 'There are plenty of farms out there.'

'There are some, but I can see no sign of smoke yet,' Simon said shortly. 'Even all the miners seem to be hidden away. With this weather, I would expect them to be hidden away in a tavern. Probably up in Chagford, most of them. That'd be the nearest to us here, I think.'

He remained still, staring about him for a long time, making sure of his bearings, and then pointed ahead and slightly left to a large outcrop of rock. 'If we make for that, I think we'll be close to the Grey Wethers. That'll give me my bearings.'

'You mean to say that you are lost,' Busse said.

'No. But look about you – if we were a mile behind us right now, would you know the difference? All is rolling hills, with occasional rocks at their summits. It is easy to become confused, and always best to make sure of your bearings. However, once we hit the Grey Wethers, I will be happier.'

'Why, are they safe?' Rob asked innocently.

Simon shot him a look, then glanced at the monk beside him. Busse, he saw, was nervous. Good! Well he might be, Simon reflected.

'No, but their spirits may lead us to safety,' he said at last, and kicked his horse to greater speed.

Exeter City

Baldwin and the coroner had to stop a while for refreshment, for, said Coroner Richard, his belly was so empty, they would soon hear it rumbling in Cornwall. After some persuasion, Baldwin agreed to visit a pie shop on Cooks' Row, and then the two could head down to Stepecote Street, where there was a man, so the watchman said, who practised magic.

It was hard to curb his impatience as the coroner prodded at all the pies on sale, before settling on a pair of matched pastry coffins filled with beef in gravy. Richard de Welles munched happily as they walked. If he had had his way, they would have been ensconced in a tavern by now, and eating and drinking their fill. Although that was by no means Baldwin's plan, he was fully aware of the dangers of an investigation with the coroner. He had witnessed the hung-over anguish on Simon's face every morning only recenlty when the coroner had stayed with the bailiff in Dartmouth. Baldwin was extremely keen to avoid such pain.

Stepecote Street was the main thoroughfare to the west of the city. It took all the traffic from the city out to the great bridge of which Exeter was so proud, so was well metalled. As in all the streets, the centre held the kennel, the great gutter which took all the rainwater away from the houses before they could be flooded in severe weather. However, the kennel here stood out more, because the street was so steep that the tracks on either side were flagged as a series of shallow steps. It meant that little traffic other than pack-horses could come this way, but that held the advantage to Baldwin and the coroner as they walked down that there were no wagons or carts to be avoided.

Richard de Langatre's house was halfway down the street on the southern side. Baldwin had stopped a priest on their way, and he had confirmed where the man lived, although he cast an eye over Baldwin as he spoke. He seemed of the opinion that men should not consort with a necromancer.

Seeing his look, the coroner had smiled broadly. 'Don't worry, Father. We're only going to consult him about a murder.'

The priest's smile fled his face, and he hurried on his way up the hill.

'Coroner, please,' Baldwin moaned.

'What? What did I say? Eh?'

'What is going on down there?' Baldwin wondered, seeing a small crowd. 'Do you think that is the house?'

'Looks like it,' the coroner said. He took a massive bite from his remaining pie, then threw away the crust. 'Let's go and find out,' he continued, showering Baldwin and the road in crumbs.

There was a pair of young urchins, perhaps ten years old, standing on a cart's wheel to peer over the heads to the door. As the coroner moved forward, trying to force his way through, Baldwin asked one of the boys what was happening.

The lad, a scrawny, Celtic-looking fellow with black eyes and a shock of unruly brown hair, looked down at him with a speculative gaze, but his companion, a mousy-haired fellow with a pale and unhealthy complexion under the filth on his flesh, snarled a curse. Only when the first noticed that Baldwin was weighing a penny in his hand did the two become more interested. Brown hair nodded towards the house.

'There's a man in there, they reckon he's been summoning the devil. And now his servant's been killed, and they're taking him up to the castle. Serves him right, too.'

Baldwin nodded. 'This servant – what was her name?'

The boy curled his lip in disgust. 'Girl? It was a lad called Hick.'

'Oh? Was he about your age?'

It was the second who answered this time, with a dismissive contempt for all knights. 'No. He was younger. Poor little shit!'

Baldwin nodded. 'How did he die?'

'I think he was strangled. They heard his screams from over the road, so I heard.'

'I thank you,' Baldwin said. He flipped the coin and the first lad caught it quickly, holding it in his fist and watching Baldwin as though half expecting to be deprived of this unexpected largesse.

Moving to the edge of the crowd, Baldwin leaned against the wall of a house and waited. He could see – and hear – the coroner a short way away, bellowing at the top of his voice, but this small group was formed of interested Exeter folk, and they would not give up their places here at the ringside for any stranger with a loud voice. No matter how much the coroner tried to force his way on, the people hemmed him in so securely that he could make but little headway until at last there was a shout and the people began to swear and curse, one or two flinging stones or rotten fruit. It was clear to Baldwin that the man who lived here was being pulled out to be taken to the gaol.

Baldwin waited a short while, but when he judged that the noise of the people was growing a little dangerous, he took a deep breath and shouted, ''Ware the sheriff's men! 'Ware! The sheriff's men are coming!'

A few heads turned, some anxious at the thought of being arrested for rioting, but others saw him and glowered, one beginning to move towards him. Baldwin took hold of his sword hilt and drew his riding sword slowly. It flashed from the scabbard with a sibilant rush, and when he held it out the bright blue of the blade caught the dull light, the edge flickering grey and deadly.

Now the crowd was thinning as the small party was pushing through from the house, and soon Baldwin was face to face with a beadle and three nervous-looking watchmen.

'Who are you?' the beadle demanded, his attention fixed on Baldwin's sword.

'Sir Baldwin de Furnshill, Keeper of the King's Peace, friend,' Baldwin said calmly. 'And this is the coroner of Lifton, Sir Richard de Welles. Who are you?'

The rather red face of the coroner loomed over the beadle, glaring with irritation from being thwarted, and the beadle tried to square up to him, but one freezing look from Sir Richard made him appear to shrivel like a salted slug.

'I am Elias, sir knight.'

'Come, friend Elias, let us find a place to talk a while,' Baldwin said.

'Got to take this man to the gaol. He's killed his servant,' the beadle said.

'Let us speak to him first, eh?' Baldwin said with a calm smile.

Robinet had seen them at the house, and he was tempted to speak to them, but an in-built reluctance came to the fore even as he considered it. The two had looked reasonable men when he saw them, first out by the body of poor James, and now at the necromancer's house. But there was a conviction in his heart that told him that he would have to be cautious. There were many who would be keen to believe that he might have killed James.

Christ knew, there were plenty of times he'd have been glad to kill the bastard. Every time he'd thought of those days incarcerated at the king's pleasure, he'd dreamed of doing it. The man he'd trusted for all those years, and the one who betrayed him.

Flashes of the previous evening were returning to him now. He'd met James first two days ago, when he was walking about the city. James had been walking up from Cooks' Row towards the guildhall, and Robinet had just left the little church of St Petrock, and was outside in the grim, cold morning, feeling the chill and considering returning to his room for a drink of warmed, spiced wine, when he felt himself jostled, and the clumsy tarse walked straight into him – *literally* walked straight into him.

'Can't you look where . . .'

'Newt? Is it you?'

It was some satisfaction to see how James's face fell at the sight of his old mentor. His face, which had been frowning in deep thought, blackened as he barged into Newt, but then there was a glimmer of appalled recognition before his face crumpled into utter horror.

Newt noted the transformation from arrogance to terror with secret delight. There was a delicious aspect to this – revenge was so close! His hand was already at the hem of his cloak as he tried to pull it tight over his breast, but the temptation to whip his hand down to the hilt of his dagger and draw and stab . . . But even as the hatred bubbled like acid in his veins, his natural caution made him still the manoeuvre. There was something . . . *pitiful* in the sight of this young man suddenly shrunken with abject fear. To kill him would be no challenge, and would serve what purpose? It would make Newt a marked man for as long as he evaded capture. Which, at his age, could hardly be for long.

It made him consider the fellow again, and the longer he stared at James, the less he saw the ambitious *nuncius regis* who had betrayed him, and the more he saw a scared, rather pathetic young man entering his middle age, who had been faced with a ghost from his past that terrified him. It was not worth even pulling his knife to scare him further.

Newt gave him a slow stare, starting at his boots, passing up his body, pausing at the pouch on his hip that held the king's own arms, and then travelling on up to meet his eyes. With an expression which he fondly hoped reflected withering scorn, Newt turned on his heel, and would have been long gone, except he heard steps following him in a hurry, and then felt the hand at his arm.

'Newt! Come on, old man. Let me buy you a beer!'

Exeter Castle

'Wife? You were away a long time,' Sheriff Matthew said. 'Are you well?'

'Yes, dear. I went to look at the shops.'

'What have you bought?'

Alice looked at her husband and for a moment she was at a loss. She rallied quickly, though. 'My dearest sweeting, nothing! I looked at all the cloths on display, and they were poor indeed compared to what I wished to buy for you. Why? Are you anxious that I may spend too much? You know I am a good, thrifty woman!'

He laughed with her as she left the room, but when she had gone he took on a more serious demeanour. Seeing Sarra, he summoned her with a jerk of his head.

'Right, maid, tell me where you have been with your mistress.'

'Nowhere, my lord. But . . .'

'Yes?'

'She was taken a little dizzy, so I fetched her some drink, and she asked me to leave her to rest a short while so she could recover.'

'She was alone?'

Sarra looked up at him with perplexity. 'Of course, my lord.'

She could hardly tell him he was being cuckolded.

Exeter City

In the street not far from the castle, the man stood looking at the place with a professional's eye.

It was not in good repair. Tumbledown would be a better way to describe it. Two towers were disintegrating, and the gatehouse itself would scarcely survive a puff of wind, from the look of it. No, it was no great shakes as a fortress. Not like Berkeley.

This city had seemed a quiet little shire town, more or less a little market town, really, and to see it like this, a hotbed of political unrest and sudden violence, was curious.

Alice was quite right to seek any help she could, but he wasn't so convinced that a sorcerer was the kind of man to give useful advice. In his own experience, fortune-tellers and future-seers were the worst kind of charlatans. They took money and preyed on the innocent. He disliked the whole breed.

And just now he had little else to do. Perhaps in the morning the man Langatre would be back again. Ready to prey on others.

It was disgusting. Yet there was little he could do about it.

Chapter Thirteen

North-East Dartmoor

Simon was anxious now. The weather was closing in as the sun sank behind them. Although he didn't slow to peer over his shoulder, he could gauge the sun's position by his shadow, and now that it was reaching out for yards before him he knew that they must seek shelter for the night, and that right soon.

Busse had grown more quiet as they continued, and his face was strangely drawn. When Simon glanced over at him, he was reminded of de Courtenay's words, how this man had apparently gone to one of the dreaded necromancers and sought, by means of some sort of foul spell, to have his election guaranteed. It turned Simon's stomach to think that a man – especially a man of God – could attempt such a thing. Simon's was a simple faith, reinforced at every opportunity by the canons at Crediton church, where he had gained an education. Their exhortations, often delivered at the end of a switch to make the lesson more instructive, had rejected absolutely the idea of conjuring demons to help with any worldly acts. It was heretical to believe that an agent of the devil could assist a true Christian.

Perhaps it would be better if Simon and Rob could leave Busse out here to die ... and yet Simon had always rather enjoyed his companionship before. It was odd that he should have fallen so far that he could sought the help of the black arts ... he was a bloody *monk*, for Christ's sake! In God's name, how could he have done such a thing?

Even as he was thinking this, he saw the monk's eye upon him, and he cleared his throat without knowing what on earth to say to the man. Then he sighed in relief. Ahead, through the gathering gloom, he could just make out the lines of trees moving in the wind. There was a wood ahead, and he began to try to work out where he was. From the direction he had taken, this should be the large wood just outside Gidleigh, where the moors lapped up against cultivated lands. Not far from here was Chagford, the bustling stannary town where they could be assured of a warm bed in an inn.

The first light flicks at his face woke him from a mild daydream in which he saw a roaring fire, a pot of warming ale, and a heavy joint of beef or shoulder of mutton slowly roasting. The scene was so distinct and alluring, it was hard to dismiss it, but the insistent soft patters at his cheeks soon told their own tale.

'Shit! Of all the foul fortune!' He rested a hand fore and aft and turned in the saddle. Behind them, the sun was almost touching the horizon. They had only a very short time. 'Right, Master Busse, you must continue straight ahead, and do not hurry. Keep with Rob there, so that he doesn't become lost himself, and do not let him flag. Keep on in this direction.'

'What of you, Bailiff?'

'I am going to ride on to make sure that we have a store of firewood before all the light fades. In God's name, I only pray I have time to gather enough.'

'Then go, in God's name!'

Exeter City

Master Richard de Langatre should have been grateful to meet these two men, perhaps, but just at the moment he was feeling more than a little disgruntled. It was humiliating to be grabbed by this beadle and his shabby little watchmen! What did they think they were doing? Was any poor professional to be man-handled like this without excuse?

'We shall go to the Suttonsysyn near the guildhall,' Baldwin decided. It was easier to ensure the cooperation of the coroner if mention was made of an alehouse of some sort, he knew.

'That would be a good one,' the coroner said approvingly, perking up considerably.

The beadle Elias if anything looked even more harassed. 'I can't allow that, master . . .'

Coroner Richard beamed down at him, but there was a steely glitter in his eyes. 'I think you should remember to call us "sir". Or perhaps

"Keeper" and "Coroner"? Either way, my fellow, you will remember what your station is, and what ours is. Sir Baldwin here has just made an excellent suggestion. We will follow it.'

'But I was ordered to deliver this man to the gaol.'

'By whom?' Baldwin enquired.

'The sheriff. He ordered us himself. He said we had to come here, take this man, bring him up to the castle's gaol, and keep the body of the dead boy at the house until the coroner could be called.'

'Right, and now the coroner is arrived,' Sir Richard boomed. 'So do you go about your duties, and leave me to mine, eh?'

'But I am to . . .'

Baldwin stopped him. 'You have delivered your charge into my custody. Now return to the house and take care of the poor fellow's body. I shall see to this man.'

With a nervous reluctance, the beadle finally agreed. He made one last effort to have a watchman or two remain with the knights, but Sir Richard was so scornful in his response to the idea that two armed knights could not subdue such a feeble-looking piece of human flotsam that the man soon gave up and submitted to their commands.

'At last,' Baldwin said. Coroner Richard was already signalling impatiently to the wench serving at the bar, and Baldwin sat on a barrel which served as a stool, and studied the creature before him. 'Now, what manner of man are you, I wonder?'

Robinet had seen them walk into the tavern, and now he saw the beadle and his men leave the place and begin to make their way back down to Stepecote Street and the house where the dead servant lay. Making a quick decision, he followed them.

Outside the house there was one remaining watchman, a youth of maybe twenty, who stood nervously eyeing the crowd. Newt could hear him clearly as he called to the beadle, and even when the beadle was at his side, a hand on his arm, trying to calm him, the lad's voice remained high and loud enough for Newt to hear every word.

'They've been trying to get past me! There's some want to stone the place and others will have it burned to the ground . . . they were going to beat me to get me out of the way, if I didn't do what they wanted. That one there, look! He's got a stone! Make him put it down!'

Newt smiled to himself at the sound of the lad's voice. There was enough anxiety in it to make a whining puppy sound bold. He was not sure what was best for him to do. At first he had an inclination to go to the beadle and ask him what was happening, but the sound of a foreign voice in the area might make one or two men wonder where he came from and what he was doing in Exeter. That was the easiest way to have himself taken and questioned he could think of. And he couldn't afford that in case people had seen him with James. Perhaps seen them argue – or fight.

No, walking up to a nervous law officer was not a good idea for him just now. Better that he should leave well alone . . . and yet he wanted to learn if there was anything about the man who lived here that could suggest he could have been guilty of the murder of James.

His problem was solved when he saw the beadle jerk his thumb at the youth. Nothing loath, the fellow gripped his staff firmly and eyed the crowd with the truculence of a rabbit before squaring his shoulders and setting off up the hill towards Robinet.

Newt turned and began to walk slowly up the hill, bent over as he went, his frame the very picture of decrepitude and weariness. When he heard the swift-pacing approach, he groaned and let himself sink slowly to his knee in the street.

'Are you all right, father?'

'Ach, fellow, it's my old feet. They give me gip on occasion. Today I've been walking from the coast, and my old bones are weary,' Newt lied, smiling bravely.

'You want some help?'

'Your arm as far as the flat way on top of this hill would be kind. My name is Jan, by the way.'

'I am Ivo Trempole.'

'It is kind of you, but I am sure you'll be busy. You don't really have time to help an old fool like me. You were down there at that house, weren't you? Are you with the watch?'

The lad grunted. 'Not that I want it. I was voted to be the constable here, but it wasn't my choice. I don't like having to stand in front of a crowd of angry people for no reason. That lot were ready to throw rocks at me, you know? Why'd I want to do that, stand as a target for all the hotheads in the city?'

'It must be hard. Is the man who lives there rich and important, then? Is that why the city has to guard him?'

'No, he's not all that important, no. He's a *necromancer*,' the fellow said, his voice dropping. 'His servant is dead, and they say it was the master who was angry with his man, and killed him in a rage, if you can believe that! Imagine!'

Clearly Ivo's imagination was doing enough work for both of them, or so Newt felt. 'Terrible. So he stabbed the lad and bolted?'

'No, he didn't stab him. He used a thin wire or something, and strangled him. Almost cut through his throat.'

'But the master has run away, I suppose? A fellow known for using magic would hardly be popular, would he?'

Ivo shook his head. 'He didn't run, the fool. His servant was there, still warm. It was obvious as the sun in the sky that he'd done it. No one else would go and kill a fellow for no reason, would they? No, it was him.'

They had almost reached the top of the hill now, and Newt began to chat about other matters as though the murder was of little importance to him, and soon after, when they reached Bolehille, he took his leave of the watchman and hobbled slowly along Cooks' Row towards the High Street. When he turned, once, to wave, Ivo had already disappeared. Still, to be safe, Newt continued hobbling and walking slowly until he reached the Carfoix, and only then did he start to walk in a more easeful manner.

There was not much to be gathered there, he reckoned. But he had learned one useful point: the lad had been throttled with a thin ligature of some sort. Perhaps the same weapon as the one used on James; perhaps the same man was guilty of both murders.

Yet so far as Newt knew, there was no one in the world who had any reason to dislike James apart from he himself. James had been a mild man, a calm lad with hardly a bad word to say about anyone. The idea that someone could have taken such a dislike to him seemed incredible. Yet, of course, he had managed to make Newt's life a misery. If it hadn't been for those unwary words of his, Newt would have kept his post, not been thrown in gaol, not suffered for months. And perhaps still be employed even now.

He looked up and saw how the sun was fading fast. All the shops were closed already, and there was a bustle about the city as people prepared for night. He must find a refuge.

Yes, instead of being happily employed, here he was. A corrodian from a far-off priory, all but friendless. Fortunately he still had one friend. Or did have until last night. He must go and make his peace with the man.

North-East Dartmoor

Simon's feet were out of the stirrups as soon as he reached the first of the trees. There was a low wall, but it had tumbled down long ago, and his horse trotted cautiously over the remaining rubble before stopping to crop the grass. Simon quickly took off the saddle and harness, and slipped a halter on him, tying it to a sapling nearby. The last thing he needed now was to lose the beast.

As soon as that was done, he started to search for timber. The snow wasn't falling in earnest yet, and he had some little while to gather firewood. In his breast, between his shirt and his tunic, was a thick handful of tinder which he'd found earlier on their way: old, dry grasses and some fine, thin silver birch bark he had pulled from a tree on the way out of Tavistock. These were wrapped in a fold of cloth with his flint, and he prayed that they would be dry and warm enough after being protected all day.

There was time to worry about that later. First he had to find firewood. There were several fallen boughs, but each, when he touched it, felt sodden. They were too old and had been rotting and soaking up moisture for over a year. However, he soon came across a tree that appeared to have been recently struck by lightning. It was tall, a good thirty to forty feet, and he was cautious at first, in case a branch might fall on his head, but when he got closer and gave it a good push to test its strength, he heard the cracking. Grinning to himself, he pushed it, rocking it carefully, until at last it gave a creaking complaint, and toppled, crashing and crackling as it smashed through the other trees nearby, until it was down. All about it were the branches which had been snapped off, and now he started to hurry about, collecting them quickly.

Hearing Rob and Busse, he snapped at them both to help, and continued stacking thicker branches which seemed to have some strength in them. The rest he tossed into a pile nearby Then he began to lay the longer, straighter stems against the main tree trunk lying on the ground.

'What are you doing?' Rob demanded, watching him as children often watch the antics of their parents.

'If you want to survive this night, Rob, find every small, dry twig you can. The best are those which have been dried on the tree and not on the ground. Those will be too damp. Just fetch as much as you possibly can. When you've built up a good pile, we'll start a fire with them.'

Rob shrugged and set off half-heartedly. Meanwhile Busse was watching Simon with an appreciative eye. 'And what of me, Bailiff?'

'Brother, if you could just help me to fix these boughs to the tree here, that would be a great help.'

'You are building a low shelter?'

Simon nodded. He had stayed out in the open before, usually with a large tree trunk to make a wall, and then built up a lean-to wall and roof with boughs to create a low but cosy hovel. However, it would not do for all three of them. Instead, he would have to form a shelter that used the trunk as a side wall, but which also had two walls with a roof.

He found a large branch with a fork in it, and smiled. After hunting about, he found three more, and began building. First he gauged the wind, and moved to the leeward side of the trunk. Here he thrust the two shorter sticks into the soft soil, the forks uppermost. He found a sapling of more than six and a half feet, and took his knife to it, placing his knife's blade against it and using a branch to hammer at it, ringing the bough, and then cutting a notch at the very bottom. Soon he could hear it crack as he pulled it, and then it came down. He set this in the forks, and braced them with the last pair of forked branches.

Running to his saddle-bags, he pulled one open. He always carried some hempen cord for emergencies, and this was just such an emergency. Soon the whole was lashed together, and he could start to set thick branches from the trunk to his supported beam. These he tied with simple loops, and used all the spare branches he could find to make a side wall and block the bottom. Now there was a basic shelter.

'Very good, if a little leaky,' the monk observed.

Simon said nothing. He was searching in the gathering darkness for Rob and growing fearful for the lad's safety.

'Don't worry, Bailiff,' Busse said. 'He's bright enough.'

'He has little sense of direction. He has never been on the moors before,' Simon said through gritted teeth. Bellowing Rob's name, he was relieved to see a figure jerk upright only a few tens of yards away. 'Hurry up!'

'You see?' Busse said.

'Yes. Now, I need you to gather up as many ferns as possible.'

Busse was startled. 'Me?'

'If you want to sleep dry and not freeze, you'll help me now. We need to cover this shelter in ferns and leaves – anything. And we need to be quick, before that snowstorm starts!'

Chapter Fourteen

Exeter City

As the light outside faded, Baldwin and the coroner demanded candles, and remained sitting with the man who had dared to make use of demons to achieve his ends.

Or so it had been said.

Baldwin was not prey to fears about men such as this. He was perfectly comfortable with the notion of an all-powerful God who would remove the foolish from the world without any need for his help. And there was not too much to be fearful of about this fellow. He did not inspire terror in Baldwin's breast.

'How long have you lived here?'

'In Exeter, you mean? Or Stepecote Street?' His voice was harsh and rasping, and sounded forced, as though it took a great deal of effort to speak at all. The pain he suffered was clear: he kept swallowing, each time wincing, and his eyes were watering freely.

'Either,' Baldwin said, but this time more gently. 'Take your time, friend; your voice is clearly giving you trouble.'

Langatre was a chubby fellow who was little more than thirty years old, Baldwin decided. He had the weakly chin of a man who was not destined for greatness of any sort, but there was little enough malice in his eyes. Rather, he displayed more the appearance of a man who laboured under a great fear.

'I was born in Langatre in Kent. I suppose I arrived here in Exeter about ten years ago, and I've been plying my trade here ever since, although it was only two years ago that I learned the deeper, more subtle arts, and that was when I took on the house down the street.'

'The dead boy?'

'Oh, God! Don't remind me! Poor lad! I don't know how I'm going to tell his mother about this!'

'Tell us first, then,' the coroner rumbled, unconvinced. Like Baldwin, he had seen too many felons deny their crimes and then burst into tears in an attempt to evade punishment.

'Gladly, lordings. I was in my workshop when there was a knock. I heard it distinctly, and heard my fellow go to answer it. I was involved in some important work at the time, making a special potion for a client, and could not pay attention. Well, I heard this strange tapping, as though someone was knocking on my workshop door, but ignored it, because Hick knows – *knew* – not to interrupt me when I was working, and then, as I was carrying my alembic to cool, someone dropped a noose about my neck and tried to draw it tight.'

Baldwin motioned with his hand and Richard de Langatre shrugged, lifted his cowl, and opened the front of his tunic.

Immediately Baldwin was struck with the similarity of his wound to the one on the king's messenger at the South Gate. 'You saw his face?'

'No. He was behind me all the time. I don't mind telling you both, it was a terrifying experience. I thought I would surely die!'

'Why didn't you? He was pulling hard,' Coroner Richard commented.

'I know that well enough! He was pulling so hard, I couldn't even get a nail under the cord.'

That much was true. Baldwin could see where he'd tried to jam a finger under the weapon: there were several scrape marks where his nails had scrabbled. 'What did you do?'

'I destroyed a perfectly good alembic . . . lost a valuable potion, rot his soul! I swung it over my head at his, and I fancy he'll be well scalded by now.'

'He shouldn't try to rob people, then, should he?' the coroner growled.

'What then?' Baldwin pressed him.

'When I was free, I grabbed for a knife, but he saw me and kicked me in the belly. God, but it hurt! Well, as soon as I could get up again, I realised he'd fled. I grabbed a weapon just in case, and went out, and that was when I almost fell over poor Hick's body. He was just lying there, right by the door. And he'd been attacked in the same manner, with something round his neck – a leather thong, I think.'

'Well, I wanted to call for help, so I went to the door and threw it wide, but when I did so, I couldn't speak! No one could hear me, and I had to wave my hands about and make a fuss before anyone noticed me. And when they did, the damned fools thought I'd gone mad. When they saw poor Hick lying there dead, they assumed I must have killed him myself, and they looked on me as a dangerous madman! I was going mad, to think that the killer had escaped and might even now be hiding about the place, so I tried to explain, and then tried to go to find him, but all I got was a poke in the ribs from some cretin with a staff, and then a crack on my head to keep me quiet. Then the bastards wanted to put me in the gaol! When my voice is back, I shall have words with that man. Bloody Elias!'

His voice had dropped, and now it petered out altogether. He swallowed painfully once more, and took a long pull of the strong ale which Coroner Richard had ordered. 'The bastard will be long gone now, I suppose.'

'Perhaps so,' Coroner Richard agreed, 'but in all of this, who do you know who is enough of an enemy to hire a man to kill your boy and then try to kill you? What on earth would someone gain by killing you?'

'You think it was a paid assassin?' Langatre asked, visibly paling.

'Hard to see who else it could have been,' the coroner said imperturbably. 'Surely you'd have known who it was, if it was someone who hated you that much, eh?'

'I never saw his face.'

'You don't need to, do you? The smell of a man's coat, his sweat, his breath . . . if it was someone you knew well, you'd have recognised him, sure enough.'

'Perhaps, and perhaps not,' Baldwin said. 'However, I am intrigued by something I was told. The people opposite your house stated that they heard a scream and as a result people began to flock to your door.'

'That must have been when I hit him with the alembic,' Langatre guessed.

'So I would presume.' Baldwin nodded. 'But in that case, it is scarcely likely that he ran away from the house. A man appearing, dripping with some foul concoction of yours, and clearly badly scalded, would have excited some comment, I think, unless your street is very different from all the others I know. He alerted the neighbours with his scream, according to your story. How else could he have escaped from the place?'

'Well, he couldn't. I only have a small house, and there's no way out at the back.'

Baldwin was suddenly tense. 'You mean there is no exit at all from the rear?'

'No. Nothing.'

'In that case, we should hurry back there! The man might still be inside the house!'

The beadle was surprised to see them all back so soon, and he eyed the necromancer with suspicion. 'I thought you were going to take him to the gaol for me?'

'Complain to the sheriff,' Coroner Richard snapped. 'Have you searched the house?'

'Searched the . . . no! Why?'

'Because the murderer may still be here,' Baldwin said sharply. 'Come!'

Leaving the nervous beadle at the door gripping his staff with both hands as though clinging to it for life itself, Baldwin and the others walked inside. Once over the threshold, Baldwin rested his hand on the hilt of his sword, and looked to Langatre.

The man was staring down at the body on the ground at their feet still, but he nodded grimly, and led the way into his workshop. 'This is where he attacked me.'

Baldwin could see the mess where the alembic had been smashed. There was a foul odour of mustiness and sourness, much of which came from the pool of solidifying stuff among the shards of pottery.

The room was a good size, but the accumulation of curiosities had made it appear to shrink. There were shelves along one wall, filled with various forms of herb. Above their heads were gathered dried and wilted leaves, while a table groaned under the weight of skulls and parts of dissected animals. Another table held the tools of his trade: there was a needle, a staff, a sword – all strange items that stank with the same smell.

'What is that foul odour?' Coroner Richard demanded, picking up a black tunic with strange symbols on it and sniffing at it doubtfully. He drew it away from his face with a wince. 'Christ's bones, that is foul!'

'Do not blaspheme!' Langatre hissed. 'You have no idea how dangerous such behaviour can be in a place like this! I depend upon God's good mercy to protect me when I am working. I will not have myself endangered because of a coroner's insolence.'

'Fine – but what is that smell?'

'I have to fumigate all the instruments before I can conjure up . . . it is just to cleanse everything, that is all.'

'It smells disgusting.'

'I seem to remember I thought the same the first time I smelled it. When you become a wise man like me, you tend not to notice such things any more.'

'Rots your nose, does it?' the coroner observed, and walked about poking at things periodically, before grunting to himself that there wasn't space for a man to hide in there, and leaving the room.

'Is he always like this?' Langatre asked, watching him go.

'N-o-o. Today he is being well behaved and inclined to kindness,' Baldwin answered honestly. He gazed about him. 'Is there anything missing in here?'

'Look, what would a man take from . . .' Langatre noticed Baldwin's cold expression, and decided that his words could be saved. He made a show of walking about the place, casting an eye over the tables, but it was only when he was almost back at Baldwin's side that his face took on a frown. 'That's strange . . .'

'What is gone?'

'My daggers. I have two knives – one black-handled, one white. They're used in some of the magic preparations . . . they were here, but . . . my hat! Where's my hat? There was a white leather hat here when I was taken by that moronic beadle!'

He was at a table far from the door. Baldwin glanced at it, then at the mess on the floor where the alembic had smashed. 'You were here? So after he attacked you, this man would have had to step over you to steal them? Could he have done?'

'No! There is no possible way . . . but why would anyone want them?'

It took little time to search the rest of the house. The place was small, with a larder and buttery opposite the door to his main room. At the far end of the building was a narrow wooden staircase which led up to the solar area. Warily, Baldwin left his sword sheathed, but pulled out his dagger, and cautiously ascended.

The chamber was a tiny space up in the eaves. Here the smoke from the fire rose and tainted all with the scent of charred logs and tar. Gripping his dagger, Baldwin climbed quickly inside. There was a palliasse on the floor with some blankets thrown messily to one side, and a small chest stood in the angle of the wall. Baldwin gazed about him, but there was nothing to see. No one could hide in this small space without being instantly spotted.

He returned to the ladder, and began to climb down again, but there was something that caught his attention: a faint odour catching at his nostrils. Stopping, he hesitated, and then climbed back.

'What is it?' the coroner called.

'He was up here.'

Exeter Castle

Matthew was too unsettled to sit and drink. He went out into his court and, crossing over it, entered his kennels.

The dogs were slumberous after a long run with their master that afternoon, and although some eyes opened, and four tails twitched, there was little more by way of acknowledgement.

It was impossible to concentrate. His wife was lying to him, going and visiting that damned magician, just at the time when it was vital that they were quiet and avoided any such people. She was in enough trouble because of her family, and he was in a potentially lethal position because of this affair of the necromancer from Coventry. There was little he could do to control matters. They were controlling him.

At least there was one thing he could do. It would cause some anger when she heard what he had done, but he couldn't explain why it was so perfect. He had ordered that fellow Langatre to be arrested on suspicion of killing his servant. That was fine, but the man wouldn't be held for long, unless Matthew could continue to have him removed from the city entirely. And how better than to have him sent to the king to be questioned in case he had any part in the assassination attempt.

Yes, Matthew would have him gaoled here, and send a man to take a message to the king.

Where were they? Langatre should have been here by now. The sheriff walked to the door, but there was no sign of the beadles who should have been bringing him to the gaol. No matter. They wouldn't be long. No. He turned back to his hounds and scratched a bitch behind the ears.

Send Langatre to the king, and it would divert attention. And his wife would not be going out to see him any more.

Two birds.

North-East Dartmoor

Simon gathered a massive pile of leaves by the simple expedient of kicking them into a heap. Here the wood was thickly laden with them so soon after the trees had shed them all, and in a short time he had several mounds ready to be used.

'Are you finished?' he called to Busse.

The monk was throwing fronds of fern atop the shelter, panting slightly with the unaccustomed labour. 'Nearly.'

Simon walked to him and eyed the structure consideringly. It had grown into a shelter of some four feet wide by seven long, with a thick layer of greenery cast over it, so that it would be hard to see any of the wood that made up its walls and roof. He lined up some of the fronds more tidily, but then nodded to himself and started gathering great armfuls of leaves to bring back and throw over the shelter. He had to repeat the action many times before he was content, for he knew that to give them protection from the chill the leaves must be a good three feet thick, if he could manage it.

'That should be enough,' he said at last.

'Thanks be to God,' Busse said, and flopped onto the ground.

By some great good fortune the snow had only fallen thinly so far, and now there was a fine crust over all, like a morning's frost. It was a relief to Simon, because he still had time to make a fire. It was essential, as he knew, that they should have heat. All of them were shivering even with their thickest clothes on. It was Rob in particular that Simon was worried about. He had little in the way of decent clothing, and Simon was anxious for him.

He had built a pile of twigs and branches, and now he pulled his tinder from his shirt and set it on a platform of thicker twigs. Taking his steel, he struck at it with the reverse of his knife's blade, striking sparks and watching as carefully as he might. It was hard work, for the sparks blinded him in the gathering darkness, and he was unable to see the gleam of the tinder catching. Usually he was quick to strike a light, but tonight, with his fingers frozen and his belly empty, it took longer. Yet at last there was a small yellow-orange mote glistening, and Simon picked up the ball of tinder and began to blow carefully, softly at first, then more strongly. It took some minutes, but then, suddenly, he had a small explosion, and the middle of the tinder flared.

Setting it down, he began to set small twigs over it, and as they glowed and flamed he set slightly thicker twigs over them, until he had to break twigs urgently to keep up. Then, at last, he started to use thicker stems and set them about the fire until it represented a cone, the outside twigs all pointing upwards. Now, he felt comfortable enough to let Rob see to it. The boy lit the fire each day in Simon's house at Dartmouth.

'Well done, Bailiff. I don't know that I would have survived without your help.'

Simon yawned. All he knew was that as soon as the fire was roaring and he had toasted himself before it for a short while, he was going to settle down in the shelter and sleep. He was exhausted.

'What did you say about the spirits of the rocks at that place on the moors?' Rob asked after a few moments. He was feeding the fire steadily, cracking smaller twigs between his fingers to build up a bed of ash. Already the first outer layer of twigs was burning through, and he must hurry to construct the second cone of larger twigs.

Busse smiled to himself. 'It is a sad tale of the misbehaviour of children, I fear. One winter's Sunday, the children from the area went out there to play at a game of some sort. Well, we all know that playing games on a Sunday is frowned upon by God, don't we? So He came to them, and struck them all into stone. All the little boys from a whole vill. Just think of it!'

Rob was thinking of it. His face wore a look of shock.

'Keep feeding the fire,' Simon called, and Rob quickly jerked back into action.

'But why were there two circles of stones there, then?'

'Oh, the Grey Wethers are the first circle – the second was not the children, that was some youths who also went there to play on the Sabbath,' Busse said. 'And God was no more pleased with them than he was with the others.'

An owl called from deep in the woods, and Rob's head spun towards it.

'Don't worry, though,' Simon said. 'There are no rocks in this wood. Not that I know, anyway.'

'Oh. Good,' Rob said, and then edged a little closer to Simon. He continued to set twigs on the fire, but now Simon could see that his eyes were as often on the woods all about them as on the flames.

Simon, nodding already, was only relieved to think that Rob would stay awake and keep the fire going for longer.

Chapter Fifteen

Exeter City

Robinet was soon at Master Walter's house, where he knocked quietly. After a short period, there came the sound of bolts being drawn, and then the door opened a crack.

'So you decided to come back?'

'Walter, may I enter, please?'

'I suppose. What's happened to your old friend, then?'

Newt swallowed. 'Someone murdered him out by the South Gate.'

Walter had been walking back into his hall, but on hearing that he stopped and turned slowly to Newt. 'You kill him?'

'Of course not!'

Walter gave him a sour look. 'You leave here a day and a half ago, saying you were going to see the little shite, and now he's dead, right? And where were you last night, then?'

Robinet held out his hands, palms up. 'You know me well enough. Would I have grabbed him from behind and strangled him with a cord?'

'Christ no! That would have been *my* way, not yours.' Walter chuckled grimly. 'You were always the kindly fellow who sought to placate people, and when you failed you just drew your sword and stabbed them while looking them straight in the eye. I was the devious bastard who made people disappear.'

'So did *you* do it?'

Walter of Hanlegh turned to face him, a man slightly shorter than Newt, with a sharp, narrow face and close-set black eyes. As he met Newt's stare, there was sadness in them, an expression almost of wistfulness, as though he missed his past calling. It had certainly paid him well over the years, as was proved by his house, a smart, new building with tiles on the floor, a brick fireplace and his own chimney, and even a solar chamber for his bed. His clothes were finely embroidered, the shirt made from the best linen, his hosen soft lambswool, his tunic bright and unfaded.

'No, Newt. It was not me.'

'Thank Christ for that, at least,' Newt said with relief. 'I thought you'd killed him just to save me from my stupidity.'

'I would have – but a man has to make his own mistakes.'

'Yes,' Newt agreed. It did not help him learn who *had* killed James, but at least Walter had not succumbed to temptation just to help a friend. Not many men would have considered murder purely to aid a companion, but then not many men had been assassins in the pay of the king.

They were still in the house when the beadle appeared in the doorway. 'Sir Baldwin? Sir Richard? There's a man here for you.'

There was a tone in his voice which Baldwin instinctively disliked: a leering, amused note that jarred.

Sir Richard was not the sort of man to notice a subtlety like that, and he shrugged, grunted, and went to the door. Baldwin glanced at the still-anxious Langatre, and followed him. Outside stood a sergeant, but not one of the city's men. This was one of Sir Matthew's.

'Well?' Sir Richard snapped. 'Be quick, man! I have been working too long already today and need my rest and relaxation. You are delaying me!'

'Coroner, I have been told to come here to bring the necromancer to the sheriff. He is not to be tolerated any longer.'

'He isn't, eh?' Sir Richard said with a sidelong look at Baldwin. 'He is in my custody at this moment, and he's staying with me.'

'Sir Matthew wants me to take him. There are some matters about him which make the sheriff demand that you turn him over to his personal custody, sir.'

Coroner Richard's face underwent a rapid change. The benevolent expression with which he had been surveying the world suddenly became as bellicose as a Bishop of Winchester whore's when she learns her client has no money.

'You tell me that you are demanding this fellow when I have already said he's safe with me?'

Baldwin quickly interjected. 'Sir Richard, this fellow has no responsibility in the matter. He is only the messenger. Perhaps we should go with him to see the sheriff.'

'That man?' Sir Richard muttered with a leery glare at the sergeant. 'Very well.'

The sergeant walked to Langatre and took his upper arm in his fist. 'Try anything and I'll brain you,' he said.

Baldwin shook his head. 'At the moment, sergeant, he is in my and the coroner's custody, not the sheriff's, and not yours. You will release him now.'

'I have my orders, sir.'

'I have no doubt you do. However, my orders to you are to release him. This fellow is innocent of the murder, and I for one want to know what the sheriff wishes to speak to him for, but I will not have him paraded through the streets like a common felon. I hope that is clear.'

North-East Dartmoor

In the event, it was Rob who succumbed to the cold first and went into the shelter to sleep.

They had set off travelling light, but Simon always ensured that he was prepared for foul weather. He could still remember one of his earliest experiences on the moors, when he had ridden out on his old bay rounsey and been caught by a sudden mist.

The fogs could appear from nowhere, and when they came down a man was hard pressed to know anything: the compass, his direction, even whether he was going up- or downhill. It was disorientating to be so completely lost, and for a lad as young as he had been, perhaps only nine years or so, quite scary.

Ever since then, he always took more clothing and provisions than he thought he might need when he crossed the moors. Usually there was no problem for him. After all, he knew all the miners and where they lived, so in the worst case he could usually find someone to provide him with a refuge, but every so often, like today, that was not possible. And here he was now in a rude shelter with two others who had little experience of such affairs.

Rob's feet looked all right in the firelight, although Simon would be happier when he had checked them again in the morning, but he was anxious enough about the lad to give him his thicker blanket and his spare riding cloak for protection. Rob wearily crawled into the shelter, and Simon could see him wrapping himself up before resting his head on a thick pile of leaves. In a short space of time there was regular snoring from inside.

'You are a very capable man,' Busse observed after a few moments.

'A man does what he must. Only a fool is unprepared on the moors.'

'I can quite understand why the good Abbot Robert, bless his memory, put so much trust in you.'

'I am grateful, but I have done nothing that any other Devon man used to the moors would not have done.'

'Do not belittle your skills, my friend. It is plain to me that you see and understand much about this land. More than most.'

Simon shrugged. 'I have spent a lot of time on the moors since I was a child.'

'I have been spending as much time up here as I can since I arrived too, of course, but I've only been here – what? Maybe twelve, thirteen years? I have nothing like your experience.'

'Yes, well, you are a monk. You can hardly expect to gather as much knowledge about the moors as someone who's worked on them for as long as me,' Simon said uncomfortably. After all he had heard from John de Courtenay, he didn't feel he could trust this man, no matter that he had such an apparently amiable disposition, or that his behaviour so far had given Simon no reason to mistrust him.

'What would you like to do when the new abbot is installed?'

'Me?'

'Yes. From all I've seen of you, you aren't a man suited to sitting in a customs house and counting coins. When you are in the town, you have an appearance of frustration, as though you want to be away, but here . . . here you look like a man in his element.'

Simon had to control himself. It was too tempting to let his jaw drop. No one else had ever noticed his irritation and dissatisfaction with the job in Dartmouth, he was sure. 'I certainly like the moors,' he said cautiously.

'So I always believed! I never thought you were ideal for the post of keeper of the port. So, if I were to become abbot, would you prefer me to put you back up here as bailiff? It is entirely up to you, but if you wish it, let me know and I'll do what I can.'

'Do you think you will win the election?'

Busse was blowing on his hands. Now he stopped and held them to the fire, looking away from Simon as he did so. His eyes were crinkled at the corners, and he smiled faintly as he spoke.

'Oh, don't listen to what others say, Bailiff. Just because a man is born to a noble family doesn't mean that he is himself very noble. I know the sort of rumour that brother John has been spreading against me, and I will not allow it to upset me. Better, I think, for me to behave as a real monk should, and continue to perform my duties to the best of my ability, rather than sinking to low political rumour-mongering.'

'I didn't mean . . .' Simon began, distressed to think that he had been so transparent.

'Of course you did, and you would be right to worry about me, too. If I were to become the new abbot, and if I were a thief or an untrustworthy soul in any way, I would merit caution from any man. Naturally. But I say this, Bailiff,' and now he turned and faced Simon, still with the little smile on his lips, but with shrewd, serious eyes, 'I say this: I am no liar, fraud or thief. I seek only to do the best I may for the abbey and for God. I have no other interests. However, I am driven by one consideration, one motivation that urges me on with ever greater determination.'

Simon nodded. 'And that is?'

'Dear God in heaven! To keep that blasted idiot de Courtenay out of it, of course! You know how the abbey was when Abbot Robert was first elected?'

Simon could smile at that. Abbot Robert had taken on an abbey that was collapsing under its debts. His first act had been to borrow money to maintain the fabric of the place. And now? At his death it was probably the wealthiest institution in the whole of Devon.

'Precisely. The abbey is safe for now – but if brother John takes on the abbacy, how long would that last? He would spend all he could on his wine and his hunting. Under him, I could imagine Tavistock having the best bloodlines of every rache, alaunt and rounsey in the country, but no money to buy candles or bread! God forbid that that spendthrift and fool should ever be in charge of the place.'

A little while later, he apologised to Simon, but begging the age of his bones and his inexperience of such long days he crawled into the shelter and rolled himself up in his own blanket, close to Rob.

It was hard to know what was best to do in these circumstances, Simon told himself. De Courtenay had been right when he told Simon that Simon had a loyalty to the family. His father had been so devoted, it was hard for Simon to consider being even remotely disloyal. And yet Busse had hit the nail on the head when he spoke about the man's interests. Simon didn't know de Courtenay intimately, but he was quite sure that the man would be an unmitigated disaster if he was responsible for the abbey's finances.

However, as he crawled backwards into the shelter, his blanket and cloak in his hands, as he wrapped himself up in them and closed his eyes, all he could see was Busse's calm, affable face offering him the chance of throwing over life in Dartmouth and returning here, to the moors he loved. He could live with his wife again in Lydford, see their daughter, see his little son growing . . .

For that he would support any contender, no matter what John de Courtenay felt.

Exeter Castle

The sheriff's chamber at the castle was a small, comfortable affair, but there was nothing kindly or welcoming in the sheriff's expression as Baldwin and the coroner entered, Langatre behind them.

'I hear you released this man? On what grounds?'

'Sir Matthew, it is delightful to meet you again,' Coroner Richard declared.

'And you. What is the meaning of releasing this man when I had ordered him arrested and brought here?' He had stood now, and walked past the two knights to stand staring at the wilting Langatre.

Baldwin glanced at Sir Richard, but he could see that the coroner was as bemused as he by this display of anger. 'You had a man ordered arrested on the basis that he had killed his servant. After a brief investigation, it was clear not only that he had not killed his servant, but that he was himself the victim of a fierce assault, and would have died were it not for the fact that he defended himself with vigour.'

'And he convinced you of that, did he?'

'Show him your neck, lad,' Coroner Richard rumbled.

Langatre obediently lifted his hands to his throat, but the sheriff knocked them away.

'I don't care what fatuous evidence you have given these two good knights. I know who you are and what you do, man. I won't have your kind in this county, and for now I want you held in my gaol until the little matter of your guilt or innocence has been confirmed to *my* satisfaction. Take him down, sergeant!'

Baldwin protested. 'Sheriff, this man is innocent. You cannot seriously believe that he could have killed his servant. I have seen the scene myself, and it accords in every detail with this man's evidence. If you hold him here, the people in his road will assume that he is guilty, and his life will become impossible.'

The sheriff watched his sergeant ungently pulling the shocked Langatre through the door and closing it after them. 'You may feel that this is unjust, Sir Baldwin, but it's only the latest in a series of insanities, so far as I am concerned. However, I have a writ from the king himself demanding that people such as this Langatre should be arrested and presented to him.'

'Where is this writ?' Sir Richard grated.

The sheriff looked at him with surprise – although Baldwin was not sure whether it was because the coroner had questioned his veracity, or merely that he didn't think the coroner could read. Whatever the reason, he had soon pulled out a small parchment with the king's seal broken on it. He passed the small cylinder to Sir Richard, who unrolled it, his eyes all the while on the sheriff, as though doubting that the man was safe.

'Good God in heaven!'

'Yes,' the sheriff said. 'Dated the sixth of November at Westminster.'

'What does it say?' Baldwin asked at last, frustrated beyond tolerance.

'There has been an attempt on the life of the king and the Despensers. All those who could have had anything to do with it are to be held.'

'You say that this pathetic little man who pretends to be able to make magic – that this little fellow might be involved in assassinating the king?' Baldwin asked.

'According to the king's messenger, the dead man, the fellow responsible for this attempt to assassinate them was a man called John of Nottingham, who was living in Coventry at the time,' the sheriff admitted. 'But that does not mean others were not themselves involved.'

'You mean even a man so far away as here in Exeter?' Baldwin said, and chuckled.

'You find it amusing?'

'I find the idea that you could think him guilty very amusing!'

'Langatre had sold his services to many clients. He is known to conjure spirits to tell him the future, as well as summoning demons to do his bidding.'

'And yet an assassin could almost have his head off with a string?'

'There is little to laugh about,' the sheriff said. He took the parchment from Sir Richard's hand. 'This message was delivered, ordering me to arrest those who could have had a part in a magical attempt on the lives of the king and his favourite companions, and a short while later the messenger was found throttled. That, to me, seems a great coincidence. And in matters of the law, I don't like coincidences, Sir Baldwin. Especially when they affect my lord the king.'

Chapter Sixteen

Exeter City

Walter drew a large jug from the barrel of strong ale at the rear of his buttery, and poured two pottery drinking horns full. Passing one to Robinet, he lifted his own and they clashed them, the ale inside splashing about and spattering the floor.

Drinking deeply, Walter eyed his old friend over the brim. 'So, come, now. What is all this about? Who'd want to kill that youngster?'

'I don't know. He wasn't known here in Exeter.'

'He was hardly known anywhere, was he?'

'This way, no. He tended to get the circuits north of London, rather than the longer ones westwards.'

Both men knew how the messengers tended to work. There were two groups: the *nuncii regis* and the *cursores*. The former were the men on horseback, the latter the men on foot. Both would cover the same distance in a day, about thirty-five miles, because a man with a horse would have to allow the beast a certain amount of rest, while a man on foot could keep going all day.

'Was he booted or horsed when you knew him?'

'When he was under my wing, he was mostly on horseback. He didn't start out like me.'

'Those fellows have it too easy,' Walter said, refilling their horns. After another toast, he glared at the floor thoughtfully.

'It is strange for a messenger to be harmed in any way whatever. You know that.'

'Aye, I do. I've only heard of one being molested, and that was by the Scots, I think.'

'Few would dare cause such offence to the king himself.'

'Yet someone did.'

Newt nodded, and leaned his elbows on his thighs. 'What is odd is that when I woke up this morning, I was in a small stable, and my knife was beslobbered with dried blood.'

'He bled?'

'I told you: he was strangled, but later stabbed as though to make sure. And someone had cut off a finger or two.'

Walter scowled. 'This grows more and more unpleasant.'

Yes, confusing. The messenger was a pathetic little fellow – he'd seen him with Newt on that first day, when he walked straight into Newt. Walter wasn't impressed by the fact that he stood up to Newt. That could well have been terror rather than courage. Walter had seen it before, with men who were startled. When they reacted, they could sometimes behave as though bold as a knight in a tournament, when in truth they were simply acting.

Newt shook his head. 'There's something about this. He didn't deserve it. He screwed me, I know, but he didn't deserve to be throttled and left out there.'

'No one does, Newt. No one ever does,' Walter said, and his eyes were black wells of memory as he spoke.

It was very late when they returned to the Suttonsysyn, and the innkeeper was not welcoming, but the coroner made full use of his size and anger, and soon they had a table in a quiet corner with a jug of the inn's best ale and two large cups, while a servant was sent to see what food was still available.

'What do you think?' Baldwin said as soon as they were alone.

'Me? That prickle has something on his mind. This is nothing to do with the poor sod found dead, or I'm not from Welles. Ballocks to that! No, the blasted idiot thinks that he can gain advantage with the king if he holds that poor dolt, and if the good sheriff sees profit in it, he'll do it. I know him of old.'

'So do I, and I hate to think that I might one day be at his mercy,' Baldwin said. 'If there has truly been an attempt on the king's life, and that of his ... friend, then you may be assured that our little necromancer here will be sent to the king.'

'I would not reckon his chances, were he to be sent before the Despenser, not if it's true that the Despenser thought his life had been endangered by a magician,' Sir Richard said.

'I think not,' Baldwin said, with a sense of inner relief. It was always a fearsome thing to talk openly to another about the king and his favourite. The rumour was that the King and Despenser were lovers, but that could well have been nonsense. However, the power and authority of Despenser was something that could not be forgotten. He had a long arm, and an infinite ability for hatred, so Baldwin had heard. Merely discussing him was hazardous, for if another overheard their conversation, and they were derogatory about him, he could be expected to seek them out. And Despenser did not seek mere punishment: he sought to destroy his enemies and take all their treasure for his own, impoverishing the families for ever.

'Of course, it is none of our business,' the coroner muttered. 'We were asked to help investigate the murder of a king's messenger.'

'Why were you here?' Baldwin asked. Coroner Richard was not usually in Exeter. He hailed from Lifton.

'I happened to be up here for a case before the Justices of Gaol Delivery, and when the body was found I was asked to come and view it. I suppose it was known that I was a coroner for the king's estate, so it was fitting that I should hold inquest on a king's messenger.'

'So it was known that he was a *nuncius regis* before you had even come to view him?'

'No . . . at least, no one told me. I realised he was a messenger when I saw him – no one warned me that he was.'

'Whereas I happened to be here in the town, so the bishop thought to engage me to help him,' Baldwin mused. 'It is peculiar that he should seek to ask me to aid you.'

'Means the man thought the theft of this roll could be embarrassing either to the Church or to him personally.'

'What could be so embarrassing, I wonder?'

'Be careful that your wonderings don't catch you out!' Coroner Richard laughed drily. 'You know what they say: if you wish for something too much, you might just win it . . . and live to regret it! This thing must be something of great importance to the bishop, whether it involves national or Church matters. Either way, if you learn what is in the roll, you will surely come to regret the fact!'

'We must find the roll. That is the charge laid upon us.'

'Aye. But if we want to learn what has happened to that, we have to find the murderer of the messenger. The man who killed and mutilated him must know about the thing.'

'I wonder. I wonder.' Baldwin sat with his chin cupped in the palm of his hand as he stared at the dying embers of the fire.

'I should think that the fellow was most likely unfortunate, that he ran into some desperate footpad, and was killed.'

Baldwin slowly raised his eyes and stared at him. 'You believe that? This messenger was caught by a stranger who knew nothing about him, was held, had his finger cut off, and was then throttled while he scrabbled, even with his mutilated hand, to save himself? And then, when the murderer had concealed his body and rested, he went to that necromancer's house and killed his servant in an attempt to kill Langatre too?'

'Think of the alternative, Baldwin,' the coroner said quietly, leaning forward and meeting Baldwin's serious stare. 'The alternative to this being an unfortunate mistake is that it was intentional. Someone knew that this messenger was carrying a secret, urgent roll that could seriously embarrass the bishop, if no one else. And then the same fellow went to the necromancer to execute him for some reason.'

'That is how I read the riddle.'

'It supposes that the young fool in the sheriff's gaol had an insight into matters far above his station, Baldwin. It means that fool has an understanding of national or Church affairs. Can you really believe that?'

'Not for a moment.'

'Nor can I. However, if the murderer thought that he was being pursued, he could have entered a house to escape? Perhaps he was hurrying past the necromancer's house, saw a man following him, and walked inside. He saw the servant, killed him, and then heard that fellow Langatre in his room, so slipped in to do away with him too. The pursuers ran on . . .'

'They could have assumed he was heading for the city's gate. Stepecote Street leads down to the West Gate,' Baldwin considered.

'And then he hoped to escape. Except the neighbours heard something and ran to the house, and found one corpse and the necromancer standing over it looking guilty. There you are! A simple story, well told.'

'True. And it chimes well, but for one problem. As soon as the pursuers reached the gate, they would know he had not been that way. And they would have doubled back to seek him, and in doing so, they would have passed by a house outside which there was a large crowd gathering. They would have thought to find their man inside.'

'Perhaps. Yes, that is possible. And why not? Perhaps they did indeed find him?'

'And there was no sound of a posse, either.' Baldwin frowned. 'If there were, we should have heard of it. So no. I don't believe your tale. In which case, there is still a murderer loose in our city.'

North-East Dartmoor

Simon shivered himself awake at regular intervals through the night. It was freezing, and although he was relieved, each time he woke, not to have the added misery of rain, he was conscious of the light sprinkling sound of snow falling gently on the trees.

In their shelter, there was so little space, it was hard to imagine that any of the three could roll over without hitting the others, or knocking down a wall, but Simon was relieved to see that there was no sign of any gaps in the thatch over his head. It seemed that nobody had knocked the shelter's walls so far.

However, he was also aware of a growing sensation of pressure in his bladder. He hunched his shoulders, turned away from the other two, and faced the wall. Then he turned back and faced in to the middle. He lay on his back. No matter what he did, or how he lay, the pressure seemed to grow, like a wineskin that was sat upon. By degrees, the wine would leak from it . . . and that was how Simon felt now. That the building discomfort must find release.

At last the inevitability of his position became clear, and he grunted quietly to himself as he unwrapped his cloak and blanket and crawled from the entrance.

The fire was glowing gently, but there was no flame now, and when he looked up at the sky he could see only white-rimmed clouds. There was no way to tell what time of day it might be, and at the moment he hardly cared. All he knew was, it was the sort of hour of the night that was only good for monks. He grunted as he felt the chill of the cold air at his cheeks, and pulled his cloak from inside the shelter. Wrapping it about his shoulders, he walked a short distance from their camp, and with enormous relief opened his hose to empty his bladder.

As he retied the thongs that held his hosen up, he glanced about him. The snow had fallen, although mercifully not too heavily. From here, although the sky was clouded, he could still make out the moors just beyond the fringe of the trees. The top of the nearer hill gleamed with a light of its own, the snow shining grey.

'I should be at home with Meg,' he grumbled to himself, feeling how the cold air was tightening the skin on the backs of his hands.

Rather than re-enter the shelter, he decided to warm himself up again. The pile of logs remained near the fire, and it took only a little shaking of it to clear away the snow. Then he spent a little time setting thin twigs on top of the embers, blowing determinedly to reignite the flames. Soon, mercifully, he had a few flickers, and he could set larger twigs about the pile. Only then did he sit back and hold his hands to it, feeling that the fire was doing him some good.

'May I join you?'

He groaned inwardly, but grunted a more or less polite acknowledgement to the monk.

'This weather! You know, I had a friend in Tavistock some years ago, and he was removed to be sent to a monastery in Italy. Have you ever been there?'

'No.' Rather than sound entirely bound to this land, he added defensively, 'But I've been to Galicia.'

'Compostela? I am jealous. I always intended to go there, but I doubt I shall make it now. I am growing a little long in the tooth to make such a pilgrimage. What tempted you to go so far?'

'It was a while ago,' Simon said. He could not explain that it all stemmed from a friend's accidental homicide of an innocent man.

'I see. Well, my friend will be sitting back in a pleasantly warm room, I am told. No matter what the season, the weather is always more clement than ours. Ah! But I am fortunate to be here in the land I love. Although the moors are daunting, do you not feel?'

Simon glanced over through the trees at the hills beyond. 'Daunting, you say? I suppose so. They are certainly dangerous for those who don't appreciate the risks.'

On the cool air, there came a weird, shuddering cry. It wavered on the air like a sob, and then died.

'What, in God's holy name?'

'Sit down again, brother. It is a horse. You can often hear them at this time of year. They wander the moors, and every so often they'll go into a mire and drown.'

The cry came again, a long drawn out wail of terror and misery.

'Are you sure? That sounds human!'

'It's a horse.'

'Christ have mercy!' Busse sat quietly, his eyes moving swiftly about the moors in front of them, hands clenched before him.

'At least you're used to being up at this time of night,' Simon muttered. 'I'm normally long asleep by now, and it'd take more than a horse to wake me.'

'Well, yes, I suppose so. But a sound like that . . . it reminds me . . .'

Simon heard a note of uncertainty in his voice. He glanced at the monk. In the firelight, Busse looked wide-eyed and terrified, like a man who was listening at the brink of hell itself.

'I was talking to a necromancer not long ago. He was an interesting man, in many ways. And pious. He believed that in order to compel a demon to do his bidding, he must make full use of the irresistible power of certain divine words. He would fast, too, and prepare himself with a long period of chastity and prayer before embarking on such a perilous act.'

'You spoke to him?' Simon asked, shocked.

'Of course, Bailiff. If I, as a monk, am to pray for those whose souls most need God's help, it is best to understand them. That was my first feeling. And then I realised that this man was a great proof of the strength of God's power. After all, even a man who wished to make use of a demon must needs first show his devotion to God.'

'It hardly sounds the sort of behaviour God would support,' Simon said. His was a simple faith: God was good, and all demons were evil and to be shunned.

Busse appeared not to hear him. 'It was that poor creature's cry that reminded me of him. He told me, you see, that there was a magician called Philip about sixty years ago, who was challenged by a knight to show what he was capable of. He took the knight to a crossroads in the middle of the night – I believe that mid-night is supposed to be propitious for those involved in such works – and there the knight endured what he had never before dreamed of. The man Philip made a circle in the dirt, and warned the knight that if so much as a digit of his finger were to stray outside the circle, he would inevitably be drawn out and pulled apart.

'He sat in this circle for some while, and then he heard voices approaching. They were obscene voices, shrieks, squawks, all manner of foul bestial cries. And then they reached him, and he found himself surrounded by the full evil of Satan's hordes. Demonic creatures of all kinds. At last a massive, foul demon appeared, so repellent and terrifying that the knight fell on his face in a dead faint.'

'Did he recover?'

'I suppose so. I didn't ask. But that sound reminds me of the tale.'

Simon pulled a face as he listened to another cry. 'It won't be there for long. Soon drown now. He's too tired to survive.'

'Doesn't it scare you too?'

Shaking his head, Simon threw a few more twigs onto the fire. 'When I was a lad, I heard that sound, and I was petrified. I'd been told stories of the wild hunt when I was little, by my nurse. She always told me that if I didn't eat my food, or if I didn't go to bed when she said, or some other little thing, then the devil would surely come and get me. The wish-hounds would appear first, riding over the moors, and then the devil would ride up on his fire-breathing horse, and catch me, and I'd be taken away to hell with them. But I'd never seen the devil down here.'

'I wish you hadn't told me that,' Busse said.

'You must have heard the stories about the moors,' Simon said. 'You've lived here long enough.'

'I think that many of the tales are told to children who are raised here, but the same stories are not thought suitable for a middle-aged monk like me. Too racy, I dare say.'

'Not even the stories of the pixies?'

'Enough! I think you are taunting me intentionally. Perhaps I should go and rest again.'

'You should. We travelled far yesterday, and tomorrow we'll still have another seven or eight leagues or so to get to Exeter.'

'I don't think I could sleep just now,' Busse said. 'The cold, and that screaming, would stop me. And, of course, I am used to being awake at this time of night. This is my usual waking hour for Matins. To think that all my brothers are even now leaving their cots and making their way to the church . . . It is a beautiful service, Bailiff, when all the voices lift in praise of the Lord.'

Simon nodded, studying the monk from the corner of his eye. It seemed so peculiar to be talking so normally to this man, who had admitted to consorting with demon-conjurors and magicians. For anyone the association was curious, but for a man of God to confess to such behaviour was bizarre.

The two men stayed together for a little longer, quiet for the most part, simply sharing in the atavistic pleasure of holding their hands to the fire, and then, as Simon yawned and stretched, Busse declared himself tired once more. Simon wished him a good night, and his eyes followed the monk as he crawled backwards into the shelter.

Yes. Busse was an odd character, certainly. And yet likeable in some strange way. Not that it mattered to Simon a jot. As far as he was concerned, the only thing that mattered was looking after the man on the way to Exeter, and then back to Tavistock again. And he preferred not to think about the references to demon-conjurings or knights sitting inside small circles . . .

It was only as Simon considered that tale again that he wondered whether Busse was giving him some kind of warning. Perhaps he was telling Simon that if he intended to spy on him for John de Courtenay, he should be careful. Busse could have a man set a demon onto Simon himself.

As he had this thought, there came another shrill, shuddering cry on the wind, but this time, for all Simon's level-headed protestations and explanations, a freezing shudder ran down his spine and trickled into his bones. He threw a last log on the fire, and hurriedly returned to the shelter.

He did not feel comfortable lying in the same tiny space as Busse, but he liked still less being out in the open on his own.

Exeter Castle

And in the sheriff's bedchamber, although Matthew had rolled over and was soon asleep, content with a hard day's work satisfactorily completed, his wife lay on her back at his side and stared at the ceiling.

Langatre had nothing to do with anything dangerous, she was sure. He was an innocent man. A fellow like him did not deserve to be caught up in the mess that was English politics.

She had been astonished when her husband accused her of trying to use necromancy again. He was desperate for children – surely he must understand her despair? But no. He said that she must not visit such men ever again. Better that she remain barren than that she risk their souls.

Yes. It was a shame. She would try again tomorrow to use her influence on him to have Langatre released. His imprisonment could help no one.

At least it had taken her mind off the other man and her fear that he, a genuine traitor, could be found and captured.

Chapter Seventeen

Thursday Next after the Feast of St Edmund[6]

Exeter City

In the cool of the early morning, Robinet woke with a tongue that appeared to have been expertly employed in cleaning the street overnight. It was thick, foul-tasting, and rough, which seemed to match perfectly his feeling of general nausea, as though he had been drinking too much for several days.

He opened his eyes with some reluctance, wondering what he might find. If the previous day was anything to go by, he could expect to be in a strange room, with no sign of his friend, and perhaps a knife fouled with another man's blood.

Fortunately, there was nothing of the sort when he peered about him. Instead he saw his old companion at the fire, a cauldron already warming, filled with a fresh porridge that scented the room with the delicious aroma of oats and barley.

'You slept well. It's past dawn now,' Walter said, stirring the pot. 'Thought I was going to have to kick you or eat it all myself.'

Robinet grinned as he drew the blanket away. Sweet Christ, but it was cold enough to shrivel his cods to the size of hazelnuts! He pulled on his shirt and tunic in a hurry to cover his nakedness, and took time to pull on his old hosen.

In the past, he would have proudly clad himself in the blue and striped particoloured uniform of one of King Edward II's messengers. Those had been glorious days. He had lived with the king's household, eating and drinking at the king's expense, all against the day when he might be sent post-haste across the country with messages held in his

---

[6] 22 November 1324

little pouch, bound by his oath to deliver the king's letters until he was released or death took him.

If a messenger was ill, the king would send his own physician to help them. King Edward was always a compassionate, friendly man. He enjoyed the company of his men, and they loved him for that. So what if barons said he oughtn't to hedge and ditch with the churls on his estates, or act, or sing? He was the king, in God's name!

'Any nearer an idea what happened the night before last?' Walter demanded.

'I swear, all I know is, we were in a tavern for the night, and then I woke in a stable. Someone had looked after me well enough. I had a comfortable straw bed, and apart from a headache, I was perfectly well.'

'Headache from the wine?' Walter asked.

'I don't know. It still hurts now, but that'll be your ale last night.'

Walter set the spoon down and walked over to him, studying him with his head on one side. 'Where does it hurt?'

'All over the back of my head – but it's not a bruise. It just hurts as if I had too much to drink.'

Walter ran his hands over Robinet's skull, ignoring his protestations, but as his fingers ran over the area above and behind the left ear Newt had to wince and draw in his breath quickly. 'That hurts!'

'I'm not surprised. There's a lump like a duck's egg there. No, old friend. You've been knocked down. Perhaps it was the wine that saved your life. You fell so quickly, you were no threat to anyone else.'

'But that's mad! Who would knock me down?'

'Someone who wanted to kill James? If they were happy to kill him, perhaps they knocked you down first?'

'That would be stupid. Would you have done that?'

'No. I'd have killed you too, just in case,' Walter said, and his eyes had that quality again which Newt had seen before when they discussed murder: a quality of emptiness. 'Better always not to leave witnesses behind. They can be messy.'

'There is more to it than expediency, old fellow; if they were content to strike me down, they would have left me where they had hit me: in the street. Who would have carried me into a stable and left me there, nice and comfortable? Certainly not this assailant who murdered James.'

'True enough.'

'No, I think it must be more simple,' Newt asserted with a frown. His head was painful still. 'Perhaps I was merely horribly drunk, and rather than carry me home James saw a stable and installed me comfortably there.'

'Perhaps – although what were you both doing out in the open at that time of night anyway? Weren't you drinking in the tavern where he stayed?'

'Yes. In the Noblesyn.' Newt frowned.

'But he was down at the South Gate, and you were near the Palace Gate yourself when you came to, weren't you? What were you both doing down there?'

A flash of memory came back to Robinet. 'There was a man at the inn who made James anxious. He said something . . .'

If only he could remember. The whole of the evening had been a blur, but now he knew his head had been struck, at least there was an explanation for that. And perhaps if he could concentrate, he might remember something. 'There was a man in there. That was it. And when he left the inn, James wanted to follow him. I went too.'

'What then?'

He was frowning now with the effort. 'I thought he was mad. I wanted to get away, anyway. Meant to come back here. So I left with him . . .'

In his mind's eye he was there again. He could see the streets, wet with the thin sleet falling, smell the woodsmoke from a hundred fires, but the whole was tilting as he stared. The wine he'd been drinking was strong, and there had been plenty of it, and now he felt sickly as he stumbled over the cobbles.

At his side, James, who seemed more competent on his legs. Watching all about them as though fearing an attack – although perhaps it was only the natural caution of a man who feared that the watch might see them and try to arrest them for being out after curfew.

'He was carrying a message from the bishop. It was a reply to a message from the king, I think. He'd have left that night if he'd had a chance, but the bishop was so slow in composing his note that he only received the message as dark was falling. Too late to do anything then. He had been going to ride off at first light. And then, I think, I was hit on the head. I seem to remember it now, a blow, and then I was falling.'

'To get here from the Noblesyn you'd have gone along the High Street, and then carried on westwards,' Walter pointed out. 'You woke up nearer the South Gate, didn't you?'

'Yes. Perhaps I'd got lost . . . or James led me the wrong way?'

'Perhaps he did, at that. Where was he when you fell?'

'At my side, I think.'

'I think that explains a lot,' Walter said. He picked up his wooden spoon and began stirring again. 'He knocked you down when you were near a place he knew would be safe for you.'

'Him? Why'd he do a thing like that?'

'Perhaps James didn't trust you entirely, and sought to protect himself. Or . . .' Walter paused, chewing at his inner lip.

'What?'

'I was just thinking – if he thought he was going into danger, and didn't want to lead you there too, perhaps he sought to protect you?'

'If he thought it was dangerous, any man would have kept a friend at his side,' Newt scoffed.

Walter shrugged pensively.

Newt shook his head gently, and offered to fetch a fresh loaf.

Outside the roads were icy, and he had to mind his step as his leather-soled boots slipped over the cobbles. The way to the bakers' shops was easy enough, and he was soon standing in a small stall off Bakers' Row where the scent of fresh loaves filled the air.

It was only as he walked back that he recalled something else. While they had been walking out from the inn, he had seen someone at the mouth of an alley – a slim figure in dark clothes. The body itself was all but hidden, but he was sure that the figure had a gaunt, sallow face.

And he was just as convinced now, as he recalled it, that James had seen him too.

Baldwin woke with a sense of gratification that he had managed to avoid any further contact with the good coroner.

When in trouble, Baldwin had always felt able to trust and rely on the coroner. He had been in some tight situations earlier in the autumn with Simon and Richard de Welles, and de Welles had always been a reliable and honourable friend. However, although his strength and ability in a fight was not in question, Baldwin was perfectly aware that the man was ruinously hazardous when it came to drinking with him.

Almost any man alive could drink more than Baldwin. It stemmed from the time when he was a Knight Templar, many years ago. He had early decided that moderation would ensure that he was as effective as possible at performing God's will and defending pilgrims on their way to the Holy Land. Abstinence in the heat had left him more capable during weapons training than those who had imbibed too strongly the night before.

In the event, of course, there had been no need to worry. He joined the Templars because they took him in, wounded, when he was at Acre, trying to protect it from the massed hordes who sought to capture it. The siege of the city had marked him for ever, and the fact that the Templars had saved him left him with a profound sense of debt. As soon as he could, he had taken the threefold oaths, firm in the resolve that he would fight and lay down his life, if need be, in the reconquest of the Holy Land to save it from the Saracens. It was an ambition that was to be cruelly crushed when the French king and the pope dishonourably perverted justice in order to persecute the Templars out of nothing more than their own intolerable greed.

His order had been hunted and destroyed, so that their chests of treasure could be raided and plundered. Many of Baldwin's friends and companions had been tortured to death, some slaughtered, and all for declaring their innocence. There was no defence against the accusation of heresy. They were not permitted to know the charges raised against them, nor who had levelled them. Instead they were invited to confess, and when they declared that they had no idea what crimes they could have been guilty of, they were put to the torture.

That gross, obscene injustice had coloured the whole of the rest of his life. It left him with an enduring hatred – of politics, of greed, of unfairness.

There were many who had turned to ritual magic after the destruction of Acre. The fall of the city was a cataclysmic event for the whole of Christianity, for if God Himself had so turned His face from His own people, their sins must have been enormous. Some turned to flagellation, others to intense prayer, while a few sought solace in ancient learning. They tried to conjure demons and bind them to themselves.

It was nothing new. It was rather like alchemy, and Baldwin had the same regard for both. He thought that they were nonsense.

From his early days in the Templars, he had studied when he might, and he had read some of the philosophical tracts written by Thomas Aquinas. He recalled that Aquinas felt that any attempt to conjure a demon, for whatever purpose, was in effect forming a pact with that demon. It was heretical, and an act of apostasy.

For all that, though, men, and sometimes women, would try to make use of magic to achieve their ends. Since the apparent weakness of Christianity was exposed by the fall of Acre, perhaps more fools had turned to these supposedly 'older' crafts. Baldwin neither knew nor cared. All he was worried about just now was the one man.

It was always possible, after all, that the fellow was less of a fool than he appeared. If he was not actually a dolly-poll, and instead was a shrewd man, he might have pulled the wool over Baldwin's and Sir Richard's eyes. It was not impossible. Baldwin was always unwilling to support authority against a churl because of his own experiences, but just because he had once had a miserable experience did not mean that all in authority were inevitably corrupt. Some were no doubt as honourable as he.

And even those, like the Sheriff of Devon, who were undoubtedly corrupt in certain spheres of their professional life, might be perfectly justified in prosecuting a man like Langatre, who was a self-confessed dabbler in the occult.

'Rubbish!' he muttered to himself. There was never any good reason for persecution. Never.

Chapter Eighteen

North-East Dartmoor

Simon woke with a pain in his hip where the unyielding soil had been an inadequate cover for a large stone. Busse was snoring gently at his side, but when he peered out into the cold daylight he saw Rob shivering at the fire, Simon's spare cloak pulled tight, his arms wrapped about himself, a thin smoke rising from the twigs and tinder he had worked at.

'Did you sleep well?' Simon asked quietly as he crawled from their shelter. It looked quite solid still, he was pleased to see. It gave him a feeling of quiet satisfaction to think that he had managed to construct that at short notice.

Rob nodded, but his face was pinched, and Simon could feel the chill air at his own back.

The landscape had altered over the night since Simon and the monk's conversation. The snow had kept on falling, and now there were a few inches covering everything. Usually Simon enjoyed the sight of snow. It was lovely to rise in the morning, look out from the window and see all covered in the unmarked blanket of white. To see the trees bowing, to hear the branches cracking with the weight, and then to see children skating on the ice of the ponds . . . it all made a man's heart leap. Especially when he could return to his own house and stand in front of his own fire to warm himself. That certainly helped.

Not all would view it in the same light, of course. Some, he knew, hated the snow and feared its arrival. Mostly it was the older folks. Each year the winter would carry away the older, the more infirm and feeble. It was natural, but sad. And when the snow fell, there were other deaths too: men fell through the ice while playing on the ponds; children fell prey to the cold; some folks would drink themselves stupid and then die on the way home from a tavern, only to be found the next morning by a passer-by, lying at the roadside with their bodies frozen to the soil. Aye, there were plenty who had cause to dislike and mistrust the weather, but for his part Simon loved it, and there was nothing he enjoyed more than the fresh, crisp air and the crunch of compacted snow underfoot when he was well prepared for it.

And that was the trouble. Today he and his companions were not ready. 'Rob, go and see how the horses have fared,' he said. 'I'll attend to this.'

The lad walked away without even a sharp comment about masters who preferred to hog the fire, which showed Simon just how jaded the lad was feeling. He set to with determination. The fire had been banked up well last night, and the embers were still good and warm, so he set about rekindling it. The tree which had supplied so much of their needs last evening was of little use. All the fine twigs were hidden by the snow. Instead he walked about the encampment seeking small sticks, and soon had found a fair collection, getting himself thoroughly smothered in snow in the process. He bound them together into a faggot and bound it tightly together with green withies wrapped about it, and put it onto the hottest part of the fire, kneeling down and blowing steadily to waken the sparks. Soon he could feel the warmth, and there was a hissing and spitting as the twigs began to take the heat.

He had brought a clay pot with him – he fetched it now, and filled it with the wine left in his skin. Setting it in the midst of the fire, he hoped the pot would warm gradually and not shatter.

'Ho, Bailiff, and a fine morning to you,' Busse grunted as he thrust his head from the shelter. 'In God's name, but this is a cold dawn!'

'As a whore's heart,' Rob muttered. 'Horses are all right, master. All stood together, and kept their heat in.'

Simon nodded, but his mind was already on other matters. 'Prepare them, then. We shall leave here as soon as they are ready.'

Rob nodded, too cold to argue. It was Busse who protested as the boy walked back to the mounts. 'But should we not break our fast? Surely it would be foolish to set off without something in our bellies?'

'Brother, I fear it would be more foolish to remain here in the open. We'll soon start to freeze. Better to ride on and see how soon we can find a house. A farm or cott. It matters little where we shelter, but we must get moving – if only to keep ourselves warm.'

'How long will it take us to reach Exeter?'

'With luck, if the weather off the moor is more clement, we might reach the city soon after noon. It depends upon the mounts. If they can cope, we should hurry. It is only one league to the edge of the moor, I'd guess. Maybe a little farther. And there are roads down there, which will make the going easier.'

'Thanks be to God.' Busse began to settle himself on the ground.

'Brother, there isn't time.'

'I am a man of God. I have to pray at first rising.'

'Look on this as a special dispensation, Brother. There isn't time.'

Busse looked at him long and hard, and then began to pray, muttering a hasty *Pater Noster*, and adding sarcastically, 'I hope that is not too slow for you?'

Simon shrugged. He had retrieved his pot, and now he sniffed at it. About to take a long swallow, he remembered his manners, and offered it to Busse. The monk drank with his eyes closed, as though this was the finest drink he had ever tasted. As well it might have been, Simon reckoned. When the pot came to him, he sipped slowly, rolling the warmed wine about his mouth and feeling the sensation of heat strike at his belly. It felt as though every inch of the liquor's journey to his stomach was distinct, and every particle of his being thrilled to the sensation.

The rest was saved for Rob, whose need was the greatest of all of them. Today, when they mounted, Simon lifted Rob up before him on the horse. In this weather it would be better for him to ride and keep his feet out of the snow. Simon was happy that he would soon be able to lead his little party off the moors and down into the warmer lands that encircled them.

It was a thought which had clearly occurred to Busse too. 'Will it be this cold and snowy all the way?'

'No. Usually the moors catch all the worst weather. We used to live north of Crediton, and there we could be enjoying a bright sunny day, and when we looked to the south we'd see Dartmoor with clouds above. Often in the spring we could be working in the warm, but Dartmoor would have snow. You could see it like a white coat lying on top. So I am hoping that when we leave the moors we should find the way a great deal easier.'

Busse nodded, but Simon could feel the man's eyes on him, and he was struck with that anxiety again – not fear exactly, but just the faint nervous premonition that this man could be dangerous to him.

He could have cursed brother John de Courtenay.

Exeter Gaol

It had been a miserable night for Master Richard de Langatre.

He had spent evenings in poor dives before now, what with one thing and another. There had been a deeply unpleasant little cell just outside Oxford where he had been incarcerated for a couple of days before the error of his arrest had come to light, but notwithstanding that, this had to be the very worst pit in which he had ever been forced to spend a night. The walls were dank and mouldy, the floor a foul mix of substances which were best forgotten, the toilet facilities non-existent. Not even a pail!

He knew why he was here, of course. It was that devious shit Sir Matthew. The sheriff had made it clear enough that he didn't like men like Master Richard. Well, that was the sort of thing which he had grown all too used to – but he never expected this! The man had seemed almost beside himself last night when he shouted at him. Sweet Christ in heaven, how could Langatre have guessed that the sheriff would fly off the handle like that! The worst that anyone could say about Langatre was that he had been attacked and robbed, and yet here he was – *he* was – in gaol for his trouble! It was grossly unfair.

There was a skittering noise, which he had grown to recognise as rats, and then he heard the scrape of the bolts on the great door outside that gave onto the castle yard. The screech of the door's hinges was like a knife dragging down Langatre's bones: a hideous, drawn-out metallic squeal of agony. He wondered if they soaked them in water daily to give the sound that timbre.

Footsteps crunched along the paved corridor, and stopped, so far as he could tell, outside his chamber. There was a silence for a moment, then the rattle of a key in the lock, and the door suddenly opened.

He winced in the sudden light from a torch, peering up at the shadowy figures before him and fearing what the sheriff might have in store for him, but then he heard the welcoming bellow and felt his courage return.

'Christ alive, man! What sort of sty have they kept you in overnight? Eh?'

'Coroner? Sir Baldwin?'

The two slipped inside, and Baldwin looked about him with distaste. 'I am truly sorry to see how you have been treated, Master Langatre. I shall ensure that you are released as soon as is feasible.'

'I am grateful to you. I am not used to such conditions.'

'Better get used to 'em, then,' the coroner stated cheerfully. 'If the sheriff keeps to his word and has you held for questioning by the king's men, you could be here a while.'

'But that would be daft! What could I have done? I've never even seen the king!'

'The sheriff seems determined enough,' the coroner said. 'Perhaps he knows something else you've been doing?'

Langatre frowned down at his boots. These two seemed friendly enough, although that was an attitude which could all too easily dissipate. Still, he was in no position to conceal anything from anyone. The very worst thing for him would be to continue to be held down here.

'My lords, look, I have done nothing wrong. I have certainly never tried to summon a demon.'

'Tell us what you have done.'

'Nothing! I swear! All I have ever done is try to earn a small living. That's all. There's nothing secret about my work. Sir Baldwin, you saw that I was robbed – my knives, my hat, all gone!'

'You have been said to have been involved in telling the future,' Baldwin said.

'Oh, that! It's mainly a knack of letting people tell me what they want me to say, and then telling them what they want in a different manner. Easy, that is. But there are many in town who profess to be able to do the same – even one of the monks in St Nicholas's Priory is supposed to be able to do that.'

'Is there something in particular that could have irritated the good sheriff? Anything you have done recently?'

'Nothing I know of. What is this all about, anyway?'

'Someone has attempted an attack on the king and his friend Despenser, from all we've seen,' the coroner rumbled. 'I should take it that the king is not happy with anyone supposedly associated with the magical arts.'

Langatre stared about him helplessly. 'Oh, cods!'

'So if there is anything – *anything* – you can tell us which might help,' Baldwin prompted seriously, 'it might just assist us to help you.'

'Oh, God in heaven!' Langatre gazed from one to the other. 'You want me to be honest?'

Exeter City

Master John of Nottingham was happy with his work so far. The models were taking on their own appearances already, and he felt sure that they would be as successful as the originals.

He put the final touches to the first of them, using his knife to remove a small flaking of wax from the little crown he had placed on its head, and setting it upright on the table before him, then bowing his head and pinching at the top of his nose where the headache seemed to be starting.

It was one of the problems he had suffered from for a long while now: he was sure that his eyes were beginning to fail him. In the past he had been graced with perfect eyesight, and there would have been little difficulty involved in doing this kind of work by candlelight, but more recently it had started to take its toll. Perhaps it was just that he was still tired from his long journey down here from Coventry. It had been a hard effort. A sore, hard effort.

He had not expected to be released. The sudden opening of his cell door in the middle of the night had been a terrible shock. At first he had been convinced that he was about to be dragged out to be tortured. Or pulled out to the gibbet and hanged without an opportunity of putting his own case. When he was grabbed by the arms and dragged out, he could not command even his voice. The words he tried to utter pleading innocence were stifled by his terror. There were steps, harsh orange light from the flickering torches, then a long corridor, and he was brought out into the open air. It made him want to shriek. As soon as he arrived out in the open, he saw a tall post, and the sight made him begin to swoon, his head pounding, his heart thudding as though trying to break free.

Before the post he saw the tall figure of Croyser.

The Sheriff of Warwick was standing by a huddled mess on the ground, and as he was pulled forward John saw that it was a man, a man of John's own age, his face white, his lips blue in death. That was when he became sure that he was being brought here to be killed.

'Master John,' Croyser said. He was pulling on gloves, and John automatically thought of a murderer covering his hands so that no blood should pollute them.

The hold on him was released, and John fell on all fours, where he remained with his head hanging, waiting for the blow to fall. He daren't look up into the eyes of the man who was to kill him.

'Get up, fool! Do you want to die here? Get up, I said.'

John hesitated, fearing a trick, but then he noticed that the two men who had brought him had left. Their feet were not at his side any more. Hardly daring to hope, he looked up.

Croyser pointed at the body beside him. 'See him? Do you know him?'

'I have never . . .'

'He is Master John of Nottingham. Do you understand? I'm going to put him in that cell, and when the gaoler arrives in the morning, he will swear on his mother's grave that it was you. Or who you once were. You are safe. You are free.'

'I . . .' John's mouth hung open, and then he slowly closed it. 'What do you seek, sir knight?'

'You were paid to perform a task, were you not? There are many in the land would like to see that mission completed. If you have the stomach for it, man, fly from here and complete it. You were paid for it, weren't you?'

'Yes, but the money is lost. How can I start afresh?'

'Here!' Croyser tossed a purse to him. It was heavy, a ponderous weight, and John dropped it. Picking it up, he could feel the coins inside. Croyser nodded. 'Yes, the balance of your twenty pounds. The money you were promised. The same men who paid you before want you to succeed, but you will have to leave Coventry. Go somewhere else, where you may be safe. But in God's name, be quick. The country cannot survive much longer with this corruption at its heart.'

John had needed no second bidding. There was a pack of food and drink with a blanket and heavy cloak against the weather, and he had taken them, stammering his thanks while the sheriff gave him some instructions for his own safety. There was no doubt that he was risking much, for if John was discovered, it would be the sheriff's own neck that would be stretched.

'One thing I do need, though,' he said.

'What?'

'My book . . . without that I cannot do my work,' John had said despairingly.

He looked over at the waxen image once more, remembering that night, flying from the gaol and the city of Warwick, guided by a man wearing the sheriff's own livery. The man took John out by a small postern, and then led him along filthy, dark streets until they reached the road south. There the man gave him his book and left him. John attempted to thank him, but in return the man merely spat at the ground and turned on his heel.

It had been a terrible flight, but at least he had escaped. And now he would do as he had promised, and make these models. Four pounds of wax. Enough for four images.

One of the king, one each for the two Despensers, and one for the Bishop of Exeter commissioned.

They would all die.

Chapter Nineteen

Exeter Gaol

Master Richard of Langatre looked from one to the other, and he finally gave in with a grunt. This was not the way he'd foreseen his own future.

'Look, I am no necromancer. Let us be quite sure of that. All I do is try to use some of God's own power to help those who need it. For a fee.'

'So you divine their futures?' Baldwin asked with a mild smile.

'Well . . . yes, I suppose. Although the most important thing is to gain their confidence, and then tell them what they want to hear. Usually.'

'How so?' Coroner Richard asked. He was leaning down like a great cat preparing to pounce.

'Well, there are ladies who come and ask if their love is in vain, for example. I cannot always give them the answer they want.'

'Why?' the coroner demanded.

'Sir, if you heard a maidservant who was convinced that her master was in love with her and would run away with her to start a new life elsewhere, would you want to let her continue in her delusion, or would you try to help her come to terms with the fact that the bastard had been pissed and fancied a tumble with a well-proportioned wench? At least, told carefully, that story could have power: the wench was attractive, after all. But there was no possibility of the . . . man's leaving his wife.'

'I see,' Baldwin said. 'This has happened recently?'

'The damned sheriff's own servant girl. She saw me the other day for just this reason, thinking he fancied her. She wanted to know how to keep his love.'

'So this kind of work requires little in the way of magic?'

'Little of my work has any element of magic, further than my skill to understand people and what they want to hear,' Langatre admitted dolefully.

'So the tools of your trade are unnecessary?'

'They look good,' Langatre said defensively. Then he nodded. 'But they aren't necessary. They just help to make people think that they have been sold something of value.'

'What do you know of real necromancy?' Baldwin asked.

'I don't do anything like that,' Langatre countered instantly.

Baldwin held him in a long stare, and the man had the feeling that he was pinioned under that shrewd, intense gaze. It was almost as though the knight could see through Langatre's eyes and perceive the world as he did: a venal place, filled with those who sought only to take whatever a man might earn. Someone like Langatre was not evil: he was merely making a living in the only way he knew how. Just now the only way he could do so was by making up false futures for gullible women in the city, or selling them potions and salves that would hopefully do them little harm.

Langatre wanted to look away, but he felt sure that to do so would only persuade this knight that he was not reliable or honest. And there was something compelling about his eyes, too. It was hard to drag his own eyes away.

'Tell me: do you know how other men perform their works when they are supposed to be authentic?' Baldwin said.

Langatre felt as though a little of the pressure was immediately removed. 'There are many ways a man might prepare, master. Some will just offer a potion or make a few mumbles and wave their hands about, but they're the counterfeiters. They don't really do anything. They're in it for the money.' He had the grace to look away as he spoke, but then he nodded to himself. He had nothing to hide in all this, after all. He was a man of integrity.

Continuing, he frowned a little, considering the tools of the men who tended towards magic. 'There are a number of different types, I suppose. I have met many of them. There are those who seek to cure by the power of God and His works, men like me, who will pray and fast for days to achieve our works. We only seek positive outcomes. Using God's authority to bring about a foul or evil deed would be bound to redound on us, I would think. But there are some who don't care. They try to exercise their skills to call up demons, and they do so with various spells and commands, much as I do, but their aim is to have the demon do their bidding, so they are using God's power to produce an evil effect.'

'How would they achieve that?' the coroner demanded. 'It sounds as if these fellows should be punished.'

'They will take the white-handled and black-handled daggers, they would have a sword, a staff, a rod, a hook, a lancet . . . many tools. All would have to be fumigated and asperged, and then the magician would consecrate them too.'

'How so?'

'He would recite seven or eight psalms over them. I have heard that the usual manner would be for the man to undergo a period of fasting, chastity and intensive prayer. A couple of days before the act, he would confess his sins and then fast again, because if a man tries to conjure a spirit he must do so in a state of grace. Otherwise, instead of being able to command the spirit, it might command *him*! Only then, after all this preparation, would he be ready to consecrate the tools. After reciting the psalms, he would offer prayers to God and His saints for a successful outcome.

'When it came nearer to the date for the conjuration, he would prepare his body. Consecrated water would be used to wash himself, and then he would clothe himself in the robes for the ceremony. A long robe and a white leather hat with the names of God written on it, like mine.'

The coroner looked blank. 'How many names does he have?'

'Many,' Baldwin said. He spoke quietly, meditatively, as he recalled his education with the Templars. 'There are Jehova, Adonay, Elohim, El . . . very many are given in the Gospels.'

'That is right,' Langatre said approvingly. 'And then the celebrant would perform the conjuration itself.'

'Which would be to have a demon do his bidding?' Coroner Richard asked. His voice was growing quieter and more thoughtful.

'Yes . . . or not. Sometimes a powerful man might be able to take a demon and confine it. Perhaps in a crystal, or in a mirror . . . anywhere, really. So long as he uses the right words to bind the foul creature, it will remain under his control and must do his bidding.'

'So if a man were to want to kill another,' Coroner Richard said slowly, 'he would have to have one of these creatures there ready to do it for him?'

Up until that moment Langatre had been enjoying his exposition on the theory and practice of the magical arts. Now there was a sudden leaden sensation in his belly and bowels. 'I've done nothing like that.'

'I should hope not!' Coroner Richard said.

'You are accused of nothing by us,' Baldwin said mildly. 'We only seek to learn what we may about other methods of magic. Would the necromancer need the assistance of a demon necessarily?'

'I should think so – at least, in all the arts I've heard of . . . Unless he used some other form of magic.'

'What other sort could there be?' Baldwin asked.

'There are many types of magic. Some is good, but some is . . . less so. All magic is simply harnessing God's power to do what we wish. It's only when a man turns to its misuse that there is a problem.'

'So how else might a man kill another?'

'There are probably many ways. I do not profess to know them,' Langatre said warily. He was not going to condemn himself out of hand by merely admitting that he knew too much about the arcane arts.

'Come! This is no time to grow diffident, Master Langatre,' Baldwin said. 'This is the crime you will be accused of and questioned about. Questioned professionally by the king's men. You know what that would mean.'

Langatre swallowed. 'I have heard of men who compose models of the man they wish to kill. They perform the preparation as I have explained, with much fasting, prayer, celibacy, and invocations to bring God's power down upon them, and then they have a ritual at which they will ceremonially kill the image.'

'How so?' Coroner Richard rumbled.

'They will stab it with a splinter, or a pin, or perhaps just shatter it. If the preparation is right, and the likeness is good, I dare say, then the attempt should succeed.'

'And this thing, this model, would be made of something rare and valuable?' the coroner asked hopefully.

'No.' Langatre smiled. 'It could be made from candle wax if need be, although . . .'

'What?' the coroner demanded irritably. He was growing bored with this recitation.

'Well, for something like that to work, the man would need to have something of the man he intended to kill.'

'Not the finger of another man?' Baldwin asked.

'No.' Langatre smiled. 'That would only confuse things. Only a little hair, or skin from the man whom the wizard wished to see dead. Not much. It would be mixed in with the wax to give it identity.'

'Who would be able to do such a thing?'

'Very few have the skill.' Langatre shrugged. 'There are few enough men in the city who can manage even the most simple tasks. To take on control of a demon powerful enough to kill a man – that would be a great task indeed.'

'I am not interested in your self-congratulation on your own skills. Just tell us: who here in Exeter could do it?' Baldwin rasped.

'In honesty . . . I do not think any necromancer in this city could attempt such a work of *maleficium*. It would be the work of a great magician. You would have to go to London or York for a man like that.'

Baldwin nodded, and tried to feel comforted.

'Keeper, you look like a man who's bitten into a medlar and found it was a sloe!' the coroner said as they both tramped up the stairs from the gaol. 'What is it? Surely it's good to know that there are no more fools like him in the town?'

'Yes. Of course it is.'

'So why the long face?'

'Because a man can always walk or ride from one place to another. Just because Langatre knows no one who could attempt such a business does not mean that someone has not arrived here recently who would be interested in trying it.'

Exeter Castle

Sir Matthew rode back to the castle gate in the middle of the morning, famished. He threw himself from the saddle and left the reins dangling for a groom. It was his usual way of returning. If the horse was to be left too long, and ambled back out of the gate, the grooms would learn to regret their laxness, and that was that. For his part, Sir Matthew expected his men to be prepared for him at all times, and when they failed him they paid for it.

The morning's ride down to the bishop's house at Clyst St Mary had been enough to make him start to sweat, and he was just thinking that he ought to arrange a fresh hunt when he caught sight of the new servant girl. Strange chit: she'd taken to staring at him, slightly goggle-eyed, like a fish just pulled from the water. He had wondered whether she might be a little dull-witted, but the child seemed to be all right in all other ways. There was nothing to suggest that she was a cretin, only that curious expression on her face.

She was there now, at the top of the stairs to the main hall, just standing and gazing at him. It was disconcerting, having her up there, but Sir Matthew was no fool, and it was safer for a man to maintain a calm attitude before the people who worked for him in the castle. Punish those who were disobedient, froward, or felonious, by all means, but it was hard to have a servant girl beaten for merely looking at him. Actions like that might start to upset the staff. They would grow sulky and petulant, and that was no good to anyone.

He crossed the yard, pulling off his thick riding gloves as he went, and climbed the stone stairs. She waited at the top, as though expectantly, her bright face turned to him the whole while.

It was damned uncomfortable. The girl was staring as though there was something wrong with him. It made him wonder whether his cods were untied, or his tunic was rucked up under his belt or something. Damn the child! What was the matter with her? He could feel his face reddening as he came close to her, and the knowledge made his voice harsh and brusque.

'Do you want me?' he asked.

She gaped, and then turned away, flushing scarlet, he saw.

The fool had been wool-gathering. Nothing more than that. She didn't even realise it was him she was staring at. That was the meaning of it all: she was in a daydream and hadn't known she was insulting him. That was a relief, anyway, he told himself. For a moment there . . . but no. That would be daft.

'Sir Matthew?' his steward called quietly from his table near the door.

'Well?' he responded testily. 'I haven't much time. I need my dinner.'

'It is only that the good keeper and his friend the coroner were here today. They visited your prisoner. I thought you should know.'

'Did they?' Sir Matthew's face turned dark. 'What did they want with him?'

'I took the precaution of having a clerk follow them and listen as best he could. They were talking all about the methods of having a necromancer fashion figures in the likeness of a man, and have that man murdered by means of it.'

Sir Matthew clenched his jaw. 'I want that man kept locked up. No one is to see him without my express permission. Ensure that it is so.'

'Yes, Sir Matthew.'

'And now, if you don't mind, I should like to enjoy my meal!'

Chapter Twenty

Exeter City

Baldwin and Coroner Richard had enjoyed a leisurely meal in a tavern near the castle while they absorbed Langatre's tale of how a necromancer might summon up a demon.

'To me, it sounds half-baked. Stodgy in the middle like a poorly cooked pie,' the coroner said with satisfaction as he finished his own meat pie. The crumbs and gravy on his beard were wiped away with a massive hand and brushed onto the table. Some fell into his quart pot of ale, and he glared at the pot as though it was the pottery's own fault that it had been polluted. He fished out a couple of crumbs, then shrugged. 'Ah well, it's all going down the same hole! I didn't like the idea that a man might confine a demon in a chip of glass or diamond, either.'

'The whole thing sounds extremely unlikely to me,' Baldwin said. 'If it were not for the poor fellow in the dungeon, I should treat the whole thing as a joke, but clearly for Langatre it is deadly earnest.'

'Aye. If the king and Despenser believe that a man like him has been making models to murder them, Langatre can look forward to a warm end over a couple of cartloads of faggots. Reminds me of a story I heard . . .'

Baldwin hastily interrupted. 'He is in trouble, yes, but we also have the bishop's paper to find. I am still struck by the matter of that other man dying there. I wish to speak to his wife. What was her name? Ah, yes, Madam Mucheton.'

'You'll almost certainly learn that he fell to a footpad, Baldwin. That message has been taken and it will appear in some place which is entirely guaranteed to embarrass the good bishop. We can do nothing about it, and nor can he. There's little point worrying about it.'

'I agree, but I dislike coincidence when it is so blatant,' Baldwin said. He sipped a little ale and his face twisted with distaste. 'What is this stuff?'

The coroner peered into his pot. 'Tastes good to me.'

Baldwin gave him a long, sour look. 'Anyway, I have a feeling that there is something about that first murder that will help us. The idea that there could be two murders in the same area that were entirely unconnected is fatuous. There must be something about them both.'

'Perhaps. If you say so. Hmm. Personally, I think that the main thing will be to hold the inquests as soon as possible.'

'You have them arranged?'

'I had planned on holding them this afternoon.'

'Very well. So we have a little time.'

'To see this woman?'

Baldwin pushed his ale away. It was undrinkable, it was so vinegary. 'Yes, briefly, and then to go on and speak to the watchmen as well. I want to learn where all the other alleged necromancers are.'

North-East Dartmoor

Simon had been careful all morning to keep his conversation to a minimum. Busse appeared content to sit upon his mount and continue on his way with an expression of pinched coldness on his features. Somehow in the last day his face appeared to have lost much of its chubbiness. Where he had been red-faced and cheerful, now he was pale, almost blue, with a faint pinkness at his cheeks, his head hunched down into his robe, his hood up and over his head.

For Simon, the more important of his charges was young Rob, though. The boy was on his feet again now, having argued that even with the snow he was more comfortable walking because it kept him warmer.

They had found a homestead soon after leaving the moors. The farmer, a young man with two toddlers at his legs, had been suspicious at first, until he saw the state of Busse and Rob; upon seeing whom, he called urgently to his wife, and helped the three into his little yard. They had been able to pause in front of a great fire, drinking hot spiced cider with honey to give them strength. Although Simon had offered money, the kindly farmer and his wife had refused to accept anything. They both agreed that it was their duty to help weary and chilled travellers out on the moors, and helpfully provided the three with replenished wineskins and a loaf to keep them going for the rest of their journey.

After that, though, as they began to make their way downhill and head out towards Exeter, their passage became a great deal easier. Before long the snow was noticeably thinner, and they found that they could move much more swiftly.

Simon was only glad that Busse appeared to be happier to remain on his horse and reach Exeter than to stop and pray like the day before.

Exeter City

Baldwin and the coroner reached the widow Mucheton's house as the sun began its slow descent to the west. Its passage high overhead took Baldwin's mind far from here, to his youth in the Mediterranean.

At this time of year, the keeper was all too often reminded of the delights of sitting in warm sunshine and drinking warm wine as the sun glinted off the sea. That was when he had lived as a novice Templar on the island of Cyprus, immediately after the fall of Acre, when he had offered his sword in the continued struggle to protect pilgrims going to the Holy Land. First, though, they must win back the Crusader kingdoms, and for that Baldwin must learn to fight as a Templar, a single member of a greater host.

The training had been hard, both mental and physical. Even though he had been learning the arts of a warrior from an early age, there was a difference between a single mounted man in hand-to-hand single combat and a knight who responded instantly to the command of his master, wheeling into attack, turning to hasten away at the order, only to strike together again at another point. This discipline, and learning how to wield swords, maces and war-hammers in unison, was exhausting. It was not the physical work that tired, it was the constant repetition, having to learn a whole new method of fighting, that wore out the recruits.

Then came the proudest day of his life. He was at last accepted into the order. The ritual was ancient: fasting, a night of prayer, then the ceremonial robing in the uniform of the Templars, and the oaths. And all had been made to sound evil and foul in the accusations made by the French king.

Baldwin would only ever remember that man with loathing. Driven by his own intolerable greed, he had seen the most holy order destroyed, her members harried and tortured, many burned at the stake, and all for his own self-aggrandisement. All to make him appear more holy as he tried to create a new crusading force – fused from the Templars, the Hospitallers, and all other orders – that would be mighty enough to win back Jerusalem. Under his own leadership, of course. Such power could never be left by the French king in the hands of others. With a force like that, he would be invincible.

The strength of the accusations lay in their terrible nature. Whereas a simple theft of plate or the suggestion that brother Templars had been involved in corruption would have earned the individuals concerned a period in cells followed by eviction from the order and installation in another, harsher regime, the charges levelled against Baldwin and his companions were so atrocious that the whole order must be destroyed. They had all been accused of heresy and worse. It had been said that they had worshipped an idol, that they had indulged in obscene rites at their initiations – even that knights had been persuaded to urinate on the Holy Cross.

That was the thing that worried at him always: the idea that a man like him, who had been raised as a Christian warrior, a man who had been so devoted to Christ that he had been prepared to risk his life in the journey to Acre, there to try to defend the city against the hordes of enemies who stood at the gates – that a man like him, who sought only to serve God, could become so easily diverted in the space of an initiation ceremony as to discard the beliefs which had built in him in the past eighteen years and perform such a hideous act. It was beyond belief. If any man had asked him to do such a thing, he would have had their head off in a flash. It was ridiculous.

Was it as ridiculous as thinking that a man might try to murder another with waxen images? Perhaps. Baldwin shrugged. The fact that a man was accused of a crime did not mean that he was guilty. There were necromancers in the land, but in Baldwin's experience they were mostly men like Langatre: not evil, but usually well educated and clerical men who sought to increase their knowledge. Mostly Baldwin had thought them mildly lunatic, but that was only because he classed them in his own mind with a similar group of madmen, the alchemists.

Both trailed a faint but unpleasant odour with them wherever they went, the inevitable concomitant of their trades, but Baldwin had never seriously considered them dangerous.

No. If there was a danger about the city, it was surely more prosaic. No demon had stabbed Mucheton, and no devil had throttled the king's messenger.

The house they were directed to was a narrow building with a jetty overhead that would disable any poor soul who tried to ride beneath it. Just in front of it, the road had a dip where years of ill-use had caused the surface to collapse. Riders would ride down into it, and duck, only to find, as their mount clambered up the farther side, that there was not enough height for them. Many men must have fallen here, he thought.

'This the place?' Coroner Richard boomed.

'Friend, please.' Baldwin winced.

'What?'

'Please try to be quieter, my friend. This woman has only just recently been widowed. She needs care and tact.'

'Of course she does!' Coroner Richard exclaimed. ' 'Strordinary thing to say. What, do you think I would be clumsy or rude to her? Hey? Hah! Come, now. Let us know whether the wench is in before you begin to give me instruction in manners, eh?'

John of Nottingham woke with an ache in his belly. It was a dull, annoying sensation, the sort of mild griping that would make a man unsettled in his spirits, but John was strong. He stood, walked to the little altar he had created in the corner of his room, and prayed for some little while, asking for God's strength in his enterprise.

If he had been asked, John would have been surprised that anyone could look on his prayers as anachronistic. To him, the authority of the spells he attempted came from the power of the divine words he was using. These words, when woven into certain specific spells, could so terrify a demon that he would instantly fall under the power – the spell – of the necromancer. But if a man were to use God's own holy name, how could he hope to achieve anything unless he was himself filled with a love of God and reverence for Him? So even if he were attempting *maleficium*, the fact of his own belief made John convinced that he was a pious man. It was just that the use of demons offered a faster route to success.

His belly was empty, though, and today that would interrupt his work. He had been through this before, oh, so many times. Today he would take a break, drink a little water, and visit the local church. Celebrating mass always had the effect of calming his nerves when he was at this late stage of work.

Later, when he was soothed by the rituals, he would return. Already the first of the figures was complete, and the second and third were roughly formed. Soon all four would be ready.

Exeter Castle

Jen was walking past the main hall as her master ate his lunch. As she entered, she saw him again – oh! He was so perfect, sitting there in his great chair, like a king on his throne! The sight of him made her feel weakly. There was a feeling of warmth in her groin, a rush of blood in her heart, and she was almost ready to faint for a moment. Then, with fortune, Sarra arrived behind her, and pulled her away.

'What are you doing?' she hissed.

Jen raised her chin. 'What did you pull me away for?'

'Look, Jen, I don't know what's got into you, but you mustn't stand staring at him. He'll grow angry and throw you out. Me too, if he's in the mood.'

'Honestly, you have nothing to worry about.'

'Are you mad? We are just servants here. You talk as if we're secure!'

'Master won't throw us out,' Jen said confidently. 'We are perfectly safe here.'

'No, Jen. You don't know the man like I do – he'd throw you out in a blink if he thought it would make his life easier.'

'He loves me.'

Sarra was silenced for a moment. She stopped and turned slowly to face Jen. 'What did you say?'

'I said: "He loves me." '

Sarra stared for a moment, and then, disconcertingly, laughed aloud. 'Are you mad? Look at the way he watches his wife, Jen! He has eyes for no one else at all.'

'You haven't seen how he looks at me. I have seen it in his eyes. Even this morning, when he arrived back from his ride, he offered himself to me. Asked me if I wanted him, and it was only my shyness stopped me from asking for him there and then!'

'Jen, honest, he'd not do anything to upset his lady. If he offered you a tumble tonight, well, that's one thing . . .'

'A tumble? You're *stupid*, you are! If you can't see the love in his face, you're blind! Don't you know that every time he sees me his whole face lights up? Haven't you seen how he thrills when I walk into a room? He is embarrassed when his wife enters. She is so hard and cruel to him, it is a miracle that he never beats her. Better that he did, perhaps. Or just asked for a divorce. Then he and I could . . .'

'No!' Sarra grabbed her upper arms and shook her. 'Jen, you mustn't think like that. If you want, let him have you some night. Let him – well, you can't stop him. But don't try to convince yourself that you're his lady love. You are his servant, and nothing more than that. You won't ever be more than that to him. You can't be! He's married, and he's not going to leave his lady.'

'You just don't understand,' Jen said calmly. She glanced down at Sarra's hands, and gradually Sarra loosened her grip, standing back, eyeing Jen with mingled alarm and concern. Jen shook her head. 'Don't worry. I'll not forget you, dearest Sarra. Even if I marry him, I can't forget my oldest friend.'

Sarra shook her head and began to weep as she realised she was serious.

Chapter Twenty-One

Exeter City

Baldwin had knocked on enough doors asking to see the recently bereaved to recognise the signs, but there was something about widow Mucheton that struck him more than almost any.

It was not that she was beautiful. Even when her face was not ravaged with grief she would have been plain at best, with a face slightly too round, her eyes a little close-set, her mouth thin and hard. Her complexion was pale, but that was probably largely due to the grief, Baldwin reckoned.

No, it was the obvious distress that affected him. So often women were so inured to the idea of death – it was such a major part of life, after all – that even when a close and loved person died, they would steel themselves and try to show little of their misery. People simply did not show their feelings like that. A man or woman had to have pride, and believe in the promise of the Church that they would see their loved ones again.

This woman would have none of that. She was distraught, and she was content that her neighbours should know it.

'Mistress?' Baldwin said quietly. 'Would you mind if we were to ask you some questions? We seek your husband's murderer.'

'Come inside,' she said after a moment. It was not that she was reflecting, more that she could only think slowly now, since the loss of her man.

It was a small room, but well maintained. The floor actually had some tiles set into the dirt to walk on. They ran to the edge of the hearth, which was delineated by a circle of little red stones, much the same rough stones as had been used to make Exeter's walls. A single chair stood near it, clearly Norman's own, while a stool sat by a table in the corner. That Norman had been wealthy was proved by the two tapestries on one wall, but more generally by the feeling of comfort. There was a sideboard with pots and three pewter plates on it, a large box for clothing, and a pantry cupboard in a corner. Candles illuminated the room, and Baldwin could see that there was a ladder climbing to the floor above. When he glanced up at it, he saw a pair of faces peering down at him: two children.

She made an effort to show that she was functioning, and offered them some food and ale, which Baldwin quickly declined, glaring ferociously at the coroner as he did so. All to no avail.

'Mistress, if you have a little good, strong ale, that would be most kindly received.'

The barrels, two of them, stood on a trestle at the far wall, and she took a pot from the sideboard to fill. But as she walked from the shelves, her apron snagged at the edge. The whole structure moved, and two pots tumbled down to the tiled floor, where both smashed.

She stood as though stunned by this latest disaster. Pots and pans were not overly expensive, but to a widow with no income, to lose two at a stroke was a disaster. As Baldwin watched, her face slowly wrinkled with despair, and then her eyes closed as her misery overwhelmed her again.

'Coroner, fetch her some ale,' he commanded harshly, while he himself stood and took her hand to try to comfort her. It took some little while, but at last she drew some deep, shuddering breaths, and drank deeply from the cup which the coroner proffered.

'Thank you, masters. I am sorry to be so weakly.'

'Mistress, you deserve only sympathy after your sad loss,' Baldwin said.

'You are kind. I miss him so!'

Before she could dissolve into tears again, Baldwin patted her hand. 'What did he do, your husband?'

'My Norman? He was an honest man.'

'Of course.'

'He was an antler worker. He made combs and other devices.'

Baldwin nodded encouragingly. He knew of such workers: they would take a complete set of antlers and cut them carefully into discrete parts, and then saw each down to specific sizes. A comb would be made as a composite, with two blanks for each side of the handle, more inserted between them with cuts to create the teeth, and usually another composite section, a sheath into which the teeth would be thrust for safekeeping. An antler could be used for making almost anything. Even the harder, bonier part from near the skull itself could be cut into cubes and dots burned into it to create dice. Little would go to waste.

Seeing his calm interest, the widow wiped at her eyes and concentrated, sitting on her stool and sniffing.

'Had he been working on the night he died?' Baldwin asked.

'That was Monday last. Yes, he'd been here in his room all day, and then when it grew later, he walked out to the tavern for a fill of ale.'

'There was nothing apparently upsetting him?'

'My man?' She smiled. It made her look a little younger. 'Nothing ever got to him. So long as he had his work in the daytime and an ale or two at night, he was ever happy. So were we . . .' Her eyes were drawn up to the children overhead. 'We all were.'

'Why should he have travelled along that alley? Do you know?' Baldwin asked.

Her face fractured again, and her mouth was drawn down into an upturned bow. She closed her eyes, but then opened them again, and now there was an angry glitter in them. 'Those bitches over the way have been saying he was going to the stews, to visit the draggle-tails in their brothels – but, sir, he wouldn't have. He never did before. Always home here, he was, as soon as he left the tavern. You ask any of the men there. They'll all vouch for him. He was as honest as a man could be.'

Baldwin nodded soothingly, but he was not convinced. Many a man, in his experience, would find it easy enough to go and see a doxy after too many ales. His courage would increase with proportion to the ales drunk, and all fear of consequences – the pox – would disappear until morning.

She saw his doubt. 'It is true, he never used to go to them. I gave him all he needed.'

'Did he have any enemies? Did he owe money to anyone?'

'Bless you, sir! He was successful. A better provider I could never meet. He always had money for us. That was how we could afford this house.'

'So he never worried about money?'

'No. Only that day he had made plenty of money. He was off to the tavern to celebrate.'

'But when he was found, his purse was gone.'

'I know. And we needed that money without him.' She sniffed. Then she shrugged resignedly. There would be many more disappointments in the years ahead, she knew.

'We have heard that he used to wear a bone brooch, too. Is that right?'

'Yes, sir. A great circle of antler, it was, with a long, thin pin to secure it. A lovely piece of his work.'

'But not something which could easily be sold on?'

'Bless you, no! Anyone who saw it would know it was my Norman's.'

It was late that afternoon that Simon and his companions arrived at the West Gate. Weary and hungry, the three rode up Stepecote Street towards Carfoix at the centre. Simon intended to see that Busse was delivered safely to the cathedral, and then he would find a place to rest, while he tried to work out how on earth he could keep an eye on the man as John de Courtenay had asked. At the moment, he had no idea whatsoever how he might be able to do that.

The sun was already low in the west behind them, and the token warmth it gave was already a memory as they reached the Fissand Gate and asked the doorkeeper to let them through. Soon they were in the close, and could release their horses to wander and crop the grass. Rob was left with them while Simon and Richard Busse walked stiffly towards the bishop's palace.

'I am most grateful to you, Bailiff, for your efforts on my behalf,' Busse said.

Simon nodded absently. 'Are you going straight away to see my lord the bishop?'

'I must. It would scarcely be right to leave him all unknowing that I have arrived, and I wish to give thanks for our safe delivery.'

Simon nodded again, but wondered whether he ought to try to stay with Busse even as he spoke to the bishop. John de Courtenay had made it clear that he wanted Busse watched at all times, but he could scarcely expect Simon to be able to listen in to every confidential discussion Busse had even with Bishop Walter. That was stretching things too far.

Busse's next words solved his little dilemma. 'Why do you not come with me, Bailiff? You should also make your presence known.' Thus it was that Simon and the brother were soon in the bishop's palace, while Rob dealt with the horses and saw to their effects.

Sitting at the bishop's table in his hall, Simon felt the anxiety of the last day slipping away. In its place was a marvellous somnolence. As Bishop Walter spoke to Busse, Simon drank some of the strong wine with which they had been plied as soon as they entered, and knew it was having its effect. He could feel his eyelids growing heavy in the wonderful heat, and his head started to tip forward without his being able to prevent it. With a jerk, he drew himself up again, and took a deep swallow of wine to try to waken himself, but the result was not as he intended. He felt his chin fall to his breast, and then he had a struggle to keep his eyes open. Only when he felt his hand slip from his lap to begin its journey towards the floor, with his goblet of wine still in his fist, did he lurch upright again.

'Do we keep you awake?' the bishop asked, but not angrily.

'This good bailiff kept us all alive,' Busse said eagerly. 'My lord, he was able to construct a shelter in the midst of the storm, and with that and a little fire he kept us healthy. It was a miracle, out there in the wilds.'

'This is true?' the bishop enquired, his head tilted as he peered somewhat short-sightedly at Simon.

'Our passage took us longer than it should have,' Simon mumbled. 'We had to halt up near Scorhill in the woods there. Otherwise we could have been caught in the open, and we would have died.'

'I owe you my thanks, then,' Stapledon said. 'It would have been a great loss to Tavistock were this excellent brother to have perished.'

'I did my best,' Simon said.

'Good. I have rooms set aside for you all – but, Bailiff, your good friend the knight of Furnshill is here in the city. Would you prefer to join him at his inn?'

After a short discussion it was agreed that Simon and Rob would take rooms with Baldwin, and the bishop sent a message to the innkeeper to make a room ready.

Then, 'So, Brother Robert,' the bishop said, turning back to the monk. 'Will you need anything from me while you are here?'

'No, my Lord Bishop. All I need is a few little items, and a consultation. When that is all done, I shall be returning to Tavistock. However, if the good bailiff doesn't mind, I think that I may ask to return by the slower, but perhaps more reliable, route, over past Crediton, and thence to Oakhampton and Tavistock.'

'Perhaps you ought to consider that, eh, Bailiff?'

Simon opened his eyes and looked at the kindly bishop. 'Yes. Yes, of course, Bishop.'

What sort of consultation did Busse need, he wondered.

John of Nottingham returned to his small chamber as darkness fell in the alley outside.

It was a peculiar little twilit world, this. The sun was long over the horizon before it could make any impact here in the alley. The buildings opposite were only two storeys high, but that was enough to blank off the sun most effectively in the mornings. By the time it had struggled over them, it was already close to noon. And then the full daylight lasted for a mere hour or so, before the sun had traversed the alley and moved back towards the west. All that could be seen down here was a narrow gap of blue high overhead between the jettied upper levels of the houses.

But that was all good for John. He liked the dark. The anonymity which he craved was here, and the result was effectual safety. Nobody who would want to harm him ever came down this way, and if they did, they would be hard pushed to find him, search however diligently they might.

In the chamber, he wrinkled his nose at the smell of dampness, and then set to lighting his candles. He had some old tinder, which he struck his flint over, and by God's good grace, after only ten strikes, he had a spark alight. Wrapping the tinder within a handful of dry wood chips, he blew steadily until a flame appeared, and then it was only a matter of lighting the first of the many candles. Taking it up, he walked about the room, lighting all the tapers and rushlights, and when he was done he set the candle on his table, and reached for the image.

It was good. There was no doubt about that. The crown was a perfect symbol to guide the demon to the king. There was only the one king, after all. John's prayers would make that clear enough even to the most simple of demons. Setting that aside, he set himself to crafting the next man. This one and his father were hard. One was large and heavily paunched, while his son was taller and slim, strong and powerful. It was frustrating, and after working on them for a while he set them aside to form the fourth man.

This was easy enough: he had to fashion the correct features first, but that was no trouble to the necromancer. He had seen this man's face often enough in the last few days when he had gone to celebrate mass. The clothing was easy. Clerical robes were long and designed to be practical, rather than objects of fashion. The hat was easy too, of course. A mitre was no trouble to a man like him. And as he worked, he felt sure that the stooping appearance was perfect. The way that the mommet peered from narrowed eyes caught the essence of the fellow perfectly. Before he came to Exeter, the last time John had seen him had been when he had been walking the streets of London after attending a meeting of financiers, and John had almost been knocked down by the man's henchmen as they cleared the road for his passage. Stapledon had not even glanced in John's direction as he walked on, his eyes set into that little frown as he tried to focus on the way ahead.

Soon he would be finished, and the bishop could take his place beside the model of the king.

Chapter Twenty-Two

Exeter City

The coroner had left Baldwin soon after they walked from Madam Mucheton's house, muttering about having to go and ensure that the inquests were properly recorded. Meanwhile Baldwin had walked slowly and musingly along the street up to the Carfoix, where he stopped and looked about him.

This was a strange, bustling city. Baldwin had been to many European cities in his life, and most were similar: noisy, boisterous places, filled with excitable people who were devoted to making themselves a little more money every day. It did not matter whether they were traders, merchants, hucksters, whores or thieves, all had the same motive: to win money from another.

Exeter had impressed him from the first time he had seen the city. It was spacious, secure within its walls, and for the most part filled with good, righteous people. But one man he could never bring himself to trust was the most senior in rank: the sheriff.

Sir Matthew de Crowethorne was a politician, and Baldwin detested those who put politics above all else. Sheriffs were notorious for their corruption, but there was something about Sir Matthew that struck Baldwin as worse.

All sheriffs would occasionally misuse their powers. Some did it to take money – in bribes, or even in corrupt handling of legal cases, charging money to release known felons. Others would not require direct financial gain: they committed their crimes to demonstrate their loyalty to or support for a lord. There were many sheriffs who were in the pocket of the Despenser family.

This Sir Matthew was certainly happy to take money in return for favours, so far as Baldwin had heard, but he was also keen to leave this city and make a name for himself in the king's court. Not for him the daily trudge about the city performing his ceremonial and legal duties. Better by far to recline on a seat in the king's household, drinking and farting with the rest of them. The decadence of the king's court was almost legendary. The trouble with such a man was, he could not be trusted in Baldwin's estimation. Most men would be keen to behave as their pockets dictated, moving with the whim of their financial advantage, but Sir Matthew was not like that. He would be more likely to consider any decision with a view to how it might impact on the Despensers and, accordingly, how his prospects might be improved by judicious leaking of information to the king.

Baldwin frowned. There was still no connection, so far as he could see, between the murders of Mucheton and the messenger. It was possible, perhaps, that he was mistaken to jump to the conclusion that simply because the two men had died on successive nights, and their bodies had been discovered so close to each other, they must have been victims of the same killer. Perhaps he would be better served by considering both deaths as individual and reviewing them in that light.

It was not good for him to wander the streets like this, though. He craved peace, and just now he craved above all his wife Jeanne. Being apart from her was . . . *unsettling*. Curious, because in past years he would not have thought it possible that he might so swiftly grow dependent upon a woman. He had desired them, yes, but would never have thought that one could so entirely win over his heart. That was a surprise.

And yet perhaps it was not just Jeanne – it was also this situation. It worried him that the bishop appeared so determined to have Baldwin sent to the next parliament, that Walter Stapledon was so keen to see him thrown into the bear pit of national politics. Baldwin wished to have nothing to do with the affairs of the realm. He was a contented rural knight, when all was said and done. Others sought glory and power, but not he. He wished to be left alone to manage his estates. That and a little hunting was all he craved. There was nothing better in life, he believed.

He recalled the bloody stumps where fingers had been cut from that dead messenger's hand. Could they have borne rings? Might a man have detached the finger to gain access to a bauble of some kind? Or was the man simply being tortured for some reason – to say where he had money kept back, or perhaps to explain what he held in his pouch: which was the most valuable message? After all, Baldwin knew already that there was one important message in the pouch of the *nuncius*. The bishop had hinted as much. If the bishop were offering advice to the king that could be construed as disadvantageous to the king's friends, or his wife, perhaps, either of them could be provoked into attacking Bishop Walter himself.

Which meant that a fellow who sought advancement, someone who knew of the bishop's note, could easily betake himself to acquire it and sell it to the highest bidder.

But why harm the messenger? Perhaps because there was a verbal appendix to the note itself? Suddenly Baldwin felt close to an answer.

Simon was already halfway through his second quart of ale when he heard the booming voice out in the road. He paused, his jug near his chin, mouth partly opened as he listened, and when his ears told him for certain who it was outside, he closed his eyes in silent despair. He waited, listening intently as the coroner spoke. Every word was as clear as if he was standing in the room next to Simon, and the bailiff gained the impression that Sir Richard's voice could quell any other sound and force it to submit.

'Have the bodies seen to. There's no point leaving a corpse lying in the street leaking blood and guts all over the place, is there?'

There was a mumble in response, and then a guffaw. 'You think the poor fellow would give a piss for that? Dear Christ in heaven, I know he's dressed in a good suit. The watchman wants his suit? Tell him he can have it – but it belongs to the king, and if he wants to argue the toss with the king, he is welcome to do so. It's none of my concern. The clothes are off him, anyway, so have them set aside in case the king feels a need for them, but I'd give the king a fortnight to decide. If your man doesn't hear, perhaps he could take them without trouble. Still, have the messenger wrapped in some good linen and have him taken to the church nearest. They can look to him . . . no, better than that, have him delivered to the care of my lord bishop. The fellow was carrying a message from Bishop Walter, so I'm sure the good bishop would want to see to the man's body as best he might . . . *WHAT?* Speak *UP*, man! D'you think I can hear you when you squeak like a mouse? Who's to pay? *EH?* How do I know? Ask the good bishop to pay for the linen if the city won't. Not my concern, is it?'

With the rattle at the latch, Simon felt his heart sink even as he heard the voice roar aloud, '*BLESS MY CODS!* Bailiff Puttock! Now there's a sight to cheer the heart of a thirsty man in the desert!'

Baldwin had not enjoyed a fruitful afternoon.

Upon leaving the widow and Sir Richard, he had decided to seek other necromancers in the city, but had met with no success. Rather than speak to the sheriff or his men, he had sought out the beadle. At Langatre's house he had met young Ivo Trempole guarding the house, who had given him some names, but he looked dubious when Baldwin began to talk about *maleficium*.

'If there was a man like that, I'd have heard,' he said doubtfully. 'Folks here wouldn't have much to do with a man who tried that kind of thing.'

'I have no doubt,' Baldwin agreed. 'But if there were someone here, perhaps he could keep his arts secret?'

'Perhaps,' Ivo agreed, but without conviction.

Baldwin soon had a list of three men to talk to, but although two admitted to telling the future, and one asserted that he could perform certain veterinary functions for cows with sore udders or horses with colic, all looked blank when asked about more advanced magic. Either they were very good at acting, or there were no men in Exeter who actively sought such assistance, Baldwin thought.

The third of these had lived a little farther down the road from Langatre's house, and as he passed by, he saw Ivo Trempole again.

'Any fortune?' Ivo asked when he caught Baldwin's eye.

'None, I fear,' Baldwin said.

'I was thinking . . .'

'Yes?'

'Well, if there was someone in the town, we'd have learned about him. People always spot someone nearby who's doing strange things.'

'Yes,' Baldwin said. After walking about the city all afternoon learning that no one knew anything that could help him, he was in no hurry to be told that he had been on a wild goose chase. He moved to walk away. Even Sir Richard's company was preferable to this.

'It occurred to me, though, that perhaps this man, if there is one, isn't a local? Perhaps it's someone who's only recently come to the city.' Catching sight of Baldwin's expression, he apologised quickly. 'I'm sorry, sir knight. It was silly. I was just thinking . . .'

'No – you are quite right. This could so easily be someone who has only recently come to the city. It would explain much. But . . .' His face grew more lugubrious as he considered the problem. 'How would I learn whether there was anyone who had recently come to the city and might practise the magical arts?'

Ivo screwed up his face. 'I'd speak to the keepers of the gates. They ought to know if there were any real strangers coming in. They know the regular visitors, like those who supply the markets, and they'd be sure to notice strangers. Try old Hal at the South Gate. That's the main way into the city for anyone usually.'

'I shall – and, friend, I am most grateful,' Baldwin said.

As he left Ivo, another thought struck him. If a man was recently arrived in the city, in order to make no noise as he walked in he must have travelled light. A fellow with a packhorse or a cart would be more noticeable. But a necromancer had need of his tools. Perhaps a necromancer without his tools had come, and required replacements?

It was an interesting hypothesis, anyway.

Robinet stood in the street and stared again at the place where he thought he had seen the man on the night James died.

Ach! It was one thing to think that a man was there in the middle of the night, when it was silent, all the people back in their homes, probably in their beds, but now? With all the noise and bustle of the city in the middle of the day, it was near impossible to bring back to mind that strange memory. The only thing he thought he could remember was that the figure was shortish, but beyond that the darkness and the ale had wiped the details from his mind.

He had been walking here for hours now, just walking the way that they had come, trying to prompt something – *anything* – that might help; but nothing occurred to him. At last, now, he was meandering about the place and eyeing the people milling all round, wondering whether a face or shape might prompt something. So far nothing had worked.

'You still here?'

'Just looking about.'

Walter looked at him and shook his head. 'Look, the man who killed him probably had no knowledge who it was he killed. It's not as though James was a man who would be missed.'

'He was a king's man,' Robinet said obstinately.

'He was an arse. He ruined you.'

'It was largely my own fault.'

'And had you gaoled fine, didn't he?'

Newt shrugged. It was true, and he had hated James for it at the time. Christ Jesus, the first moment he saw James here in Exeter, he had thought to kill the man. But then he had seen the shadow of the lad he had helped train in the job, and suddenly all that had been less important. Especially when James had apologised. It was a little thing, but Robinet was not the sort of man to bear a grudge unnecessarily. If James was contrite, and he did appear to be, well, there was little worth in being angry or bitter about things. The king had forgiven him a long while ago, and Newt was well protected now, with his corrody.

'Just leave him be, friend. There's a murder every few weeks here. What's the point of seeking James's killer when there are so many others? They never get resolved, and I doubt this one will either.'

'He was once a friend,' Newt said softly. 'That makes it worthwhile for me.'

Walter nodded, but gave a twisted grin. 'Not for me, though. I'm back for some food. You coming?'

Robinet was tempted. He had been walking and thinking all day without a break, but he shook his head. 'I'll stay here a little longer. Just to see if I can recognise anyone.'

Walter gave a chuckle and shook his head as he strode off towards his house. He was clearly of the impression that Newt had lost his senses over this matter.

Well, his opinion was not important, Robinet thought to himself. No. The main thing was that he felt as though he had a duty to find his apprentice's killer, no matter who that man might be.

From Langatre's house, it was a short walk up the hill to the main South Gate Street, and thence down to the gate itself. On the way,

Baldwin wondered whether he might meet the coroner again, and found himself hoping against hope that he would not. The coroner was a kindly soul, it was true, and generally had a shrewd mind, but his loudness and constant attempts at telling jokes were wearing after a while. Baldwin was happier to try to find out all he could without his company.

The keeper of the gate was standing before the arch with his thumbs stuck in his belt, grinning broadly at the sight of a carter shouting with rage and kicking at his horse. His exhausted old nag stood patiently, head hanging in the shafts, and as Baldwin approached he saw the man aim a kick at her flank. She moved with the pain, but was too tired to do more than shake her head and whinny.

'Damned fool. Has turds for brains,' was the gatekeeper's assessment. 'Came in here with his cart overloaded, and then complains when the poor beast can't carry it all.'

'Does it often happen here?' Baldwin asked, seeing other splinters and shards of broken wheels about the place.

'Fair bit. If a carter's an idiot. The way up here is not so steep as Stepecote, but it's bad enough. Look at her! She's carrying far too much on that cart. It's his own fault.'

Baldwin could only agree. 'Master Hal? I have been advised to speak to you.'

'What about?' His eyes had hardened instantly, and now Baldwin was aware that the fellow's smile was gone like frost in the sunshine. 'If it's anything to do with my lad, I'll . . .'

'I am trying to learn whether anyone has come to the town recently who might have looked suspicious. I was told,' he improvised shamelessly, 'that you were the most astute of all the gatekeepers, and if anyone was a stranger, and looked up to no good, you'd be the man to spot him.'

'Aye, well, that's as maybe. True enough, I suppose, but what would you want with the man?'

'I am the Keeper of the King's Peace, friend,' Baldwin said silkily, with just a hint of menace. 'You can be assured that I have my reasons for wanting to speak to him.'

'Well, there's no one I've seen entering by my gate,' the man said shortly, and would have left, but Baldwin shook his head.

'What does that mean? Hal, you say that no one entered by your gate, but the very way you say it seems to imply that you have seen something – what?'

'I don't know what you mean.'

'Let me guess, then. You know about the two dead men. One was a local man, who had few enemies from what I have heard. He could have been killed by anyone – but more likely a stranger with a knife than someone who knew him. And then there was the other: a king's messenger, no less. Someone with a pouch full of important notes for other people. Surely a man who would dare to kill such a one would dare anything at all. He must be a most dangerous fellow.'

'Perhaps. Nothing to do with me.'

'Ah, but a man who knew something and didn't let me know, that sort of a man would be of great interest to the king himself, wouldn't he? Because a man like that might just be in league with the man who killed his messenger. The king would most certainly want to speak to him. Or have his expert questioners come and speak to him.'

At the thought of torture, Hal's face changed. 'Now, Keeper, there's no need to think such things. I wouldn't deceive you . . . I have seen a man who looked most odd, but it's surely nothing to do with the murder of the king's man. I wouldn't have held back anything from his majesty.'

'Tell me all.'

'It was Tuesday evening. I was off to the tavern early with my son. I like a drink or two with him, and we were off to the little place near Bolehille that's just opened. Well, we had some of the strong ale there, and when it came to be time to get home, I was a little weak on my pins. Art, he was all right, and he helped me along. I seem to remember seeing a fellow up in front of me. At least, that was what I reckoned at first,' he added more quietly.

'What was he like, this fellow?'

'A shadow. Nothing more than a shadow. He moved along with the speed of a ghost. Slinking along in the darkness, he was. I thought at the time that he was just a silly dream I had because of the ale, but now . . . the more I think of it, the less I think I was dreaming.'

'It was not the dead messenger?'

'Master, if I'd seen *him*, I'd have said so. No one wants to upset the king about the murder of his messenger,' he said sharply.

Baldwin nodded. That much was almost certainly true. 'What else?'

'That is it.'

'No. You are embarrassed or ashamed by something. What was it?'

Hal was about to repeat that it was nothing, but then he lowered his head and stared at his boots. It was hard to confess. He was a stolid man, and proud of his commonsense, but that sight had given him more of a shock than he wanted to admit.

At last he nodded. 'I heard about my neighbour. Old Willie Skinner there. He saw something too, the same night, I think. A figure. I mentioned what I saw to him, and he told me he'd seen the same thing. A low figure. Except when he approached the figure, it disappeared. Just like mine.'

'Porter, any man can sidle into a shadow or into an alleyway without resorting to the occult,' Baldwin growled.

'Maybe so. But they do say that the devil can make his servants disappear. And witches can fly through the air.'

'You say you saw a witch?'

'You can laugh, but there are necromancers about who can look just like ordinary people if they want to. And they will kill people, so they say.'

'Who says that?'

'You know,' Hal said gruffly. 'People. Will said he didn't see where his man went, and neither did I. You can't explain people disappearing like that.'

Baldwin looked at him with pursed lips. It was tempting to say that he could explain such manifestations all too easily, usually by the expedient of a convenient rope, ladder or trap door, but this man was already embarrassed enough. Instead he clapped his hands together.

'Good. In that case, come and show me where this all happened. Let us see whether I can conjecture a more natural agent for your vision.'

'You might have all the time you need, but I don't!' Hal spat, bitter at the impression that the keeper was amused by him. He waved a hand about him. 'Look at all these people here! I have my duty to do until the gates are closed.'

Baldwin eyed him, and then he smiled. 'I know, then: fetch me your son. He can take me to see where you saw this . . . this thing.'

Chapter Twenty-Three

Exeter City

It was done. John of Nottingham scraped away the last pieces of wax and let them fall to the floor as he stood back and stared at the last of the little models. Only when his hawkish face had studied them all for some few moments did he finally give a sharp nod to himself. If not pride, there was at least professional satisfaction in a job well done.

The mass he had attended at church had been enough to make him realise that he would have to make this last figure more . . . *realistic*, for want of a better word.

It had been a marvellous occasion. The crowd of city folk all standing and listening as the canons and vicars sang their refrains, murmuring the prayers . . . it made him feel quite nostalgic. All that part of his life was gone, though, naturally. He could hardly return to Nottingham now. Everyone would be looking for him, the noted necromancer who had dared to attempt the assassination of the most powerful men in the country.

Still, the ceremony had soothed his soul. The broad open space of the nave, cluttered and spoiled as it was by the rebuilding work, was yet so enormous that it stilled a man's heart to think of the effort that had gone into it, the adoration of God which had impelled men to undertake such a project. All too soon, the mass was done and he was ushered out again with the ebb of the congregation, listening to people discussing the priest who had officiated. Most concluded that he was still too new to his job. They felt sure that the following Sunday would be better. It was Saint Catherine of Alexandria's feast day, an auspicious day for any church. Surely the bishop would attend. Perhaps John should have him in full episcopal rig in honour of the feast day?

Others he knew would have taken a piece of the man's elements.

They'd have paid to acquire some of his hair, or some parings from his nails, and incorporated those into the figure while making it, so that when the ivory pin was thrust into the heart, the little mannequin would transfer the damage all the more easily. Yes, that was necessary for those who were less powerful than John.

He had no need of such hocus-pocus. John of Nottingham was an artist. He did not require any paltry little additions, because he could make use of less tangible exhibits of the man's soul. But accuracy was important. When he had been in the church today, he had seen an error. The king was clear and obvious: his crown would make him stand out. But a bishop, a man who remained in his cathedral close all the while, would be more difficult to pinpoint. Surely the demons sent to destroy him would need more than a mere image of the man, they would need a closer likeness.

So, he had fashioned a bishop's mitre, given him the elements of his regalia, and finally – this was a touch of brilliance on his part, he thought – crafted a pair of spectacles on his nose. No one but Bishop Stapledon in the whole of Exeter would have them, he thought. He had seen the bishop wearing them in the cathedral a couple of days ago, and it had made him frown at the time, but apparently they were for reading pages close to his nose. After all his work in the king's exchequer, it was probably no surprise that the man's eyes were suffering.

The bishop was carefully, almost reverently, picked up and set alongside the king.

He pinched at the bridge of his nose as he thought about the work he had yet to do. The tools of his trade were all laid out on the bench, where they had been fumigated and cleaned assiduously. Soon, when all his preparations were complete, he would set in train the process by which he would have the four men killed. And then he would have his money in full, and he could travel to extend his understanding of his magic.

It was then that he had the idea, and the marvellous perfection of it made him catch his breath. Looking at the figure, he nodded as though already personally acquainted, and gave a dry smile. Yes. That was how he would do it.

His head was hurting, and he wandered to the grille which gave out to the roadway above. The light was fading. He could just see the sturdy legs of a man standing near the wall above him. Stepping backwards to avoid being noticed, he knocked against the table with the tools, and carefully rested a hand on it to keep it stable. One item only rolled to the edge, and as it was about to fall from the table he managed to catch it.

Closing his eyes in relief, he carefully set it down again. It would have been terrible if it had become contaminated with dirt from the floor, because then all that time spent in cleaning the damned thing would have been wasted.

No, the fingers of a man killed a few moments after they were removed were far too important to be allowed to get dirty.

Art was no fool. When he saw the knight talking to his father out there in the space by the roadway, he knew that the man must have guessed about him, and he was half inclined to bolt. The door to the yard was in plain view, but Art was fairly confident that he could beat a knight carrying a sword over a short distance, let alone a longer one. This man, the Keeper of the King's Peace, didn't live here in the city. He was just an occasional visitor, that was all. All Art had to do was run now, and then come back in a week or two when things had calmed down. Or maybe he should just go. There was little enough to keep him here now. The bleeding city was a prison to a man like him with ideas and schemes. He had a good mind, him.

There was no love between him and his old man. Hal didn't understand him at all. Never had. He seemed to reckon that a boy like Art should be well behaved all the time, like Hal always was. But Art wasn't some crusty old wrinkled shell like his father. He was young, and his blood fizzed with energy. Hal? He was a worn-out old husk, he was.

He could see his father talking with that self-righteous manner he had, like he was always so perfect. Well, he wasn't any better than Art himself. Art had heard tell of the scrapes his father used to get into when he was a lad, too. Which was what made it all the more galling that he tried to beat Art when Art went out and had a good time.

When he heard them discussing the figure Hal had seen, Art gave a wry grin. Old fool! The thing was just a trick of the light, that was all.

There'd been nothing there. Nothing at all. If there had, Art would have seen it too, wouldn't he?

Art leaned out to peer at his old man again, and saw the knight's gaze fix on him. 'Shite!'

If he was going to run, he'd best get on with it right now. He took a deep breath, dropped his head to his breast, and was about to set off when he heard a step very close – too close.

'So you are Art? I would like to speak to you.'

'Why?'

'The night that the messenger died you saw someone. Your father told me about it. I want to know all about it.'

The Bishop's Palace

Robert Busse had completed the business he had with Bishop Stapledon, and was glad to be able to take his leave.

It had been an excellent idea to come here, he thought with satisfaction as he walked from the palace into the close. That dunghill rat John de Courtenay would find it hard, very hard, now that Busse had already won the bishop's ear.

His rival was a fool, that was the thing. He never understood the simplest point of organisation, he couldn't manage an account to save his life, and his sole interests were his damned hunting animals and his clothing. Had to follow every damned fashion – as soon as the court altered the length of their hosen, so did he. Under him, the abbey would collapse. Busse was convinced of it.

Still, the good thing was, Busse was ahead of him now. There could be no doubt in the mind of any of the brothers that the better was going to win the throne, and it wouldn't be de Courtenay. And one of the first instructions that Busse would give, when he had the abbacy, would be to command that all brothers adhered to the rule's commands, and all hounds, raches, alaunts, whatever the blasted slobbering mutts were, would have to go. If de Courtenay wanted, he could send them all back where they came from, his father's household. Personally Busse had nothing against them; it was only that de Courtenay was flaunting his wealth for no reason. And when that God-cursed monster had come into the refectory last month and taken the food from Busse's very bowl, Busse had known, absolutely for certain, that he would rather die than see the poor abbey fall into that man's hands.

There had been many things to be done, of course. Busse had managed to deal with many of the other brothers long before poor Abbot Robert, God save his soul, had died. He'd already won the agreement of Richard de Wylle (he would become prior under Busse); Roger de Pountyngdon (who would become sacristan); William de la Wille (almoner); Alexander . . . the list was endless. All had agreed, though, to vote for him at the election, rather than for de Courtenay.

But now he had just one last little task to ensure that all was done. He'd already checked with Langatre, and now he wanted to make sure once more. Just to see that his future was as secure as he thought it should be. Langatre was competent enough to read the signs for him. Not that it was necessary, of course. But it would make him a teeny bit more comfortable . . . John de Courtenay was a powerful man, after all. His father was a baron . . .

The roads were clearing now in the gathering dusk, and he could smell the delicious odour of cooking pies and meats as women prepared their last meals of the day. During the summer months, they would do so at this hour, and he somehow much preferred the summertime, and smelling the cooking in daylight. There was something wrong about the odours in the darkness, he always felt. When it was dark, people should be in their beds. God! As he ought to be now, he thought, pulling his robes tighter about him. The thought of rising for Matins was most unappealing. But Langatre was never about much during the day. He reckoned that most of his work was achieved in the dark, and slept for much of the morning. Probably a load of old guff, so far as Busse was concerned, but the man was a competent fortune-teller, so who cared. Let him think he was convincing. The main thing was, he helped clear Busse's mind and allow him to think logically.

His path was in darkness, and he almost fell full-length at a loose cobble, but managed to save himself at the last moment. Still, it left his ankle giving him gip, and he hobbled the rest of the way.

Passing a man leaning against the wall, he nodded and absently made the sign of the cross, before walking to the door and knocking on it.

'He's not there, Father,' the man said.

'Hmm?' Busse grunted enquiringly.

'The man used to live there. He's been taken by the sheriff's men. Held up at the castle, so I heard. If you want to see him up there, you'd best pray your hardest. The sheriff's not minded to let him have visitors, so I reckon!'

Langatre taken! Sweet Christ! 'Why?'

'He's been dabbling with evil magic, they say. Getting demons to obey his command. I heard tell that he's been trying to kill men with waxen images. *Maleficium!*' Elias said solemnly, as though it was a word he had known all his life, and not something he had heard for the first time that morning.

Busse muttered a hasty 'Thank you. God speed!' before turning and hastening as fast as his limp would allow back up the road towards the cathedral. And all the way he could only think that God was sending him a sign. With his fortuneteller arrested and held for summoning demons, all of a sudden Busse felt that his plans were beginning to collapse about his ears.

He could have wept.

Exeter City

Baldwin was sure that this was the same boy. Yes, he had the same pale, rather unhealthy-looking face that he had glimpsed while standing over the dead messenger, and, as he eyed Art, Baldwin was impressed by just how shifty a lad in his late teens could appear.

There was none of the arrogant self-confidence he would have expected in a lad this young, only a kind of anxiousness. Baldwin had seen that in the faces of others: it was a natural result of someone's realising that they were in the company of a man who, after the sheriff, was one of the most powerful in the country. Often, of course, the lads he met were those who had something to hide, he reminded himself, and wondered about Art. It was natural for a keeper to suspect everyone, though, and he tried to put his suspicions aside.

Apart from that, there was little else to impress. The boy was thin and would have been gangling, were it not for his bent back. It did not look like a hunch, but was more an affectation which appeared to be there to highlight his disgruntlement with the world. He had a pasty complexion enlivened by a small mountain region of yellow-headed spots about his mouth and chin, grey, watery-coloured eyes, and a shock of thin sandy hair that only served to emphasise his glowering demeanour.

'All I wish is to see where you saw this man, and to hear what exactly you saw,' Baldwin said soothingly as Hal left them, muttering darkly about being 'not too big to be clipped hard round the ear if you're cheeky . . .' and similar dire warnings.

'I didn't see the one he's telling about. Didn't see anyone that side of the road. Anyway, doubt whether the old man did either. Silly old fart's too pissed to see anything clearly. He prob'ly saw a dog in the shadows or something.'

'Let us go and look, eh? Surely your eyes are keener than your father's, and you will be able to tell me much more.'

'Wouldn't be hard,' Art admitted grudgingly.

Baldwin was always being surprised by youngsters. Some could look as helpful and quick-witted as any, and then prove themselves tongue-tied by the sight of a knight, or more commonly by the sight of a woman, while others would be cocksure and a pain but then, when a posse was needed, the first to lift their hands to volunteer to help. They were also the first to get into a fight as well, though, sadly.

First impression aside, this fellow seemed bright enough. He wasn't one of the nervous, overly self-aware boys who would retreat into a blushing shell at the first sign of an argument, but neither was he the sort who would respond with violence to any perceived threat. In short, he was moderately quick-witted. Baldwin had the feeling that anything the lad said would be trustworthy.

'Your old man was drunk?'

'Yeah. Usually is. He thinks I'm going to get into trouble if I go to an alehouse without him, so he always comes along. But he can't handle his ale like he used to.'

'No mother?'

Art squinted sideways at him. 'She met a merchant, so they say, and left the city to be with him. Look at the old man. Not hard to see why.'

Baldwin nodded. It was depressing how often a woman could have her head turned by someone who was interested in a buxom breast or the length of a thigh. So often these fellows would ensnare a wench, then prod her and leave her, despairing, with a babe. At least Art's mother appeared to have left with her man. Baldwin wondered whether he would have kept her, or had perhaps left her at the next city he visited. It had happened before.

'What did you see that night, Art?'

'We'd been in the tavern some while, and the old man had been throwing the stuff down his neck like it was gone out of fashion, so when I could, I grabbed him to take him home. He didn't want to come, though. He was right pissed off,' Art said. He was speaking slowly, musingly, as he walked, his face introverted, as though he could see the scene in his mind as he spoke. 'I think it was that man – you know, Norman Mucheton. Dad's not used to seeing things like that. It was a shitty sight. It was like his head was about to fall from his shoulders.'

'You were all right about it, though?' Baldwin said as a picture of the man's body sprang into his mind.

'Yeah. Seen a few corpses in my time. Well, you know. This *is* a city.'

'Of course. What then?'

They had reached the little tavern now. A decaying holly bush was bound to a stake over the door to advertise its business, and Art glanced up as it squeaked. 'We came out, and walked down back that way. Didn't take long usually. Well, you've seen how near we are.'

Baldwin reckoned that they had walked a scant two hundred yards from the gate, but they had turned into a little alley to reach this place. The gate was hidden from view.

Art continued: 'It was when we got into the road. Look, come up here . . .' He led the way back along the alley, until only a few yards from South Gate Street. 'Hereabouts, it was. The old man saw something down there on the right. Shook, he did, and fair gave me a shock. Said it was a man, but when I looked there was nothing there.'

Baldwin walked to where the lad pointed. In the gloom, he could see little. There was a bundle or two of faggots lying at the foot of a wall, and the overhang from the jettied room overhead concealed anything else until Baldwin was right underneath. Gradually his eyes grew acclimatised, and he peered about him carefully. 'Your father said the thing was where? Here?'

'Yeah. A bit up that way.'

Moving to his right, Baldwin saw that the building here did not quite meet its neighbour. A gap of eighteen inches separated them. 'Where does this go?'

'Right along to the next alley. Why?'

'I think your father was not so drunk as you imagine,' Baldwin said thoughtfully.

Art gazed about at the alley. 'You joking? You think there was some sort of . . .'

'Not a ghost, not a demon, nothing like that,' Baldwin said. 'But there was probably a man here, yes.'

'That what Will saw too?' Art asked.

'Perhaps,' Baldwin mused. 'He was very nervous about it, certainly.'

'It was him telling my dad about it made him see things that night.'

'You mean your father spoke to Will yesterday and his story prompted Hal to think of what he saw as a demon?'

'Yesterday? No, Will said all that to us on Tuesday, after finding the body outside his old house.'

Baldwin stopped and peered at him. 'I think you and I need to discuss this further.'

Chapter Twenty-Four

Exeter City

'Did I tell you the joke about the man who wanted his neighbour's wife?' Coroner Richard asked Simon rhetorically, and continued before Simon could respond. 'He waited until his neighbour had gone on a journey, and then knocked on her door. "Madam," he said, "I have fallen in love with you. My life holds no promise for me unless I can have you. I will do anything – command me and give yourself to me!"'

'Well, this woman was honourable, and she was shocked to be addressed in this manner by her neighbour, so she gave him the turnabout right away. "I love my husband, and I've given him my vows. I won't dishonour myself and betray him. Begone!"'

'So off he went, the flea biting his ear, until he had a thought. There was a clever woman in a wood not far away, and maybe she could help. Off he went, and spoke to her thus: "Old woman, there is a wife I adore, but she will have nothing to do with me. I'll die if I can't have her. Is there anything you can do?"'

'The old woman looked him up and down, named her price, and when she had it in her purse she told him to wait there in her cottage. She took some string, and set it about the neck of a piglet, and walked off. When she approached the woman's house, she rubbed soil in her hair and down her face, and pinched herself to make herself tearful, and then carried on, the piglet behind her.

' "Old woman, what is the matter?" the woman asked when she appeared.

' "My daughter! Look at her! Turned into a piglet by that evil man!"

' "What evil man? What has happened?"

'This dishonourable old woman said: "A man arrived yesterday and no sooner had he seen my daughter than he decided he must have her. He told her he would pine without her . . ."

' "But that is what happened to me!"

' "My daughter was a good, honourable chit, though, so she refused him."

' "As did I."

' "And although he told her that without her, his life would be worth naught, still she refused him. And when he set to her to try to force her, I beat him away. And as he went on his way, he roared at us most fearfully that if he couldn't have her, nor would any other man. My daughter would henceforth be turned into a pig and would never know a man. And this morning . . . this morning, when I awoke . . . this had happened to my little child!"

'The wife turned pale on hearing this, you see, and she cried out, "But this all happened to me! Good woman, tell me what I must do to save myself! There was a man here today who asked me to lie with him, and told me he would pine for love of me if he didn't have my body, and I sent him away with every curse my heart could summon. What shall I do?"

' "Good wife, there is only one thing you may do: find him and promise you'll do all he desires so long as he doesn't turn you into a sow."

' "Should I leave at once?"

'The old woman shook her head. "You wait here. I shall fetch him to you. I think he lives near here. Do you prepare yourself for him."

' "Old woman, you are kind."

'So the old woman sauntered back to her cottage and told him to get back to his neighbour's house, and he had a high time. And it only goes to show, you see, that if you want a vain woman, while she tries to protect her looks there is always a way to her heart!'

Simon looked up at him. 'You think that was a joke?'

'Just a story to lighten the heart,' the Coroner declared confidently. 'Hoi, host, where's your wine all gone? Is your barrel empty that you leave your customers dying of thirst in this hovel? Eh? Ah, Bailiff, it is good to see you again. I like your friend the keeper, but he can be a cold soul of an evening. Much more fun to have a congenial companion.'

'Yes,' Simon said meaningfully. His own thoughts were on his wife again after that joke. At least Meg would never fall for so foolish a tale. Turned into a sow indeed!

'Yes. I was not glad to be sent here just now.'

'What did bring you?' Simon enquired.

'Ah, thank you, my fine fellow!' Coroner Richard declared happily as more wine was poured into his jug. 'To answer you honestly, Bailiff, I do not know. There must have been something, for the sheriff asked me to come here to meet him. When I arrived, I learned that the city's coroners were both away, and as soon as I got here there were these bodies about the place, so it was fortunate I *was* here.'

'But the sheriff . . .'

'Saw me briefly at the bishop's palace, then at the castle too, but that is it. Since then, nothing. Still don't know what he wanted with me.'

Hearing how his voice had grown quieter, Simon shot him a look. The coroner's eyes held a cold glitter suddenly, as though his thoughts were not pleasant to him. 'What?'

'Oh, nothing. Just musing,' the coroner said. 'Aha, who's this?'

'Baldwin!' Simon said with relief. 'It is good to see you once again.'

'And you, old friend. This man is Art, son of Hal at the South Gate. He has an interesting tale to tell about a body or two.'

Christ Jesus, but his feet hurt! The way here with all the newer cobbles was hard on the feet, especially after two or three days of solid walking. Rob didn't know what was so exciting about marching from one town to another. From what he'd seen, walking and seeing other places was greatly over-valued. Better by far to stay in one place, and if you had to travel, then best to do so by ship. The less of this stomping over moors and cobbles, the better.

Where was he off to now? Rob watched as the little hunched figure of the monk scurried across the lane in front of a horse, which shied and made the rider curse, and thence passed over Carfoix and continued along the High Street towards the castle at the farther edge of the town.

'Why couldn't you stay at the bishop's palace?' he grumbled as he walked. 'Hot rooms, beds, blankets, food, ale . . . what more does a man need?'

But the monk merely hurried onwards, and Rob had to stifle his complaints to keep up.

Simon had been quite explicit. 'If he leaves the close, you have to stay with him. Don't let him see you, but keep behind him and watch where he goes and who he talks to. All right? If you do this well, there will be a reward for you. Fail, though, and you'll get a thrashing!'

The threat was meaningless, as Rob knew perfectly well. The bailiff wasn't the sort of man to punish a lad for trying his best and failing, but still he seemed to be happier for sounding like one of those modern knights who only ever knew how to get men to obey by threatening dire punishment.

If he were to be honest, he rather liked the tall, dark-haired bailiff. Simon Puttock was a great deal kinder than most masters he'd seen before. Usually they would be content to issue a command once, and then beat a fellow with a suitable rod. Only last year a young apprentice had died after being whipped by his master. The man had explained that he had been trying to show the boy the error of his ways after he had done something wrong – probably drank too much one evening or something. There were so many reasons why a master could beat his charges.

Puttock was different. There were times when he had been so bound up with his work that he had been ridiculously easy to fool. Usually when there were too many new ships in the port, all waiting for their goods to be assessed so that they might be unloaded. At times like that, Rob's life was much easier. He could rise later and not worry about preparing too much food, for his master would snarl about going to a pie shop, he was in such a hurry, and that would be all. Still, the fact that he was trusted tended to make Rob more protective of his master, as though Simon was in fact his charge, not he his.

The monk passed through the castle gates and Rob could see him inside. He was speaking to a guard, but when he was finished he didn't go to the steps that led to the little hall. Instead, he was taken to another building. Even Rob could recognise the entrance to a small gaol-house. He watched as the monk entered, and then he sauntered over to a log by a wall to sit down and wait.

Bailiff Puttock would be interested in this, he reckoned.

* * *

There was a short pause after Art had told his story, and then Baldwin and the coroner glanced at each other and nodded.

'He has some questions to answer,' Coroner Richard acknowledged, and soon the three men were marching back down South Gate Street towards the old watchman's house, Baldwin speaking quickly to Simon to explain what he and the coroner had already learned.

'The trouble is, old friend,' he said as they approached the gatehouse itself and turned right to stand before Will Skinner's dilapidated property, 'we have no idea why anyone should want to harm a king's messenger. The idea that a man should cut off a messenger's fingers, too, is bizarre. I can only assume the fellow was being harmed in order to force him to answer some questions – simple torture.'

'Why would someone want to torture the messenger?' Simon scoffed. 'The pouch was there to be taken. No need to harm the fellow first.'

'What if the messenger was aware of some other aspect to the note? Perhaps the bishop decided not to put all into writing? If there was some other part to the message that he dare not even commit to paper, something so dangerous that he could only put it into the messenger's head – what then? Perhaps a man might cut off his finger just to prove he was determined enough to stop at nothing to learn what the messenger knew.'

'It's possible,' Simon admitted. 'But it is too wild. Who would have learned of something of that nature?'

'If the bishop had a man in his room while he briefed the *nuncius*,' Baldwin pointed out, 'that man might have heard something. And then, if he had a brother, or a friend, out here in the city itself, he might have been able to contact him, tell him to take this fellow . . .'

'And then he caught the wrong man on the first night?' the coroner rumbled.

'Many thieves and felons are less bright than the common dog in the street,' Baldwin pointed out. 'It would not surprise me if one of them caught the wrong man. In the dark along an alley, they could have mistaken him, I suppose.' In his mind he was reviewing the two men: the messenger was a lot taller, but Baldwin knew that gauging a man's height in the dark could be very difficult. Yes – it was possible.

Considering, Simon said, 'It at least makes sense of the poor man's losing his fingers, certainly. I'd be happier knowing that there was someone in the bishop's household who could have done such a thing, though. It is far-fetched to say that someone was in a position to learn about this theoretical message, and happened to know a friend in the city who could kill the messenger. You might as well suggest some supernatural agent. What?'

Simon had caught sight of Baldwin's quick look at the coroner. Coroner Richard grinned to himself and knocked on the door as Simon set his hands at his sword belt and glowered. 'I wasn't saying this *was* a ghost, Baldwin!' He knew how his friend looked down upon the idea of malevolent spirits of any type. In Baldwin's world, all was easily explained by rationality. 'Look, all I was saying was, you may as well suggest that it was the devil who came and killed the fellow. Until we have more information and a genuine possible suspect, I think that we ought to . . .'

'Consider other possibilities. I know,' Baldwin said coolly.

Simon was silent. He was annoyed at being treated so dismissively at first, but then he saw a strange look in the coroner's eye, a look almost of anxiety, and the sight was enough to make him pause. There was something about this matter that he was not yet aware of.

'Well,' he said, 'I can at least offer some help with the bishop. I have a young lad with me, and if Rob can't sniff out a conspiracy at ten paces, no one can.'

'You mean that boy from Dartmouth?' Coroner Richard boomed unenthusiastically.

Simon shook his head. 'Coroner, he has spent his life in the company of the most devious, thieving set of people in the realm – sailors. If he cannot recognise when someone sees the possibility of making money from a situation, I doubt if anyone can.'

'Very well,' Baldwin said. 'Where is this fellow? Would he have gone on his rounds already?'

Art was leaning against the wall, picking his nose. He shrugged now and looked about him. 'Doubt it. Too early for him. He's probably up at his old place.'

'Where is that?' Baldwin asked.

'Where that man died – Mucheton.'

Coroner Richard's face screwed up as his brows knotted. 'What do you mean? Will used to live in that road?'

'Yes. Before the fire. Then him and his wife had a good place up there. But the fire killed his family while he was out drinking. I was quite young then, but that's what I heard.'

'What do you want?'

The voice took Baldwin by surprise, and he could see that the coroner was struck the same way. Sir Richard's head snapped round so quickly, Baldwin half-expected to hear the bones in his neck crack.

In the doorway was a bent figure. It was Will's wife, Baldwin saw. 'Mistress, we are looking for Will Skinner. Is he home?'

There was a faint light in her eyes as though she harboured some long-held hope, but as her gaze went from one to the other, the spark faded and she appeared to sag a little. 'He's not here. You want him, you go to where he left us that night.'

She walked with immense difficulty. One hand gripped the doorframe to steady her as she gazed at them all, her back so badly deformed that her head would only have reached Baldwin's middle chest.

'He left you?'

'To burn. Aye. I'm still his wife, but if I had courage I would leave him. He did this to me! I won't suffer much longer, though. The good Lord will take me away from this vale of sin and horror. And I'll be glad to leave!'

'It must be hard to live here when you used to live so close by with all your family,' Baldwin said. He was trying to sound understanding and compassionate, but even to his ears his words sounded empty and cold.

'Hard?' She looked up at him from her twisted frame. 'Hard? You think it's hard to lose everything? Yes. It's hard.'

'Mistress, I meant no offence to you. I was merely . . .'

'Hard! Yes, we had a good life before. Will was a merchant and life was good. Yes, it was fine. We had our house, with three little children, and plenty of money coming in every day to support them all. Yes, it was good. And then one night my *pathetic* husband stayed out late to drink with his friends, and we had a fire. It took my children, it took our treasure, and it even took my body. So now he's a watchman and I'm the twisted wreck you see today. Burned until all my skin was falling away. Because while my useless prickle of a husband was singing with his friends, I was in the house trying to save my children. But they're all gone. All gone!'

'Mistress, we shall leave you. I had no idea you were here. You have my deepest sympathy,' Baldwin murmured.

Usually his calm and respectful manner would soothe even the most truculent woman, but this evening his words only inflamed Will's wife.

'You had no idea I was here? No, almost everyone thinks I'm dead. And they're right! Yes, I'm dead. I've seen what hell is, fine sir. Yes, the devil has visited me once and taken my little sweetings, although he left me to suffer for them. And he left me my husband, too, so that I might see every day the man who destroyed my life when he wasn't there to save our children; and that I might make his life as miserable and cheerless as possible with my constant rebukes and sniping. Yes. The devil made a fine job of me, didn't he?'

Baldwin could not meet her eye. He turned and left, trying not to listen to the cackling laugh that followed him.

'So, Keeper,' the coroner asked as they trudged up South Gate Street, 'Should we wander up that alley to find Will now?'

Baldwin stopped and glanced back at Will's house. 'In Christ's name, the poor devil has enough already with her in his home. No. We can speak to him later.'

Simon felt only relief to hear that, thinking he could do with some sleep. But when he caught a glimpse of the coroner's sturdy frame, he began to wonder. He had had experience of 'quiet' evenings with the coroner.

At least the drinking was delayed a little when they reached the door of the inn and Rob called to him.

'I think you'll be interested in this.'

Chapter Twenty-Five

Exeter City

The alley was quickly darkening now, and Will was ready to return home and gather up his staff and lamp, when he heard the steps approaching.

At least now the body was gone. It had been hard, standing here with the corpse and Tom atte Moor in the background, watching, and Tom probably chuckling to himself.

Everyone laughed at him. He knew that. Back some years ago, they'd all been sympathetic as they could be, but then as he grew unable to continue with his normal work, as the demands from his wife increased, the compassion of his friends started to dull a little. While the fire was fresh in everyone's minds, that was one thing. When he went to the tavern after that, he couldn't put hand to purse without a drink appearing and a muttered, 'Sorry to hear about them, Will,' accompanied by a hand on his shoulder. That all changed over time. Margie accosted some people in the street and shouted at them because they hadn't helped save her wains, and then the tales of her shouting and screaming at others grew more common.

Will had enough problems already. As soon as it grew obvious that he wouldn't be able to keep his business afloat, he had started to decline, but that had been halted by the appreciation of his wife's dependence upon him. Before the fire she had taken in a little spinning and hawked some goods about the city, but that was all in the past. After her appalling injuries, she could do nothing of that kind. Suddenly he had an adult to provide for.

It was the spur he had needed. He could see that now. With a little more luck, he might have been able to return to his trade, but the fact was, he needed to be there almost every day to look after her. At night it wasn't so bad. She grew tired easily, and once she was asleep it was all right for him to leave her. She couldn't keep abusing people when they were all in their own beds.

When he first spoke of taking on the post, she had been driven almost lunatic by the thought of his leaving her at night. Yes, that had been hideous. The filth that came from her lips . . . accusations of his whoring, of his having other children to visit, of his being ashamed of her, of his being determined to go and drink himself to oblivion to forget what his shameful drinking had done last time, when he had condemned his wife and children to their fates.

Through it all, he had to try to forget the sight when he had first returned to the house.

Now, peering at the place where his house had once stood, he could almost hear their voices: the children in the front yard by the door to the hall, shouting and screaming with delight as they kicked a ball about. There were so many happy memories: of digging round a tree trunk with Tom and then setting a fire about it to remove it from their little garden so that they could start to grow their own vegetables; building a small shed for logs; seeing all their faces alight at Christmas as the house was decorated . . . so many happy memories. And memories of his wife, too. Because that was all he had left. Memories of those wonderful times when he had been whole and happy.

At least in his mind his family was still there.

And as Will began to sob once more, the man clad in the worn and tattered old cloak watched him with dispassionate speculation as he waited for his messenger. And when the woman arrived, he turned from his contemplation of the weeping watchman to go with her into a darkened doorway.

Friday Next after the Feast of St Edmund[7]

The Bishop's Palace
Baldwin and Simon were at the bishop's palace as soon as the close opened its gates the next morning.

---

[7] 23 November 1324

To his disgust, the coroner had been called away, and the two were relieved to be marching across the cathedral green together, although neither spoke much. Simon was feeling light-headed and foolish after drinking with the coroner last night, while also trying to make sense of Busse's wanderings. For his part, Baldwin was still feeling bruised after his first discussion with the bishop. It was hard to believe that the bishop had asked him to begin to investigate the death of the king's messenger only a matter of hours ago.

If he was honest, though, he was also petulant after the treatment he resented so much: being told that he must go to join the parliament when he had neither desire nor interest to do so. All he really wanted was a peaceful time far away from politics and the dangers of the king's household and court. There was no useful purpose in his taking the place of so many others, and all the reasons in the world for him to avoid going. To be noticed now was to be in danger. If a man went to the king's parliament and spoke in any manner against the interests of the king's friends, he risked his life.

The bishop was up and waiting when they reached the palace, and they were shown in together. He sat at a table, with a soft woollen cap on his head, a great gown trimmed with fur, and warm, high boots. At his eyes were his spectacles, as usual, which he drew away as they entered. He smiled genially at them both, but Baldwin was sure that there was a hint of steel in his eyes as well.

'Sir Baldwin – I had hoped to hear from you sooner than this. Have you told Simon about our little problem?'

'I think I intimated that I would report as soon as I had something *to* report,' Baldwin said firmly. 'There was all too little until last night.'

'Really? And what happened last night?'

'The watchman who discovered the body of the messenger had also found the body of another man only the previous night. This victim was a worker in bone and antler, and was murdered on his way home after an evening in the tavern.'

'A common enough occurrence, sadly,' the bishop observed. 'Now, about the messenger?'

'He died the night after the other man. That is too much of a coincidence,' Baldwin stated. 'They were both murdered within a few yards of each other. And a short while later, during the day following the messenger's murder, a man climbed into Master Richard de Langatre's house, killed his servant and tried to kill him too.'

'I believe I have been told of this matter. Brother Robert has brought the case to my attention, and I am inclined to advise the sheriff that Langatre is in holy orders.'

'The sheriff seems dead set on having him taken to the king at the earliest opportunity,' Baldwin observed.

'A sheriff is a sheriff,' Stapledon noted; there was a trace of sudden steel in his voice as he added, 'but a bishop is a lord. I have jurisdiction over this man.'

'I am convinced that he is innocent,' Baldwin said. 'I even discovered traces which showed a man had been in his sleeping chamber after the attack.'

Suddenly Baldwin felt as though the air had left his lungs. A strange light-headedness assailed him as he realised what he had just said, and what he had failed to do.

Fortunately, the bishop had not noticed his brief abstraction. He continued, 'Sir Baldwin, I am not worried in the remotest by these two others. The dead antler carver and this fellow Langatre . . .'

'And Langatre's dead servant,' Baldwin reminded him.

'Yes, him too. They are of secondary importance. The crucial matter which should be at the forefront of your mind is the singular murder of the messenger and the theft of my note. You *must* find that roll. It is vital . . . I cannot emphasise enough just how important it is. If news of it were to become common knowledge . . .' He picked at a splinter on the table before him. 'You cannot understand how crucial this thing truly is.'

'Perhaps you should tell us, then, so we can assess its significance for ourselves,' Baldwin said.

The bishop looked at him for a long moment, but then shook his head. 'It is a matter of the highest national importance. I think it's best that the information is not shared.'

'Someone already shares it,' Baldwin said coolly.

'Perhaps.'

'Have you heard from anyone about paying a reward for its return? A ransom?'

'For the note? No.'

'No. Not for the note. For something else you told the man. Something so secret you did not wish to put it in writing,' Baldwin said.

The bishop was clearly shocked by the question. 'Why in God's name . . .'

'The messenger was tortured, I believe, and the only reason could have been to learn something. They could open his pouch with ease. What would they torture the man for? Clearly if he had some knowledge they desired. Or another message. Which was it, bishop?'

Stapledon opened his mouth, but then closed it again and raised his spectacles to his nose. He peered at a paper before him as though trying to concentrate, then shook his head. 'No. It would not be safe for you to know what I put there.'

'Bishop, soon it is very possible many people will know what it is you told this man,' Baldwin said. 'If you tell us now, though, we may be able to guess who could have exhibited enough interest in it to be willing to kill a king's messenger. Unless you tell us, I think it extremely unlikely that we shall be able to find your note, or the man who learned what was in it and the messenger's mind.'

'He swore he would tell no one,' the bishop said. He was not meeting Baldwin's eye, but instead stared off over Baldwin's shoulder as though at a tapestry hanging on the wall.

'Bishop, have you ever seen a man being tortured?' Baldwin rasped. 'He will tell anything to stop the pain. And if a man is shown that his torturer will put him to exquisite agony, and still kill him, even the weakest will choose a swift death without much pain over the alternative. He lost two fingers. What more would you expect of him?'

Bishop Stapledon looked at him again. He gave a slow nod.

'Very well, Sir Baldwin. I shall take you at your word. I was asked to advise on some matters a little while ago. One such matter was the likely threat from Mortimer while he lives abroad.'

'The man has escaped barely with his life,' Baldwin commented. Simon looked puzzled, so he explained briefly, 'Lord Mortimer was the man who escaped from the Tower of London last year. He was one of the leaders of the Lords Marcher who lifted their standards against the king and his allics.'

'He is a greedy, dangerous warrior,' Stapledon said. 'Crafty and sly. He has already made one attempt upon the king's life. Did you know? Only a year ago a man was captured in London – he had been paid by Mortimer to assassinate the king! And there have been other attempts on the king's life, and those of his friends, since then, too. This is not an isolated incident.'

'What of it? If a man is captured trying to kill the king, he will be caught and killed,' Baldwin said.

'But what if the enemy is within his own orbit? What if the person whom he should fear most of all is actually nearer to him than any other?'

Baldwin shot a look at Simon, who returned his glance with an expression of happy incomprehension.

For Baldwin the bishop's words could mean only one thing: that the bishop had at last realised, along with most of the population of the country, that Despenser was a malign influence at the heart of government. With the power that Stapledon held, surely there could be some means of removing Despenser before he caused any more hardship to the people of the realm.

'Yes. I fear that the king is in great danger,' Stapledon finished. 'His wife is too untrustworthy.'

Baldwin felt the breath leave his body in a great gasp of horror. He stared at the bishop dumbfounded.

Stapledon continued thoughtfully. 'There are many who mistrust her. I have myself been anxious about her for some while, especially since that nonsensical affair over Saint Sardos in the summer. The French are trying to provoke us. The matter could have grown much more dangerous. Fortunately, cooler counsel prevailed, but we cannot be assured that it will again in future. I have already had to propose that the queen's household should be disbanded, and all her French friends have been arrested and are held, but she can still write to her brother. Who can tell what sort of dangerous information she may provide? Perhaps her brother might decide to come and support Mortimer in an attack on our country? If he did, what could we do to protect ourselves against his host? And if he was being warned in advance of our lack of defences in different parts of the realm, that would itself be of signal benefit to him. Thus I advised the king in my message. And in addition I advised him, through the sealed lips of the messenger, to put his mind most boldly to the idea of an annulment of his marriage.'

'You suggested that?' Simon blurted. 'But what good could that do? The king and she both made their vows before God!'

'Simon, you have no understanding of international business,' the bishop snapped. He was himself most concerned, Baldwin saw, and biting the head off another man was a simple means of assuaging his own feeling of guilt at having exposed himself so gravely.

'But I do,' Baldwin said. 'So, this must mean that you have a spy who can keep an eye on the queen at all times, so that when she begins to write a letter there is someone there to read it, or who can open it and read it later, perhaps?'

'I do not know, nor do I care, what procedures have been imposed upon her,' the bishop said. 'All I do care about is that the message I sent to his majesty remains entirely confidential and secret! It must never become exposed to all!'

It was some while later that Baldwin realised that the bishop had never admitted whether the message he was so concerned about was the one in the messenger's mind, or the one put in his hand in writing.

Chapter Twenty-Six

Exeter Castle

The sheriff was keen to fetch his horse and go for a ride when he was distracted by a guard.

'Yes? What is it?' he demanded testily.

'There is a man here to see you from the cathedral, sir.'

'What of it? Tell him to be here again later when I may be able to see him for a little while. I am busy.'

'I do not wish to wait, Sheriff, not when I can see you right away,' Robert Busse said firmly.

The sheriff groaned inwardly. He didn't know this old man from the cathedral, but he recognised the type all too well: he looked the sort who would consider any necessary restrictions of the church's powers as a personal affront. There were all too many of them about the city. When a murderer ran from the scene of his offence and into the cathedral close, the men there would close ranks and do anything in their power to obstruct the city's men in their attempts to arrest him. Even though, by harbouring a murderer in their midst, they were risking their own lives as well as those of all the men around them. It was lunacy, in his mind, to allow such ridiculous abstract demarcations as borders of cathedral responsibility compared with those of the city, when the result was that known felons could evade justice. Bloody sanctuary! It was a mad way to organise things, and gave people an escape when they had committed the most outrageous crimes.

Not only menfolk from the city made use of the church to escape their rightful punishments, either. Christ in chains! It was only a little while ago that one of the canons from the cathedral, that thieving scrote John Dyrewyn, broke into a painter's house and stole five pounds' worth of goods. Not because he was owed money or anything, but because he was a thief. No better than a common draw-latch. He was seen, the crime was witnessed, and yet there was nothing the city could do to bring him to justice because, oh dear, the man was a canon, and therefore answerable only to the Church court. And you knew what sort of judgement he'd get from his own kind.

Then there was that foul, venal piece of dog-turd, the Rector of St Ive. He kidnapped the wife of John de Thorntone and robbed him as well, adding simple theft to the brutality of his treatment of the woman. And he blankly refused to return his ill-gotten gains or apologise to the lady. Sweet Jesus, you couldn't invent some of the crimes these supposedly 'godly' men were guilty of.

The memory of all these past offences, and more, made his tone chill. 'I am very busy just now.'

'Ah yes. Going hunting?' Busse said sarcastically. 'You have a man of mine in gaol for no reason, and you are going to leave him there just because you wish to enjoy a good day's hunting? I scarcely think that to be honourable behaviour for a Christian.'

The sheriff bridled. 'You suggest that I am holding someone unfairly? Let me tell you . . .'

'You have a member of the Holy Catholic Church held in your gaol. That itself is illegal, for you took him without informing my lord bishop. He is aware now, and may seek damages from you.'

'You will not threaten me, Brother. Are you from the cathedral? I do not recognise you.'

'I am Abbot of Tavistock, Sheriff,' Busse said with as much pomposity and presumption as he could manage. It was shortly to become true, anyway, he told himself. And to console the twinges of guilt still further, he reminded himself that he may be telling a technical untruth, but it was in order to release one of God's clerks, and that could not be wrong. The greater good demanded that he did so. 'As such I have responsibility for God's flock.'

'I am sheriff, and I have a writ from the king himself demanding that all those who practise necromancy be arrested and sent to him.'

'Then why have you taken Langatre?'

'Because, Abbot, I . . .' Sheriff Matthew stopped. There was a glint in Brother Robert's eye that he didn't like. It was like the glint of steel in a bush at the side of a road: warning of an unexpected ambush. He quickly recovered himself and his conviction. 'Because he is known to practise magic, and is thought to have murdered his servant. You in the church may have a different view on such matters, but, for me, to commit man-slaughter is a crime – and I don't care whether his servant answered him back or not. If he was guilty of something, his master should have brought him to his own tithing, not wrung his neck like a chicken.'

'If I thought he was guilty, I would bring him to you myself,' Busse said with asperity. 'I am not considered an easy judge. It was only two years ago I had a man hanged for stealing oxen.'

The sheriff's eyes narrowed. He recalled that case. The judge at the time had overstepped his authority, having a man sent to the gallows without referring the matter to his local coroner. Even the Church was supposed to have the approval of a coroner before execution, and the coroner should always be invited to be present at the hanging to ensure that it was legal. In that case the justice was remarkable for its swiftness. The church did not approve of people who took its own goods, no matter how assiduously they would protect those who stole from others. Hypocrites!

'David de Cornilii? I remember that. I seem to recall that the judge had to be reprimanded for his decisions. Was it not that same judge who had a man's ears cut off for a petty offence?'

'Those tales are vastly overblown. But I am not considered to be a gentle, mild fellow when it comes to criminals. I am known to be enthusiastic when it comes to punishing those who merit it. This man, however, is innocent. I know him personally.'

'Then you may speak for him in the king's court when he comes before the justices,' Sir Matthew said dismissively, and would have continued on his way, but Busse stepped nearer, blocking his path.

'Langatre is a good man who has been of great use to me. I think he will be again. He is not guilty of any *maleficia*, but rather has saved people from the effects of them. And you should know, Sheriff, that he can see into a man's future.'

'What of it?' Sheriff Matthew grinned. 'You going to tell me that I need his help now?'

Busse did not blink. 'I spoke to him last night, Sheriff, in your gaol.

I wanted to consult him about my future, but the spirits and demons who aid him needed to tell him about the dangers to others. I have been at risk in my life, but there is nothing in my immediate future that could put me in danger . . . whereas, Sheriff, you are in great, mortal peril even as we speak.'

The sheriff tried to respond, but although his mouth opened, no words would come. There was a deep sincerity in Brother Robert's eyes, and the sheriff knew he had much to fear always. Sheriffs were never popular, and had never been held in more contempt than they were now. There were always those who objected to the way that men like Sir Matthew lined their purses through demands for cash in order to swing a court judgment one way or another, and victims would complain bitterly when they saw convicted criminals released in exchange for a small contribution. Yes, there were always those who sought to bring retribution to a sheriff. Not to mention the other matter. He was aware of a curious sensation, as though he had a lump in his belly. A lump of lead.

Busse watched him closely, and then nodded. 'You know, don't you? You know that your life is in peril even as we stand here debating the future of this young idiot Langatre. And yet while you hold him, he will not explain to you how he might help you. You are punishing unnecessarily the only man who might save you.'

Exeter City

Robinet woke with his head less painful than it had been since the attack. For the first time he felt as though he could eat something almost as soon as he awoke, rather than suffering the queasiness which had afflicted him yesterday.

Walter was not about yet, so Robinet lay back under his thick blanket. He put one hand behind his head, but incautiously allowed the other to fall onto the blanket itself, and winced. It was always the same: when the weather was cold, a man's blanket would be covered with a thin layer of moisture in the morning, just like the dew on the grass in summertime. He wiped his hand on the bundle of clothes under his head.

No, he couldn't lie here all day. He had work to do. Rising, he dressed quickly and walked to the pot dangling over the fire.

Yesterday Walter had muttered about the quality of his latest wood, and Newt could see why as soon as he put his head over the fire – Walter had run out of good burning wood, his oak and beech, and this birch was foul. It burned with an acrid stench that caught in a man's throat and lungs, and Newt was forced to slam his eyes closed and turn away as it seared them.

The bowl's handle was hot, so he took a fold of his robe to carry it away, and sat on a stool to eat a bowlful of the pottage. At least the smoke hadn't made that too foul.

'Up, eh?' Walter said when he walked in a short time later.

Newt had already finished his first bowl and was sitting nursing a second, feeling the food slipping down his gullet and warming him. It was one of those rare pleasures, this sensation of heat as a man ate. 'Where have you been?'

'Out seeing if I could learn more than you. I don't know if I have succeeded,' the older man admitted, leaning against a wall. Over the years, he had gradually saved enough money for stools and a bench, but he had spent much of his early life as a poor churl living without such luxuries, and he had grown accustomed to standing. Now, even though he had the items about his room to enable him to sit, he still preferred to stand. There was a sense in him that to sit was to be more of a target, and he had no desire to be that. No, it was better that he should stand and be ready to fly or attack in a moment.

'Where have you been?'

It was easy to see how Robinet was affected by James's killing. Robinet was so easy to read, it was astonishing. Of course, that was how he got himself into trouble, because he was such a transparent fellow. The damned fool. Others would have been much more circumspect, but not him. Even here, in the dim light of the house, Walter could see Newt's pallor. Perhaps it was in part the effect of his ordeal, when he was knocked down so violently. Some men would keep their wounds better than others, it was true, but Walter reckoned it was nothing to do with that. No. It was James's death.

The trouble was, Newt had spent so many years wishing to repay the debt. James had hurt him badly. But since the two had bumped into each other in the High Street, Walter had seen a change come over his old friend. Suddenly Robinet had grown less colicky and pinched. It was as though meeting James had brought back to his mind what sort of man he really was, and all that jealousy and vengefulness had gone, to be replaced by an easiness in the companionship of an old friend. Newt had rediscovered such a one, only to have him stolen away in a moment, for a reason he could not comprehend.

'I've been to a couple of taverns and alehouses in the last day or so,' he said. 'There's a lad I know, Art, who often knows who could be involved in crimes like James's murder.'

'Whoever killed James wouldn't be there bragging about killing a king's messenger, would he?'

'You'd be surprised how thick some churls can be,' Walter said with a slight grin. 'I've known men do just that. And then they look shocked when they realize you have slipped a knife into their chests for their boasting. I killed a man once who spent all the evening in an alehouse regaling me with stories of how he planned to kill the king. He was going to sit near the roadside and plead for alms like any beggar, and when the king was near enough, leap forward to stab him. As if the king wouldn't have enough men all about him to protect him from some adventurer like that! It was doing him a service, killing him quickly as I did. The cretin would have suffered for days at the hands of the king's torturers else, and died a bad death as traitor to the king. Aye, I did him a favour: a quick and easy death.'

'Did you learn anything?' Newt asked eagerly.

Walter gave an inward sigh. His mate wouldn't listen sometimes. Perhaps Walter shouldn't bother, but Newt ought to realise that James's death was not so bad. It was fairly quick: a cord about the neck, pulled tight in an instant, and suffocation would have brought about a speedy end to his life. Better than many deaths Walter had seen in his life as an assassin.

He shrugged. 'There was no one who admitted to seeing anyone kill him, no. But there are some hints that a man was in the area at the same time as you two. A stranger to the city.'

'Do you know who it was?' Robinet demanded.

'No, but some I've spoken to have said that he seems to be an oddity. Tall, scrawny, pale – does it sound like the one you saw?'

Newt considered for a long while. He had only the vaguest of ideas of the man he'd seen – it had been such a fleeting glimpse . . . and yet, if he were honest, the man he'd seen had appeared shorter, more thickset. Not at all like a slim, tall fellow. 'I suppose if he was seen by a very short man, he might appear tall?'

Walter laughed. 'No! These men I spoke to were sensible enough. They know the difference between tall and short, believe me!'

'How can you be so sure?' Newt asked, stung by his amusement.

'They are thieves. If they noticed this man, whoever he was, they'd have made sure of him. They don't go about robbing a man if he looks as if he's going to thrash them. They can tell at a glance whether he's too big or too strong.'

'If he looked so weakly, why didn't they attack him, then?' Newt wanted to know.

'Because he clearly had little or no money about him. If he had anything, they would have captured him.'

Newt stood. 'Where is he, then?'

'Hold hard! Before you decide to run off and attack him, what will you do?'

'If he's the man who killed James . . .'

'That is the problem, Newt. The "if". You don't know it was him any more than the pope.'

'The pope isn't here in Exeter.'

'Perhaps not, but just because a stranger is down here doesn't mean he killed James.'

Newt sat down again, more heavily. 'Then what should I do?'

'Watch him. The men told me where he is staying, and if we go there and wait, no doubt we'll see something if he was the one.'

'And how will we be able to tell that?' Newt scoffed. 'Look to see whether he's got plenty of blood all over him, or just wait and watch to see whether he's likely to kill someone else?'

Walter turned his full attention on him, and Newt was suddenly aware of him. Those firm eyes were unsettling at the best of times, but just now Newt felt transfixed by that look – it was like being pierced by a lance and pinned to a wall.

'Walter, I did not mean to say . . .' He wasn't sure what he meant, but he was quite sure that this man was too dangerous to upset, and at the moment he felt sure that he had done just that. 'Walter, I am sorry.'

Gradually the intensity of Walter's stare declined, and he nodded.

'That is how we'll know,' he said. 'When I have studied the man, I'll be able to tell you whether he killed James or not. And when we know that, we'll know what to do.'

Robinet agreed effusively. He believed his old comrade. No one would be able to endure that stare for very long. He had himself felt like a rabbit caught in a snare, being watched like that.

But then, he knew that Walter was a professional killer.

Chapter Twenty-Seven

Exeter Castle

Jen was in the bedroom, tidying and shaking out blankets and pillows, when it happened.

Afterwards there was only shock, utter, utter shock, that she could have behaved so, but at the time it was just natural.

She was there, in the bedroom, and she could see the side where Madam Alice slept, all neat, her slim body outlined in the dips and curves of the mattress. The other side was where *he* slept. The impression was broader, with the indentations of a masculine frame, and Jen stood looking down on it for a long while before she did it.

Bending, she put her nose to it, snuffing his strong, musky odour. She started at his pillow, and slowly, teasingly, drew her face down the bed, tormenting herself with the protracted investigation. *That* was where his neck would have lain; *that* where his breast began; *there* would be his upper belly; *here* where his middle belly rested . . . and this, *this* was where his groin lay. She sniffed long and hard, and then merely smelling him wasn't enough and she had to do more. Placing her hands on the mattress reverentially, she allowed her face to touch the linen. She rested it there, feeling the thrill of being there, where he lay naked each night, until the excitement was too much and she had to do more. Rubbing her face in his scent made her quite light-headed, and she almost purred for sheer delight as she moved her cheek up and along like a cat in catmint. It was marvellous.

She climbed onto the bed, her body naturally resting in the outline of her master, eyes closed, dreaming that he was there under her, in her, and then there was a scream.

'What are you doing there?'

Jen leaped from the bed, flustered, flushed, but not scared. 'Mistress, I was cleaning in here.'

'You were resting on my bed, you hussy!' Lady Alice spat.

'I haven't finished,' Jen said haughtily. This woman was soon to be giving up her place. She didn't realise it yet, but her husband had fallen hopelessly in love with Jen. Jen knew it. Perhaps Jen should have been more compassionate, but it was not easy with a woman who was so foolish and didn't give her husband the love he so richly deserved.

'You *are* finished, wench! Fetch your belongings right now, and be gone! I will not have a lazy churl trying to sleep in my bed.'

'It's not yours, it's the sheriff's bed,' Jen said.

Alice was silent a moment, but then the worst imaginable thing happened. She glanced from Jen to the bed with a small frown; her mouth fell open as she took in Jen's disrespectful demeanour, and then she laughed aloud, long and hard.

'You don't! Surely you don't think that my husband could desire you, do you? He is a great man, a knight, sheriff and representative of the king, and you think he could desire you, a scruffy little maid-servant from the back of beyond? Child, you are more stupid than I had thought!'

'I'll finish here, then,' Jen said with determination.

'No. You will go. Now.' All humour had left Alice's face. Instead there was a steely firmness. 'You are not wanted here any more.'

'Your husband won't have me leave him,' Jen said.

'Child, he won't even notice you have gone,' Alice said with conviction.

Jen had ignored that, and carried on with cleaning the bed, and after a few moments Alice had moved. For an instant, Jen thought that Alice would attack her, and she prepared herself to resist and defend herself, but then she realised that Alice had left the room.

It gave her a feeling of satisfaction to know that her mistress had given up the cause and fled the field. Victory here was definitely Jen's. She pulled the pillow from her master's side of the bed and drew it to her nose, inhaling deeply. So that was how his hair smelled: faintly acrid, but with a warmth under it, a little like a dog, she thought. Setting the pillow down, she pummelled it fiercely to make it plump and comfortable. The other pillow received a cursory shake. There was no point making Lady Alice's side welcoming. She wasn't welcome, and that was that. Perhaps she ought to spend more time on

Lady Alice's side, because the poor woman was soon to lose her husband, position, everything, but Jen couldn't bring herself to do it. The crabbed old bitch was as vicious as any harpy from an alehouse, and she didn't deserve any more than she already got. No, let her work on her bed herself if she wanted to. In time, perhaps she would be maidservant to Jen and Sir Matthew ... but Jen would rather have someone kindly and friendly as a maid. Perhaps she could have Sarra as her personal servant? That would be much more fun.

'Hey, you, Jen! What are you doing here?'

It was the master's steward. He stood in the doorway with an anxious frown on his face. Jen smiled at him. 'Making the bed, of course. What does it look like?'

'I don't care what it looks like, wench. You have to gather your things and go. I've already spoken to my lady Alice, and she tells me you are to leave. Get your stuff, or it'll all be burned.'

'I don't think Sir Matthew will be pleased to hear that you've done this,' Jen warned. 'You should be more careful who you listen to.'

'Sir Matthew? Child, I've just seen him. It was him ordered me to have you thrown out. Madam Alice had told him about you, and he wants you to go right away. Come, child, there is nothing for you here.'

Jen gaped, and fought hard, but the tears assaulted her cheeks as the import of the man's words struck home. 'No!' she said, and then louder, '*No!*'

She ran from the room, almost knocking the steward over as she went, down the steep stairs to the ground, and thence into the hall, where she found the sheriff talking with two other men. Hurtling to him, she threw herself at his feet.

'Your wife, she's told me to leave!'

'Get off me, woman! Christ's bones, what is the matter with you? Are you mad?'

'She wants to separate us, Matthew!'

There were few things in the world that scared Sir Matthew. In his life he had entered the lists and won some bouts to go with the many he had lost, but the memory of the buffeting never stopped him from trying again. He had faced the Scottish schiltroms, the mad Welsh, even some of the flower of French chivalry, while serving his lord the king, and he had never flinched. Not even at Bannockburn, when the arrows fell like rain and the men all shrieked as yard-long wands penetrating their mail and leather and piercing them, men and knights together, squealing like hogs in their death throes. No, he had not flinched, and his courage was a matter of pride to him.

But insanity was different. In war, a man could stand with his companions against any foe, safe in the knowledge that all must fall together if so much as one ran. All remained rooted to the spot. Yet just now, he would have fled from the room. There was something so appallingly terrifying about madness.

'Take her away from me and throw her outside.'

'Matthew, my love, what do you mean?'

'Sweet Christ, just get her out of here, will you?' he bawled at his steward, and a man at arms leaped forward to help. The two men gripped her arms and started to pull her towards the door, and yet, although the two were burly enough to control most, she managed somehow to wrest herself away from them, and flung herself at the sheriff once more. He shifted his legs away before she could grab them, but fast as he was, she caught hold of his rich tunic, and held it to her face, then to her throat.

'Please, my darling, don't send me from your side! I only ever wished for all that was good and right for you. Throw over the old harpy – you don't truly love her. It's always been me. I've seen it in your eyes. You love me best. You know that. You mustn't send me off and let her win. Our love will . . .'

'Christ's pain, will you not take this mad bitch away? Must I kill her myself?'

'Don't speak like that, Matthew, my love, my sweeting . . . let me just . . .'

He stood and sprang away from her. It was all the time the steward needed. He and the man at arms caught her arms again, and this time they were not going to let her fly from their grasp. They hauled her off, through the hall's doors and into the yard. There she was pulled and thrown through the gateway into the city of Exeter itself.

'If she tries to come back, you have my permission to kill the sow,' the steward said to the gateman. 'She's mad. Completely mad. If she comes back, run her through.'

But Jen had no intention of running back. She had seen the look in

Matthew's eyes, and she knew it was not love. Fear, yes; incomprehension too. But no love. No reciprocal adoration such as she had so often thought she had seen there before. No, there was only revulsion. A loathing bordering on utter hatred.

Her life was over.

In the hall Sir Matthew wiped at his brow with a sleeve and blew out a long, nervous breath. 'My *God*! As I hope to achieve life eternal, I swear I have never been more worried by a woman than I was then. She was quite insane. Did you see her? Telling me I must throw over my own dear wife for her? Christ Jesus!'

Robert Busse nodded, and glanced at his companion. 'So you see what importance there is in being forearmed? If you make use of Richard Langatre's skills, you will be better able to protect yourself from her. Make no mistake, that woman would need but a little prompting to take after you with a knife. I have seen it before, and I am sure that I will see it again. I only pray it will not be here and with your blood and gore open to the roadside. That would be a tragic end to one who has spent his life in service.'

'Don't overdo it,' Sir Matthew growled. 'I was born three and forty years ago, Brother Abbot, and I can tell when I am being cozened. You! Wizard! Tell me what it is that puts my life in danger.'

'You expect me to summon a demon here, before your eyes? Do you not realise the preparation and effort that must be put into such a conjuration?' Langatre said with feeling. 'Dear God, as I live and breathe, I swear that such a service must be accompanied by the strictest fasting and prayer. Do you think such knowledge as I possess can be called upon at a moment's notice?'

'I thought you fellows could hold a demon in a ring, or have demons change their appearance into the mould of a cat so that they might be with you at all times,' the sheriff asserted, trying to appear casual but quickly surveying the man's ringless fingers.

'Yes. However, I have no cat and, as you observe, no rings either. No, if you wish for my expertise, you will have to give me time to prepare. However, I should have thought that the young woman's outburst just now proves that you already have enemies.'

'One woman? Pah!'

'One woman who enters the city and spreads the malicious story that you were after her fine young body and deflowered her here in the castle would be all that was needed to make a certain kind of youth wish to test himself against you. She would not lack for champions.'

'Sweet Christ!' Sheriff Matthew muttered. It was all too true. 'You seem to have the ability to understand women better than men like me who've been married for years.'

'I am fortunate that many of them wish for the advice that only a man of God like me can give,' Langatre admitted.

'Has my wife been to see you?'

Langatre hesitated only a moment. 'Your wife would have no need of my services, I am sure.'

The sheriff peered at him closely. 'Very well. I am convinced. You are free, but only if you swear that you will deal honourably with me. Understand? If I learn that you have been dishonest, I will have your lying tongue torn out and your throat cut. Clear?'

Exeter City

It was easy to find the place, and Robinet was about to walk to the door when his friend took his arm ungently and drew him away to the farther side of the street.

'Are you absolutely without brains?' he hissed. 'If this is where the murderer is staying, we don't actually want him to know we're here, do we?'

Robinet nodded. 'Er, no. So what are we doing here, then?'

'Watching, old friend. Watching. So that if a man comes here whom we recognise, we can follow him, perhaps knock him down and call the hue and cry to have him attached, or maybe see to it that he never rises again. Whatever strikcs you as the best option at the time, I suppose. Whatever else, though, we want *him*, and that means we have to find him.'

'Yes. Of course.'

It was while he had been a messenger that he had first met Walter. Back then Walter had been a dour, stolid character, with a black expression much of the time, but Newt had early on seen that there was another side to the man. He was entirely trustworthy, for one thing. Under the old king, and this one, he had been unswervingly loyal, and that was more than could be said for most of the king's own household.

They had first met because Walter had been in Winchester, and Newt had been surprised to be sent to him with an urgent message. He found the man in a dark alehouse, a foul, noisome little place with nothing to recommend it, and as soon as the message was delivered Walter had read it and burned it at a nearby candle. Then he stood and left the room without a word. The fact that such a churlish fellow should be in receipt of messages from the king himself made him fascinating to a young *cursor*, and when they next met, this time at the king's household while it was at Eltham, Robinet had been further impressed by the firm, unsmiling man. Others muttered darkly about him, but none dared to speak directly to insult him. There was a certain aura about him that dissuaded men from being too forthright in their criticism.

It was that which had made Robinet feel he ought to befriend the man. That and an aggressive ambition. A man who was so favoured by the king was a man whose friendship was worth fostering. Accordingly Newt sought him out, being so unsubtle in his methods that Walter was instantly on his guard. Then, one morning while walking out, Newt found himself grabbed from behind, a knife held at his throat, and a cold, ferocious voice demanding what he was after.

When he confessed, Walter was quiet for what felt, with that knife at his neck, like a very long time indeed, and then Newt grew aware that the knife was moving. It terrified him for a moment, until he realised that it was not drawing a line across his jugular, but wobbling as the holder laughed silently.

From that moment on, Walter appeared to look on Newt in the same way that a man might view a small pet dog. He was tolerated so long as he never made a mess. Then, as the two aged in the service of the king, Walter's tolerance became a genuine affection, and it was reciprocated. The future Edward II himself once told Newt to be wary, that the man he was befriending was much more dangerous than he could ever know, but Newt was too sure of himself to be warned. He trusted his own judgement, and he had never had cause to regret it. Walter was his closest friend.

Now that the two men were retired from their past occupations, it was interesting to look back on their history. It gave a man more perspective, Newt thought.

Walter was certainly a most dangerous man. If ever a fellow wanted a lethal and resourceful opponent, Walter was the ideal. Newt had no interest in upsetting him or causing him grief, but he had seen others who had succeeded in exactly that, and generally they regretted it. Some of them for only a very short period.

Any king had need of a man like Walter. He was the ultimate control for the king over his population. Completely focused, Walter would ensure that the king's most embarrassing problems were removed. When a man preached treachery, or threatened the king's life in some other way, Walter would see to it that the annoyance was soon eradicated. There was nothing personal in it, and he did not kill all the king's enemies. Often there was no need if the target knew of Walter. Then all he needed to do was make it clear that the king had asked him to speak. That in itself was perfectly adequate for almost all situations and all men. However, there were occasions when more forceful arguments were required, and when they were, Walter was an expert with a dagger. He always said that it took only an inch or two of steel to silence for ever an irritating voice. Newt had no idea how many irritants had been stilled in that way by Walter, but he knew it was many tens over a career that lasted more than twenty years.

When he had been a *cursor*, eating at the king's expense, he had always been well fed. No matter what else happened, the king's messengers had to be given their fill of the best of all viands. They had been good days for him. For them both.

'Now, I am proud of my pottage, but there's no doubt that a little meat sets a man up for the day, is there? And just now, a bit of meat would be good. If there's going to be some knocking about later, we'll need our strength.'

Robinet couldn't argue with that. For all that his belly was filled, he yet felt a little hungry, as though the pottage had been unnourishing, and the thought of a minced beef pie beneath his belt was most attractive.

'One of us will have to stay.'

'Aye. You want the head or the tail?' Walter asked as he flipped a coin.

Chapter Twenty-Eight

Exeter City

It was some little while later that Alice's brother Maurice returned and stood eyeing the dilapidated building over the road with a frown of some perplexity.

If he was not outlaw, he would have already blown his horn and chased after the man, but not in his present situation: that would be suicidal. And yet he wanted to. It was rare that a man witnessed a robbery or murder, and for him, a man of noble birth, to watch and allow a felon to go free was at best galling.

He had been here, hoping to see something of Alice again, when he saw the furtive-looking man stand at the way to the rear of the building. Maurice's attention was taken immediately as the fellow sidled down some stairs which appeared to lead down into the undercroft, only to disappear in the dark.

Maurice was not the only man who had noticed him. Only a short while afterwards he saw another man, cloaked and hooded against the cold, armed with a good staff, move to the top of the stairs and stare down. He descended quickly enough, and Maurice glanced about him, satisfied that the thief – he must be a drawer-latch because from his demeanour he could have had no legitimate business down there – would soon be caught.

For a little while he waited to hear the inevitable sounds of arrest, the blasts of a horn or the hoarse demand for assistance, but to his surprise there was nothing. Instead he saw, after some time had passed, the second man reappear and set off briskly towards an alley.

Maurice watched him for a moment or two, torn between the undercroft and the hurriedly departing man, and then, his interest piqued, he set off after him.

The alley was narrow and dingy, but at least there was less breeze.

In Stepecote Street the wind whistled about a man and drew all heat from his body, or so it seemed. Here in the darkened alley, Maurice felt warmer. The buildings reached out overhead and almost touched, and there were many little corners and narrowings, so he kept losing sight of the man, but then, as he came to a wider stretch, he caught sight of him again a short distance away. The man drew off his cloak and let it drop to the floor. Then he pulled off his surcoat and stared at it as though with revulsion, before balling the cloth and using it to wipe at his arms and feet. He dropped it into the cloak and wrapped it up tightly, before throwing them over into a corner and striding away.

Maurice waited until he was gone, then trotted to the clothing where it lay. He unwrapped the cloak and felt the stickiness of the blood at the same time as his nostrils warned him. Quickly he drew his fingers away.

He could not remain here with that incriminating evidence. Turning, he hurriedly walked back to the street. There, he could not help but notice that there was no shouting or calling. The hue and cry was unaware of the crime.

And then, as he stared about him, he saw another figure come back up the stairs, glance about him and cross the road with slow, pensive steps.

Maurice watched with a frown, then leaned against a wall to watch. He had no idea what was happening here, but he was intrigued enough to risk staying and seeing what happened.

Baldwin and Simon met the coroner a short way from the Palace Gate, and all three turned south towards the great city gate and Will Skinner's house.

His wife was there, sitting on their stool at the table. 'What do you want here again?'

'Where is your husband?' the coroner demanded.

'Fetching food. What do you want with him?'

'We have questions for him. How long will he be?'

'Not long. Not long.'

She was as good as her word because very soon there was the tramp of feet outside, and the door opened. In the doorway stood Will

Skinner, and he shot a look at his wife, then stared at the three men. To Simon it looked as though the older man shrivelled at the sight of them, and he felt a certain sympathy for him. He was old, weary, working ridiculous hours in the attempt to earn some money, and now he was being questioned by three officers as though he was himself a suspect in their enquiry. Which Simon supposed he was, if an unlikely one.

'Skinner,' Baldwin said, 'I want you to tell us again what happened on the night you found the first body.'

'Why? Do you think he lied to us all?' his wife cackled.

'There, Margie, my love, be still,' Will said. He tried to pat her hand, but she snatched it away, her eyes blazing with hatred.

It had been the same every day since that terrible one when he had got home in time to see the walls collapse. Even from the road the heat had been appalling, and he had felt as though his brows were going to be scorched away. It was a scene from hell. Margie had done all she could, running inside to try to rescue the children, because as the fire took hold they could be heard inside, screaming for help. But no one could get near them. By the time Will got there, thank Christ for His mercy, the screams had already been stilled. If he had heard his little children pleading for help and rescue, he wasn't sure that his mind could have coped with the strain.

Just as Margie's hadn't.

'I was there in the lane that night. I often stop there, just to look at my house.' And to pray for my dead children, he added to himself. 'While I was there, I saw the man lying on the ground. I thought he had a great cloth about his neck. It looked like it. But when I approached him, I saw that it was blood. So much blood from one man . . . it was terrible.'

'And no surprise,' his wife added.

'Why would it be no surprise, woman?' the coroner pressed her.

'Because in a place like that, where God could let my little babies burn to death, any man is likely to be murdered. If the sweet innocents were killed, why not an older man whose life is full of sin and corruption?' she wailed, and now she had her arms wrapped about her misshapen torso, and was rocking back and forth, her eyes fixed on the distance – or perhaps the past.

The coroner cleared his throat and, unusually for him, appeared to be struck with shyness in the face of her grief. 'Perhaps that is so,' he allowed. 'But for now, I need to deal with the actual agent of the man's death.'

'I told you before: I saw no one. But I did see that strange thing earlier. That was when I should have gone down the alley, but when that thing became a cat and walked up to me like a demon stalking a soul, I fled. I am sorry, but the thought of standing there with that creature staring at me was too terrifying. That is why I only went down the lane later.'

'So you returned on your rounds,' Baldwin said, listening with a glower of concentration fixed to his face.

'Yes. I knew I had to go there again, and this time when I stood at the top of the alley I saw nothing. The cat was gone, and so was the shape I thought I'd seen. I was very fearful, masters, but I can't afford to lose my wage as watchman. I entered the alley and until I reached my old house there was nothing to make me scared.'

'You told me that the shape and the cat were things you saw on the next night, when you found the body of the king's messenger. Why did you lie?'

'I don't know. I didn't think it mattered that much, and the things were still in my mind all that night, and since then too. It preys on me, sir. I cannot help it, it's just always there. I am scared that some night I'll be there outside my children's death place, and I will be struck down too . . . *oh, God, I wish it might happen soon!*'

He collapsed, his hands going to his face as the tears ran down both cheeks and his voice faltered. Baldwin sucked at his teeth to watch the display of grief. He had known loss himself, and he could feel compassion for a man who had lost so much, but then he caught sight of the man's wife, and had to look away.

The woman's face showed only fierce, brutal glee at her man's suffering.

Exeter Castle

Lady Alice had been feeling rather light-headed and uneasy since the little hussy's departure, although, to be fair, she had been up until late the night before. It was better to think that her sense of subtle dislocation was due to the deprivation of sleep than to the foolish behaviour of one silly chit of a girl.

Yet for all her inward protestations of calmness and the fact that she had not been upset in the least by the servant's sudden display of lunacy, there was a small part of her that felt an unreasonable anxiety.

Lady Alice had floated serenely through life. Nothing that she had ever needed or desired had ever been withheld from her, and she had the knowledge that at all times she need only mention a whim and it would be fulfilled. She was enormously fortunate, and sometimes that sense of good fortune could leave her with this little – well, *doubt*.

She knew full well that she was considered a beauty. The admiring glances of men followed her like the inevitable tribute due a queen, and she was aware of the reaction of men to her features and body without being tempted by any. She was content with her match. No, more than that . . . she could happily state that she was very fond of her lord. And he did all he could for her. She was fully aware of that. He had raised himself from a position of near poverty as a mere rural knight into this post of power and influence by his assiduous political negotiating.

The first rung on the ladder had been his acceptance as a knight of the shire when parliament had met some years ago. At the time she had thought little enough of his sudden elevation, but after his return she had realised how much it could help them. He had been careful and cautious, measuring the influence of others, assessing the strengths and weaknesses of the different groupings, before coming to the conclusion that John of Lancaster was weak and incompetent. He would not challenge the king in any serious manner. No, Lancaster was a petty, jealous man, driven by trivial complaints into a ridiculous corner from which he could not retreat. As soon as he returned from that parliament, her Matthew had told her that he would not support him, but instead would turn his loyalty to the Despensers, father and son, because he thought that they were ruthless enough to command the respect of all.

And so it had come to pass. Whereas the other men in parliament were shown to be cretins or callow, the Despensers soon managed to acquire all authority under the king and with the king's own support. They began their long government of tyranny, taking all that they desired from those who did not give them their full backing, and some of those who were more fulsome in their praise and support were rewarded. As was Sir Matthew.

Lady Alice had no care for politics. Hers was a world of calmness, secluded from the rude work with which men must occupy themselves, although it was true that she was concerned on occasion when she heard of those whom the Despensers had deprived of lands, wealth – or life itself. Yet when she had met Sir Hugh le Despenser, the son, she had been entranced. There was an *aura* about him, a power that filled a room without effort. There, with him, she had been convinced that she was in the presence of a truly great man. Yes, it was easy to see how her husband had been convinced by him.

Soon Hugh le Despenser had noticed Matthew, and then suddenly their lives changed. Rather than being given somewhat demeaning functions, Matthew found himself with serious responsibilities, even finally receiving this post of Sheriff of Devon, with all that that conferred on him. Before that their income was limited, and they were utterly dependent upon the money that they got from their manor, but now all that was changed. They had much more.

But there was an aspect which Alice could not fail to notice: the power made her husband a great deal more attractive to other women.

It was odd. Beforehand men had flirted with her while Matthew watched. Now their roles were reversed. Not that many of them would dare to try to throw themselves at him. If they did, Alice would soon have noticed. But it did leave her feeling . . . what would the word be? Threatened? No, that was too strong. But on edge certainly. After all, she had no children yet, and that lack was the sort of thing that could make a man turn to another. And if he did, and she gave him a child in the place of the woman he had married, then his wife's life could grow unbearable. Especially with a strong-minded man like her Matthew. If he turned against her, she felt he would become a relentless opponent.

But even the lack of a child would not tempt him from her bed. She had received too many proofs of his adoration for her to be fearful of that.

That foolish wench's declaring her love for him had been proof. She had been quite ridiculous, almost demented, throwing herself at his feet as though he had actually professed his love for her. And that was *absolutely* impossible. The notion that he would give himself to a lowly serving maid was risible. Quite insane.

And yet the girl had appeared to be convinced. Totally convinced. As if she really expected Sir Matthew to protect her.

On top of her brother's arriving in town, this was one complication Alice really could live without.

Rob had followed Busse all the way to the castle that morning, and when he saw the brother leave the castle with Langatre he immediately rose and watched the two march down the roadway, across the empty space where no buildings were allowed in case they gave succour to attackers of the castle, and down to the High Street.

Swiftly Rob was up and after them. This was more interesting than sitting back in Dartmouth and cleaning the bailiff's rooms or preparing his meals. Usually by this time of the morning he would be growing bored, wondering where the next diversion would be: whether he could escape the house for a couple of hours and find a game of dice to join. There was always gambling of one sort or another going on in the town. It was the great thing about sailors, he reckoned. Where they went, there was money to be traded for fun. But this was better. Being the eyes and spy of an important local official, that was even more fun.

The two men went along the road as far as Carfoix, and then walked past the cooks' shops and thence westwards down the hill. It surprised him, for he had expected the brother to want to return to the cathedral, but no, they continued down the lanes until they came to a small house in an unremarkable position, and both entered.

He idled a few minutes, walking further down the lane to see what else there was, but it just carried on down to another gate, so far as he could see. He wasn't going all the way down that hill: it was far too steep to want to descend only to have to ascend again later. No, bugger that. Instead he looked about for a good point to stop and watch the place. There was one ideal location, but there was already another man there. And although he made a pretence of idling, he couldn't fool an expert lounger. As Rob watched, he grew certain that the man was staring at the house with grim determination, as though he was expecting to see his wife in there committing an act of adultery.

Rob stood staring at the house for a moment or two, but before long his interest was divided between the house and the man who stood gazing at it with such interest, and soon he reasoned that if anything was to happen in the house, he would see it in the man's eyes anyway, and he gave up any attempt to view both. In preference he settled down in the angle of a house beneath a jetty and devoted himself to watching the stranger.

He had a feeling that this man was to become useful, and he was ready to stay here and consider the fellow for as long as it proved necessary.

The man's wife cackled suddenly, and she aimed a slap at Will's shoulder. 'Perhaps you fool them, but you don't fool *me*!'

'Leave him, woman,' Coroner Richard snapped. 'He is answering our questions.'

'You don't know what to ask, though, do you?' she sneered. 'He knows more than all this! Why don't you ask him what he conceals?' She stood and hobbled painfully from the room, spitting on the floor as she went, turning once at the doorway and staring at her husband for a long period, then saying to no one in particular, 'If you take him, do it and be damned to him! He was ever a poor husband, and now he's nothing!'

'Perhaps she is right. I don't trust you,' Coroner Richard declared when she was gone. 'You are withholding something, I am sure of it.'

Baldwin was less convinced, but when he glanced at the watchman he saw that there was something in his eyes that he did not like. There was a strange attentiveness and cunning there – not at all what he would have expected from a man suffering God alone knew what torments after losing his entire family in a fire. It was almost as though he was using his grief as concealment. 'Well?'

Will had apparently believed his efforts had succeeded already, and now he gave a little start at the tone of sharpness in Baldwin's voice. 'Master?'

'You are keeping something from us, are you not? We need to know what it is that you are holding back, and with the deaths already we have enough reason to take you.'

'There is nothing I can do to help you! I am only the watchman!'

Simon had propped himself against a great timber set into the wall, and now he glanced at Will with a frown. 'The king's messenger lies dead, his messages stolen. It will embarrass our lord bishop if those messages are not recovered. If we wanted, we could have you arrested and taken to the king to be interrogated by his men. If you do not assist us, we may order that.'

Will shook his head with apparent despair. 'How might I help you further?'

'You know something,' the coroner rasped, and now he crossed the room and gripped Will's shoulder. 'Tell us what it is, or as there's a God in heaven, I'll take you to the castle and question you more fully there myself!'

The implication of torture was all too plain, and Will paled. 'I'll tell you all,' he protested. 'Just leave go of my old shoulder, sir knight, I beg! It's sore enough.'

'Come, then. What have you been keeping from us?'

'Look, a man who serves near the South Gate sometimes will learn things that others may miss. I have been in the city for many years, and I remember something from a long time ago, ten or more years. It was when the men of Bristol rebelled against their tallage – you recall?'

'Aye.' The coroner nodded. 'The city mutinied against the king's lawful taxes, and he had to lay siege to the city until they submitted.'

'Yes. Many were anxious at that time. And even down here in Exeter there were men who said that we should avoid paying the tallage. The rates were set so high. Well, there was one man in particular, Piers de Caen, who said that he rejected them, and he began to seek support among the people to join with him and refuse to pay. Except a short while after he made his feelings known, he was killed.'

'What of it? Men are killed all the time,' Baldwin said.

Will's head was hanging slightly. He looked at Baldwin from beneath lowered brows. 'There was a man came into the city at about that time. He was thickset, strong, powerful-looking. He made me nervous just to see him. And as soon as Piers died, he left the city again.'

Simon grunted and sucked his teeth with dissatisfaction. 'So a man was here when another died? How many others were there?'

Baldwin held up his hand. 'You are saying that this fellow killed Piers? Was there ever any proof of it?'

'Piers's wife. She saw the man. She denounced him before the world, told the men of the hue and cry, told the coroner and the sheriff ... but he was released. It was said that he was a king's man. He'd been sent to leave a message for all those who disobeyed the king's lawful commands.'

Baldwin gave a sidelong grin. 'You think that the king of England can command the death of any man he wishes on a whim? That he has men who will obey his every little desire?'

'Ask the sheriff. See what he says,' Will said seriously. 'The man's name was Walter. Walter of Hanlegh.'

'Aye, and what of it now?' the coroner asked with frank bewilderment.

'It is said that he is back here again. He's been seen in the city. He's a killer, Coroner, and if he killed Piers, perhaps he may have killed again.'

Chapter Twenty-Nine

Exeter City

'I do not care for that man. I don't think we can trust a word he says. D'you think he's told us the whole truth? I feel sure he is holding something back,' the coroner grunted as the men walked up South Gate Street towards Carfoix.

'Perhaps he is,' Baldwin conceded, 'but after the suffering he has gone through, I am scarcely surprised. And look upon it in this way: if you were married to a woman who blamed you for her own pain and the destruction of her body, as well as the deaths of her children, and were asked questions before her, what would you sound like? I rather think that if my own wife were to treat me with such open contempt and hatred, I should also appear to be concealing something. I should think that the poor fellow conceals much. He is too distraught to be rational.'

'This Walter of Hanlegh could be worth finding, none the less,' Baldwin said. 'Although what he could want to kill a king's messenger for, let alone a mere comb-maker, is beyond me.'

Simon nodded, but his eyes were narrowed as he considered. 'Yes. But if this Walter is a genuine killer, perhaps the man Mucheton merely offered some sort of insult? He could have done so entirely unwittingly, but still have given grave offence.'

'Eh?' The concept of subtle affront was alien to the forthright coroner.

Baldwin nodded, considering. He was about to comment when they all heard the shouting and horns. 'Come! That sounds like the hue and cry!'

The three hurried their pace, and soon they were trotting down the hill towards the source of the noise.

'Not this place again!' Baldwin breathed.

'You know it?' Simon asked.

'It is where the necromancer was attacked and his servant killed,' Baldwin said heavily. 'It is a place of ill-repute.'

Simon grunted. 'And here's a lad of ill-repute.'

'Bailiff—'

'Speak up, boy!'

'No, I—'

'I said speak up! Good God, boy, I can't hear a word you say over this row.'

Rob looked at him, and then bawled: 'There's a man up there who was watching this place when I got here. He looked really upset about . . .'

'Don't shout, Rob, you'll scare him away!' Simon hissed, his eyes over Rob's shoulder as he studied the crowds. 'Point him out to me.'

The noise was appalling, and it smothered the disturbance as Simon pushed his way through the crowd, whistling a little tune he had heard a while before in a tavern, his hands in his belt, until he was at the opposite side of the street. There he instantly saw the man Rob had told of.

He was clad in well-worn garments, a thick-set fellow who had lived long in that face. Simon drew down the corners of his mouth. The man was fit, but Simon reckoned he would have the advantage of some decades. With that conviction, he approached the man cautiously and slowly, stepping briskly but quietly until he was only a matter of yards from him.

It was plain as a pikestaff that the man was watching the house. He gazed at it almost hungrily, and as the crowds in front of him moved he swayed with them, his head straining to stretch his neck so that he might peer over their heads. With his height, there was little enough need, Simon thought privately.

Making a decision, he went to the man's side. 'What's happened in there?'

'Another dead man, so I'm told.'

'Really? Is that why you were watching the place so carefully?'

The man turned and considered him. 'There are many watching it now.'

'Yes,' Simon agreed reasonably. 'But you were here long beforehand, weren't you?'

The man moved abruptly. If Simon hadn't expected it, he might have succeeded in making his escape, but if there was one activity at which Simon did not excel it was running, and so as soon as his quarry tried to bolt, Simon jumped. He caught the man's neck with one hand, and gripped his tunic, while the other grabbed him by the belt.

What Simon lacked as a runner, he more than made up for in wrestling, and now he swung hard, pulling the man over his hip and throwing him to the ground. 'Good! Now, let's start again, shall we?'

Jen was inconsolable with grief. She didn't know what time it was. There was no meaningful passage for her: all she knew was that she was no longer in the castle which she had come to look upon as her home, and that the man whom she had adored from the first moment of setting eyes on him detested her. The ugly old cow he had married must have poisoned him against her.

The roads were quiet, but she was oblivious. Her despair was so acute, she would not have noticed if the road were paved with burning coals. There was nothing which could ever ease her torment. Not now – not ever. Her life was a long stretch of grey misery without redemption. Nothing could ever give her joy again.

When Busse and Langatre had entered the house, they strode straight through to the main hall.

'Very well – tell me! What was that all about?' Busse demanded as soon as they were inside the door.

'I couldn't tell you in the street, Brother,' Langatre said. 'When you asked me, we were inside the castle still, and it would have been dangerous to talk. No, I was anxious when I heard the sheriff ask whether his own wife had visited me, because she had – several times.'

'Why?' Busse asked with the eagerness of a man to whom an entire sex was a mystery.

'She was anguished, for her husband and she have no children,' Langatre admitted reluctantly. 'She came to ask me whether she ever would bear children, and I had to tell her that I thought she would not. It is a sad problem, but the conjuration was entirely convincing to me, as a professional. She will have none.'

'Why would that make you so anxious?'

'She did not want her husband to hear of her visits to me. If he were to learn, just think how he might react. Knowing that she was barren, and learning that she'd been here and had told me about their problems ... it is not the sort of news which a man would appreciate, much less when it means a man's wife has been consulting a known magician – especially just *now*. You have heard of this suspected conjuration with the intention of harming our own noble king?'

'Sweet Christ on the Cross!' Busse said, crossing himself hurriedly.

'Yes. So we should be cautious, Brother. I must not see her again. Perhaps I could send a message to her, explaining, but I do not know how.'

'By sending her a note, of course!'

'And who would open it? Probably her husband or his steward!' Langatre said scathingly.

Busse nodded distractedly. He could quite see that this was a matter of some delicacy. A mistake, and thereby letting her husband know her business, would inevitably lead to recriminations. And Busse had no intention of losing Langatre – not when he was still so useful. 'Give me writing tools. I shall write to her and have a priest deliver the note to her alone. That will be best.'

'Of course. No one would open a letter sent from a priest,' Langatre agreed with delight. He fetched a small square of parchment and a quill and ink, and watched as Busse scrawled laboriously. Then, when it was done, Busse melted some wax from a candle and thrust his ring into it to seal the note. He went to the door and walked the short distance to the church of St John Bow. Soon he was back again.

Langatre spun on his heel, startled by Busse's abrupt return.

'What is it, man? Do you think to be taken again when I have only just had you released?' Busse said acidly.

'Brother, I have been attacked in here, my servant murdered, and then I have been arrested for harming him, and all the while the killer stood upstairs in my chamber. I am nervous in the place!'

'Perhaps so, but you have work to do!' Busse snapped. 'I cannot afford to be here too long. I must return to the abbey and make sure that my rival doesn't steal my supporters away from me by the use of heavy bribery or threats. All the time you stand here gazing around like a lovesick owl, you are wasting mine. Get on with it!'

Langatre nodded disconsolately. There was a large cauldron in the corner of the room, and he went to fetch it. The brazier was gone out, of course, and he must take scorched cloth and flint to start another fire, blowing hard to light it. Soon he had a spark caught on the cloth, and could set it amongst some light tinder: feathers and hay. These he placed in the brazier, and as the flames sparked and crackled he began to set twigs about them, and then reached for his little pail of coals. 'Oh!'

'What now?'

'My pail's empty. I need more charcoal.'

'Good God! Then get it, man!' Busse barked.

Langatre set his jaw, but did as he was bid. The coals were down in the alley that ran from the street to the garden, and he took the pail with him as he left the room, walked into the street and thence to the alley.

It was always dark here, but today it felt very close, as though the weather was about to change. A strange smell reached him, and he twisted his features at the odour. Something was different – odd.

The little sack of charcoals sat deep in the alley, away from the wet, and he lifted it and poured the contents into his pail, cursing quietly as some coals missed the pail and fell to the gound. One or two toppled over the edge and slipped down to the entrance to the undercroft. There they splashed in the rainwater by the door.

He peered down, tutting to himself. No doubt the new lodger there would complain if he stood in Richard's discarded waste. Some tenants about here were astonishingly fussy, and would moan to the landlord at the slightest infraction of whatever rules they felt supreme. He considered, then tutted once more. Carrying the pail to the top of the stairs, he walked down, collected the offending coals from the strangely viscous pool, and carried them up. He set them in the pail and picked it up, wiping his hand on his gown as he walked to his door and entered.

The little fire was burning merrily, and he began to set more dry sticks on it, building up the pile before setting a ring of coals about it, putting more and more on top until he had a small, smoking pyramid. Then he began to blow at it until the coals spat and gleamed.

Busse had been wandering about the room as he prepared his fire, but now, as Langatre stood again, he peered at him. 'What's that?'

'I dropped some coals,' Langatre said absently. 'I had to pick them up, so I wiped my hand. Why?'

'What were they lying in?'

'Just some rainwater.'

'*Red* rainwater?'

Busse led the way. Soon they were in the street, and Busse saw the steps at the front of the alley. He approached them nervously, and stood studying them before tentatively putting his foot on the top step and descending.

It was cool down here, and well shaded, and soon he found that the noise of the street was left behind him. The steps were good sandstone, moving but little with his weight, and he was soon at the bottom. Here there was a pool of liquid, which in the dark was merely a puddle. It had no apparent colour, and it could easily have been water, were it not for its apparent thickness and the odour of tin. It seemed to run from beneath the door, a good, board door to the right, that had a latch. He set his thumb to the latch and pushed.

He burst from the undercroft like a rabbit before ferrets, and it was his sudden appearance which caused the first ripples of delicious interest through the people in the street.

'You all right, Brother?' a man asked, and Busse stared at him wildly.

'Get away from me!'

'You look like you've seen a ghost,' another said, and there was a little laughter, but it was stilled when someone noticed his hands.

'Have you cut yourself?'

'That's blood!'

Busse felt his heart pounding like a wild deer's at the hounds' approach. He was distraught, confused, desperate, uncertain what to do for the best. He should have taken a horn and blown the hue and cry, bellowed for men . . . but the first idea to come into his head was to fly from here. He couldn't now. He'd been seen, and even as thoughts of flight came to him, he felt hands grip his rough tunic. 'Release me!'

Where was Richard de Langatre? Where had he gone?

'Not until we've seen what's in there,' someone said, and then there was a nasty chuckle from someone. 'We don't believe in benefit of clergy here, Brother. If you've killed an Exonian, you may just fall down a ladder or something on the way to the gaol.'

Others were sent inside as he spoke, and amidst the muttering Busse heard some cries, and he tried to struggle free at the noise. He had to get away!

They had found the body!

Chapter Thirty

Exeter City

Sir Richard de Welles and Baldwin saw Busse pulling this way and that, and although the coroner wore a happy smile on his face at the sight, he remonstrated gruffly with the men who held him.

'What is this, eh? A man of the cloth being held by you horny-handed peasants? Eh? Have you no respect for the Church? You should release him at once.'

'He was in there, Coroner. We saw him come out just a few moments before, and there's a dead man inside.'

'What? Is it murder?'

The man who had spoken glanced around at his peers, but it was clear that none had been inside to see whether it was murder or not.

But Busse knew. 'It was murder, Coroner. His throat has been opened from one side to the other.'

'What is this, Brother Robert?' Baldwin asked. 'Have you had a part in a murder?'

'It's nothing to do with me! I had no part. I was with the sheriff until a very few moments ago. I came back here with Langatre, and we found this . . . body when we came here.'

'A body in Langatre's house?'

'In the undercroft. We saw that the door to it was open, and there was a pool outside . . . blood, Keeper. Blood in a puddle like rainwater. It had drained from his body . . . Good God! I hope never to see a sight like that again.'

'He's lying!' One of Busse's captors had no doubts. 'He bolted from there like a quarrel from a bow.'

'If he is telling the truth and the man in there was killed by having his throat cut,' Baldwin said mildly, 'then God must have performed a miracle indeed.'

'Eh?'

Baldwin stepped nearer, and gestured with a hand that encompassed Busse's torso. 'To have cut his throat and not been smothered in the fellow's blood.'

The men gripping Busse gradually allowed their hold to loosen. It was clearly true. Although Busse's sandalled feet showed signs of blood, there was none on his body or his hands. 'Sorry, Brother.'

'You are forgiven, friends. You had no reason to consider me innocent,' Busse said, although it was partly through clenched teeth. However, that was less from anger than from an urgent need to stop his teeth from chattering. The sight of the body had shocked him more than he could say.

Baldwin beckoned the coroner. 'Let us go and view this latest body.' He looked about him for Simon, but he reasoned that Simon was never at his best in the presence of sudden violent death, and the bailiff would probably prefer to be saved studying yet another. He would no doubt return shortly.

'Yes,' Coroner Richard agreed, but he shot a look at the miserable monk. 'Don't go anywhere until we're back, though, Brother. Wait for us here, eh?'

Busse gave a dejected nod as the two men made their way to Langatre's house.

Although the front door gave onto Langatre's own little hall and the stairs which led up to the small second storey, there was a passageway to the left side of the property. Originally Baldwin had assumed that this must lead to the garden at the back, but now he realised that there was another staircase here that led to the basement beneath the house. He stepped to it, and saw that there was indeed a series of stone steps leading down below the main house. And on all the steps there was the unmistakable sign of bloody footprints. Peering down it was easy to see where they came from. At the bottom, as Busse had said, there was a thick pool of blood.

Descending, Baldwin mused that this must be how hell itself smelled. There was a strong, tinny odour from all the blood, but as he came to the rough elm boards of the door at the bottom, that was overwhelmed by the stench from within. Brimstone, sickly decaying foulness, all with the cloying, repellent tang of death. He wanted to pull a fold of his tunic over his mouth to protect himself from infection, for all knew that bad air, *malaria*, could kill, but it was impractical to try that down here. Instead he took a deep breath before entering, hoping to be able to take in less air within the room, and carefully stepped over the blood.

It was dark. Even with the candles set about the place at different vantage points, it was still gloomy. There were two windows at the front of the building, but the sun was at the rear of the house, and there was no ingress for light from that direction. Instead the two front windows served to provide all light and air. They were inadequate.

'Christ's balls, Keeper, I've been in brighter caverns!' the coroner rumbled. 'Fetch more light in here!'

There were four men in there, all standing about the body on the floor, which was only a matter of two feet or so from the door. When the owner of house had built it, the undercroft had been constructed with a drain from the staircase leading away from the place. Otherwise water could have flowed into the undercroft from the road whenever there was a heavy downpour. That was why the blood had flowed in a stream from the body to lie outside at the bottom of the stairs. Baldwin could see that, and take it in as he crossed the threshold, but then he was at the body and squatting to one side so that as much light as possible from the doorway could fall on the corpse.

'Langatre,' he said coldly.

'I was here with Busse, but he bolted,' Langatre said. He was reserved, but Baldwin had seen many men so in the presence of sudden death.

Clearly this had been an older man. He was pale, a little thin, but powerful in appearance. His arms had been strong, and his jaw jutted with an obstinate look. Baldwin was not certain, especially in this light, but he reckoned the man must have been at least five-and-fifty. His eyes were wide – with shock, perhaps? – and the gaping wound where his throat should have been was foul. Blood had sprayed all over the room, smothering the table top in front of the door, spattering the ceiling . . . and yet there was nothing on the door itself or the wall behind Baldwin. There was a beam of oak sitting propped at the wall, and Baldwin saw that this was used to lock the door. He wondered whether this man could have opened the door to someone he knew, turned his back to lead the man inside, and been grabbed from behind and slashed with a knife. That would clearly explain the wide pattern of blood: the killer had the victim's forehead in his hand, pulling back his head and so stretching his neck. When cut, the vessels all gaped and gushed like fountains.

Baldwin had seen enough men die to know that this one would have had no chance to protect himself. Once the knife had severed his veins, he would have been unconscious in moments.

'Someone in here has been toying with sorcery,' Langatre said.

'Why do you say that?' Coroner Richard asked.

'These tools. Look at it all.'

Baldwin was peering at the table. 'What was all this wax for, I wonder.'

Langatre didn't answer. His mind, like Baldwin's, was fixed on the attempt to murder the king by necromancy.

The room was filled with strange items. Baldwin saw some implements lined up on a table; a robe which had curious symbols stitched onto it, similar to Langatre's upstairs.

Langatre jerked his head. 'I think we may have solved one murder, at least.'

The coroner was still standing and studying the body, hands on hips, as Baldwin crossed the room and gazed down at the thing on the table. 'Eh?'

'Master Langatre has found a finger,' Baldwin said.

Simon did not think that his captive merited much concern. After allowing the fellow to stand, and dusting down his own jacket, which had become spattered with mud and dirt from the ground, he sniffed. 'Who are you?'

The man met his look with a fixed consideration, then threw a look back towards the house over the way. Eventually he grunted, 'I am called Robinet of Newington. Friends call me Newt. Who are you?'

'I am a bailiff. Why were you watching that place?'

'You're a city bailiff? You don't look like one.'

'No, I'm not from the city. Why were you watching it?'

With a quick glance about them, as though anxious, he said, 'If you want to talk, why not do it in more comfort? Let's find a tavern or . . .'

'Ah, no, friend Newt. This will do us fine, unless you want to talk in the gaol.'

Simon found he was being submitted to a minute inspection, from his worn and stained boots to his soft felt hat. 'You threaten me with that before you know anything about me?'

'You just tried to run like a felon. I don't need to know much about a felon to have him gaoled.'

That brought a twisted grin to his face. 'Fair enough. So let's find somewhere to sit while you judge whether I am a felon or not, eh?'

'Perhaps we can do that later, Master Robinet. For now there is the matter of a dead man in that house over there,' Simon pointed out. 'What do you know of it?'

'Absolutely nothing. I was here to meet a friend, and as I arrived these men began running out and screaming.'

'Who was your friend?'

'A man of the city. He's called Walter.'

'Of Hanlegh?'

'You know him?' Robinet said with a smile.

Simon shook his head. 'No, but we have been hearing a lot about him.'

'Ah, that is a relief. Walter was here, but when I went to fetch pies for our dinner he disappeared. Where is he?'

Simon contemplated him. 'Do you know who owns this house?'

'I've met him a couple of times. A man called Michael, I think. Why?'

'We will need to ask him about the man we just found in the basement, that's why,' Simon said. 'Come with me.'

'I'd prefer to wait here – I am worried about my friend.'

'We'll find him later.'

To Simon's relief, he submitted. There was no point in trying to evade a so much younger man while he was alert and ready.

Simon saw that the monk was still in front of the house, encircled by a small group of men with staffs held ready. Simon eyed him as they pushed their way through the crowds. The monk looked quite petrified, and from the grim expressions on the faces of the men holding him there, he had cause.

As they came closer, Baldwin and the coroner reappeared from the undercroft.

'I am Sir Baldwin de Furnshill, Keeper of the King's Peace. This is Coroner Richard de Welles. Who are you, and for what reason were you watching this place?'

'Robinet of Newington,' he answered, studying Baldwin and then glancing at the coroner. He had known many king's officers in his life, and none had justified trust. These men looked decent, but felons often did. 'I was waiting in the street for my friend to return. I was to meet him here.'

'Rob?' Simon said.

'I followed the monk here, and when I arrived that man was already stood over there and staring at the place.' Rob's voice held a heavy larding of glee. He was triumphant to be the centre of all attention. Even as he spoke, he was aware of other people coming closer to listen.

'Where is the monk?' Baldwin asked.

'Here I am, Sir Baldwin! Sir, we have met before when you visited my beloved lord, Abbot Robert at Tavistock. Do you remember me?'

'I know you,' Baldwin responded coolly. 'But let me ask you the same question I asked of this gentleman: what were you doing here?'

'My good friend Richard Langatre had been arrested in error, and I had a lengthy conversation with the sheriff to ask for his release. Naturally when I secured that release, I wished to talk to him for a while, so we came back here. And when we did so, we had been inside only a short while when my friend needed some coals. I think he dropped some into a puddle, and I later saw that it was blood. It appeared to come from beneath the door, so I went to investigate, as any good citizen should, and there I found a dead man.'

'Where is Langatre now?' Coroner Richard called.

'I am here.'

Richard de Langatre stood in the doorway to his own rooms, pale and faintly green about the face. He was wiping at his mouth, and his eyes were red-rimmed. 'Sorry. I had to throw up. I'd had my hand in the blood, and it made me sick to think of it. I've been sick. Several times . . .'

His eyes took on a faraway look, and he would have fled back indoors had not several men taken hold of him. Their grip appeared to drive off the urgency of his need for a pail, but he was still apparently enfeebled.

'He has spent the last night in the sheriff's gaol,' Baldwin reminded himself as he watched the man being tugged towards him. It was clear enough that Richard de Langatre was feeling weak, but Baldwin had seen others who had been pathetic and enfeebled after committing murder.

'I know nothing of this man's death,' Langatre said. 'I was in the sheriff's gaol all night, in God's name. I only returned here a little while ago.'

'And I was with the sheriff myself,' Busse said eagerly. 'I was with him all this morning until we arrived back here together, me and Richard here. I couldn't have had a part in that man's death!'

'He is still warm,' the coroner stated. 'He has been dead only a very short time.'

'But he can't have been killed since we got back,' Langatre protested. 'We should have heard something.'

'Perhaps. Perhaps not,' the coroner said, his eyes going from one to the other. Coroner Richard was often thought to be a fool because his voice was loud and he had an amiable demeanour – except when he felt he was being obstructed – but his mind was as sharp as any, and it had been honed by listening to men who lied to him. Just now he was unsure how much these two men knew, but he wasn't convinced of their guilt. 'What were you doing in your rooms?'

Busse leaned forward as he attempted to respond before Langatre could speak. 'My friend here was offering me ale to thank me for rescuing him from the gaol. That is all.'

Coroner Richard looked at Langatre. 'What else?'

'There was nothing else,' Busse said quickly.

'I asked the man here, not you,' Sir Richard shot back. 'Well?'

Richard de Langatre licked his lips nervously. He knew that the monk wanted him to remain silent about his work, but as he studied Sir Baldwin and Sir Richard he was suddenly reminded of the evening when they had come to his cell and promised to help him. Yes, even then he had been reluctant, but they had not been false. 'I feel I can trust you to deal fairly with me, lordings. We came back here because brother Robert here wanted to consult me on a matter. He wished to know some details about his future, and it was for that consultation that he came here.'

'Can you tell the future?' Coroner Richard asked dubiously.

'Better than anyone else in the city,' Langatre said with certainty.

'Did you learn anything interesting?' Sir Baldwin asked.

'Before I could perform the act, we discovered the body. It was brother Robert who insisted that we should investigate, too, I should say. He would hardly have done that unless he was innocent.'

Baldwin smiled. 'I have known men who were bold enough to do just that. There are some who feel so safe in their brilliance at concealing their act that they bring it to the attention of the law without expecting to be discovered. Some even wish to be discovered. But I dare say you are correct. Brother Robert does not look much like a murderer.'

'So who was the dead man?' Simon asked.

'I do not know,' Busse said.

'I had heard that there was a new tenant there, but I never met him,' Langatre said. 'My landlord, Michael, should know.'

'Your fortune-telling fails you today?' Baldwin asked suavely.

'Who is this Michael, and where is he?' Simon asked.

'I am Michael.'

Chapter Thirty-One

Exeter City

'You will be arrested soon, and when you hang, I won't be worried. I may die soon without any money, husband, but the knowledge that you, who put my children into their grave, are dead, will be enough for me,' Margie Skinner said.

She was sitting at her stool, back resting against the wall with her head jutting as it always did.

Will looked at her, then away. It was shameful. He ought to be able to look her in the face, but he couldn't. To see those features, which were still so familiar and lovely in some ways, attached to this ruined body was enough to make his mind want to burst for misery and horror. She had once been his lover, his beauty. Now she was a foul image of her former self, twisted and deformed by the heat of the fire, like a wax doll.

He had to get out.

'Where are you going? Trying to run away from them? That coroner won't let you escape him, husband. He'll catch you and have you dangling. Not the sort of man to let such as you escape justice, is he? No!'

Her poisonous cackling followed him down the street as he walked away, his head hanging over his breast, blinking to clear the tears.

This afternoon was quiet compared with some, and the air was crisp but dry. He was thinking about finding an alehouse, but somehow his feet drew him back *there*, and soon he was standing at the posts that blocked off his house.

The space where Norman Mucheton had lain was clear now. Ivo had gone home as soon as the coroner had declared the inquest closed and the men had carried the body off, so now there was just the stain on the ground where the man's neck had bled over the dirt. Will looked down at it and sighed.

From the ruins of his house there came a rending sound, and, as he turned to look, a beam that had once supported the upper jetty creaked round and started to move. Ponderously, it slid sideways, and suddenly fell to the ground. It crashed to the earth, raising a brown cloud of mingled soot and soil, which almost instantly dissipated.

The ruins were falling apart. Soon even this little memorial to his family would be gone. And then, when Margie and he had died as well, who would remember his children?

No one. No one would remember them.

Michael stood before them perfectly content. There was nothing even these corrupt bastards could do to him. He'd done nothing that would earn him a rope, and if they tried to hang him, he'd get the best pleader in the court to protect him. There was nothing that couldn't be bought with enough cash. He knew that if little else.

'You are the owner of this house?' Baldwin demanded.

'Yes. It's mine. Top rented to this fellow, Langatre. Undercroft to a stranger to the city, called John.'

'From where?'

'He said he came from Nottingham.'

'Sad to say, he won't return,' Coroner Richard said. 'He's had his throat cut.'

Michael blinked. 'When?'

'You answer *our* questions, man! When did you last see him?'

'Earlier today. I was here, and I visited him. He was perfectly all right then.'

'How long ago was that?' Baldwin asked. 'It will help us to learn when he died.'

'Only a short while after the end of mass. I attended the church as I do each Friday, and on my way homewards I saw him in the street here. I exchanged a few words with him, and then continued. There were plenty in the street here who would have seen us together.'

Baldwin studied him. Short and dark, this man enjoyed life, from the look of him. He had the florid complexion of a regular visitor to the tavern, and a paunch to match it. From the look of him he was a moderately successful businessman, but there was an odour about him. 'You are a tanner?'

'Yes. What of it?'

Baldwin shrugged. 'You have been successful.'

'Is that a crime now?'

'If success is the reward for theft or illegal acts, yes.'

'Do you accuse me of illegal acts? Do you think I am a . . .'

'What?' Baldwin asked silkily. 'Do I think you are a . . .?'

'Nothing, *sir*,' Michael said, with as much sarcasm as he dared. 'I should scarcely dream of accusing any man in the city of taking bribes or promises of money in exchange for favours. A man who did a thing like that could look to a short life, eh?'

'Do you mean to accuse me of breaking the law?' Baldwin asked, and he was genuinely surprised rather than offended or angry. The idea that a man might dare to think that he might have done such a thing was startling to him.

Michael stared at him. His small eyes were strained with his poor eyesight, and his peering manner, together with his lowered head, made him look like a belligerent ox preparing to charge. 'No,' he said at last, reluctantly. 'I've heard nothing about you.'

'Then who?'

'There are stories.'

Baldwin nodded. There always were. If a man won a certain post, it was sure to be because he had paid well for it; when a man took on a new office, invariably the grantor of that office was thought to look prosperous. And often it was true.

There was no position in the country which did not depend upon a gift. And other officers made their own profits. The sheriff, for example, would often rig a jury at court, either to free the men who had paid him, or to see condemned those who were enemies of powerful lords. A man could be taken and confined for no reason beyond a bribe paid by his enemy to the arresting officer.

It was interesting that this tanner should have taken such matters so to heart, though. Baldwin would expect it from others, but not a lowly leather worker. 'Forget these "stories" for now, man. What can you tell us of this dead man?'

'I have already told you all I know.'

'There was a finger in his room. It could be a finger cut from a king's messenger. Why would your tenant have that?'

'Master, I inherited this house many years ago when my father died. He was a brewer and had run it as his own little tavern ever since he first arrived here from Warwick years ago, but when he was gone I saw no need to keep it as a drinking house and rented it out instead. The undercroft is damp and cold, and it is hard to coax money from any man for that. When this John of Nottingham came and asked for it, I was happy to rent it to him.'

'How long has he been there?'

'A matter of days. No more.'

'But you say that he asked for you?'

'He asked me for the room, yes. I suppose he had enquired in the city where there might be a room he could use.'

'Did he say what he would use it for?'

'No. I didn't ask. Why should I? If it suited him, he suited me.'

'Yes. I am sure he did,' Baldwin said. 'And tell me: you say your father came here from Warwick. Was he a freeman when he arrived here?'

'Yes. He was no runaway serf.'

'A man of some position, then, to have acquired his own house. And you turned to tanning.'

'So?' Michael said defensively. It was not an occupation that would appeal to all, but he had never regretted his choice of career. 'It makes me a good income.'

'Yes, I am sure.' Baldwin sighed a little. 'Tell me, do you know anything about a man called Walter of Hanlegh?'

'I have heard of him,' Michael said suspiciously. He could sense Robinet tensing, and looked his way. The old messenger was gazing at him with a scowl.

'What do you know of him?' Coroner Richard boomed.

'Little enough. I never wanted to meet a man like him. Always reluctant to tell what he used to do, apparently. You can't trust a man who won't even say what he does.'

'Is that true?' Baldwin asked Robient.

Robinet shrugged. 'He and I worked for the king. We did as we were commanded.'

'You worked for the king too?'

Robinet set his head to one side and grimaced. 'Keeper, I was a messenger. Like the man you found the other day down at the South Gate. I was one of the king's men.'

The world looked a little improved, at first, from the bottom of a leathern jug, but soon the warming flood of ale was depleted, and all that happened was that Jen's tears felt all the more unsupportable.

He had given her to believe that he loved her. That was the thing. Whether or not she had any feelings for him, he had made her believe he adored her. It was his languishing expression that had made her begin to feel affection for him in the first place. She was quite sure of it. Not that Sarra could see it, but Sarra was so short-sighted, she wouldn't have seen a knight's shield if it stood in front of her.

It must be cowardice. That was it. He didn't want to risk his marriage to the harpy. When Jen had flown from the bedchamber and sought him out in the hall, he had been surprised and then shocked and fearful, because his wife was there too and could hear every word. Oh, she should have thought it through! If only she had considered, she would have seen how it must affect him. He was too kind to want to hurt his wife, even if he didn't love her any more. Surely he wanted Jen still. Perhaps even now he was searching the streets for her, trying to learn where she had gone so that he could protect her and plan with her how he could win his freedom. There was no possibility that she could live in an adulterous marriage with him. He must discover a means of divorce if it were at all possible.

Although the bitch, his wife, might try to prevent him. It was the sort of poisonous thing a woman like her would do. Women like her, like Alice, who were born to high families, were frigid. They had no idea of great love. They were bartered and sold for position, like heifers. Surely she couldn't seek to make him unhappy for the whole of his life, though. She had been a failure as a wife so far, not giving him his children. He needed them. All men did.

But if he was searching the streets for her, she must get up and make herself visible to him. Yes. She stood and left the tavern a little unsteadily, gripping the door-frame as she passed into the street.

There was a gap in the clouds, and the houses on the northern side of the street were lighted with a shaft so bright that it hurt her eyes. She had to shade them as she made her way over the street and into an alley that led south to the High Street. There she turned left towards the castle.

The High Street was busy now as people hurried to find food for their dinner, and she was knocked about a little as she struggled onwards. And then, as she was coming closer to the castle, she stopped.

There in front of her was her friend Sarra, and as Jen was about to rush to her to beg for money, advice, *help*, she saw the other face a step or two behind: her old mistress, the poisonous bitch Alice, walking towards her.

'So, master,' Baldwin said. 'Perhaps you should tell us your whole story.'

They had left the street, and at the suggestion of the coroner had walked a short distance to a small alehouse towards the West Gate. Now they stood inside, all with ales in their fists except Baldwin, who had eschewed the drink in favour of a cup of hot water with dried mint leaves infusing in it. He sniffed the brew every so often, as though the vapours could remove the foulness of the death he had seen in that undercroft.

'I was born Robinet of Newington, although everyone calls me Newt,' the man began. 'Many years ago I was recommended to the prince, as he then was, and he took to me, and brought me into his household as a *cursor*, a runner. He'd use me to fetch and carry messages all over the country. As his household grew, so did my duties, and when he became king, he kept me. At all times, he was a good, fair and decent master, too.

'When he was into his second year as king, he had need of more messengers, and he had me take a man on for him, to teach him what was necessary. That man was poor James.'

'You could have saved people some time if you had come forward and told us all you knew at the time of his inquest,' the coroner growled.

'And if I had, you would have arrested me for being his killer.'

'Why should we?'

'I was with him on the night he died,' Newt said. He shivered. Telling his life story was the last thing he had intended to do, but once he began to speak, it was hard to stop with all their eyes upon him. 'If I had come forward, I thought men would point to me and say: "He was with James, he must have killed him!" '

'It should take more than proximity to have a man arrested,' Simon observed.

'Should it? I taught James all I knew. How to find the best resting places, how to make up time when one day goes slowly, where to have boots mended . . . for a man walking thirty-five miles a day, there is much to take in. At the end of it all, when he was as good as I could make him, I saw him clad in my master's uniform. I was proud for him. Proud! And then, with the end of the Scottish wars after Bannockburn, for a time all because confused. There was less need for messengers to go north, and many men-at-arms sought new posts, since without the wars they had little to do. And it was rumoured that some of us would lose our jobs.

'The easiest thing would have been to get rid of the older men. All of us knew it. Anyway, it was my own silly fault. I was in my cups one day and admitted to the bailiff of my local vill, Saer Kaym, that the king had been forced to retreat from Scotland because he didn't bother to attend mass, he was lazy, and indecent. Christ's saints, the man enjoyed playing at being a serf, making hedges and digging ditches. Well, news of my words got back to the king. I was imprisoned. It was not a good time for me.'

'And the man who allowed this tittle-tattle to reach the king's ears?' Baldwin asked mildly.

'As you guessed. My friend James was with me when I said those things to Saer, and he told the king. But the queen interceded on my behalf, and I believed my friend when he told me on the night he died that she only did so because he had told her what had happened to me. Otherwise I might still be there now.'

'Still, you did have good reason to wish to curse James at the time,' Simon noted.

'Yes. And when I bumped into him here in Exeter, I wanted to grab a knife and end his life there and then for what he did. Except then I saw his eyes, and instead of remembering that one crime against me,

I found myself recalling all the evenings by a campfire, or at an inn. All the dinners we'd taken together, all the ale we'd drunk . . . it made it hard to stick steel in his belly. And then I saw another thing – he was terrified of me. Terrified! Of me! It made me want to slap him about the face, seeing that. So when he offered to buy me an ale, I had to accept.'

'Did he tell you what he was doing in the city?' Coroner Richard asked.

'He was bringing messages to the sheriff mainly, although there was something for the bishop too. It was mainly the sheriff. Have you heard of the arrests in Coventry? There has been a necromancer there, who, with twenty or more others, plotted to kill the king and his advisers, if you can believe it! James said that he was here with special writs for the sheriff to arrest any other culprits down here, and then to have them sent to London to be questioned by the king's own men.'

'I see. Do you have any idea who could have wanted to see your old companion dead?' Baldwin enquired after a moment.

'Ah!' Newt said. He took a long pull at his ale and wiped his mouth. Speaking thoughtfully, he told them all he could recall from that last night when he had wandered drunkenly homewards with James, only to wake the next morning alone, and with a broken head.

'Do you think James could have done that to you?' the coroner demanded. 'He plied you with ale all night and then struck you down? Hardly credible to me.'

'Or to me, unless he thought that there was danger ahead. I think he saw someone or something that made him fearful. He struck me to keep me quiet, and perhaps leave me safe, before going on. Or he set me down somewhere safe and someone else knocked me down.'

'He was drunk?' Baldwin shot out.

'We both were.'

'Was there blood near you when you woke?'

'Yes,' Newt remembered. 'And on my knife.'

'Then the riddle is easily explained. The messenger was the target, Master Robinet. You gained your lump when you were knocked down by an assailant – or two or three – who wanted information from James. I imagine they cut off his fingers while he was alive in order to prise that information from him. If they wanted to torture him extensively, that would have taken time, and perhaps they had little enough. Still, they got such information as they felt they needed, so they drew a cord about his throat and killed him. Perhaps in the barn with you, perhaps at the rubbish heap. And then they simply hid him. And there he might have lain for some while, if a hog hadn't taken a fancy to his hand.'

'That is all clear enough. Except, why should the messenger be killed?' Simon muttered.

'I think this man has answered that for us already,' Baldwin said. 'John of Nottingham was the man Michael said was renting that undercroft. And now we hear of a necromancer from Coventry who caused writs to be sent all about the country. Do you not think that perhaps this John could have escaped, only to see the messenger who was carrying messages to have him arrested? What would John do? He paid an accomplice and hunted down the messenger, bringing him to a place where he knew he could overwhelm the fellow, and when he was sure he had all he needed, he killed James and threw away his body. A callous and barbaric way to treat a Christian corpse.'

'What of John's murder today?'

'I should think that someone who wanted revenge against him must have decided to take action,' Baldwin said quietly.

'Me? But I swear, I wouldn't recognise him if I saw him,' Robinet said hastily. 'You must believe me, Sir Baldwin. I had no idea. All I was doing there was watching for the stranger, to see . . .'

'Yes?'

'I wanted to see whether it was the same man I thought I had seen the night James was killed. But from the description, I don't see how it could have been. The man I saw was not too tall. But others said the killer was over there at the house.'

'Well, let us hope he was the killer,' Coroner Richard grunted heavily. 'Rather than some poor innocent, eh?' And he looked at Newt with a contemplative air.

It was plain enough that he thought Newt had taken the law into his own hands and removed a murderer. And did not disapprove.

Chapter Thirty-Two

Exeter City

Alice saw the crowd outside the house from the top of Stepecote Street, and she glanced at Sarra with a perplexed frown. 'What is all this? I thought he was released today.'

'I shall go and ask, mistress, if you want,' Sarra suggested, and soon she was pushing her way through the mass of people. She could not reach the front of the crowd, but from a vantage point – which was a small wooden crate she found lying in the street – she was able to see that there was a beadle standing nervously with a polearm in his hand, surveying the crush with wariness bordering on alarm. Sarra recognised him, but there was no possibility of getting to him and asking what was happening, not with all these people about. However, there was a small, scruffy urchin nearby. She stepped down from the box and walked up to him.

'What is happening over there?'

Rob had been happily engaged in studying a pair of pigeons on the roof and wondering whether he could hit one with a stone when the young woman prodded him with her foot. He looked her up and down, lifted his eyebrows, shrugged, and snorted to himself. 'What's in it for me if I tell you?'

'A smack on your head if you don't answer sharply,' Sarra said sweetly. She had two brothers.

He scowled. 'There's a wizard lives here – he's been murdered. Say his head was almost taken off his body.'

Sarra gave him a close look. She only knew of one necromancer in this street. 'I heard tell he was all right this morning. He had been kept in the gaol overnight and released earlier today – and now he's dead?'

'Look over there and you'll see the beadle guarding the body until the inquest can be held,' Rob said. He was waiting here for Busse to reappear. The man had retreated into the house with Langatre a short time ago, and Rob wanted to follow him again. It was growing chilly out here. Even in the midday sun it was cold.

'Do they know who killed him? Or why?'

'Nah! You know how people are. The fornicating churls from this roadway are all clucking about like gossips from any other, but they won't help the coroner for nothing.'

'Wait there!' Sarra said, and hurried to her mistress. 'Langatre priest is dead, my lady,' she gasped as she reached Lady Alice. 'Apparently someone murdered him this morning. I saw the beadle there with my own eyes.'

Lady Alice felt as though she had been buffeted by a heavy blow. She rocked on her heels and blinked, momentarily overwhelmed by nausea. There was only one thought in her mind: that her husband had somehow learned about her visits to Langatre and had taken his own revenge for her discussions with the magician.

It was no surprise. If a man learned that his barren wife was seeking the aid of a magician, he might well imagine that the latter could have taken advantage of her. And although she had been the soul of propriety in all their negotiations, she could all too easily comprehend that her husband might have flown off the handle at the thought that she had been here to consult a known sorcerer. It must have made him mad.

Unless it was something to do with that little whore Jen.

Alice felt the breath catch in her throat at the thought. What if Jen was in reality her husband's lover, as the mediocre-minded little hussy had implied? If Matthew was in love with her, he would not want Alice to suddenly conceive, and he would ruthlessly remove any man who might be able to help her . . .

No, that was ridiculous. And yet, if he heard that his own wife was consulting a necromancer in order to achieve something, just at the time when he had learned of the attack on Hugh le Despenser, he would want the fact suppressed. And he could be ruthless in pursuit of his career, as Alice knew. It was foolish in the extreme of her not to have seen this! So stupid! For her to see a magician at just this time was asking for trouble. Of course her husband could not possibly condone her visits to Langatre when his own master, Despenser,

THE MALICE OF UNNATURAL DEATH

would be made so angry by the idea. It was just a matter of bad fortune that she had decided to come here today to see him, after reading that curious little note.

Be careful! she had read. *Your husband knows all our business.*

Fortunately she had had the presence of mind to throw the offending thing straight onto the fire, and then, calling for Sarra, had felt a little foolish in leaving so swiftly, but now she felt more than ever vindicated. It was merely a shame that she had not managed to get here sooner, or that the message had not been sent earlier so that she could have come and protected Langatre from her husband's men.

'Mistress? What would you have us do?' Sarra asked.

'We should return to the castle,' Alice said with a catch in her throat. She turned, and was about to make her way up the street when she saw the twisted features only a pace or two away. As the steel flashed, Alice screamed and lifted both hands to protect herself.

Michael Tanner felt tired as he left the keeper and his companions. They had questioned him quite fiercely, he felt, and the experience had left him drained. And it was all for nothing, sod them all!

The last days had been exhausting. Ever since the shock of hearing that the attempt to assassinate the king and his bastard sons-of-the-devil, the two Despensers, had been betrayed, Tanner had been on tenterhooks, waiting for the men to arrive at his door and take him away. Yet nothing had happened. Life had continued as though nothing untoward had occurred. While he knew that men were being tortured in Coventry, he heard no signs here in Exeter that anything was wrong.

And it was good to reflect that while all the associates in the attempt were arrested, the one crucial man in the whole enterprise, John of Nottingham, had escaped and made his way here.

Sheriffs tended to be corrupt, but among such a dishonourable rabble there could be one or two exceptions. And Croyser was one such. A deeply religious man, who believed with all his heart in the life to come and the Gospels, Croyser hated what he saw the Despensers doing to his land and his people. He deplored the way that the king acquiesced to each and every demand made by the Despensers, and he refused to see all the conspirators taken, hanged and displayed in order to satisfy their lust for revenge. Instead he had released John of Nottingham and given him instructions on where to go: to Croyser's old servant's son and still loyal retainer, Michael Tanner.

A message had already arrived, warning Michael to expect John soon, and it was a good thing it got to him. Otherwise he would not have considered talking to such a bedraggled figure.

He first saw the fugitive necromancer outside the tavern. There was little enough in the sight to inspire confidence. Shabby clothing, gaunt features . . . little enough to speak of power and importance. Michael would have left him there, had he not already been contacted, and as it was he at first thought that this was only some beggar who had appeared by coincidence, and would have left him to the mercies of the night. But then he caught sight of those eyes, the deep-set, dark eyes of a man who held inconceivable power. There was a force which emanated from his soul and fired the eyes with authority.

This was a truly awesome character, and fearsome. He gave off a sense of command that was not human, as though any insult would be rewarded immediately with a punishment more ferocious than even the Despenser could imagine.

Yes. There had been much to fear, looking into those eyes. Not as much as some, of course. The man who killed him was clearly even more to be feared than his victim.

Tanner walked to his barrel and poured himself a strong ale. He felt light-headed and not a little emotional. The idea that the effort, all the planning, all the terror at the idea of discovery, had been in vain, was enervating. He could have toppled over for lack of command over his legs. Sitting was impossible. If he sat, he might never rise again.

All that work, he thought, and drained his cup.

And as the cup was raised, he heard a knock at the door.

His heart lurched like a rache seeing a cat. 'Fool, fool, fool!' he swore at himself. Christ Jesus! If John was dead, obviously they'd known where he was, and that meant they probably knew where all the conspirators were. They must have been following John or someone else, and now they were going about the city and capturing all those who'd ever had anything to do with the conspiracy. Why had he come back here to his house? He must have been mad! He was a cretin!

The knock came again: urgent, demanding. With leaden feet, Michael Tanner started to cross the floor to the door, but before he could reach it the door sprang open, and in the doorway was only emptiness. He gaped, staring, and even as he did so a figure, tall, slim, clad in dirty grey and black, slipped round the doorframe and into his house. And as Tanner took in the sight, he felt his reason slipping.

'In God's name—' he began.

'Yes, friend. In God's and all the saints' names,' said John of Nottingham. He drew his lips back from his teeth and bared them briefly. 'But before we start our prayers, do you close that door and keep all unwanted eyes from us, eh? Because we have work to do.'

Lady Alice fell back, away from the dagger, and cried out in alarm. Jen smiled to see her so fearful, and advanced, her long knife waving from side to side, before suddenly lunging.

It was Sarra who stepped between them, a hand up to protect her mistress. 'Jen! *Jen!* Stop this! What do you think you're doing?'

'It's her, *her* – she's poisoned my lover's mind against me,' Jen said through gritted teeth. 'Get out of my way, Sarra.'

'So you can kill her? No, I won't! You can't kill her, Jen. All she's done is stick to her vows. It's not her fault she married the sheriff before you ever heard his name, is it?'

'He loves me. He always has loved me, and she's in our way. Without her we can be happy.'

'Jen, he doesn't feel anything for you at all. Why should he? He's a knight, Jen, a God-fearing knight – and what are you? You believe he'd leave his wife for you? Look at yourself, Jen! How can you think he'd leave her for you?'

'Shut up! You don't understand! *You* haven't been in love, have you? He and I love each—'

'Has he kissed you? Has he called you his sweeting? Has he touched your body? Has he moaned for love of you? Has he visited your bed at night? What is this, Jen? You are mad if you think he feels anything for you. All he knows right now is that you're insane. You're lunatic. If you go back, he wouldn't even want to be in the same room as you–you have to be sensible, Jen! Put the knife away and leave my mistress alone. Otherwise all you'll get is a painful death for your treachery to our master.'

Jen slowly turned to face Sarra, ignoring Lady Alice for a moment. Her face registered her dumb astonishment. As though Sarra could comprehend the depth of feeling that existed between her and her master! 'You say he wouldn't want to be in the same room as me? He would leave his position, his wife, his *life*, if I asked him to . . .'

'He didn't even speak up for you when you went to him yesterday, did he? He wouldn't protect you then, would he? Because he loves his lady. It's Alice he adores, Jen. Never you.'

'No! *No!* That's rubbish. His only trouble is, she's like a limpet! If he tells her how he loves me, she won't let him go. She cleaves to him like a contagion! Well, I'll kill her now and save him from her. Then he and I may leave and find ourselves our own happiness.'

Sarra shook her head. Her heart was already thudding painfully in her breast, and she put her left hand to it even as she turned her right palm upwards in the sign of good faith. 'Please, darling Jen, don't do something you'll regret. This isn't you! I know you – you wouldn't hurt another person for no reason. My lady has done nothing to harm you, Jen. All this stuff about Sheriff Matthew, it's in your head. It's not real, Jen.'

At last she could see her arguing was achieving something. Jen's face went blank for a moment, and then her eyes screwed up and tears began to flood from them and course down her cheeks. She stood there some little while, hands clenched at her sides, the knife forgotten, her entire body rigid and unmoving. And some of the people who had been watching saw, and one or two men started to step towards her in a bid to capture and restrain her. One, Sarra recognised: it was her mistress's man. She turned to see whether Alice had seen him too, and then . . .

And then Jen's eyes snapped open, and Sarra's relief turned to horror as she realised that Jen's mind had finally broken.

'It's all right, Sarra,' she said reasonably, and then gave a gentle smile. 'I can see you're worried about your job when I am wife to the sheriff and this sow is in her grave. You don't have to worry. I'll keep you in your post. All will be easier when this woman is dead, never fear.'

Maurice slipped on a cobble, and Jen suddenly became aware of her danger. She shot a look over her shoulder and saw him coming close. Her jaw clenched, and she turned a furious look upon Sarra. 'You should have warned me!' she hissed, and then sprang forward with all her anger behind her blow.

The knife flashed grim and deadly, and Sarra felt nothing, only a desire to save Lady Alice. The moment dragged past slowly, like a lifetime. She saw the knife in Jen's hand, and she felt herself move to block Jen's path to Lady Alice. It was instinctual, not a thing she intended to do, and as the knife shot forward to reach past her flank, Sarra felt it hit her, a slow, dragging blow that hurt like a punch, but which hardly felt dangerous. No, it was more like a blow one of her brothers might have given her. And then she had Jen's forearm in her hands and held it tight. 'Jen, come, leave us here. You don't need to get into any more trouble,' she said.

She saw Jen's face twist with rage, and felt the arm in her hands twist. At first she had a good grip, but then somehow her grip loosened, and she felt the knife hand pull away from her, saw it gleam like red oil in a wide arc to keep the men at bay, and all hold up their hands, watching that wicked blade as it passed in front of them. And Sarra tried to go to Jen to capture her herself, wrap her arms about her so as not to hurt her, and try to bring her to her senses, but she heard a sharp, piercing squeal and spun on her heel to see her lady staring at her with a hand to her mouth.

'Lady, I . . .'

But no more words would come. In a bleak inspiration, she knew what Alice had seen. The pain throbbed at first, like a bruise, but then she was racked with a white-hot searing deep in her bowels, and as she put her hand to her side she realised she was dying. There was a gushing from the wound, and a hot, burning feeling at her groin and heart, and as she fell to her knees she saw Jen baring her teeth in impotent malice at Lady Alice before springing away from the encircling men and darting up an alley.

Then she toppled over, and even as Maurice reached Alice, Sarra's sight was fading. She just couldn't focus. It was so irritating. And there was a roaring noise in her ears . . .

Chapter Thirty-Three

Exeter City

Maurice reached his sister as her legs began to buckle. 'Sister! Sister, did she cut you?' His arms went about her, and he gripped her in a hug.

Her eyelids fluttered, and as his panic communicated itself to her she shuddered, and then pushed him away. 'Sarra! Sarra!'

Maurice had seen enough death already in his life. He glanced down at the maid where she lay twitching on the ground, eyes wide but unseeing. 'She is dead, Alice. I am sorry.'

Alice gave a short scream, instantly quashed as she realised who was holding her. 'Maurice, you must run! Fly from here. My husband's men will be here any moment. Please, run!'

Maurice looked over at the house. He could see all the people in the roadway about them staring at the body at his feet. 'I cannot . . .'

'Leave me! Just go!'

He nodded dumbly. Slowly and reluctantly he let his sister free from his arms, and saw her sink to her knees on the roadway at Sarra's side, weeping as she reached out to Sarra's face, stroking it gently as the life left her.

And then he turned and set off in pursuit of the bitch who had tried to kill his sister.

Baldwin sat musing for a long while after Robinet had finished. It was plain enough to him that this man had reason enough to kill the messenger, but he was less convinced of his ability to do so. For one thing, unless Robinet managed to have James overwhelmed with drink, it was clear enough that James was the younger, the taller, and the stronger of the two. In a straight fight, James must surely win. Then there was the other aspect: the fingers removed while James was yet living. He couldn't see why Robinet should want to torture the man.

It was Simon who voiced his feelings. 'How would this fellow get the messenger to submit to losing a finger or two?'

'Money, Bailiff,' the coroner said. 'It'll always bring in a hireling to help do your business. This is a large enough city. There are plenty of men here to do a man's bidding.'

'It would take a strong man to hold down the messenger while his finger was taken off,' Simon said musingly.

'What of this fellow's friend?' the coroner said, as though reluctantly. He was averse to bringing to justice those who acted from good motives, clearly.

'Walter of Hanlegh,' Baldwin murmured. 'The man who would do the king's bidding. Where is he now, fellow?'

'I do not know,' said Newt. 'I suppose he saw someone whom he sought to follow or something . . . Perhaps the man he thought might have been the killer of James.'

'He too was a friend of this James?' Baldwin ventured.

'Alas, no. He considered James a traitor to me, and for that reason he refused to speak to him. Walter is a man of firm views.' Newt smiled thinly.

'Firm enough to avenge the injustice done to you?' Simon queried swiftly.

'No,' Newt said firmly. 'He denied it and Walter is a man of honour.'

'Was he a local man? Was he born Exonian?' Coroner Richard asked. 'I don't remember the name.'

'No. He was here some years ago, and liked the city. When he left the king's service, he had money to buy a house, so he came here to live.'

'What was he doing here before?' Simon said.

'It was a service to the king, that is all I know,' Newt said. 'He would not discuss his tasks with me, and I won't speculate with you about him. He is honourable and fair-minded. I will say no more.'

'Let us go to his house, then,' Baldwin said, rising. 'Perhaps we shall find him there.'

Newt nodded, albeit unhappily. He already felt as though he had betrayed his oldest friend, but there was little else he could do in the face of their suspicion, and just now all he wanted was to ensure that these men accepted his own innocence.

They made their way from the tavern, and as they did so they heard the all too familiar sound of the hue and cry.

'Sweet Jesus, what is the matter with this city?' Coroner Richard boomed as he heard the regular blasts on a horn. 'Come, Keeper, we should go and investigate this, too.'

Baldwin shook his head, grunting. 'I would prefer to see this Walter . . . but is not that noise coming from the east? If we continue on our way to Walter's house, we shall surely pass the place from which all this noise is coming.'

Newt was content to have their visit to Walter's house delayed. For all he knew, this was another little incident in a large city: a churl caught trying to snare a purse in a crowd, or an urchin grabbing a loaf and bolting. There were always little felonies being committed in a city the size of Exeter.

They made their way up the lane towards Carfoix, and it was as they turned a corner in the street that they came across the little group of people. A woman stood weeping loudly at the side, being comforted by Langatre and another man, while others peered and spoke in hushed voices.

'*Stand back!*' The coroner stood in the road with his hands on his belt and bellowed with full force, and the men in the crowd moved away hurriedly. A woman at the far side of the road gave a small shriek on hearing him, and dropped a basket of eggs.

'Well? What is all this?' Coroner Richard demanded. 'Oh! Good Christ!'

'Who is this child?' Baldwin demanded as he dropped to a knee at her side. There was a terrible wound in her flank, he saw. It looked as though a long blade had stabbed in, and then been torn out through her stomach wall. Blood oozed slowly through the mess of intestines, and although her hand remained over the gash, her eyes were already dim, lips pale, flesh waxen. She was past rescue. 'You poor, sweet child,' he murmured.

A priest hurried up, unstoppering his bottle of water as he flung himself at her side, making the sign of the cross and beginning his ritual. It was enough to bring Baldwin back to his senses. He brought himself up from his knees and cast about him. 'Langatre – what can you tell us about this?'

'This is Lady Alice. I heard her scream, and when I came to see what was the matter, her maid here was lying as you see her. Another servant did it, apparently.'

'It was Jen. She was cast from our household this morning,' Lady Alice said, and shuddered. She was cold, so cold! Wrapping her arms about her, she managed to prevent herself from succumbing to the waves of nausea which threatened. She wanted to throw herself into Maurice's arms, but that would only cause more comment, and she dared not. She must be strong! 'I thought she was a little unhinged – she said my husband had promised himself to her, and that he would divorce me in order to win her. I was so furious that I decided she must be sent away, but I had no idea . . . no idea . . .'

'What happened?'

'Jen appeared. She had a knife, and tried to stab me. It was only because I moved quickly that she didn't kill me.' Alice held up her arm. There was a slash in the rich material of her tunic, and a little blood had stained it. 'As soon as I was away and safe, Sarra tried to speak sensibly to her, but she wouldn't listen. Wouldn't hear anything. Just kept repeating that I was in her way, or something. I don't know . . . I can't truly recall her exact words . . . and then she lunged and tried to stab at me, but caught little Sarra instead. She did that . . . and then fled.'

'Where?'

It was Langatre who answered. 'Up that alley there. She has half the men from the street after her, though. I doubt she will escape them all.'

Baldwin looked at Sir Richard. 'You are coroner, old friend. What should we do with her? You have seen her body already. Is there any need for her to remain here until the jury can be collected?'

'No, of course not! Let us set her down in the undercroft with that necromancer. That would surely be best,' Coroner Richard said, quietly for him. He kept gazing down at the little body, and Baldwin saw the glistening at his eyes. It made his own begin to well.

Activity was always the best cure for such emotions, and he quickly sniffed to himself, then called to men to fetch a few boards or a door to carry the body down the stairs. In a few minutes a door was provided and Baldwin helped the priest and Langatre to lift her little frame onto it. It was not a heavy job. She was little larger, so Baldwin felt, than his own Richalda. No. Nonsense. Richalda was only an eighth the age of this young woman. Still, the feeling of sadness would not leave him as he watched Simon and Robinet pick up the door with its sad burden and begin to march to the undercroft.

The dark was like a clammy blanket after the open air in the street, and as they walked inside Baldwin heard Simon bellowing for a candle. Baldwin felt the cool lick up his cheeks as he trailed in after them, cursing as he felt his boot squelch in the mess of dirt and blood at the doorway, and then he was feeling about for tinder and a flint. Soon he managed to strike a glow, and blew it gently until he had fanned it into flame. Setting a candle to it, he lighted two more and placed them on a shelf before helping to clear a space on a table. Simon and Robinet lifted the door up, and carefully rolled Sarra's body onto the table before bowing their heads respectfully and moving away.

Baldwin was already cupping a hand about the first of the candles to snuff it when he heard the explosion of shock.

'Christ's cods! *Sweet Mother of Christ, NO!*'

And then Robinet fell to his knees beside the body on the ground.

'Walter! Walter, no!'

Jen was strangely cold. There was the noise of the people chasing her along the alleyway, and that made her heart thud like a hammer in her breast, but that wasn't it. In some way it felt as though she wasn't here at all, as though she was relaxed and unconcerned, floating high over all the people and the city, observing with the detachment of an angel as her body pounded along the cobbles.

Sarra would understand. Given time, she'd understand. This wasn't some silly infatuation like so many girls had every so often, this was real love. Love that could scorch a couple when it ignited. Sarra couldn't see that yet, but she would when Matthew declared his love for her. Trying to tell her, Jen, that he didn't care for her! Hah! She must have thought Jen was *blind* not to have seen it. His adoration was there in his eyes at every moment when he was in a room with her. There was no concealing it. The only obstacle was his first wife, and she must leave him. She would go one way or another.

There was no guilt in Jen. Not now. Not ever. She was only fighting as any woman must to protect her love and her lover. Alice was nothing. A mere encumbrance to him. Jen was his real soulmate. She would have him, too. And when Sarra saw how happy they both were together, she would understand.

But there was this odd feeling in her. It was like a panic, as though she was anxious or something. But that was daft. She was not worried about anything. Except escaping from these people. It was maddening that she must run from them as though she was some common felon, when all she was doing was trying to protect herself. That was it. She was protecting herself. Didn't any woman have the right to defend her man against other *whores* who might seek to take him away? Yes. And she would, too.

The alleyway ended in the second street, and she had the presence of mind to thrust the knife into her bodice. Looking down as she started up towards Carfoix, she saw the redness on her hand and for a second her eyes opened with horror. She thought, she really did, that she had cut herself – and then she almost laughed aloud at the silliness of it. Of course, it was only the scratch she had given Sarra. She'd have to apologise for that later, but Sarra would understand. She was a kind girl, Sarra. It would be nothing once she saw how happy Matthew was with his Jen.

She hid her hand in a fold of her dress and ducked her head a little as she made her way on, pushing through the crowds like any other native of the city. Yet there was a constant irritant. Behind her she would keep hearing the blowing of horns and the shouts of the men in the hue and cry. Once she risked a quick glance over her shoulder, and saw a man glowering ferociously at all the people in the street. He almost caught her eye, but she turned away and continued, her head lower still on her shoulders.

Near the crossroads in the middle of the city, she heard more calls and shouts. At first she thought it was merely the hawkers up there, but then she understood that someone had already made his way to the place, and there were three or four men standing and peering at the approaching women with intent, serious expressions. She could not stop; she could not continue, and returning was impossible. That man with the brutal glower might do her harm. For a moment she actually considered taking him into her confidence and telling him that it was all right, the sheriff had sanctioned her actions – but then she shook her head. She hadn't been able to tell him yet what she was trying to do to help him, hadn't told him that she was going to remove his wife so that they could be together for ever.

There was a stall to her side. It was a butcher's from the shambles opposite, and she acted almost without conscious thought. A foot lashed out and the trestle holding up the table on which the wares were displayed collapsed. Amid the shrieks of rage from within the shop, Jen hurried along the street to the opposite corner and darted over the main intersection, thence up and along the High Street.

She had only the one thought: she must reach her lover before anyone else could get to him and lie about what had happened.

The man was inconsolable, and it was some while before Simon and Baldwin could persuade him to stand, leave the body on the floor, and go with them up the stairs.

People outside had heard the unearthly shriek and wailing of despair as Robinet caught sight of his old companion, and they stood blocking the way as the men left the undercroft. It took some curses and the threat of Baldwin's sword before they were given a free passage. In preference to the street, Baldwin crossed the way, grabbed Langatre's arm and hissed urgently, 'Up to your rooms now, and bring the sheriff's wife with you. Don't argue, just *do* it!'

In a short while they were inside the room and Langatre was fussing about heating water over his brazier for some concoction for the lady, while Baldwin secretly wished he had a good quarter-pint of burned wine instead. In his experience that colourless distillation was a supreme cure for almost all ills and panics.

'This maid, my lady,' he ventured at last, when Lady Alice was seated more or less comfortably on a chair, 'is she a local girl from the city?'

'No ... I think she came from north of here ... Thorverton, perhaps, or Silverton. I had no reason to question her on it. Master Langatre – could you permit me a little of your wine?' With her hand she pointed to a small dresser. Langatre nodded and opened a curtain.

Behind it was a quartet of pewter goblets and a jug. He poured a measure and passed it to her.

'Of course not.' Baldwin smiled reassuringly, thinking that he knew the names of all his serfs, their parents and their offspring, let alone which homestead they had sprung from. 'Has she shown such violence before?'

'Never. I would not have allowed her into my house if she had.'

'You have no children, though. That at least is a mercy.'

'A mercy?' Lady Alice snapped.

'I meant only that she could not have harmed a child, since there were none there,' Baldwin said, but now he eyed her more closely. A woman with no children would often be sharp on the subject, as he knew only too well. His own wife had been accused of barrenness by her first husband, and he had made her life miserable, refusing to accept any blame for her inability to conceive. Although he had reasons to dislike the sheriff and mistrust him, Baldwin was a rational and fair man. The fellow was no bully to his own wife, he felt sure. No, any pressure this woman felt was more than likely self-inflicted.

And yet . . . many a man had unknowingly put his wife under strain. Women could attach significance to the least matter, and then live in despair while refusing to explain what it was that made them upset.

'My lady, what was it that made you consult this magician?'

'I? What makes you . . .'

'It is clear that you know each other, and you are familiar with his room here. You even knew where he might keep a jug of wine, lady. I am sure that your reason for coming to such a place as this is honourable, and I suspect it must be a natural woman's concern. Am I right?'

She shot an accusing look at Langatre, as though she expected him to confess to betrayal, and then eyed Baldwin more haughtily. 'What of it? I admit nothing, but yes, I know this man and his rooms.'

'I ask again: why? You have to understand that at the moment there is a murderer, a most ruthless murderer, loose in the city. He has killed a king's messenger, the man who lies in the undercroft below, and possibly another, not to mention striking down this magician's servant and trying to kill the magician himself. His throat still bears the mark.'

She could not help but look up at that. Langatre's throat was visible above his tunic as she glanced at him, and she could see the mark about his neck, a dark bruising that encircled it like a necklace. Except here there were bruises at the front too, where his fingers had scrabbled for purchase on the cord. She met his look and let her eyes slide away. 'I know nothing of this.'

'Really? The man who was living downstairs was a magician too, by repute. Did you know that? He left the tools and trinkets of his trade, which makes me wonder what he was doing down there.'

'I know nothing of this.'

'One thing was not found. Did you know who the first victim was in this miserable little charade? A mere carver of bones and antlers.'

'I know nothing of him,' she exclaimed in astonishment. 'Sir knight, I do not understand what you are trying to suggest! But I am a woman, and if you have an accusation to make, you should speak to my husband, and not badger me without his being here to defend me. This is unseemly.'

'No. Dead bodies are unseemly,' Baldwin said heavily. 'The murder of innocents is unseemly. Questioning a woman who may be able to help resolve some of these issues is not unseemly. It is sensible.'

'Except I know nothing about any of this. I have enough other affairs to concern me, Keeper.'

'Did your husband know you were consulting this fellow?'

Her face told him all he needed to know. This, then, was another complication, Baldwin told himself.

Chapter Thirty-Four

The Palace Gate

It had taken him some effort, keeping up with the old bastard, but Rob was nothing if not persistent. A lad growing in a town like Dartmouth could be rewarded for being persistent. Standing out of reach of a sailor and watching a ship could show a lad when to slip up to the dock and casually slide a hand into a bale of goods to retrieve some little item of value. Yes. A lad with determination and grit could get far.

Today it had brought him right back to the bishop's palace, though. No further. He'd seen Simon and Baldwin walking away with Robinet, but he reckoned his place was still following Busse. Simon had promised him a penny a day for performing that duty, and that was worth a bit, that was. With any luck, he'd soon get a whole shilling if Busse kept on wandering about, because Rob was competent at merrills and other games of skill or chance. There were few lads of his age who were more capable of palming a die when necessary.

There was no telling what the monk was doing in the bishop's palace. It was plain enough even to Rob that the man had received a severe shock when he hurried from the house where the body was discovered in the undercroft. Anyone would have thought he had never seen a dead man before, the way he darted up the stairs after finding him with that man Langatre, and then stood about like a whore in a church, gaping with a daft expression on his face as men eyed him up and wondered whether he was mad or murderer.

Rob didn't much care which he was. So far as he was concerned, the man was a source of money, and that was all. He hadn't got to know him on the way here, other than to be insulted by his reference to the 'boy', and that had not endeared him to Rob in any way.

There was a noise from a little shed near the gate to the bishop's palace, and when Rob went and peered inside, he saw a group of lads, all a little older than him, standing about an upturned barrel, playing some game or other. It made him grit his teeth. He had two pennies already saved in his purse, and with them he felt sure he could fleece these fools and make his fortune.

He turned and stared back at the palace, chewing at his lip. If he was any judge of a man, that monk was staying put in a nice, safe, comfy palace with no risk of sudden death. He wouldn't want to run out into the streets again, not alone, not for a long time.

It decided him. He fitted an amiable, slightly foolish smile to his face and leaned round the doorway. Using his broadest coastal dialect, he said, 'I'm new here, only up for a couple of days – are you playing a game of some sort? It looks like fun . . .'

Exeter Castle

Sir Matthew left the hall in a foul mood, and bellowed at his grooms to prepare his rounsey. He would ease his soul with a sharp gallop down the road towards Bishop's Clyst, then on the road out towards Powderham and back. There was little enough business to keep him in the city today, and he could do with the break. Sweet Mother of Christ, he deserved a little time away after the affair of the mad woman this morning. He could still feel the hairs stand up on the back of his neck at the thought of her staring eyes. Jesu, but that had been terrifying. Better to stand in the way of a host of chivalry than remain in the same room as a woman like her.

When his horse was brought, he took it without comment, mounted, and rode away slowly. The bridge over the first defence, the gap in the ramp before the gate, was falling into disrepair. He would have to have the under-sheriff look at it and have the thing replaced.

It was the same with all the basic fabric of the castle. Only a few of the buildings actually had roofs. Most had lost them over the years, and no one had bothered to replace them. In the same way, the towers were all so dilapidated that they were gradually collapsing. There was nothing to be done with a place like this.

If he had the money available, he would have razed the place to the ground and replaced it with a good, new, warm castle on the lines of the late king's castles in Wales. Good, substantial fortresses with firm, grey walls of moorstone rather than this soft sandy stuff. But a place like that would cost far too much. The king would never agree to it, not while the city was so quiescent. In the past, there had been risings here, and men had revolted, but not for many years now. Not since the tallage riots of 1314 had there been any popular gatherings in mutiny – and even that had been in Bristol, not down here in Exeter. At least the Bristolians had the courage of their anger against that tax. Down here the men were more bovine.

He clattered down towards the High Street, glancing about him at the clear space around the castle. On the north and east, the castle was bounded by the city's own walls, but to the south and west the walls gave onto the city itself. For protection there were no houses allowed nearby, and this clearing meant that any attack would be visible for some distance. Now, though, there were a few apple trees permitted. And city-dwellers were allowed some rights of pasturage on the slopes. There was a flock of sheep there now, grazing quietly on the very last of the year's grass.

It was a calming sight, a pastoral scene such as he had witnessed for so many years, and a little of the tension he had felt started to leave him. The horse under him was eager, and he was growing keen to get out of the city himself. They would both be better for a good ride.

Already soothed, he was almost smiling by the time he turned east on the High Street and rode up to the East Gate. He acknowledged the porter at the gate, and was about to ride on when he heard the sudden shriek.

He whirled in the saddle and gazed behind him, and saw the woman again. His heart seemed to freeze, and he felt a wave of ice smooth its way over his back as he took in her uplifted arms, her wide eyes and slobbering mouth. He was tempted to ride straight back into her and run her down, or, better, to draw steel and run her through, but even as his hand strayed to his hilt, he was aware of the porter and all the others there in the gateway. No, he couldn't do that. But he needn't hang around here like a cretin.

Turning away, he set spurs to his horse's flanks and felt the power of the beast as he surged forward, under the old gate, and eastward on the old roads.

Exeter City

She stopped, gaping, feeling foolish in amongst so many others who stood and stared at her as though thinking she was mad. Had he not *seen* her? Perhaps he couldn't see her in such a group, with all these others about her. Yes. That was probably it. He had surely heard her voice, because he had turned as soon as she called out to him. 'My sweet!' she had cried when she saw him, and instantly he had paused and looked for her. She had seen that: he must have been upset to have missed her. That was it. He had looked for her, and when he couldn't see her he had ridden off in a hurry.

It was tempting to go up to the castle now, to walk straight inside as though she was already married to him, but she knew that she shouldn't yet. Her ascendancy was not in doubt, but a certain wariness was making itself felt. Perhaps it would be better to wait until Alice was already gone.

She gazed longingly after the man who, she was convinced, loved her more than anything. There was a soft, wistful smile on her face at the thought of him, but then she turned about and began to trudge back towards the city centre. She had nowhere to go just now, and the only thing she could think of doing was making her way to an inn and staying there for a night. In the morning she would be able to seek out the sheriff again and make sure that this time he saw her.

'Are you feeling a little better now?' Baldwin asked Robinet.

Newt stood at the side of the room, away from the strange devices and implements lying all about the place. There was an unfamiliar emptiness in his soul as he looked about the room. It made him feel desolate. For some reason it reminded him that he would never see his friend again.

After considering him for a few moments, Baldwin suggested that the sheriff's wife should be taken home again, and after she had gone with Langatre he stood and contemplated Newt.

'Your friend was killed for some reason,' he said. 'Is there any more you can tell us about him?'

'What more is there to say? He was remaining outside here to watch for the man he had heard of who could have been the man who killed James. He sent me to fetch pies for our breakfast, and when I returned he was gone. I thought he must have followed the man. It never occurred to me that he could be . . . there.'

'Do you know who the man was whom he sought to find? If you have any information, it would help us.'

'All I know is, he said that the man was tall and gaunt-looking. I had thought that the man I saw was shorter, but Walter heard different. I suppose I saw someone else.'

'Or you were right and he was wrong. How did he come by this description?' Simon asked.

'Walter was familiar with people I would never have come to know. It was all a part of his work. He knew those who were involved in crimes, whereas I only ever mingled with the people who were important in the city.'

Baldwin studied a long-handled sickle and shook his head distastefully. 'I dislike men like this Langatre who meddle in things they know little about. Fooling about with conjurations . . . it is ridiculous. A man should be expert in his own field and leave others to their own. I am competent as an investigator – you were a good messenger, I presume? And Walter, he was an expert in the king's household. But an expert at what?'

Newt sighed to himself. 'I have no reason to conceal anything from you. He was a man who would enforce the king's rule. Sometimes that would mean that he must kill in order to protect the king. He would remove obstacles to the king's will.'

Simon's face clouded. 'So he *was* an assassin? We had heard as much.'

'Yes. But not a mercenary. He would only ever work for the king.'

Baldwin stood and walked about the room, a hand cupping his chin, the other wrapped about his upper body. He didn't look at Newt as he asked, 'Did he ever kill a man here?'

Newt cleared his throat. 'I think so.'

'Who, and when?'

'He told me a long time ago that he had to come here when the Bristol men revolted against their tallage. You remember that?'

'Of course I do. It was the outset of the dread years, wasn't it? The city was in revolt from 1314 to 1316, when the whole posse of the county was called out against the men of the city. Was it not Pembroke who had to lay siege?'

'Yes. I think there were upwards of eighty who were outlawed. It was a disaster, especially coming on the heels of Bannockburn and other failures of the king's. That was why . . . well, I was gaoled the year before, in 1315, because the king was wary of any comments that held his authority in contempt. And it was why Walter was sent down here a while afterwards.'

'Why?'

'If you knew Walter, you'd know that there was no point asking him something like that. He'd just be quiet, and you wouldn't want to ask again. However, I have heard that a man died. A fellow called Piers de Caen.'

'And this was when?' Simon said.

'It was the same year as the Bristol riots – the year sixteen. He was calming hotheads here because the king did not want to see any more challenges to his authority. He couldn't afford them. Christ Jesus, it was bad enough that he should have lost his greatest friend . . .'

'Gaveston?'

'Yes. So Walter was here, and afterwards, when it came to his leaving the king's service because he was getting to be quite an old man, well, he thought of this city because he had liked the feel of the place when he had been here before.'

'So what you're saying is, he chose to retire to the place where he had pacified the people,' Simon said with a knowing nod.

Baldwin shook his head slowly. 'No, I don't think that's quite what he's saying, is it, Robinet? You think he came here for slightly different reasons, don't you?'

'He liked it here. He felt safe.'

'Yes. Because he could cow the people who lived here. Isn't that right?'

'I suppose that's one way to look at it.'

'Because when he was here, I don't remember any rioting.'

'There wasn't any,' Simon agreed. 'Nothing here in 1316 or afterwards – the famine was kicking in by then, after all.'

'That's not what he meant,' Baldwin said, turning back to them and sitting on the table's edge. 'No, our friend here is talking about a hired murderer who retired to the place where he felt secure because he reckoned he could kill others with impunity. That was how he "pacified" this city, after all, wasn't it, Robinet? He killed Piers de Caen.'

'I think so.'

'And that was the friend you had?' Baldwin spat contemptuously.

'He was a friend to me,' Newt said defensively. 'All those he killed were enemies of the king. He was no murderer, but a professional acting in the interests of the crown.'

'A mercenary,' Simon said with disgust.

'No. A king's man. A man from the king's household. And honourable. He would only kill quickly and with the minimum of pain. I know that.'

Baldwin's tone was dismissive. 'You may do – *I* do not. Killers are killers, friend. Once a man gets a taste for slaughter, it is a hard habit to vanquish.'

Chapter Thirty-Five

Exeter City

Baldwin and Simon walked back towards their inn with the coroner.

'My stomach thinks my throat's been cut!' Coroner Richard declared loudly as they passed the bloody stain in the street where Sarra had lain.

Baldwin was looking at the stain, and now he frowned and stared towards the undercroft. 'Whoever killed Walter, they must have invited him down there. Surely a professional killer like Walter wouldn't have let the man get behind him?'

'If it was an older man, perhaps then he'd do it,' Simon guessed. 'This necromancer is said to be tall and skinny. A haggard old man, from what we've heard. Surely a brave and brawny man would feel safe enough with someone like that behind him?'

The coroner was thinking. 'If I were a mercenary killer like Walter, I doubt I'd let my own mother behind me. I'd be inside the room and sidle round with my back to the wall. I certainly wouldn't allow a man rumoured to be a paid assassin to get behind me, no matter how old and decrepit he was.'

'That is how I read it too,' Baldwin said. 'It makes little sense to me. Do you think that man was telling the truth, Simon?'

'Yes. I trusted his word,' Simon said. 'He seemed quite rational and sensible to me.'

'Certainly rational,' Baldwin said. 'But I wonder if he told us all the truth.'

'What else could there be?'

Coroner Richard stopped and was gazing at Baldwin with his head set to one side. 'You have an idea, don't you?'

Baldwin continued walking for a few paces, then halted, his head bowed. 'I think I have the beginnings of an idea, but I am sure of nothing yet. I have to consider things more carefully.'

'In the meantime,' Simon said, 'I think that we ought to make sure that the woman who tried to kill the sheriff's wife has been captured. If she is still wandering the streets, others could be in danger.'

'Yes,' the Coroner agreed. 'We should make our way to the castle as quickly as possible and ensure that the good lady arrived home safely.'

'To check that she has suffered no harm,' Simon agreed.

'Oh, yes. And to see what they serve in the sheriff's hall for dinner. It is a fish day, and I have heard that he does not stint when it comes to a good fish pie and wine,' the coroner agreed unperturbably, a beatific smile fixed to his face.

Robinet stood watching from Langatre's doorway as the three men disappeared east up the hill, and only when they were out of his sight completely did he dart back into the house, into the magician's hall, and over to a table. There he found a knife with a good oak handle. He picked it up and weighed it in his hand. The blade was a scant two and a half inches in length, and black all over, unpolished from the forge, with only the edge keen and gleaming where it had been honed. Putting it on his forefinger, he found that the short blade balanced the heavy wooden handle nicely. It was ideal.

With it in his pocket, he peered out through the doorway into the street. He had worked in places like this often enough to recognise potential danger when it was visible. Today he could see nothing, and he soon nodded to himself and slipped out, his back to the wall for the first five paces, eyes scanning the street, where there was nothing to give him cause to shy. After that, he set off at a smart pace, up towards the Carfoix, and once there he turned southwards to the South Gate.

He knew that his friend had been grabbed from behind. He intended to see that no one had an opportunity to do the same to him.

His old friend had been in that room for a specific reason. He reckoned that it was likely that the necromancer had invited him inside, or perhaps the man had left the undercroft, and the watcher had thought it safe to essay a short investigation into what the magician was attempting. No matter. The man had killed a close friend. He would suffer for it.

First, he must find the evil bastard who had been there in the room. He wasn't sure how he was going to do that yet, but he'd think out a way soon, and then, when he had the man in his hands, he'd kill him *very* slowly indeed. He'd learn whether a necromancer could beg a demon to harm a man when his own fingers had all been cut off.

He came to the South Gate and nodded to the gateman. In the house he saw Art, and stared at him meaningfully. Art looked from him to his father, but his father was already speaking to someone else in the gateway, and Art quickly left the house and came to him.

'Boy, I need help.'

'It'll cost.'

'It always does, boy. It always does.' He smiled, and then the smile was wiped away. 'I want you to find me a necromancer.'

Exeter Castle

Sir Matthew was back in the city in the late afternoon, a little weary, but elated after a fine ride. The rounsey was still full of spirit, and if he'd wanted to, he felt he could have ridden the beast all the way to Winchester and back!

Not today, though. There was too much to be done. This was a busy time of year, and there was still the matter of the writ about the murder attempt on the king and the Despensers.

He had heard a rumour from a friend in court that the Lord Despenser had himself written to the pope asking for special protection against such attempts at assassination using supernatural means – but the pope had written back to tell him to mend his ways and stop abusing his powers, beg forgiveness for his past sins, and nothing more would be needful. Apparently the Despenser had raged up and down the corridors of his house for hours after reading that.

At the moment, though, Matthew thought he had enough on his own plate. There was the matter of his wife, then the mad maidservant, not to mention this trouble with sorcerers. It was all getting to be a little too much for him. He needed time to focus and concentrate. Stop being blown about by events.

The castle came into view, and he found himself peering about him, half expecting to find himself confronted at any moment by a mad woman with foaming mouth and rolling eyes. Christ in a cave, but that wench scared him. Madness was akin to leprosy – both were obviously unhealable, and both left the sufferer revolting to all men of good sense. And madness was the worse in some ways. It meant that the victim could not herself see why she had become the object of revulsion.

He rode in through the gate and tossed the reins to a waiting groom, then dismounted and stood watching while the man began his work. If there was one thing that Sir Matthew would not tolerate, it was any laxity in the care of his mounts. A stable boy or groom who displayed laziness or incompetence would not last any time in the castle. No one received more than the one chance to do things right in Sir Matthew's stables.

'Sir Matthew? There are some men here to see you, in your hall.'

Sir Matthew gazed distastefully at his steward. 'I have not invited anyone to visit me today.'

'These were most insistent, sir. The Keeper of the King's Peace, a coroner, and a bailiff from Tavistock. They are trying to catch the woman who killed your wife's maid.'

'My wife's . . .'

'Your wife was there, sir. It is thought that the woman wanted to harm her too.'

Sir Matthew's mouth fell wide. He recalled glancing back from the gate, seeing Jen with her hand raised, the fist and forearm painted with blood . . . he left the steward in the court and bolted to the hall's door. He threw it wide and hurried inside. 'My wife, where is she?'

'I am here, husband,' Alice responded. She lay on a bench near the fire, while a girl soothed her brow with a cool cloth and passed her a large gobletful of wine.

'My darling, I only just heard – your servant is dead?'

'Yes. She was stabbed by that little bitch we removed this morning.'

'It is true that it was her, then. And you saw it all?'

'If Sarra had not sprung in between us, I should be the one lying dead on the cobbles instead of her,' Alice said.

'We would like to speak to you about this,' Coroner Richard said.

Sir Matthew lurched, startled by the voice over his shoulder. In truth, he had been in such a hurry to speak to his poor wife, he had forgotten that he had visitors. Now he spun and saw that there were three men seated at the table at the other end of the hall. 'Who are you all?'

Baldwin snapped curtly, 'Come, now, Sir Sheriff! You know me at least, and my good friend here the coroner. And if you do not know my companion Bailiff Simon Puttock, one of my lord abbot of Tavistock's most trusted servants, it is about time you did.'

Peering into the gloomier reaches of the hall, away from the fire, the sheriff could make out their faces more clearly. He could also see that although the keeper and Simon had risen to their feet, the coroner still remained sitting at the bench. He waved a hand airily while in the other he held a salmon's head.

Matthew nodded to them, bowing as graciously as he might as Coroner Richard sucked loudly on the head. 'My apologies, lordings. You were in the gloom there – after the sunshine in my courtyard. I did not recognise you.'

'Now, Sheriff, can you tell us aught about the woman who left your service this morning? We understand she may have come from Silverton. Is that right?'

'I have no idea. Perhaps the steward would know?'

'He thought Silverton,' Baldwin said, reflecting on how little interest some people took in the lives of those upon whom their comfort depended. 'We have sent a man to the vill to see whether she might have tried to escape in that direction, but have had no luck.'

'She must be in the fields, then.'

'I doubt it,' Lady Alice said weakly. 'Why should she leave the city? If she had somewhere to go where she would be free, that would be one thing, but if she's got nowhere else to go, then why should she leave? I think it more likely that she waits somewhere nearby.'

'Why, my darling?' Sir Matthew asked.

Baldwin responded. 'Sir, we have been discussing this affair since we arrived here. It seems clear that the wench is infatuated with you . . .' He was tempted to add an acerbic comment about his own surprise at the thought, but curbed his tongue. 'It is possible that she fled after her crime, but it is equally likely that she has remained here, in which case you will have to do all that is needful to protect your lady.'

Sir Matthew felt as though he might be sick. This morning he had contemplated the grateful thanks of the king for his swift and efficient apprehension of the magician, and instead he was being advised to exercise great caution on behalf of his wife. 'Why would the child think I could desire her? It's insane.'

'Did you ever give her cause to think you might love her?' Baldwin pressed. 'Anything at all?'

'Never, on my heart! I love my wife, Sir Baldwin. Adultery would never sit easily on my soul.'

'I have heard of young wenches who gain a false impression of another's love,' Baldwin admitted doubtfully. 'They have such an intense fascination with the object of their desire that they convince themselves that their adoration is reciprocated. I have never witnessed such a one, though. Are you quite sure that you never gave her cause to believe that you might . . .'

He could not continue. One look at the sheriff's face told him all he needed to know. This was not a man ruled by his heart on most occasions, but seeing him now, Baldwin was forced to admit to himself that unless the fellow was a consummate actor, he was no adulterer. To Baldwin, who had once submitted to his passions and betrayed the love he felt for his own dear wife, it was plain enough that this man had never committed the same sin.

'This wench is very clearly dangerous. The men must be told to redouble all their efforts in the city to find her, and in the meantime you, Lady Alice, must not leave the castle grounds.'

'I would be most reluctant to become a prisoner in my own house,' she said sharply.

'And we should all be most reluctant to see you buried for lack of protection,' Baldwin said as gently as he could. 'And now, Sheriff, there is another matter which we needs must ask you about.'

It had been damnably cold at the gate when she stopped, but Maurice had steeled himself to kill Jen. The bitch had tried to kill his sister, and he would spill her blood for that.

Standing there, he'd had a stirring of revulsion at the thought of slaying a young woman, but the memory of the great blow aimed at Sarra was enough to drive away any compunction he might usually have felt. The blood . . . he could scarcely believe that the girl who had smiled at him and flirted as she relayed messages from her mistress, his sister, had been slaughtered like a hog in the street. Her sightless eyes returned to haunt him now, as though reproving him for doubting the justice of his revenge.

She had been there in front of him as he began to make his way towards her. With her back to him, she made a very tempting target. Easy enough to throw a knife at her, except in a crowded street it would be too obvious. No one could miss the sight of a man hurling a missile. Better by far to slip a knife between her ribs from closer.

As he approached, she lifted a hand to wave, and following the line of her sight, he saw the man whose attention she was trying to catch, saw the sheriff on his horse suddenly spur his mount on, and saw him clatter along the roadway and out through the gate.

Suddenly Jen's shoulders dropped. Even from behind she presented the very picture of dejection. It was little enough, but sufficient to make Maurice hesitate.

Turning, she stumbled blindly away, a hand at her face, the other clutching at the breast of her tunic.

It was that which stayed his hand. She came closer and closer, and he stood still, waiting, his hand on his knife, until she was before him, and then he saw the misery in her features, and his hand left his dagger sheathed. It was impossible to harm a child in such despair. And that was what she was: a child barely ready to be loosed from her mother's apron-strings.

She looked at him, her eyes unseeing, and then continued on her way, sobbing with deep, racking shudders of her entire frame, and he couldn't do it. A man, yes, he could kill any man – but not this child.

Wonderingly, he followed her to a little tavern, but although she went inside, it was plain enough that she had little enough money, and soon she was out again, reeling from one wall to another. Although occasionally she would look about her, it was clear enough to him that she didn't recognise him when her eyes passed over him. She had no thoughts for anyone else; she was entirely focused on her own deep depression.

He was past making an attempt on her life, and yet he would not give up his pursuit. As she walked along a narrower street, then turned into a lane near the South Gate, he trailed along behind her. Soon he saw her test a gate, and enter a small yard. She crossed it, and climbed some steps to a hayloft. With the door open, she looked about her once, and then threw herself inside, pulling the doors closed behind her.

Walking in after her, he stood a while staring at the doors. They were designed to be locked shut. There was a simple, hinged bar that rotated about a bolt in one door. The two ends of this fitted into wooden slots set into the doorframe on either side of the door. Maurice considered the doors for a long time, before quietly stepping up to them and turning the bar to lock her inside.

Chapter Thirty-Six

Exeter City

Art had spoken to his friends at the two taverns he knew, but this one was a much worse place.

It stood a short way down the little alleyway that ran from Combe Street southwards to the wall. The alley itself was foul, stinking of piss and shit, and filled with refuse from all the shabby buildings in the area. It was no surprise to Art that there was no chapel or church in this whole quarter of the city. No vicar would want to penetrate too deeply into this part.

Much happened here. The wall was always a convenient boundary, but where there was a wall there were also men with ladders, and often in the morning, after a good gambling session with dice or a little contest between fighters, a fresh body would be found thrown over the wall to lie beneath near the stews or the quay. A man who asked too many questions was also likely to end up down there, as Art knew. Still, he had been promised money to find out all he could about this unknown necromancer, and he wasn't going to turn his nose up at good money. So here he was, trying to breathe the revolting air sparingly so he didn't catch a disease from the miasma that lurked all about.

The tavern itself was only a single room with a low ceiling, little better than an undercroft. At the farther wall was a trestle table with four barrels of ale racked ready. Over it, splashes had struck the ceiling where the barrels had been over-lively, and there was a reek of stale ale that had seeped into the earthen floor over years. Men stood about with their horns or cups, for this place had no need of tables – it was not a relaxing alehouse for a worker to repair to after a hard day's effort and toil. No, it was a place to stand and drink until a man could no longer stand. Then he would merely sit or fall prostrate, and others might leave him alone, or might take their sport with his body. Art had seen one man bound and scarred by the knives of three men who took a dislike to him as he lay snoring.

He felt eyes upon him as he entered. It was unsettling, and he almost turned about and told the man that he couldn't learn anything, but then he thought again of the money and he squared his shoulders and marched to the trestle.

'Strong ale.'

A horn was filled, and he paid before taking a gulp. 'You know of this man been killed today? They say it may be the same man killed the king's messenger. I know a man will pay for news of the killer.'

'You think we'd be likely to help someone like that?'

Art could hear the voice and thought he knew the man. It was a fellow who had once been a trader in the market, but had been thrown from his pitch by the pie-powder court which found he had set fire to a competitor's wares. Arson was looked upon as one of the most serious crimes in this largely wooden city, and he was thrown out. Having lost his livelihood, he resorted to his native cunning and his dagger to earn a penny when he could, and it was said that old Hob was as willing to gut a man as a rabbit.

'Look, all he wants is to try to catch the man killed his friend, that's all.'

'I think he wants us to turn traitor to our own, that's what he wants. It's one thing to ask us to see whether we can finger the man who killed the king's messenger, but now he wants a fellow who's only looking to earn a crust, eh?'

There was a ripple of laughter about the room. Art carefully controlled his shaking hand as he took a long pull at his drink. It would not do to let people think that he was afraid of them. They could work like a pack of dogs when someone showed a trace of fear, all of them helping to pull down their quarry that they might tear him to pieces on the floor.

He finished his horn and set it down. 'I'll tell him no one here knows anything, then,' he said, and turned towards the door. The man he knew as Hob was in his way.

Hob was heavy-set, with a massive paunch that was held in by a broad belt, and he had a rough scarlet tunic and faded cowl and hood.

He had only the one eye, for the second had been lost long ago in a fight, and now he peered at Art with it as though weighing him up like a dog for a fight. 'I don't think I like the way you come in here asking questions for others, boy. I didn't like it the other night, and I don't like it now. You'll be telling the beadles all about us next, won't you? And then you'll be telling stories about us in the sheriff's court, I dare say.'

'No. I only want to try to help this man. He is paying well.'

'The sheriff may pay well too, to have us all in his gaol nice and safe. Don't think I want to go there, though. Perhaps you should be made an example, eh? We haven't had a fresh boy down here for a long time. Maybe you'd like to be bedded by us all, eh?'

Art felt a sweat of ice break out all over his body. The idea of being raped by this motley gang was enough to make his stomach turn over in his belly, and he shivered with a sudden paroxysm of terror. He wished now he'd not taken the man's money again. 'No, look, let me go and I'll just be away. I only said I'd try to learn if I could, that's all.'

'I don't think you should try to go in such a hurry,' Hob said, and he smiled. Somehow that was more petrifying than his words.

Hands grabbed him. Art felt them on his arms, rough, calloused hands on his wrists and elbows; a foot kicked his legs away, and he was on his back suspended by his arms. Someone was giggling, pulling at the cords of his tunic, pulling down his hosen, yanking at his underclothes, and he was struggling, crying, shouting, and then he was on the floor, dropped, thud, just like that, and gasping. He drew up his hosen quickly, while all the men had their attention elsewhere. And then he heard the voice.

'Leave him, I said. Anyone who touches him is picking a fight with me. And you don't want that.'

Art could see Hob above him. He was peering over towards the doorway, fingering the knife that dangled by a thong from his throat, and then he hawked and spat, and at the same time his hand took hold of his knife and he started to walk.

Hob had a lumbering walk, but for all that he covered the ground quickly when he wanted to, and now he wanted to. Art saw him move off and accelerate fast, and as he drew nearer to the door he started to bellow like a bull, and then he slashed with his hand.

There was a spray of blood, a roaring, and Art saw Hob spin, then crash sideways into a wall. His hands were at his face, and the blood was pumping in a fine mist from a gash in his temple, and Art suddenly realised that he had been hit in his remaining eye. He was blind.

'Any others want to try themselves against me?'

Art could hear the poison in that voice. It was the sound of a man who hated himself. He could ravage and kill, but he loathed it. And now he was Art's sole friend. Art could no more leave him than fly. He closed his eyes, expecting a knife in his side at any moment, maybe a kick in his kidneys, but nothing happened. When he opened them again, he saw that the men about him had gone. They were over near the barrels, muttering to each other as they refilled their cups, ignoring Art and his companion.

'Are you all right, boy? Then get up.'

Art obeyed him, staring at Hob with fearful fascination. Hob was hunched over on the floor, his head down, and Art could hear his snuffling as he wept. Then he looked up.

'Kill him! You going to let him do this? Kill the son of a Winchester whore! He's blinded me!'

None of the men moved. And now Art felt the man beside him start to twist his head, revolving his skull on his neck. 'I want to know. Who saw him. Who knows anything. I want to know where this necromancer has gone.'

'Kill him! You can take him, there're seven of you! Kill him, but do it slowly! Come on, where are you all? Are you women? He's one man!'

Art felt his eyes filling up. It wasn't the shabby figure on the floor there, it was the thought that if this man hadn't been here, he would have been spread over a table by now, with all these men covering him . . . he would have been killed tonight, and if he hadn't, he would have wanted to take his own life. The revulsion at what Hob had tried to do ate at his soul. He detested the old man, and he wanted to kick Hob into a pulp. He wanted to stab at him again and again . . . but just now all he could taste was a foul nausea in his mouth. He wanted to spew.

'I want him. One of you must know where he is.'

He stood at Art's side on feet lying flat on the ground, slightly apart, his arms at his sides as though resting, the little blade showing from his right hand, apparently gripped lightly, not tightly as Art would have imagined, but more as an artist would hold his reed.

'No one wants to help me?'

Suddenly all was silent in the room. Hob was still, listening with a pained expression on his face. Art noticed that he could actually hear the men breathing. Not himself, and not the man at his side, but he could hear all the others, the stertorous noise of Hob, the rasping, higher-pitched sound of the alehouse-keeper's son, the low, guttural tone of an older draw-latch in the corner . . . and then the man moved again.

He reached out and took a man's hand in his own, then pulled. The man fell off-balance, and as he fell the man took a grip under his chin and set the knife against his neck.

Instantly the men all spun around, two with knives already in their fists.

'Do nothing or he will die.'

'You can't make it to the door without us getting you. I think we ought to teach you about coming into our little house. We ought to . . .'

'Shut up, Saul, he's sticking it in! Jesus save me!'

'If you try to rush me, he dies. If you try to throw something, he dies. If you try anything, he will die. Is that clear?'

Art wondered whether any of the men would be concerned to see the man die, but they seemed to be unwilling to risk his life. All stood and stared as Art and the man slowly made their way backwards towards the door.

'I want to hear who. I want to know where he is.'

And at last a man spoke.

Maurice stood in the dark and stared back at the little hay loft where he'd locked the girl. There was no sound from it, and he wondered whether she had even realised that she'd been trapped.

She couldn't be left in there to die. He could not do that. Better to go to her and slay her humanely than to leave her to succumb to hunger or thirst. The idea of killing her was appalling, but little worse than the idea of letting her loose and seeing her kill his sister. That too was unconscionable.

He cursed, swearing at his miserable fortune. If it were not for the depredations of the foul Despenser clan, the fecklessness of the king and his own misfortune, he would be able to march to the sheriff or a city bailiff and tell of this chit's crime. Then the responsibility for her punishment would be someone else's. Although that would merely pass on the accountability. What he would prefer would be to give the child some chance of protection. Not now, though. In his outlaw state, that was impossible.

Unless there was someone who could mediate for the girl. That set his mind racing, and soon he was setting off towards the cathedral's close. At the entrance to the gate, he saw a rather pale-looking man in clerical clothing, and walked to him. 'Father?'

Busse was startled, and caught his breath as the stranger approached. Sighing, he closed his eyes a moment. This was one of the worst days of his life, he thought. The discovery of that body in Langatre's undercroft, the realisation that he was a suspect when the folk from the street crowded round him . . . it was a day he would prefer to forget, and that as soon as possible.

'Yes,' he answered testily. 'I am on my way to see my lord bishop. Please be quick.'

'I saw a woman enter a hayloft down this lane, Father,' Maurice said. 'It's just down here, on the right as you go towards the South Gate. Above a stable with a broken door in a cobbled yard. The latch fell and locked her inside.'

'What of it?' Busse said, but even as he turned back from staring down the lane in the direction indicated, Maurice was gone. 'Where is he?' he demanded pitifully. 'What can I do about this?'

He was in a quandary. There was no time now . . . it was growing dark, and his stomach was already querulously rumbling.

The aspirant abbot set his jaw, his mouth pursed, and hurried down the lane to the abbot's gatehouse.

'Keeper, I have just been told that a girl has been locked in a hayloft,' he declared as he saw the porter at the gate. He quickly explained what he had heard, before continuing on his way to the bishop.

The porter looked about him at the darkening lanes. 'Can't do anything now,' he said, and slammed the gate shut.

There would be time tomorrow. He'd tell the nearest watchman as soon as he reopened the gate in the morning.

Exeter Castle

Baldwin and Simon waited while the sheriff took his leave of his wife, and then led the way outside, the coroner taking up the rear, reluctant as ever to leave a still-filled table.

'Now, Sir Matthew, I have some questions for you on this other matter,' Baldwin said when they were out of earshot of any idle ears.

'What is that?'

'I am drawn to conclude that you know more than you have said about the arrival in the city of a necromancer.'

'Me?' Matthew was stunned. 'All I know is that I had a writ asking me to help the king in his investigations, and I did what I could to aid him.'

'You did? What did you do, exactly? You arrested a man who could not conceivably have had anything to do with affairs in Coventry, and had him held in your gaol for a little over a night. I do not see how that would have materially assisted the king.'

'He was a necromancer. He might have known something.'

Baldwin eyed him with contempt. 'You expect me to believe that? You seriously believe that Despenser and the king himself would be impressed with your bringing forward a benighted soul all the way from Exeter, when it was clear enough that he knew nothing about the affair? That he *could* have known nothing?'

'If there was time for the messenger to arrive here from Coventry, after he had already travelled all the way to the king, received his writ, and made his way all the way here, there was plenty of time for a foul necromancer to have made his way here from Coventry. The man Langatre could have had information that was useful. It was right to arrest him.'

Baldwin was still. 'I had not considered that – are you saying that the very same messenger came here after Coventry?'

'Yes. The man James was the same man who took news of the attempt on the king's life to the king.'

'What is it, Baldwin?' Simon asked. 'You can see something, can't you?'

'Only this: if the man who brought the message here was the same one as was in Coventry, then we have a reason why someone might have killed him. He could have seen the necromancer and any confederates in Coventry, couldn't he? If one of the assassins had made his way here, thinking himself secure from any agents of the king, how would he feel were he to suddenly be confronted by one of the men who had seen him there?'

'And the carver of antlers?'

'Perhaps this fellow from Coventry thought he took too much interest in him?'

'All this supposes that there is someone here from Coventry,' Coroner Richard said. 'We have no proof of that as yet.'

'No, we have no proof, but we have had a man break into Langatre's house and rob him of some tools used by necromancers. Sheriff, I would be grateful if you could have your clerk give instructions to all the gate porters to try to recall whether they have admitted a man from Coventry or somewhere nearby in the last month.'

'Of course.'

It was Simon who shook his head doubtfully. 'That is another reason why this Mucheton could have been killed.'

'Why?' the sheriff demanded.

'Because if there is someone manufacturing dolls in the city with the intention of stabbing them to kill people, what would he use to stab them? A white bone pin might appeal to some men.'

'*Maleficium!*' the coroner breathed.

'It would explain the black cat seen at the first murder, and the strange disappearing man at the second,' Simon said.

'A bite of strong cheese or too much strong ale would explain them just as well,' Baldwin said scathingly.

'So you may believe,' Sir Matthew said, 'but I have heard that Sir Richard de Sowe was killed by this necromancer in Coventry. A doll was made, and a little lead pin thrust into his head killed him. These necromancers are very mighty, Sir Baldwin. And I have heard that they can do all they wish with the merest glance at a man. The demons they carry about with them can do their will . . .'

'You think so?' Baldwin asked sarcastically. 'And I suppose they carry these demons in rings on their fingers?'

'That is what they say.'

'I wonder, do they have especially strong fingers?'

Sir Matthew was puzzled. 'What?'

'Well, you know how heavy a falcon is. If you were to walk about all day with a falcon on your wrist, would not your arm grow tired? Yet a demon is apparently so light that it can rest on a finger, and not make the magician exhausted. Are they so small that they can weigh so little? And if so small, do they truly have any power? Ptchah! This is nonsense, all of it. I believe in corporeal bodies causing harm. The antler-carver Mucheton was murdered by a man with a knife; the messenger was murdered by a man with a knife and another, perhaps, with a cord; the servant of Langatre was killed by a cord; Walter of Hanlegh was murdered with a knife. All weapons which are used by men, not by mystical and magical creatures. We should look for human agents here, not ghosts and demons!'

Chapter Thirty-Seven

Exeter City

Art hurried with a growing sense of trepidation. He had been involved on the fringes of violence and outlawry for some years, but this was the first time he had witnessed near-death. Hob had never been a friend of his . . . or anyone else for that matter. He just happened to be a strong man in a team who admired strength and little else. Yet he had been destroyed in a moment by this man, this stranger. And now they were hurrying towards a place where there would probably be another fight. It made him anxious, and his nervousness was making him stumble.

'Keep up, boy! Is this the alley?'

'Yes. Yes, this is the one.'

'He said it was the third door. Come! You can knock for me.'

Art was reluctant to get any further involved. He wanted nothing more to do with all this – but the man was compelling. Art had the feeling that if he wasn't careful, it would be him being held by the chin, a sharp knife point at his throat. 'What do you want me to do? I don't know who lives here!'

'The lad in the tavern said that if anyone would know where the necromancer had gone, they would be here. Let's find out.'

Art stood at the door and hunched his shoulders against the cold. Perhaps it was him, but just now he felt as though the temperature in the alley had dropped almost to freezing. He pulled his jack closer about his chest, gripped it in a tight fist, and knocked.

'Do it again!'

Art complied. While the knife was held in the man's fist, he was unwilling to antagonise him. At last, after a third bout of knocking, Art heard steps. They were hesitant, ponderous, shuffling steps, and Art heard them come almost to the door before a thin little voice called out, 'Who is it? What do you want?'

'Mistress, I need a room. Do you know where a man may rest the night?'

'Go find an inn. There are rooms aplenty in them.'

'No – I don't want to be in a place like that. I need somewhere quieter.'

The bar was lifted, and then the door opened a crack. Immediately Art felt himself propelled forward, into the old timbers, and then he was through and sprawling on the dirt floor, while his companion slammed the door behind them, barred it, and then kicked the knife from the old woman's hand.

She was older than Art would have expected. Thin, frail-looking, she was at least sixty years if a day, and her thin, hatchet face spoke of her harsh life. There had been a time perhaps when she had been young, but there was no sign of it in her pinched features and narrowed eyes. Now she cringed like a dog waiting to be kicked, and cowered away from Art's companion.

'Don't hurt me, masters! I have nothing worth taking, on the gospels!'

'You have knowledge. That will do for me. I seek a man who recently came to the city from Coventry. Do you know where he is?' He was gazing about him as he spoke. There was a staff by the door, and he moved it further from her reach, glancing at the ladder propped up against the rafter where her bed was unrolled on bare planks.

She interrupted his thoughts. 'How can I know? I am bound to my house. I rarely leave it now, with my poor legs hurting so much and . . .'

'Yes, old crone, you are a wizened old bitch. You were a whore, though, and you know where the whores all live and work, still, don't you? And you have a good knowledge of where a man might take a room to hide from the law.'

Art wondered if he was right . . . there was a slight glint in her eyes as though she was considering springing on the two men. As he watched, he was sure that he saw her right hand moving under her kirtle, and then stop, as if she had taken hold of a knife and was waiting before drawing it from a scabbard. Still she cringed, trembling, as though petrified by them. She whined, 'How can I know all this? I am only an old woman trying to make ends meet.'

'And you do so by peddling information. Very well. I have money. I will share it with you – for information.'

'There are some houses where a man may hide,' she admitted, her eyes taken by the coins now held out towards her. Art pursed his lips in a silent whistle at the sight of them all. If he'd known how much the man was carrying, he'd have joined the men at the alehouse against him.

'He is tall, thin, strong, older, and dresses in dark clothing to suit his trade.'

'What trade is that?' she asked, her eyes still on the coins.

'He is a necromancer. He was living at Michael Tanner's undercroft beneath Langatre's house. Do you know the place?'

'There was a man killed there today.'

'That is right. It is the murderer I seek.'

'Why?' Her shrewd eyes rose to his face and studied him. There was no fear in them, he saw. She was entirely absorbed by the attraction of the coins in his hands. Any pretence at cowering was over.

'He has killed my friend,' he said. 'A good friend. I will have vengeance.'

'Ah, well. That's as good a reason as any. Come back in the morning.'

'I want to know now.'

'You'll wait. You'll wait. There's nothing so urgent that you can't wait a short while, and there's nothing I can find out in an instant. You will have to wait. What shall I call you?'

'Robinet. And you?'

'Me?' She laughed drily as she straightened finally. 'Call me Edie. It's what my friends like to call me.'

The Palace Gate

Things grew a little sticky when he told them that he was leaving, because by that stage he had amassed the majority of the money from the table, but Rob had expected some dissatisfaction, and put his hand to his knife, gripping his purse in his other hand as he walked backwards from them, scowling ferociously. A schooling amongst the sailors of Dartmouth taught a lad much about life, he reflected as he turned and ran towards the Palace Gate.

There had not been much to learn, if they were telling the truth. Certainly no one appeared to know anything much about Busse, although there was the strange little snippet he had picked up on while they were playing. Beside him was a scruffy little sodomite with the face of a ferret – and the body odour to go with it. He was called Ben the Bridge, because he had been born near the city's great bridge over west, and Ben was a servant in the bishop's household.

'Not much happens there, I dare say,' Rob had ventured early on in the game.

Ben had been stung into a response. 'You think? We have enough excitement.'

'What, meetings with a monk wants to be abbot?'

'Killers and witches. That's what. There are some even here in the city want to see the king dead, that's what I've heard.'

'You have, eh?' Rob had a practised indifference when he cared to use it. Just now he was concentrating on the dice, because he was sure that if he expressed more enthusiasm, this fellow would clam up and say nothing more. The fact that he was showing no interest upped the stakes for Ben, who now fought to gain his attention.

'Yes. The steward of the household had me in there as the bishop was instructing a messenger. You know what he said? He was giving a message to the king that the sheriff here in the city wasn't trustworthy, that's what. He said that the sheriff was weak-willed and might make an attempt on the king's life.'

'A sheriff who's disloyal?' Rob chuckled cynically, and the other boys about the table joined in.

'You laugh if you want to, but the bishop reckons the sheriff plots against the king.'

'And how would he hear that, eh?' Rob demanded sarcastically. 'Suppose he's got spies in the sheriff's house, has he?'

There was no answer to that, and the very lack of any more information piqued Rob's interest. The lad must have thought that the bishop did indeed have some means of access to the sheriff's household, for otherwise he would not have brought up the matter, but the simple fact was that as soon as he realised how much interest Rob took in his words, he had become as open and informative as the cathedral's stones.

Nah, there was probably nothing in it. He was just some lad trying to make an impression on a stranger. Perhaps he was laughing about it even now, telling his mates in their room how he'd got the prick from the sticks all fired up with that ballocks. No, it had to be nothing.

He twisted his face with indecision. Probably no point telling Sir Baldwin and his master. Probably no point at all.

Nah. Best if he just made his way back to the inn. Looked like Busse was set up for the night now.

Exeter City

The old woman watched as the wary, unsettling man all but kicked the youth through the door and then walked out himself. She had to remind herself to try to look anxious, and for the most part she was happy that she had succeeded.

'Well?'

'Mother, you never cease to astonish me,' Ivo the watchman said. He had been dozing in the upper chamber, and now he peered over the boards and stared down at her.

She lifted both hands in irritation and kicked some sparks from her fire, pushing the logs nearer together, and then settling before the flames. 'Get down here, then, fool. You're due out there in the streets shortly. Do you want to lose this job of all?'

Ivo grinned and tipped himself forward, rolling out until he was dangling from his hands, which clung to the rafter. He was only a scant eighteen inches from the floor, and when he allowed himself to fall, his feet scarcely raised any dust. 'Well?'

She shot him a look to hear her own word returned to her. 'I think he's a serious man who wants revenge for the death of his friend. What Art is doing with him, I don't know, but never mind that. There could be good money in supplying him with what he wants. What do you think?'

The watchman nodded thoughtfully. 'It could be worthwhile. His purse looked full to bursting. Just the sort I have always liked.'

'What of this man he seeks?'

Ivo shrugged emphatically. 'If he wants the man and it's worth some cash, who are we to leave the money in his purse? Surely this man is guilty of *something*, eh?'

'Yes,' she said, but she wasn't listening. She had another aspect on her mind. 'Did you recognise him? He looked familiar.'

Ivo knew better than to make fun of her memory. 'I think I have seen him recently about the market or somewhere. Why?'

'No . . . this was longer ago.'

'Well, you can recall many things that happened long before my birth, mother. How would you expect me to remember all your lovers?'

She aimed a clout at his head. 'Fool. You concentrate on winning his money. You'd not be foolish enough to try to take it on your own, and then claim I did no work for it, eh?'

'The thought wouldn't cross my mind,' Ivo said lazily as he pulled on a thick jerkin against the cold night air. He set his cap on his head and smiled at her again as he walked from the room.

She sighed. Her son was an idiot, but an engaging one. She had given birth to him three-and-twenty years ago, and although her husband was already dead by the time of his birth, he had been some consolation to her. As a child he had been difficult, obstinate and surly, but now that he had reached a more mature age, he was endearing to her and others. His good looks and apparent shyness could disarm any, and his carefully learned, hesitant speech made all think that he was a borderline cretin.

As a watchman he was perfect. He would keep his eyes and ears open for any infractions of the city's rules – unless it was to the benefit of himself and his mother. And being a city's officer meant that he could always be counted upon to learn of things sooner than others.

This matter of the dead friend was interesting, though. And there was the other thing: the necromancer. She didn't approve of meddling with people's lives in that way. A sharp blade was enough for her. Killing with supernatural nonsense was for the rich. She found that for her purposes cold steel was adequate.

Edie did wish she could remember where and when she had seen that face before, though.

Only a few tens of yards away, in the little room which Michael had made available for him, John of Nottingham smiled as he set the last of the characters down on the table and rubbed his tired eyes. All was ready now.

He stood and eased himself upright to his full height of six feet and one inch, lifting his arms over his head and feeling the bones of his back settle into their more usual position. The last days of hunching over his work had not been good for them, but now the figures were completed he could rest a little. Already fasted and prepared mentally for the ordeal, he could start his conjuration, and with a task such as this the sooner he began it the better.

Cleanliness was important. He took up the besom and started to sweep the floor of the dirt lying all about. With his arm, he swept the shavings of wax from the table, careful not to disturb the four statues. They looked good. Almost his best. The king stood so regal, especially with the crown. Beside him, the two Despensers were easily distinguished, with their finery on display, the one taller and younger, the father fatter and shorter, just as they were in real life. And then there was the bishop. An evil, grasping man who would do anything to increase his wealth, no matter who else was forced to suffer that he might win advantage. All of them disloyal, untrustworthy men who had conspired against his lord.

When he had been advised to come here and seek a safe place in the tranquillity of this small, rural city, he had been happy to do so not only for the benefit of his clients, so that he could continue to carry out their bidding and earn the balance of the payment they had offered, but also for his own reasons.

There were many who would applaud the removal of this king with his cruelty, treachery and pathetic interests; more still would celebrate the demise of the Despensers. But most would be no less delighted to hear of the death of that foul thief and tyrant, the Lord Bishop Stapledon of Exeter.

For years he had tried to show himself as a moderating influence on the king. He had displayed a political liberality that was appealing to all men of conscience, but then, by degrees, his true colours had been revealed. In place of the man who tried to negotiate peace between the king and his barons, there appeared a man who would oust all of the king's older confidants, who would even presume to evict the queen herself, in order to acquire ever more power and wealth. There was nothing this evil chancre in the heart of government would not dare, so that he might gain more himself. The strength of the realm, the good of the people – they meant nothing compared with his intolerable pride and arrogance.

It was performing a sacred duty, removing these people – especially the arch-villain himself, Bishop Walter of Exeter.

It was the bishop who had stolen lands from all over the realm, impoverishing others as he lined his own purse. He was as evil as the Despensers . . . No! He was worse! They did not conceal their rapacity: he took what he wanted by more subtle means, persuading the king to deprive the queen of her manors and income, and to help – ha! – volunteering to take over her mining ventures and any other profitable opportunities while professing to do all for the good of the realm, not his own self-interest.

There was too much to be done, though, to worry about that man.

John retrieved his book – the one item he had been able to rescue from Coventry – and wiped its cover. The lettering was quite worn already, but he could feel the letters under his fingers on the embossed leatherwork: *Book of the Offices of the Spirits*. This was his own copy, written out in his own hand when he was studying in Oxford.

Satisfied with the cleanliness of his room, he sat down and began breathing carefully. He was no Satanist, and didn't seek to worship the evil lord. No, he was a cautious, pious and Christian man, who sought to control demons to do his bidding. All magicians knew that no enterprise could succeed without utter confidence in God and belief in His power.

The tools were all fumigated and asperged. Now he consecrated them, before reciting the psalms and beginning the first of the many prayers. He washed himself carefully, itself a part of his ritual, first from the bucket, and then more slowly with holy water.

It was very late when he was ready to don his robes. Standing in the cold room, his arms held high over his head, he began the invocation, the thrill of fear setting his belly quivering as he dared once more to summon the demons to obey his will.

'In the name of the Father, Son and Holy Ghost, I summon you: Sitrael, Malantha, Thamaor, Falaur and Sitrami . . .'

Chapter Thirty-Eight

Saturday Next after the Feast of St Edmund[8]

Exeter City

Simon woke several times that night. There was the insistent call to the chamber-pot, a natural result of Coroner Richard's repeated purchases of ale the previous night, and then his snoring, which was enough to make a man commit violent murder; and then, long before the sun rose and illuminated the outline of the shutters, he saw Baldwin, fully dressed, sitting in the open window and staring out to the south.

It was not unusual for his friend to sleep badly every so often, and Simon wondered if he had been suffering from a bad dream. Once in a while, so he had told Simon, he would have a mare come to him in his sleep and plant hideous dreams of the foul end of Acre in his mind. There were children and women . . . but beyond that Baldwin would not speak.

Simon knew full well that the confession of this weakness pained Baldwin, so he made a conscious effort to forget that his friend had mentioned his dreams. However, sometimes it was impossible to ignore Baldwin's behaviour, and when Simon woke properly a while later, when the sun was almost over the roofs to the east, he raised himself on one elbow, tugging the blankets up over his nakedness against the cold air.

'Are you all right, Baldwin?'

'Yes. I couldn't sleep.'

Simon considered asking about the scenes of death and destruction

---

[8] 24 November 1324

during the siege of Acre, but a look at Baldwin's pale features persuaded him that the best cure for his friend would be to ignore his memories and hope that in time they would fade.

'It was that fool of a coroner, I suppose. He makes enough noise to waken the dead. It's a miracle all the corpses from the cathedral haven't risen and walked out of the city to find a quieter cemetery.'

Baldwin smiled feebly at Simon's attempt at lightness, but then he shook his head. 'I am worried, Simon. The idea keeps tearing at me that the murderer could escape the city and punishment. We cannot permit the killer of a king's messenger to escape. It is not to be borne.'

'All we can do, we are doing. What more do you expect?'

'I do not know. But I wish to be away from here and home again. I wish that with all my heart.'

There was a knock at their door, and a moment later Rob walked in with a bundle of twigs bound into faggots in his arms. 'The host says if you want a warm, he's lighting the fire and will soon have some ale spiced and hot for you.'

'That sounds like the best offer we are likely to receive today,' Simon said with enthusiasm.

Rob nodded and was about to leave when Simon caught something in his expression. 'Are you all right, boy? You're quieter than usual.'

'I am fine, master. Just thinking, that's all.'

Simon was going to ask him what the matter was, but from experience he knew full well that Rob's concerns were more likely to be based upon brother Robert calling him a 'boy' or the quality of the sleeping quarters here at the inn than anything worthwhile, so he was more testy than usual when he asked, 'If it's just you thinking about your next meal, stop that and tell us whether you saw anything interesting yesterday. Did the man who would be abbot have any other adventures after he found the body in the undercroft?'

'No. That was all the excitement he could take at the time.'

'Fine. At least he is behaving himself. Hopefully after the surprise of finding Walter down there, he'll be a little less keen to wander the city. That would be one less problem for me.'

'In the meantime, I should go and tell the bishop what we have discovered so far, and about the body of Walter,' Baldwin said.

'Don't forget the girl Sarra,' Simon reminded him.

'I haven't,' Baldwin admitted heavily. 'But that young girl's murderer is the responsibility of the sheriff in so many ways, I cannot become worried about her. She was from the sheriff's household, and if there is one thing that seems certain about her, it is that she is seeking revenge on the sheriff himself. Surely he has enough men about him to protect him from one girl. No, I am more concerned with these other deaths. No one should dare to hurt a king's messenger – and the man who did so probably killed two others as well. Someone who would dare that must be uniquely dangerous.'

'Or driven by a powerful motive.'

'As you say.'

'Do you still believe that the murderer might be someone from Coventry?'

'The more I think of it, the more I am convinced of it. Who else would have dared to kill a king's man, if not someone who feared to be recognised? And Robinet was there with the messenger that night and thought that he might have recognised someone – it makes sense.'

'Put like that, yes, it does,' Simon agreed. 'Although there could be many other explanations.'

'Yes. But none would appear to make so much sense.'

'So what should we do?'

'Everything in our power to find this man and capture him before he can harm anyone else. We need a good description of the fellow so that we may have it broadcast to the city . . . but the only man who knew him has been killed. Robinet can hardly be thought of as reliable, since he was himself very drunk at the time he saw the man.'

'So we are no further forward,' Simon said heavily.

'No. Yet there must be some way of finding the man. There must be!'

'In a city of this size? You would have to be very fortunate.'

Baldwin nodded distractedly, but he had returned to peering out through the window at the morning. He could not see a way through the mists that enveloped the murders.

Ivo was happy as he returned to his mother's home that morning. The night had been cold, but there were three taverns which had provided him with warmed, spiced ale, and there was a brazier out near the

Palace Gate which had been enough to warm his fingers for short periods. But for much of the time he was involved in his mother's business.

There were several women in the city who, like his mother, had found themselves widowed while still young. Some would occasionally take in a man and be happy to pay a little to Ivo and Edie for recommending them to their clients. It was an occasional, intermittent trade, but welcome for all that. Then there was the other business. Ivo's position as a beadle made them a good profit from robberies.

They would learn quickly of any items that had been taken by a cut-purse or robber, and either take a commission to find the stolen goods, or at the least charge the thief for pawning them. There was little trade in the city that Edie was not aware of within a short space of time.

It was not a hard job to find out where the man had gone. There was a bawd down the alley that led north from Stepecote Street, who sometimes took in Edie's men. She had heard the kerfuffle when the body of that man was found in the undercroft, and it made her think, because only a little while before that she had been walking up the street from the river, and she had seen a man leave the place and make his way to Michael's house. She hadn't thought much of it at the time, because she had been busy, but now . . .

Yes. And Ivo thought so too. She had described him in some detail, because, as she said, he didn't look quite the sort of man Michael would have befriended. Yet there he was. A tall, thin old man with piercing eyes and a stubble of white riming his chin.

She had earned herself another penny with that news, for Ivo believed in repaying loyalty, and she could have told anyone else. He was not sure what value he could put on the information, but that it would be useful he had no doubt, and as he walked down the alley to his mother's house he whistled to himself. It was still early. She wouldn't be awake yet, but he could make himself some warmed cider with honey and set the oats to soak for his breakfast.

It was with this cheery thought that he set his thumb to the latch and his shoulder to the door. And at that moment he felt the sharpness under his ear.

'Don't shout, master watchman. I want to speak sensibly to you and discuss how much I shall pay you.'

'Shall we go in?' Ivo said hopefully.

'No. We shall remain out here for now.'

Ivo turned slowly and carefully and saw that it was the man from the night before. 'Why do you threaten me with steel, when I am doing your bidding?'

'Why did you remain up in the bedchamber instead of coming down to see me?'

'It seemed better to be up there. How did you know I was there?'

'I didn't. But there was a staff by the door. I felt sure that the old woman must have had someone there with her.'

'I have what you need.'

'And I have money. Where is he?'

'Let me fetch some breakfast and . . .'

'No. You are taking me there right now, watchman.'

'Don't you trust me?' Ivo said sorrowfully. There was no need for an answer.

The streets at this time of the day were almost empty. Only the very earliest hawkers had made the effort to rise and cry their wares. Shivering and ill-clad for the most part, these young girls and youths stood at street corners with bunches of herbs, or small hemp strings, hoping to sell all their stocks as soon as possible that they might leave and find a fire somewhere to fight off the bitter wind that blew straight from the east.

Ivo noticed that the man paid none of them any attention. Rather he hurried along the streets with his hand clamped like a vice on Ivo's upper arm. Although he didn't see the knife, he was sure that it must be very close.

'This man . . . is he likely to be dangerous?' he ventured.

'Very.'

'Perhaps you should allow me to fetch reinforcements? If he bests you, you won't want him to escape, will you?'

The man stopped, suddenly, and turned to face Ivo. He had very penetrating, dark eyes that seemed to cauterise all the blood vessels in Ivo's brain as he stared. The intensity of his look seared all thoughts in his mind and left Ivo cowed.

'You think he will escape *me*?'

They continued, but now, as they drew nearer the house where the man was staying, Ivo jerked his chin to point.

'Good. Say nothing,' he heard in his ear. He carried on walking, and soon the pair of them were beyond the house on the steep section of Stepecote Street, looking back to the house.

'That is Michael's house?'

Ivo nodded. 'That is where I was told he was staying. What will you do?'

The man stood peering up at the place with a considering expression. Then, 'I think now I should report the man to the Watch.'

Jen woke with a short cry as the door opened and bright sunlight flooded the little chamber, shining straight into her eyes and blinding her.

'Now then, maid, what are you doing here in my loft?'

She wriggled away from him, deeper into the hay, staring at him with alarm. From here, in the darker recesses, she could see little. The opening was a blinding whiteness beyond the fine green-yellow hay. There was nothing there except a confusing whirl of dancing motes. They glittered before her, and she could feel them catching at the back of her throat, making her cough. Eyes watering, she tried to blink them away as she gazed forward in the direction of the voice.

And then the air cleared as the air gusted through the room and she could see him.

He was an older man, grizzled and bent like a miner, with a bush of beard and eyes of bright blue that twinkled as he smiled. Just now he wore a felt cap to cover his old locks, and he appeared to realise that it hid his face, so he slowly took it off. He looked the sort of man who would be very thoughtful, she thought; the sort who would smile a lot.

'Come now, I won't hurt you. You can't stay up here, though.'

The events of the previous day came back with an awful clarity. Her lover had spurned her, and even when he heard her as he was leaving the city, he had ridden off as though he was scared of her or something. It was awful. That hog-faced bitch he lived with must have soured his feelings towards her. There was no telling what she might have said to him last night. No one could know what a man and woman spoke of in their chamber, and it was plain enough that the woman would have done all she could to poison Matthew and Jen's relationship.

'Maid?' Suddenly the twinkle in the eyes had gone, to be replaced by a serious contemplation. 'Maid, have you been hurt? Is that blood?'

She stared at him without speaking for a moment, then shot a look at her arm. From the hand up as far as her elbow was blackened with blood, and she frowned with mild confusion. There was a reason for it, she knew, but just now she couldn't remember where it had come from.

'Have you been harmed, child? Eh?' His tone was even more solicitous now. 'Was it a man from round hereabouts did that? Eh? Have you been raped?'

Suddenly she could have smiled and laughed aloud. 'Raped . . . yes, I've been raped.'

'You come down here, lass. You'll be safe with me. I'm a watchman, I am. They call me Will, Will Skinner. Any man tries that with you, I'll have his ballocks in my purse! Come, now. Do you know who it was? Was it last night? Well, we'll have to get you straight to the sheriff, and that's final. It's a job for him to sort out this sort of thing. We'll catch the bastard, maid, don't you worry. You give me your hand, now. That's right. Christ alive, but you're frozen, child. Let's get you inside first and warm you up as we may, eh? This way, child. This way.'

Chapter Thirty-Nine

Exeter Castle

Sheriff Matthew was up at his usual hour and, as was his wont, made a circuit of the castle's walls before returning to his hall for his breakfast. There he found his wife already waiting, and while the first messes of men at arms entered and took their places he sat, hands on the table, watching them.

There was a strangely muted atmosphere about the hall. Usually this meal was one of the loudest, with men bellowing at each other and demanding more bread or ale. It was the beginning of their working day, and the servants tended to eat and drink their fill, putting off the moment when they must get on with their duties – but not today. Today there was a quiet, reflective feeling about the place.

It was her. The mad one. Or perhaps the friend she'd killed: Sarra. They were all feeling it. Such a shame to lose a pair of girls like them – but it couldn't be helped. Jen was plainly lunatic and Sarra had been killed by her in a frenzied attack. Not his fault, that much was certain.

'Bread, my dear?' he asked, offering Lady Alice a slice before taking his own from the panter.

She looked at him, startled, and he thought to himself that she reminded him of a hart in the forest when it first heard the huntsman's horn. Wide eyes, elfin features . . . God, she was lovely.

He smiled at her, but the reciprocating easing of her face was slow and only a pale reflection of his own. 'Are you well, my dear?'

'Husband, I have to ask you – did you ever take that girl to your bed?'

He gasped at the injustice that was done to him, his knife falling from his hand to clatter on the pewter dish. 'You ask me that?'

'She was so twisted with her rage, there must be some cause for it. And she claims that you promised her . . . that you would divorce me.'

'If I had done that, the girl would scarcely need to kill you as she tried yesterday, would she?' he asked reasonably. 'And in any case, if she were to murder you, I doubt there would be a vicar in the whole of the country who would consider joining us in marriage! Can't you see that everything she suggests is mad? She is clearly out of her senses. There is no logic to anything she says. Alice, my love, you must ignore everything she has said.'

'I cannot but remember her face. It returned to me in my dreams! Oh, Matthew, I feel so scared. While she is free, she could appear in front of me at any time in the street.'

'You will be safe, my love. Do not fear her. We will catch her. And until we do, you will have the best guards from all my men here.'

'I am scared.'

'Well, you will have to remain here in the castle. That is all.' He sipped from his mazer – a good red wine – and then casually asked the question that had been uppermost in his own mind. 'By the way – what were you and your maid doing down that street yesterday?'

Alice licked her lips. 'I wished to speak to the man in the house there.'

'The necromancer?'

'Yes.'

'I thought I told you to avoid him, Alice.'

'I wanted to ask about our future. I was worried, Matthew.'

'He is dangerous,' the sheriff stated in a low voice, leaning towards her. 'In ways you cannot appreciate. Please, as you love me, do not visit him again. Or any other magicians.'

'He is harmless, though.'

'He may be so personally, but his craft makes him dangerous. Believe me, he and his type will only get us into trouble.'

And that, he reflected with some sadness as he toyed with his drink, was the understatement of the century. Suddenly his appetite was gone and he pushed his plate away, petulantly refusing any more and glaring at his silent household. He wanted to shout at them to be calm and enjoy their meal more, but he daren't.

Exeter City

Ivo had no idea what he was about. The man stood a long while, considering the place, especially, apparently, the door itself. It was a firm enough barrier, made of good elm boards that had been nailed to two cross-pieces, the nail heads all on display. Suddenly he spun and faced him.

'Master watchman, there is a man inside that house who is plotting the murder of the king and his advisers. You have a duty to arrest him.'

'What? Me? No, you have to tell the sheriff if there's someone dangerous in there. He's the man would have to look at writs and stuff. It's not my place to knock the doors down,' Ivo said. He wished he was back at home in his bed in the eaves. His job was watching over his mother while she haggled over the cost of some trinket from a thief, not risking his life in an attack on a sorcerer.

'Do you say so? Perhaps that would be adequate in normal times, but today we must hurry. There is no time to wait.'

'Let's get some help from the sheriff first. What's the hurry?'

'There is no time. The king's life is in danger.'

He would have argued more, but at that moment he felt the little knife under his left shoulder blade. 'Hey – you'll have a cut in my jack.'

'I'll cut more than your jack if you don't hurry and knock on the fuckin' door.'

Ivo hesitated, but then, as the knife dug deeper and he could feel his flesh opening, he walked forward and banged on the door.

There was the sound of feet hurrying, and then a shutter slid down in its runners. 'Who are you, and what do you want?'

'Open this door in the name of the king!'

Ivo heard the roar behind him, and turned to glance at the man. He seemed to have grown, and now his face displayed his anger for all to see. Suddenly he shoved Ivo from him, snatching at his heavy staff as he did so and gripped the latch. The door remained barred. He lifted the staff and used it to smash at the door, over by the hinges. He swung the staff again and again, the staff crashing hard into the timbers and sending clouds of dust rising. There was a creak and a crack, and the door began to move. Then, after yet another thunderous assault, the topmost board gave way. It remained in the door, pushed back a good two inches, but a final blow broke it away, and the next plank was taken. Once that too had fallen, the man reached in and pulled the bolts open, then hurtled inside.

Michael was at the far end of the screens passage gripping a sword and a knife, and now he bellowed his defiance and flew at them.

Ivo would have fled, but the man with him knew nothing about running. He waited, then used the staff in a quarter-staff grip, knocking the sword away, and coming back to thrust with it at Michael's face. It connected, striking the man's nose, mashing the bone and slipping down to hit his mouth, striking all the front teeth from his jaw and carving a great gash in his upper lip and chin.

Screaming incoherently with pain, Michael clapped his hands over his mouth and fell to his knees.

'Where is he? Here in the house? Where, man?'

He grabbed Michael's shoulder and pulled him up, holding the knife to his chin and letting the older man see his eyes. 'You may make the mistake of thinking I wouldn't want to kill you – but look in my eyes, master. You'll see that would be a foolish mistake. If you don't tell me, I'll kill you as easily as I would squash a beetle. Now: *where is he?*'

Michael drew his hands away from his mouth and spat on the floor. There was a step behind him, and Ivo saw a woman appear from a doorway. She saw her master and shrieked, high and terrified. Michael seemed to take strength from her, and held his chin up defiantly.

'Don't kill him,' Ivo said quickly. 'He's not . . .'

But the man had no intention of killing him. Not yet. He took Michael's hand and put it flat on the wall, and then set the little knife over his index finger. Michael made to snatch his hand away, but before he could, the knife pressed down, hard, and there was a little crunching sound. Held by a tendon, the finger flapped and jerked as Michael pulled his hand free, a muffled scream bursting from him because he was too shocked to even open his mouth properly.

'You want to lose another? My friend James lost two, didn't he? But I expect you think you're stronger, eh?'

Michael was shaking his head, and now he spoke, 'No, no, please, no more . . .'

'You showed no pity to my friend, did you?'

As Michael tried to fight, his hand was taken again. A snatch and a tug, and the finger flew off. Ivo could not help but watch it as it bounced on a wall, to come to rest on the ground near the servant's feet. She rolled her eyes skywards and slowly collapsed. When Ivo looked back, Michael was pulling his hand away. There was a short punch from a fist, and Michael's head snapped back. He began to fall, but his hand was held up again, rested on the wall again, and the little knife pressed down once more. There was a 'click' this time as the blade passed through the finger and struck the stone.

Michael's body tensed with the pain and horror. He watched as his finger, still twitching, was lifted before him. The man tapped it against his mouth as though tempting him to eat it, and then at last Michael spewed, retching violently.

'Where is he, Michael?'

'In the back. The barn. He's there.'

Wasting no more time on more words, the man took the staff and ran along the passage, then out to the garden beyond. Ivo gathered his thoughts and followed him.

The garden was a small affair, with four little vegetable patches set apart with decorative woven hurdles to raise them. Farther beyond was an orchard. Nearer, though, stood a small thatched barn. The man ran to it, grabbing the door and throwing it wide. With his staff held high, he entered, and then Ivo heard him curse viciously and long.

'He's not fucking *here*! We missed him!'

Jen walked with her hood over her head all the way up the little lanes and streets to the castle's main gate. She was wearing a thick, rather smelly old cloak of Will's, and with her head under the hood she was unrecognisable, she felt sure. Will spoke a little as they walked, all inconsequential stuff.

'I had a little girl. She'd have been quite like you by now, I suppose. About your age, too. Her name was Joan. Lovely thing, she was.'

Jen said nothing, but her silence seemed not to offend him. Rather, he appeared to like it. She did not realise that his friend at the bishop's palace gate had asked him to look in the loft for her. There was no need to mention her ordeal of last night he reasoned.

'She was always into things. That was why I looked in the hayloft just now, you see. Joan once climbed into a loft like that one, and the door slipped when she was inside, and if my neighbour hadn't heard her shouting, she might have been left up there until the next need for hay. So, when I saw that the door on that loft was shut when usually it's left open, I just thought, maybe some little girl has fallen inside. But there was no need to worry about that, was there?'

They were passing the ruins of an old house, and Jen heard him sigh and sniff a little. 'There. That was where she died. Her and her brother and sister. We had a fire one night. Everyone said it was an accident . . . You never stop loving them, you know. Your own children. Never stop loving and missing them, when they die. Doesn't seem natural, your children dying before you. No. Not at all.'

She had nothing to say, but as they carried on up the alleyway, she squeezed his upper arm. He patted her hand. 'There, it was a long time ago now. Who knows but that they would have died in the famine, anyway? So many other little ones did. Do you remember that? Of course you do. You'd have been eight or nine by then.'

He started talking again, about unimportant, irrelevant little things that he obviously felt wouldn't upset her too much, as they made their way along quieter lanes towards the castle, and once there she heard her helper explain coyly to the guard why he was bringing the young maid to see the sheriff, and where could they wait for him?

She thrilled within to hear the guard answer immediately, telling them to wait outside the hall, and he'd have the steward come to find them when the sheriff was ready. Already excited to be back inside the castle's court, she found herself growing faint with expectation as they entered the hall's little screens passage.

'Maid, you're coming over all weak, aren't you? Look. There's a bench here. Be you seated, and the sheriff will be here shortly. You'll be all right, maid. Don't you worry. Are you sure you don't want a physician to see you? No? Well, you be seated there, and we'll have the sheriff and the coroner come look at you. You'll soon have satisfaction.'

It was a long wait, though, with men coming and going, some casting interested glances at the woman who remained still, covered only with a blanket that her protector had given her, and the hood of her cowl. She shivered periodically, although if asked she could not have said whether it was because of the cold, her trepidation, or simple excitement.

'You the girl?'

It was a voice she didn't recognise, but then she heard Will talking respectfully, and realised he must be important. Then he said something about the Rolls and called the man 'Sir Richard', and she realised it must be the coroner. Of course – he would have to be present at any enquiry into a rape.

Suddenly she felt a panic welling up inside her. Of course her man would support her – Sir Matthew could hardly deny their love, could he? But he might find it difficult to explain her arrival in front of another important official of the king.

So be it! She would show them all how much she loved him.

At long last the steward came and spoke to the man at her side, and he seemed conscious of her condition, speaking kindly and warmly to her. It took some while for her to understand that he meant her to follow him into the hall, for she was panicked by the sound of his voice, but then she realised he was talking quietly and understandingly, and simply had not recognised her.

It was astonishing. Only yesterday she had been petrified of this man. After the sheriff, he was the most powerful man in the castle, and he ruled it with an iron rod. Any maid found slacking in her duties would soon be evicted, and she would never be permitted to return while he lived. That was her belief, anyway. He had been so stern always. Yet now he was treating her as an honoured guest, and she could do nothing but follow him dumbly as he took her arm and brought her into the hall.

'Well, maid? You have been raped?'

It was *him*! He didn't recognise her either. Ah, blessed Mary, Mother of . . .

'It's her, husband! Can't you recognise her? It's her, I say!'

Jen recognised that voice, right enough. She threw her blanket aside and stood straight again, seeking her enemy. There she was, up at the far end of the dais. With a snarl, Jen leaped up towards her, but even as she drew her knife and raised it to stab, there was a stunning crack over her skull, and she fell to her hands and knees.

Groggily, she looked up. From here all she could see at first was a shimmering vision of boots and hosen. Her vision swayed and wobbled out of focus as she tried to hold her head still, but it was impossible. And then she saw the face of her beloved. Sir Matthew was peering down at her with an expression of . . . not love, but horror, as though she was a devil or a witch . . . She glanced about her, and saw that the men in the hall had formed a ring about her as though they all feared her. They had weapons ready, as though they meant to slay her there and then. They all feared her.

She wanted to shout at them, to declare that they were mad, it wasn't her, it was the poisonous whore's whelp who stood there behind Sir Matthew and held his shoulder, the picture of matronly virtue – but she wasn't! It was she, Jen, who loved him, she who should be there now, with her man. But she couldn't work her mouth. It was too hard. She was so tired.

Letting her head droop, she panted and waited for the blow to come that would end her misery.

Chapter Forty

Exeter City

Ivo was tempted to run through the house and grab some friends to come and capture this man, but courage was never his strongest suit. Having seen how the man had dispatched Michael, he was reluctant to test his own skills as a fighter against him.

'What is it?'

'Didn't you hear me, fool? He's gone. And so have the figures, from the look of it.'

'What figures are you talking about?'

He had approached to the doorway now, and could peer in as the foreigner kicked at tables and benches, overturning them all and hunting high and low for something. The dust was rising, and he chewed at his lip as he went about the room, prising with a knife at some of the stones, seeing if they could be moved, then carefully inspecting the floor as though there could have been a trap door hidden there, but soon he stood, breathing heavily and staring about him. A shelf dangled from the ceiling, attached by ropes. He slapped his hand underneath it, sending everything atop flying, and kicked at a small phial lying on the ground. It flew away and smashed into pieces on the wall.

Only then did he seem to calm a little. Standing staring at the wall, he nodded to himself, and then called to Ivo. 'Fetch me Richard Langatre. Right away.'

Ivo was nothing loath. He turned and hurried from the barn, through the house, where Michael sat huddled on the floor with a bloody rag tied about his ruined hand, being tended to by a maid, and out into the street with a feeling of distinct relief. Up the road he hurried, and pounded on the sorceror's door.

Langatre had been sitting before his fire and thinking of the man lying dead beneath him when the banging came on his door, and now he agreed with alacrity to go and help the dead man's friend.

'I need you to tell me what this man would have been doing in here.'

Langatre eyed the wild-eyed man uncertainly. Although he was a knowledgeable man, there were limits to what he could achieve, and he was close to the limit right here. 'I don't know how much I can tell you, friend. This place is in a mess.'

'He was doing something in here. What can you see?'

Langatre sighed to himself and entered. There was a table-top on its back, two trestles nearby where they had fallen after being kicked, and all about a mess of broken pots and various tools. Some were no doubt used for *maleficium*, but in the main they looked like gardening implements. It was only as he tentatively lifted the table-top that he gave a little gasp.

'What is it?'

'My bloody knife, that's what it is! He must have taken it . . . this must be the man who broke into my house and tried to kill me!'

'He was desperate to achieve something with the things he took. What else did he remove?'

'There were any number of things . . . mainly tools that a man might use in cleansing his soul before . . . Hey, that's my leather hat!'

'So?'

It was possible. There were plenty of magicians who attempted conjurations, as he had told Sir Baldwin and the coroner the other day while he was in the gaol. Yes, some had tried such things, but the chances of success were minimal, and the dangers . . .

'Well?'

Langatre scowled at him. 'I don't know what you normally do, man, but my job is to be cautious. Leave me to work it out and I shall give you accurate information. Hurry me and you'll get something that is less use than horseshit. Is that clear enough?'

Without waiting for the response, he started looking about him carefully. If Sir Baldwin had been right, and the stories were true, there may be some wax lying about in here. He searched, but there was nothing to be found. Shaking his head, he rose again and thought wildly. Then his face lightened and he hurried outside to the vegetable plots. At the side of one was a large rubbish heap, and he ran to it excitedly, prodding at it until he gave a little whistle of glee.

'Here you are!'

'What is it?'

'Wax – like the stuff in my undercroft. The fellow has made some models of men out of wax, I'd guess. He's going to try to kill someone.'

Baldwin was still glowering with concentration as he left the inn and began to make his way to the bishop's palace.

Simon was with him. The coroner had been asked to visit the sheriff at the castle because a woman had reported a rape, or something, but Rob walked a few paces behind as usual, truculently glaring at all those about him as he went. At one point he was fairly sure that he saw one of the lads from his game the night before, but the face soon disappeared in the crowds, which was some relief.

Their path took them down Cooks' Row, and thence to Bolehille and down to the Palace Gate, and it was as they entered Bolehille that Rob saw another face he thought he recognised. Hastily he turned his head slightly, and hoped that the simple subterfuge would serve. Fortunately he could hear the master talking to his friend the knight, and so long as they kept on their musings about the dead men and all that, he'd be all right. Yes, there was the Palace Gate. Only a matter of a few hundred yards, now. Easy enough.

As he sighed with relief, he felt his legs pulled from under him. 'Aargh!'

Hands outstretched to break his fall, he felt stone on his palms, the scrape of flesh rasped away and the instant stinging pain. His knees were bruised, and his breath had been knocked from him.

'We want our money, *foreigner*!' he heard as he started to try to clamber to his feet. A kick at his legs made him fall again.

Then there was a chuckle, and he turned his head to see Simon and Sir Baldwin, both standing with arms crossed, Simon with a broad grin on his face. 'Been upsetting people again, lad? I've warned you about this before.'

'It was a fair game!'

'You're learning new concepts, are you?' Simon asked unsympathetically.

'I was doing it for you, master,' he said hurriedly.

'What?'

Now he had Simon's attention, Rob spoke quickly. 'They told me
of a rumour while we played last night – it's said that the bishop
doesn't trust the sheriff. Thinks the sheriff might be disloyal to the
king . . .'

'Quiet!'

'It was this one, sir. He's called Ben.'

Suddenly both his attackers were running away, swift as only rats
or city-bred churls could go, Rob thought to himself.

Simon started as though to chase them, but then he stopped and
looked back at Baldwin, then both stared down at Rob.

'Are you sure of this?' Simon frowned.

'Why else would they run like that?' Rob demanded reasonably.

'Why should they?' Baldwin asked. 'All they need do was deny
your story. It is foolish, perhaps, but not an offence to see a lad
hanged, telling a tale like that.'

'They got nervy when I asked them how they knew,' Rob recalled.
'It was when I asked whether the bishop had a spy in the sheriff's
house. They went quiet then.'

Baldwin nodded. 'I doubt not that the good bishop has an ear in
every important house in the city. Yet that is interesting. Yes, Simon,
it is enormously interesting! If the good bishop felt that the sheriff was
actively plotting something, he would have done all in his power to
warn the king, would he not? And what better means than to send a
messenger with a private, verbal message?'

'But what could the sheriff be planning all the way down here?'
Simon said sceptically. 'The king is many leagues away.'

'*Maleficium* is supposed to know no bounds of distance,' Baldwin
mused. 'I wonder if that is what they planned? To have the king
assassinated from insignificant little Exeter?'

Simon was eyeing his servant doubtfully. 'You are sure of this?
How drunk was the lad?'

'Ben? He was the one with the face like a ferret and the smell of a
fox on heat. I don't think he was drunk last night. He seemed all right.'

Simon looked at Baldwin. 'Should we go and ask the bishop?'

'I do not think so. The news that his affairs are common knowledge may not please the good prelate. No. Perhaps it would be better were we to keep this information private for now.'

Simon nodded, although he would have preferred to have asked the bishop about his concerns. Politics were becoming a mess, and Simon was trying still to see a way through. As a mere bailiff to the abbey of Tavistock, he was not involved, thank God, in national politics, but every man had to be aware of the currents of power. If a man were to upset even the lowliest servant of a man like Sir Hugh le Despenser, he could find himself either in a very painful place or dead. 'Does that mean that the bishop's loyalty is being tested?' he wondered aloud.

Baldwin threw a casual look at Rob, and, seeing he was far enough away, drew nearer to Simon. 'Old friend, do not even wonder aloud about such things. Simply listen and draw your own conclusions. This country is grown too dangerous for musings in public. For now, assume that his lordship the bishop will stay loyal to Despenser and the king, for it is in his interests to remain so. His star has waxed with the Despenser's, and Despenser has grown fat on the largesse of the king. Yet there are many who do now question the king's management, and who detest the overweening arrogance and greed of Despenser. Perhaps this sheriff is one such? I do not know.'

They had reached the Palace Gate, and Baldwin nodded at the porter as they entered the bishop's precinct again. And I hope I learn to read the signs correctly too, he said to himself.

Exeter Castle

Will was appalled to see how the girl was thrown to the floor. 'Wait! Don't hit her! She's been raped!'

'Sorry, man, but this little innocent slaughtered another maid from the castle yesterday,' the coroner said. 'She's not as sweet as she looks.'

'I didn't kill her,' Jen said. She spat in the direction of Lady Alice. 'She's right there!'

'You killed your own friend, maid!' Sheriff Matthew stated. 'You killed Sarra.'

'Me? I couldn't have hurt her! She is my best friend.'

'It was witnessed by many people,' the coroner said calmly, bending to pick up her knife.

'She was asleep in my hayloft,' Will said stupidly. 'I just thought she'd been attacked and went there to hide.'

'You did well to bring her here,' the sheriff said.

There was a note of dismissal in his voice, though, which Will recognised. He nodded sadly, walking to the doorway. Yet he could not help but turn and give her one last look before leaving. She was so much like the girl his daughter might have grown into, and the thought made him want to weep.

The Bishop's Palace

'A good day to you,' the bishop said as he marched into his main chamber. He peremptorily demanded wine from his waiting steward, and sent him on his way. Rob scuttled after him in a hurry, knowing when it was best to make himself scarce.

'My lord,' Simon said hesitantly, 'you seem a bit vexed this morning. Do you prefer that we leave you for a little, or come back tomorrow?'

'Tomorrow? Hah! It is all well and good for a bailiff to suggest work on the Sabbath, but for some of us that day is already the busiest in our week. No, Simon, I am not rebuking you – do not look so pained. Tomorrow is the feast day of Saint Catherine of Alexandria, though. I shall officiate at the mass to her honour, although God knows well enough that I could do with a day of rest myself just now. I am too old for all this bickering!'

This last was said with a particular fervour, and Baldwin smiled. 'You are not enjoying a peaceful time just now?'

'Just now? Just *now*, you say? Sir Baldwin, I am hedged in upon all sides. There is the master mason who looks daggers at me because I refused to agree to order thirty cartloads of marble when he admitted to me that he should only need twenty-three. My labourers are all complaining that there is not enough light for them to work, and, of course, they won't do a thing when it rains! My . . . but I can see that you are not very interested in the affairs of a bishop with the rebuilding of his church. At least I have my throne made and ready. It fits me perfectly. And a good thing too.'

Baldwin smiled, but politely did not mention the reason why the Bishop had demanded so extravagant a seat. Some assumed it was only to make sure that the bishop went one better than his peers, but in reality it was in order that he should be as comfortable as possible. He was a prey to haemorrhoids.

'So! You are here to bring me more news? What can you tell me?'

'Little enough,' Baldwin said. 'There was another murder last afternoon, when an innocent man was killed. We assume that he had surprised the assassin, and had his throat cut for his pains.'

'Who was this? Anyone of importance?'

'I do not think so ... although his past appears to be rather a mystery,' Baldwin admitted.

Simon knew that the bishop knew many in the city. 'His name was Walter, my lord. Walter of Hanlegh. He came here recently, so we understand.'

'I know of him, yes,' the bishop said. 'Hmm. He was a worthy man in the king's service. I knew him before . . .'

'Is it true that he was an assassin?' Baldwin asked bluntly.

'Yes. He was one of those who in past times would remove obstacles to maintaining the king's peace. If a man sought to upset the king's equanimity, this Walter might sometimes be sent to chastise him. And occasionally, I fear, simple words were not enough.'

'We have spoken to Robinet, who was once a messenger like James, and who appears to hold the same regard for Walter.'

'Sir Baldwin, do not judge the man entirely by your own code of chivalry. In God's name, I can swear that there are many dangerous men in the realm who would do the king harm if they but had the opportunity. Walter saved the king, very likely, and possibly that could have impacted on your life too.'

'He worked down here, then?' Simon asked.

'I recall hearing that he was here once at the outset of the famine, and because of his efforts the city was saved from disaster.'

'I wonder what led him to try to arrest the magician,' Simon said. 'A fellow like him should have overwhelmed a poxed old man like this fellow. Perhaps he was lured into a trap intentionally.'

'We may never know. Let us only pray that no more men need die and that you soon find the stolen message.'

'We shall if we may. If God wills it,' Baldwin said irreverently. 'Have you had a demand for money?'

'No. I should have told you if there had been any such thing.'

Baldwin frowned, but it was Simon who voiced his thoughts. 'In that case, I really wonder whether there has been some sort of error. The pouch was still with the messenger, wasn't it? Were there other messages in it?'

'Yes,' Baldwin said. 'This was the only one we know of that was missing.'

'Was it the only written message you confided to him?' Simon asked.

'Yes,' the bishop said, with a sidelong look at Baldwin.

'Then if it was so important that it alone was taken from the pouch, I do not understand why someone has not yet asked you for money to return it. It makes little sense.'

'It was important – but perhaps the thief did not recognise its value.'

'Then why take it? Why not cast it away and find another message more interesting to him?'

'Who can say?' the bishop said uncomfortably.

Baldwin enjoyed his discomfiture. There were two messages in James's safekeeping: the one about the trustworthiness of the sheriff, if his guess and Rob's information were correct, and another that proposed further persecution of the queen. Either of them could have caused great pain to others. If he was wrong, the sheriff could have been condemned without the opportunity to defend himself; his suggestion that the queen should be made to suffer still more indignities and humiliation was unchivalrous in the extreme.

Baldwin said, 'I told you when you first asked me to help that it would be a difficult task. I do not know whether the message still exists or has been destroyed, whether it is in the city or has been spirited away . . . nothing! For me to find it, I shall need a miracle of some sort. But we will stretch every sinew to rescue it if we may.'

The bishop's wine arrived, and he smiled wearily. 'I thank you for that at least.'

'Shall we come here again tomorrow to report what fortune we have enjoyed?'

'No. Tomorrow you must attend the mass. It will be a beautiful service, and with the work you have undertaken, you need your day of rest. Perhaps we can meet afterwards to discuss matters of lesser importance?'

Chapter Forty-One

Exeter City

The man who had murdered his friend was gone, but he could find out where with some luck. He was back in the house as soon as he realised what the magician had been attempting. Squatting in front of Michael, he eyed the bloody mess of cloth wrapped about his hand. 'You should learn to talk more quickly.'

'Please – I don't know how to help you. You must believe me!'

'Ah, but I don't.'

'I cannot tell you anything more.'

The girl had returned. She held a large bowl of warmed water from the copper, and she stood in the doorway with a terrified look on her face.

Michael shook his head at her. 'Go! It's not safe for you here!'

'Oh no, I think she ought to see to your wounds,' Robinet said with a flash of his teeth. He had the knife in his hand again now. Against the wall, he saw one of the fingers, and he picked it up and studied it. There was a crash, and when he glanced round the girl had fainted again. 'You should get her viewed by a physician. She seems too phlegmatic for words. Now – you were going to tell me where he's gone.'

Michael looked up into the man's eyes and saw nothing there but a cold intensity that spoke of his determination. 'I don't know anything, master.'

'You can do better than that. You will have to.'

'Master, I can't tell you what I don't know!' Michael pleaded.

'A man with no fingers is a sad sight. You know that?'

Michael withdrew his hand as his torturer reached for it.

'Now, naughty. If you don't help me, I may get angry, and look to something other than your finger. Do you want that?'

'Please! I don't know anything.'

'The only thing that looks worse than a man with hands but no fingers is probably a man with no fingers and no eyes.' He was speaking ruminatively, with a pensive expression that sent ice into Michael's blood. Gently, he reached for Michael's bleeding hand, and took it, pulling the linen away as he did so. 'Ah, good, clean cuts. I thought that knife was good and sharp. Now – you've lost those two already. What is it to be next? The thumb or the next finger? What? Not sure? Shall I decide for you?'

'The bishop! He's going to kill the bishop, God save me!' Michael burst out, pulling his hand away and weeping.

'Enough!'

Michael was close to puking. The interruption gave him the moment's respite he needed. He turned his head and retched emptily. There was nothing more to come.

'Leave us, Langatre.'

'I will not! You are committing a gross offence on that man, and I will not permit it!'

'You will learn to keep your silence.'

'Why? So you can execute him? What if he is telling the truth? What if he is nothing more than an innocent tradesman who rented a room to a stranger? You are performing a foul injustice on him. Out of my way!'

'You don't know what you're doing, Langatre. Leave me with him for a few more minutes. He will tell me where the murderer is.'

'You are no better than a murderer yourself. I will not leave you. I demand that you release this man to me instantly. Ivo? *Ivo!* Get in here. If he tries to harm that man even by so much as a scratch, you will strike him with your staff.'

'Master, I don't think . . .'

'I am sure you're right and fortunately there is no need for you to do so! If he so much as scratches that man, you knock him down. Do you hear me? Right, now, Master Michael, you come with me. This man will not harm you any more.' Langatre pushed past Robinet and leaned down to help Michael to his feet. 'Come, fellow. Where is the nearest leech?'

Exeter Castle

Coroner Richard was unhappy to see the girl bound, wretched and groaning with despair, but he wasn't willing to risk her grabbing a dagger and putting paid to another life. No. Best to see that she was kept controlled.

'What will you do with her?' he asked the sheriff.

'She is a murderer. She should be gaoled until the next court is held. If the bitch comes before me, I'll have her hanged in a day!'

Coroner Richard nodded. Understandable, he reckoned. The silly minx had killed off a perfectly good young servant for no reason. Well, only because she wanted to kill someone else and her blow went awry, which was not the best legal defence against a capital crime he had ever heard. No, he was fairly sure that she would soon join her dead friend.

There were some who asserted that extreme cases of dementia like this were caused by demons who inveigled their way into the body of their victim, and then began to cause mayhem. The coroner had no idea whether that had happened in this case, but he wondered whether it was possible. In some cases, so he had heard, the use of prophylactic flogging could bring on a recovery, as could the use of starvation occasionally. Perhaps this was a case where such a treatment could be considered.

'Yes. I'll have her hanged in a trice, damn her soul!' Matthew said.

The Coroner looked at him without speaking. The sheriff was visibly shaking as his wife put her hand over his shoulder and tried to comfort him. He hardly seemed to notice her, but after a little while his hand rose and took hold of hers. Still, he could not speak without a quaver in his voice.

He was so knocked back, Sir Richard wondered whether he had indeed led the poor child on. Perhaps even raped her. It was hardly unknown for a pretty maid to be bedded by her master, and if the master then thought that the mad bint was going to try to kill him and his wife, it would hardly be surprising if he was a little unnerved by the thought.

'Aye, well, I'll be leaving you now. Business to attend to,' he said, and made his way from the hall, out into the court and thence to the castle gate. 'Hoi, guard, where is the best alehouse around here?'

He was soon being given directions to the place favoured by the castle's guards, and thinking that a tavern which was patronised by the castle's men at arms would be ideal for him too, he set off over the bridge to the High Street. But before he could reach it, he saw the grim face of Langatre hurrying up the street towards him.

'You are in a hurry.'

'I have been searching for you, Coroner. You can be a most elusive person on occasion. You must come with me to hear what has been happening to the poor man Michael in his own house.'

Coroner Richard held up his hands. 'Tell me as we walk. I have a need of some food and drink first, though. If you want to tell me this tale, do so now and while I eat.'

'You must come at once, Coroner!'

'Why?'

'The man Robinet – he has been torturing Michael. I had to get him away, and have left him with a leech.'

'So he is safe at the moment?'

'Well . . .'

'Tell me as I eat, then,' the imperturbable coroner repeated, and listened as he marched at his best speed to the tavern, Langatre dancing at his side as he tried to keep up. 'You know this Michael?'

'Yes. He is an old companion of mine in the taverns. He is a kindly man. He doesn't deserve this assault.'

'Then what was he doing protecting this necromancer? It sounds to me, from what you've said, that the fellow deserved all he got.'

'It is illegal to capture a man and torture him,' Langatre said, and there was a fierce determination in his voice.

Coroner Richard looked at him for a long moment. Then, 'Very well. But first I want my companions to join us. I will send a message for them to meet us here. Now, where is that bone-idle bugger of a landlord? Ho! ho!, I am thirsty!'

Exeter City

John had heard the brouhaha as soon as the first knock came on the door. He had already packed up all his remaining belongings against just such an eventuality, although it did not please him to learn that his place of hiding was already discovered. Still, at least the man who owned the house would keep his mouth shut if he knew what was best for him.

Quickly, he grabbed his pack, now considerably heavier than it had been originally, and threw it over his back by the stout rope that bound it. He ran to the wattle fencing hurdles and pushed his way between a pair of them, then darted up the adjacent garden all the way to the end, where it gave out onto the road near the south-western corner of the city wall. Once there, he set off eastwards. That was the way to the busy street from the South Gate, and once there he could easily lose himself in the crowds.

He was still cursing under his breath as he reached the gate, and turned northwards again, pulling his hood over his face. In this cold weather, most people were doing the same, conserving their warmth as best they might, and he did not stand out. It was ideal.

Yes. It was annoying that his refuge had been lost, but perhaps it was all for the best. Now he had but one night to worry about, and for that he knew exactly where to go. In the north-western angle of the wall was the old Franciscan abbey, but the brothers had moved from the city a few years ago, to a new location outside the walls near the river. Since then, the place which had held their cloisters and dormitories had become the province of various poverty-stricken families. There would be space there for a poor wanderer like him, and no one would be the wiser. It was only for one evening, after all.

It took him little time to find the place. Soon he was traversing the muddy, icy paths, and looking for a dwelling that could accommodate him. There were several near the outer wall, but he didn't want to be too close to the edges. Better to be entirely immersed. He would keep on going until he felt sure that no one following him would be able to find him with ease.

At last he saw it. A rough lean-to, much of whose thatched roof had long ago disintegrated. However, a section of it still functioned, and when he peered in through the doorway he saw that beneath the straw there was a good space in among the rafters, and if he pushed the door up there he would be able to lie snugly off the floor, secure from the wet and hopefully warm enough.

Pushing the door up was a trial, but in time he succeeded, and then he clambered up after it, opening his pack and pulling out his book, and laying it reverently on the boards. Next was the blanket, wrapped about the first of the figures, and he took it out now, peering at it with some pride. Tomorrow it would serve its purpose.

It was almost dark already when the three men were able to sit at the table at their inn and rest.

'Not a sign of him,' Baldwin muttered as he eased his legs out before him and leaned back against the wall.

'He could have been swallowed by the earth,' Coroner Richard agreed.

Simon was more positive. 'Perhaps he has left the city to escape? After seeing what Robinet did to that landlord, I'm not surprised.'

They had gone to speak to Michael almost soon as Baldwin and Simon had met the coroner in the tavern. Langatre had taken them at an urgent pace to the physician's house where he had deposited him, and he had held back as they entered, as though fearing that Robinet might have been there before them and killed all in the house. 'He's a mad bastard, that one. He enjoyed cutting off Michael's fingers. I swear it! He enjoyed it.'

The tanner was little help. 'I don't know where he is, I rented him a room, and then he came to ask for another. That's all.'

'You were renting the undercroft to this man, weren't you?' Simon pressed him. 'You knew he was planning to murder the bishop, didn't you? Why didn't you tell the beadle? It was your duty.'

'I didn't *dare*. I thought he was a powerful wizard, and it looks as if he is, doesn't it? I mean, where is he? If he was a man, someone would have seen him by now, and yet he's disappeared. He must be a necromancer with a lot of power.'

'He could just be hiding in a room somewhere where the landlord is not fussy,' the coroner commented. 'Come, now, where could he have gone?'

'I tell you, I do not know!'

Thinking back to his terrified expression, Simon reckoned that if he had even a remote inkling as to where this 'John' had got to, he would have told them. Apart from anything else, it was clear that he wanted someone else to suffer for the pain he had endured that day.

'And he didn't have any more idea where Robinet could have gone,' Baldwin observed. 'Where can he have got to?'

'In God's name,' the coroner grunted, loosening his boots, 'I confess I find these disappearances baffling. Each time someone finds the wizard, he seems to slip away. And now that damned fool Robinet has gone too.'

'Perhaps the pair of them have killed each other,' Simon mused. 'What do you reckon, Rob?'

'Me? I don't know anything, do I? I just get sent to walk about in the cold and stare at people, I do. No brain at all, me. Except I was able to help tell you about the sheriff, of course.'

The coroner had an amiably bovine face, but it concealed a sharp mind, and there was nothing wrong with his hearing. 'Eh? What's this?'

Baldwin sighed and closed his eyes. 'If you continue to speak out of turn, Rob, you will learn that life can be unfair and more than moderately painful. Coroner, this was some information that came to us. It would seem possible that the bishop has some strong concerns about the sheriff, and has even gone so far as to put them to the king.'

The coroner whistled low. 'That could cost the sheriff dearly.'

Simon yawned. 'His ballocks would be off, wouldn't they?'

'I do not like to speculate about matters like this when the man himself has no opportunity to defend himself,' Baldwin said. 'I should like to know what has led the bishop to leap to this conclusion. There must be some reason for it.'

'I have not noticed many bishops who need good reason to jump to conclusions,' the coroner said sourly.

Baldwin smiled, but only fleetingly. He soon reverted to his frowning contemplation, which he maintained as Simon and Coroner Richard ordered food for them all. Before long steaming plates filled with pies and boiled pigeons appeared before them, along with a loaf of heavy bread. The sight and smells persuaded Baldwin to turn his attention to the table, and he slapped Rob's hand away from the food quickly, making him wait until the coroner had filled his own plate. Then he motioned to Rob to continue, watching the lad while he sipped at a strong wine.

When they had eaten their fill, and even the coroner declared himself satisfied, Baldwin returned to the matter. Simon had often thought that his friend was rather like a dog which would return to worry at a bone until all was gone.

'I cannot help but believe that a man so determined to attack the king and others would not have run far. But *why*? If the fellow is determined to commit murder by means of a demon or some other form of wizardry, surely he could be anywhere. What would be the point of proximity? If I were an assassin, and I wished to kill a man, would I not do so from a distance?'

'He's mad. That's the thing. Like this girl killed the sheriff's servant. Same thing. Quite potty. She even returned to the sheriff's hall for some reason.'

'Why?' Simon asked.

'*I* don't know!' the coroner declared testily. 'You'd have to be insane to comprehend her motives. Same with this sorcerer.'

'From what you said, the maid was in love with the sheriff.'

'No accounting for tastes.'

Baldwin gave a faint grin. 'True. But the fact is, she thought she would be receiving a generous welcome from her lover, from the sound of things. In reality, she petrified the poor fellow. There can be little similarity between her and this John from Nottingham.'

'Unless there is something unique about the murderer, of course,' Simon considered. 'Perhaps it is simply that he hates the bishop and wants to be there when the bishop is struck down?'

'Perhaps,' Baldwin said. He stifled a yawn. 'But after a lack of sleep last night, and all the exertions of searching for the fellow today, I think I must to my bed. I shall see you in the morning.'

It was later, as Simon entered the room to go to his own bed, that his words returned to Baldwin. Something about the idea of a demented assassin being in a specific place to witness the effectiveness of his murderous sorcery that stuck in Baldwin's mind. Yet even that could not prevent him from slipping into unconsciousness before Simon had even begun to snore.

Chapter Forty-Two

Exeter Gaol

Jen woke to a thin, grey light that scarcely managed to illuminate the far wall of the cell.

It was freezing down here. She tried to hunch herself into her clothing to conserve some heat, but it did little good. Not that it would matter. She was going to die down here, no matter what happened.

There was a part of her which wanted, oh, so desperately wanted, to think that this was all a clever scheme on the part of her Matthew to lull his wife into a sense of false security, so that he could remove her, and then install Jen as his lover. Perhaps it was only a plan whereby he would remove her from the public's gaze, and put her in a small cottage of her own near the castle, so he could visit her each morning, and his wife know nothing more of it? There were woman who lived like that, and although she didn't think it was completely honourable . . .

No! She had to stop that line of thought! He didn't love her. It had been in his eyes yesterday when he had told his men to bind her. It was not love in his eyes, it was not even feigned indifference; it was hatred . . . disgust – terror, perhaps – but not *love*. The sight of her repelled him.

'Sweet Mother, holy Mother Mary, save me!' she whispered. It was like having two lives: one in which she and her lover plotted to remove the sole obstacle to their happiness, a second in which she herself was the evil impediment to his joy, and the two lives constantly in dispute with each other inside her head. She didn't know which was telling her the truth at any moment. Just now it felt as though the story that she herself was at fault, that the sheriff had never desired her, let alone planned to leave his wife for her, was the more truthful, but in a moment she knew that the other side of her would return and scornfully remind her of the look in his eyes when they had passed in the screens corridor, or that time when he had met her at the top of the stairs and they had flirted . . . Which was true?

The door opened without warning, and she fled to the wall at the farthest side of the room. It was only a man-at-arms with a bowl of food, though, and he set it down near the door, as far from her as possible, before swiftly turning and leaving again.

It wasn't only the sheriff. All his men were terrified of her too.

Sunday, Feast of St Catherine[9]

Exeter City

John was already awake. He was bitterly cold, wrapped up in his clothes and with his blanket over him, but today would see the culmination of his efforts, with good fortune.

Others would have sat in the background and avoided any danger. That was not his way. It was important that he learned what happened. A man who kept away from the results of his work would never truly reach the highest level of knowledge. No. Far better that he should go and perform the operation while he could see the victim. Learn what he could from the work. Witness the result.

Robert le Mareschal had understood that. That was why he had agreed to go and view the last agonies of de Sowe. It wasn't perfect, though. The man had largely undergone his suffering out of sight of Robert and John. Better by far that the experiment should be nearer to hand, so that he could see what happened stage by stage.

The light was grey and dull. A good day to die, he reflected as he rolled over, trying to stop his teeth chattering, and let himself down from his attic with a small bump. In his hand he held the one figure. The others would lie up in the roofspace he had left. Later he would come and fetch them, when he was sure that he understood the impact of his magic. Outside, he stood a moment wrapping the waxen figure in a fold of his cloak.

Did he say a good day to die? No: it was a good day to *kill*. Especially that misbegotten son of a whore, Walter Stapledon.

---

[9] 25 November 1324

*

'So you slept a bit better, eh?'

Baldwin lurched to wakefulness, his eyes widening in shock as he heard Simon's voice. There was a chuckle as the bailiff walked round the room pulling on his shirt and hosen. 'If you want some breakfast before visiting the cathedral, you'd best hurry.'

'I'll be ready in a moment,' Baldwin said, rubbing a hand over his face. He felt rough and unrested, for all that he had slept long beyond dawn. He needed more sensible exercise, that was it. Less of this sitting in smoky taverns where the highest aspiration to hygiene was the annual replacement of the rushes on the floor; more riding his horse and practising with his sword. That was what he needed.

Not much chance of it here, though. Certainly not today. He had to get to the cathedral church to avoid insulting the bishop, and with his intention to refuse to accept the bishop's offer to become a member of the parliament, insulting him in any other way was beyond contemplation.

He got up from his bed, scratching idly at the bites under his armpit where some bug had got to him overnight, and gazed about him at the room, a wave of dissatisfaction washing over him.

In the last year or two he had spent too much time away from his own bed. He had a young child whom he wanted to see growing, and his wife had another baby in her womb even now. It was wrong for him to be here, miles away in Exeter, when she was alone at his manor. That was where he belonged, with her.

If he were honest, though, he should not be here in any case. His life was a fraud. Although he held the position of Keeper of the King's Peace, if his background as a Knight Templar became known the king would remove him from his post in an instant. And if the Templars had not suffered arrests and destruction, he would not be here. He would still be in the preceptory in Paris, a bearded knight ever training to return to the Holy Land to free it from the hordes of Moors who had overrun the Christian territories. Perhaps he would be dead, killed by a Muslim arrow or scimitar, in which case this new life was actually a rebirth of sorts. Perhaps he ought to think of new ways of working for the realm, to protect it from the ravages of barons like Hugh le

Despenser. He had been saved from the pyre . . . was it possible that he was saved for something more important?

'God's teeth!' he muttered, and completed his dressing. There was no more singular arrogance than that of a man who felt that his life had a mystical purpose to it. Clad in his red tunic, he went to join Simon and the coroner at their table.

The fire was sparking fitfully in the corner, and the smoke was forming an unpleasant pall beneath the roof. Baldwin cast a look up at it. The trouble was, so often a householder in a city like this found himself being passed off with rubbishy wood for his fires. There was sometimes little to tell whether a bough was of good wood or rotten, whether it had been properly dried, or whether it was simply wood that was bad for burning, like elm.

'I think that the good host of the tavern has been rooked by a deceitful woodseller,' he muttered as he joined his friends.

Rob looked at the fire. 'It's the fault of the boy who laid the fire. He ought to know what wood will burn and what won't.'

'And you're the expert?' Simon scoffed. 'You are hardly out of your bed in time to see the fire being laid when you're at home in Dartmouth.'

'You let the boy lie in his bed?' the coroner asked, his mouth full of bread. He cocked an eye at Rob. 'Didn't I tell you your duties last time I was in Dartmouth?'

'And I do them, sir. My master is making fun,' Rob said with a scowl at Simon.

Baldwin shook his head. 'Never let your servants get the better of you, Simon. If he's lazy, give him a good beating every so often. That's what he needs.'

'You may not think it much, but it's a lot better than other fires I've seen,' the coroner said. 'Anyway, you should pity those without a fire this fine morning.'

'There can't be many who survive without a fire at this time of year,' Baldwin said. 'I suppose that man Robinet may be without one, if he has taken refuge in some quiet little out-of-the-way place.'

'True. I was thinking of the girl, though. The demented one in the gaol. She'll be suffering for her illness.'

'Which? The one who killed the servant outside Langatre's house?'

'Yes. Didn't you know? She's in the sheriff's gaol. Poor little thing. The devil's got her, right enough.'

'Is she really lunatic, then?' Simon asked with a shudder. He hated the sight of the mad, drooling and shouting at people.

The coroner was largely of the same opinion. 'Yes. Thought the sheriff fancied getting inside her skirts so much that he'd appreciate her killing his wife to facilitate matters. Well, she'll have a while to reconsider her foolishness in his gaol, and then he'll have her neck stretched.'

Baldwin shook his head, appalled. 'That is barbaric, though. The poor chit has a demon in her, but the sheriff should be consulting people as to the best way to remove it, not trying to have her executed for something that is beyond her control.'

'Baldwin, you can't tell us that a mad woman who has killed her friend and now wants to murder the sheriff's wife shouldn't be kept secure.'

'Secure, yes – in a hospital where her demons can be exorcised without harming her any more. She is no more responsible for her actions in harming the other servant than we are, if she has a demon inside her.'

The coroner grunted affably. 'You are too kind-hearted for your own good, Keeper. Look, she must be guilty of some gross sin to be afflicted with this. Either some perversion or a crime. Why else would God have visited this dreadful punishment on her? Better, probably, that she is simply hanged.'

'What, would you punish the child for something she cannot be held responsible for? It is madness indeed to hang her for an act that was the responsibility of the demon inside her,' Baldwin declared.

'What would you do, then?' Simon asked.

'Why not bring her to the cathedral with us? Ask the bishop whether he can do something to cure her?' Baldwin said.

'You are joking!' Coroner Richard said. 'Think what harm she could do in the church with the congregation there.'

'We could do her a great deal of good, with any fortune,' Baldwin said harshly. 'The bishop should be able to drive out her demons and save her. After all, even if she did kill the servant, she cannot be held guilty. Remove the demon and see whether she could have done it on her own.'

Coroner Richard drained his cup, then leaned back and considered Baldwin, chewing the last of the bread ruminatively. It was a bizarre idea, but no worse than flogging the girl. And he couldn't help but remember how small and thin and frail she had looked when she had been knocked down. Little more than a child in reality. He swallowed and decided.

'Well, if you're serious, we'd best go to the castle and tell the sheriff that we want to try it.'

'Yes,' Baldwin said. And his eyes went to Rob.

At least it was only a short walk to the castle. But it was ruddy freezing, Rob told himself bitterly. The weather was miserable, too. Not wet, but it was surely colder than a witch's tits.

'Hi, boy. You getting the keeper's breakfast?'

He looked up to see the beadle, Elias. 'We've eaten,' he snarled. 'I'm just off to the gaol.'

Elias shrugged as Rob explained about the girl. 'Your master and his friends must be mad. Easier to just have her hanged. If there's a demon inside her, that'd let it out fast enough!'

Rob nodded as he carried on his way. Yeah, it would be better. At least he could have stayed by the fire then, rather than trudging through the cold and damp to the castle.

Waking, he looked about him sadly.

Walter had bought this place only a few years ago. At the time he had thought that his life was going to change, as he had repeatedly told Robinet over the last days until his death. Well, now it had changed.

Thinking about that sad little body lying before the door in Langatre's undercroft made him feel the sadness again. That man had been his only real friend for many years. When Robinet arrived in Exeter, the two of them had immediately felt the bond between them renewed, as though they had never parted. And, now they were parted for ever.

He left the place with a few coins from the purse on the window-ledge, walked the hundred or so yards to Cooks' Row, keeping a wary eye open for anyone who showed a little too much interest in him, and ordered himself a good meat pie. Eating it slowly, he went round the back to the little alehouse at the corner of two alleys. It was a rowdy place even at this time in the morning, and he knew that no one in there would be looking for him. The only people who could be on his tail would stand out too distinctly in here. It was the sort of place he could enjoy a form of anonymity.

Where had the murderous bastard got to? He had thought he could get some answers from Michael, but the interference of that pathetic imitation sorcerer had put paid to that. If he'd been able, he could have silenced Langatre, but there was no telling what Ivo would do while he was making the man shut up. Anyone with a stout staff was a threat to be considered when his loyalty was in doubt. And there was certainly no love between him and Ivo. No, none.

Where was John? With any luck he had fallen into a ditch and his decomposed remains would be found late in the summer. But there was no way to tell whether he was dead or not. Better to assume he was still alive for now, and find him. There was nothing he wanted more than to see John's head on a spike outside the city wall as a warning to all those who dared kill his friends.

If he didn't know where John was, perhaps the Watch had been luckier. A beadle could have stumbled over his corpse in the night. And if he hadn't, a beadle could maybe tell him what the city's officers had been doing overnight to hunt the bastard down.

He drained his cup and left the alehouse quietly by the little side door. Soon he was walking down the alley where Ivo and his mother lived, and when he came to it he stood in a doorway some distance away and surveyed the street, making sure that the measly little prickle hadn't thought to protect himself with a couple of roughs who would look for him in case he returned again.

No. There was nothing. Confident that the alley itself held no threat to him, he sauntered to the door and knocked.

It opened quickly, and Ivo stood gaping before him. A hand planted firmly on his breast gave him the hint, and he walked backwards, still silent.

When the door was shut, Ivo's mother, who had been huddled by the fire, turned and scowled. 'What do you want here?'

'Mother, I only want to learn what happened yesterday. Ivo? Did they get him?'

'No. After you disappeared we spent the afternoon searching high and low for him, but none of us had any luck. Half the time the coroner seemed to want us to find *you* more than the stranger.'

'Fortunately no one did, though. What are they going to do today?'

'They're not. They're fetching a demented girl to take to the bishop to see if he can exorcise her demons.'

'That would be worth seeing.'

Ivo nodded. He had seen plenty of exorcisms in his time. The shrieking and screaming was quite entertaining in its own way. As good as a hanging. This way, perhaps they'd have the exorcism and then the hanging later, both from the same girl. He was so taken up with his thoughts for a moment or two that he didn't notice the man's expression change suddenly.

'What day is it?'

Ivo shot a look at his mother. 'St Catherine's day?'

All knew of St Catherine of Alexandria. The noblewoman who refused to marry the emperor of Rome and defended her Christian faith even when they threatened to kill her on the wheel. She had disputed her religion with fifty philosophers and won, and had stood up for . . .

Robinet stood as the realisation struck.

'We must get to the cathedral!'

Chapter Forty-Three

Exeter Cathedral

Baldwin and Simon had a leisurely walk to the cathedral after their breakfast. Already the grounds before the great church had started to fill with city folk ready to join the Sabbath celebrations.

Practically every day of the year had its own saint to revere, and Baldwin knew that keeping abreast of which was due for honour on any day was a task that exercised some of the finest minds in Christendom. At the cathedral there was a good man who was paid a gallon of wine to call out all the different relics that were held there on the Monday after Ascension each year. It was a task that demanded a degree of perseverance on the part of the annueller concerned, calling out the piece of Mary's pillow, the splinter of the True Cross, the oil of St Catherine and all the other bits and pieces that made up the great treasury owned by the cathedral. The number of relics made Exeter a place of pilgrimage for people from all over the west country.

All too soon Baldwin saw the first of the black-robed canons appearing in his doorway as the bells began to ring, and then all the houses in Canon's Row disgorged their occupants. Entire households stood in the road, with the processions being decided by rank and authority: canon first, then vicars, annuellers, novices, servants, all clad in their robes ready for the service. They stepped over the open sewer that ran between their houses and the cemetery, and began to cross the grassy plain. A hog and two horses moved out of their way as the men passed around the new building work, avoiding the great stones lying all about, and making their way to the southern entrance. Only when all the choir had already entered did the rest of the congregation follow.

Inside it was serene, an odd silence compared with the anticipated noise of a working building site. None of the workmen was allowed to continue on the day of rest.

Baldwin and the others made their way to the northern side of the cathedral, where there was the altar dedicated to St Catherine, and stood about while the incense wafted and the singing of the choristers rose to the heavens.

Bowing his head beneath his hood, Baldwin listened to the service in the choir. The music was marvellous, as always. Although he had travelled widely and knew the forms of celebrations in the more modern and contemporary churches of France, Galicia and Portugal, he still felt most at home here in English churches, with their more restrained, simple services. In other countries there was too much extravagance, he felt. The plainer customs in English services were more suitable.

As always, the people standing all around were hooded and hatted respectfully. When the bishop came to raise the host up on high for all to see, they would bare their heads. There was a group of women near him, under the watchful gaze of a chaperon, while beyond them an older couple were sitting on folding chairs with leather seats and reading a book of hours together. The sole irritant to him was the woman behind him, who would keep up a relentless prayer for a son who had disappeared some years ago, which spoiled his concentration.

And then he saw the man: Robinet.

He was over at the southern wall with the watchman, Ivo. Baldwin recognised him immediately, and was angry to see the man here, flaunting his freedom in a church of God. It was shameful.

'Look, Simon,' he breathed. Simon followed his pointing finger and Baldwin saw his neck stiffen.

'Where's Sir Richard?'

Ivo had tagged along reluctantly, but he wasn't sure he understood what his companion was on about. There was some story about the man they'd tried to find yesterday actually being an assassin who was going to try to kill the bishop, which caught his attention, naturally enough. Where there was a job to be done saving a bishop's life, there was also a good fee to be earned as reward. He was sure of that.

But apparently the killer wouldn't have to be nearby. Would not be getting up close with a knife or anything. No, he would be a little distance away – but near enough to see the bishop.

'What, he going to use a bow in the cathedral?'

'Not a bow, no. But something quite as deadly.'

'As deadly as a bow?' Ivo said doubtfully, squinting up at him.

He didn't answer. The necromancer had to be here somewhere. Not in with the congregation, not if he was going to strike right now . . . and he *had* to strike now. It was the only thing that made sense, attacking during this special celebration.

There!

It was a fleeting glimpse of blackness up at the top of the wall, where the new construction joined the older section of the building. A flash of black clerical cloth, nothing more, and it was that very movement that told him he was right. Any other man would have stood still and watched the service. Only a man seeking concealment would disappear like that.

'He's there.'

Baldwin saw Robinet start to move towards the rear of the church, his eyes fixed skywards, and he turned to stare up, wondering what the retired king's man had seen.

'Simon!'

'I see him!'

The two pushed through the laity towards the back, but even as they moved they heard the door open and the steady tramping of the coroner's feet, the petrified girl bound at his side, his hand on her arm to stop her bolting. Immediately attention was diverted, and people craned their necks to see what was happening, some few, who were better informed, telling others that this was the mad girl who'd killed that servant over near the West Gate.

'Come on, Simon,' Baldwin muttered as he shoved people from his path. Then, at the rear, he found a clearing, and he hurried over it. At the back of the church there was a ladder set up, and he came to it just as the girl was dragged to the altar. Baldwin cast a look over his shoulder, then began to climb. Reluctantly: he hated heights.

It was fortunate that the ladder was only propped up against a lower section of the wall. While it looked high enough to Baldwin, and set his heart racing, there was a dread emptiness in his stomach as he looked overhead and saw how much higher the walls climbed.

'Come on, then!' Simon said enthusiastically as he reached Baldwin.

'Yes. Yes.' Baldwin gathered his thoughts and his courage and took a deep breath before gritting his teeth and making his way along the wall to another ladder. This one took them up to another level, and now Baldwin did not dare to look down. The sound of singing and prayer came to him, but only dimly, because there was an unpleasant rushing sound in his ears. He heard a wailing cry, and it distracted him long enough to make him glance in its direction. There, before the altar, he saw Jen kneeling while the bishop set his hands upon her head, the coroner nearby, his head bowed, but his eyes fixed on the child.

Turning away quickly, swallowing, Baldwin continued. There ahead he could see the king's man, and now he searched about for any sign of their quarry.

Up here, the walls were a mass of confusing blocks of stone. There was a great scaffold erected, with good poplar boughs lashed together, but the uneven nature of the building work made it difficult to see. The man could be anywhere along here, only a matter of feet away, and Baldwin would not spot him.

But then he did. He saw a sandalled foot between two lumps of rock. John of Nottingham was the other side of them, sitting in a vantage point where no one could see him, but from where he could see all that was going on below.

Baldwin signalled to Simon, and began to creep nearer.

It was perfect up here. John of Nottingham smiled to himself as he drew out the figure and gazed at it, wiping the brow smooth with a rough thumb. Down below, there was a sudden hiss and rush as all the congregation bowed their heads and pulled off hats or drew back their hoods, and the bishop lifted his hands high overhead with the host, praying.

John took the small antler pin from his purse and waited a moment, then set it at the figure's temple. He peered down again, and slowly pushed it into the waxen head.

At first he would have said that nothing appeared to happen. The bishop continued his prayer loudly, unfalteringly, and with determination, but then, as John pushed the pin all the way in, and felt the point at the far side of the skull, he was sure that he saw the bishop stumble over a few words. The host was set down on the table, and the bishop shook his head. Yes! It was working.

The efficacy was proved. He took out the pin, and held it over the figure's heart. Uttering a prayer of his own for the success of his effort, he was about to push it in when there was a scrape of rubble behind him. It urged him on, and the pin had just begun to penetrate the breast when a bright blue steel blade appeared in front of him. It flicked, and the pin was jerked from his hand, to whirl over and over, away from him, down to the floor.

'*No-o-o!*'

'Keep still, man, or you'll be joining it,' Baldwin said. 'Come round here, and don't be foolish.'

John was staring down in dismay. There was nothing on him. Nothing at all – not even a little knife to stab at the thing in his hands. Yet he must . . . he took the figure in his hands, and slammed it down on the edge of the wall in front of him. The head was dented badly. He did it again, and the head snapped off, falling to bounce on the floor of the cathedral.

'There!'

Ivo was behind Robinet when they both heard the voices behind them. Robinet stared, and then his brow cleared as he saw how he had walked past John without seeing him. He started off in a hurry, and almost knocked Ivo down as he hurtled along the wall to where John knelt, smiling up at Baldwin.

'Well done, Sir Baldwin. Where are the other dolls, though?'

Baldwin reached round the stone and gripped John's tunic. Pulling hard, he half pulled, half lifted the older man back to the more solid base of the cathedral wall. 'Where are they, John? You *are* John of Nottingham?'

'Yes. I am John, but I see no reason to help you. The others will be destroyed in time. You cannot stop me and my friends.'

'Why?'

'Why do you think! Because of the injustice daily perpetrated by those miserable bastards. The king was a supposititious child. You only have to look at his unnatural activities to see that! Look at his lovers. Forsaking his own wife he consorts with hedgers and ditchers, dancers and play-actors! And then he gives up the riches of this sovereign realm to his advisers the Despensers, and richly rewards the thieves. And asks your Bishop Stapledon to spy on the queen. Did you know that?'

'Enough! Come on, you're coming down with us. You have many questions to answer,' Baldwin said.

'Oh, yes.' John stared at him, a thin, gaunt man with a face like a skull. Baldwin could feel the strength of the man's intelligence as he met that firm gaze. It was almost as though John was trying to work upon Baldwin silently, by the power of his thoughts. It was alarming to see how he strained, as though by the mere exercise of will he could force Baldwin to change his mind and release him. A vein throbbed in his temple, and he brought his head down slightly, as though to add to the intensity of his stare.

It made Baldwin smile to see it. 'You may as well relax your overworked features, John. I do not succumb to witchcraft.'

They reached the ladder in short order, and Simon, knowing how Baldwin felt about heights, volunteered to climb down it first. He went, and when he was almost at the bottom, Baldwin and Ivo pushed the sorcerer towards it, Baldwin sheathing his sword ready for his own descent.

Suddenly John spun round, his fist catching Ivo full in the face. The watchman fell back, and would have toppled over the edge but for the attention of Robinet, who caught him and whirled him round, using his weight to pull him back towards the safety of the wall. Baldwin saw it, and his hand was on his sword-handle, but before he could reach it he felt something whip round his neck. It was a fine cord or thong, and on one end was fixed a small lead weight, so that it encircled his throat. Immediately John grabbed the second end and started to pull tight, strangling Baldwin.

If he had done that from behind, Baldwin would have been fearful for his life, but as it was, he took hold of John's hands and forced the older man to loosen his grip. Crossing John's wrists, he lifted them until the cord was over his head. 'It's too late for that.'

John responded by dropping the thong and grabbing at Baldwin's belt. The old man was astonishingly powerful for one so frail and thin, and he wrestled Baldwin towards the edge of the wall.

'*Baldwin!*' he heard Simon shout, but he had his mind on other things. He threw himself bodily backwards to the wall, striking his head on a stone, and suddenly he felt a great lassitude overwhelming him. There was a roaring in his ears, and his head was swollen, so he thought, to double or more its usual size. He was aware of being dragged a little, and then he realised that John had thrown himself over the edge of the wall, and his weight was pulling Baldwin towards the abyss.

'No!' he roared, scrabbling with his feet for any purchase, but they were already over the edge. There was nothing for them to grip. His hands were scratched as he tried to cling to the bare rocks, but the new dressing was so precise that he could gain no hold. Inexorably he felt himself sliding towards the edge and certain death on the floor below.

And then he saw Robinet at his side. Robinet drew Baldwin's sword and hacked down. There was a short scream, and Baldwin glanced down to see the bloody stump of John's left forearm waving, blood flicking in an obscene fountain. Still clinging to Baldwin's belt with his right hand, John stared up, and saw Robinet. 'Tell Matthew I shall see him with you in hell!'

The sword flashed down again. There was a spurt of blood that sprayed up and over Baldwin's face, then a hideous, damp sound.

Chapter Forty-Four

The Bishop's Palace
The bishop felt his headache begin to reduce as he sipped his wine. 'It was most peculiar,' he admitted.

Baldwin could say nothing to that. He was still only too aware of the great height from which he had nearly fallen. When he had reached the ground eventually, which had taken him some time, the ladder did bounce so, he had been confronted with the body of John of Nottingham, a tortured figure, oddly shrunken. At first Baldwin thought it was his headache and the sensation of sickness. Only later did he see that the man's leg bones had been thrust upward until they protruded from his torso, so immense had been the violence of his fall. It was Ivo who pulled the two hands from Baldwin's belt and threw them after their owner. Now the groin of his tunic was damp from the spurting blood as they had parted from John's body.

'Are you quite well, Baldwin?' Simon asked kindly.

'Yes, old friend. I am well enough.'

They were all in the bishop's hall: Baldwin and Simon, the coroner, and Baldwin's saviour. Baldwin had also asked Langatre to come to speak to them.

'So can you tell me what this was actually all about?' Bishop Stapledon asked.

'I think that it is quite clear,' Baldwin said. 'We know already that there was the assassination attempt in Coventry, when this John of Nottingham tried to make seven wax figures with a view to killing a number of men – among them the king, the Abbot of Coventry, a man called de Sowe and others. He succeeded in one killing, but then his assistant caught a fit of fear, and reported the matter to the sheriff. The sheriff tried to catch all those accused, but there were twenty-seven of them, and perhaps one escaped. John. He gradually made his way here, and found himself refuge in the city, where he managed to find a man who was inclined to help him. This Michael. Perhaps he knew what John intended, but it is possible he did not. Although I can quite see that it would look curious to any man to see how people died when John was near, it is possible that John had a control over Michael's mind. He was very strong-willed.'

'You mean that he did have some powers over others?'

'He tried it on me. At the time I thought he was trying to force me to release him so he could escape, but maybe I was wrong. It is possible he was bending me to his will without my knowledge, and that I was the unwitting associate in his last plot – to kill me as well as himself. If he had succeeded, he might have killed Simon too.'

'Why did he kill the messenger and take the message?'

Baldwin made a vague gesture with his hand. He still felt enormously weak after the near-death on the wall. Answering what seemed to him to be fatuous questions was hardly relaxing. 'He saw the messenger, and he recognised him, I expect. You yourself told us, I think, that the messenger had brought news of the attempt in Coventry. It is quite possible that in a city the size of Coventry a messenger would be a not common sight. Perhaps John saw James there, then saw him here, and feared that he was about to be arrested again. He killed the messenger to empty his purse, found the note from you and kept it.'

'Why?'

'I think Master Langatre is in a better position to answer than I.'

'Most magic, Bishop, relies on the use of God's own power and authority, as you know. But when there is some evil to be done, a magician would need more. He would need to have some tokens to give added force to his work. For him to harm you, he would have had to have taken some part of you – parings from your nails, perhaps, or some hair. Or, so I would think, an example of your writing on parchment. Such as your writing on the note in the messenger's purse.'

'So what happened to it?'

In answer, Langatre picked up the figure from the table on which it lay. Simon had pressed the head back on the neck, but now Langatre pulled it off again, and pushed his finger down into the body. 'Aha!' He pulled out a little roll of parchment. 'Is this it?'

The bishop tried not to appear too eager as he took it and unrolled it. With an expression of intense satisfaction, he rerolled it and put it into his purse. 'And the fingers?'

'Twofold purpose to that,' Baldwin said shortly. 'One: to provide human flesh which would perhaps aid him in some magic later; or, two: to torture poor James to learn whether or not he had been sent here with news of John. And, of course, once he was sure that he was safe, he could not permit the messenger to live, or James would have gone straight to the sheriff and told him all about John. So he died.'

'And the other man in the alley the night before?'

'He was walking in a place where John thought he might find James. He died as an example of mistaken identity.'

'I see. Then he killed this Walter of Hanlegh, because he was following him?'

'Yes,' Baldwin said. 'Although I am surprised that a strong, powerful man like Walter, a man used to serving the king, would have been so foolish as to let a murderer get behind him. I should have expected only a messenger, or someone else who had spent his life believing that he was safe from such attacks, to have succumbed to so simple a ploy.'

'Quite so,' the bishop said. 'Now, what of this girl Jen?'

'I would like to think that she might become cured, Bishop, but it is clear that she will never be entirely safe in the city here. She could have a fit at any time, and that would mean that Sheriff Matthew – and his wife – would know no peace. In any case, they would never agree to have her back in their household, so I think that there is nothing for her here. I would ask that you find a place for her in a convent, perhaps. Somewhere where the abbess has experience of looking after the ill?'

'I shall consider it. Certainly I feel sure that she is innocent of wanting to harm her friend. She has been weeping ever since I laid hands on her and demanded that the demon leave her. Yes. I agree.'

'I am most grateful, my lord. And now, if you do not mind, I would like to leave and return to my bed. Simon, would you help me? I still feel very weak.'

Exeter City

They had only walked a matter of yards from the cathedral close when Baldwin started to murmur to Simon.

'Did you like the tale? I set it up nicely, I think. What do you think?'

'I liked it, but only because I thought it was real,' Simon admitted. 'What parts were false?'

'There was little actually false, but there were some parts which were not entirely true. Ah, look, there is friend Robinet. How are you?'

'I am fine, Keeper.'

'Really? It occurs to me that I only met you after your friend had died. At the time there seemed no reason to doubt you, of course, but it is always a mistake to take a man at his word. Now so far as I know, Robinet was a tall, gangling walking man, a fellow used to strolling five-and-thirty miles every day. Yet you are stout and powerful, and you are swift to make decisions.'

'You appreciated my swiftness to decide to cut his hands off and release you.'

'Oh, yes. I appreciated that enormously. I did not appreciate your quick decision to torture Michael, though. Even if the reasons were good, your methods were atrocious.'

'If I had been successful, you would have thought otherwise.'

'Perhaps so. But tell me: why the deception?'

Walter shrugged. 'When your bailiff detained me, I already knew Robinet was dead. When we had eaten our pies he said he was going to have a look round, and when he did not return I went in search of him. When I saw my friend dead in that room, I was enraged; but then I realised that I might be able to turn it to my advantage. As a king's man, I have had to kill before, of course, and it does not scare me, but if my enemy knew of my skills, it might make it harder to find him. I thought that if he thought he had killed me and not Robinet, he might try to come to find me to destroy me as well, thinking that I was a messenger who also might have known of him. If he knew that I was the king's killer, and he had murdered the wrong man, he would be more likely to flee the city, and then I'd never catch him.'

'I see. So, what now for you?'

'I bought my little house here with a view to a new life. It would appear that events have conspired against me. Although I like this city, I do not think I could ever live here safely. I shall sell up and move away.'

'That sounds to me like an excellent idea,' Baldwin said. 'I would do so swiftly.'

'Very well. God speed, sir knight. And you, Bailiff.'

'Godspeed, Walter,' Baldwin murmured.

'Well?' Baldwin said a moment or two later. 'Does that clear things up?'

'Yes. A little.'

'Only a little?'

'There is still the first man to have died.'

'You do not think that my explanation will suffice?'

'No. No more than you do.'

Baldwin nodded, and then looked away. 'This is a sad story, Simon. I would appreciate your help in telling it. Come, let us find a friendly tavern.'

There was a favourite which the pair of them had used before, the Blue Boar, which lay a little way from the Palace Gate. Simon led the way, and soon they were sitting, legs stretched out before them, while a maid brought them large jugs of a sweet, light ale.

'Well?' Simon pressed him. 'What is this story?'

'It is the tale of an old man. He is sad, he is lonely, and he is guilty. His guilt comes from the night many years ago, eight or so, when he was the father of three little children, and owned a thriving business. He had a house in an alley not far from here. But he had extreme views. As a trader, he had friends all over the country, and one day he learned that a good, kind businessman and associate of his had died. Hanged when the king sent the whole posse of the county against one city. Bristol.'

'The tax riots?' Simon guessed.

'Exactly. And shortly after that, there were rumours from Exeter that a man here was fomenting trouble. The king had no desire to see his treasure wasted in another costly adventure, so rather than wait until matters got out of hand, he sent a man here.'

'Not Walter?'

'I am afraid so. Walter came, he saw the man, and saw how to remove this little nuisance. He went late one night, and set fire to the man's house. It killed his little children, and dreadfully burned his wife, but the man himself . . . well, he happened to be at the tavern that night. He knew nothing of it.

'This man suffered the torments of hell over his lapse that night. He was ruined, because his house was also his store and factory, and all his goods were burned along with his property, but he was also saddled with a bitter, vindictive and vengeful wife. There can be few more hideous lives than that of a man who feels such guilt. And he had even lost the love of his woman.'

Simon took a long gulp of ale. 'Will Skinner?'

'Yes. I don't know what happened that night, but I'd bet it was something irrational that simply made him snap.'

They finished their drinks and stood.

'We can leave him, Simon. We could return to the inn and leave the fellow alone.'

'We would never learn what made him do it, though,' Simon said.

'Do we need to? I am not so sure. And there is another thing,' Baldwin added, looking about him. 'Before Walter, or Robinet, whoever he is, managed to cut John's hands from him, John shouted at us. He said he would see Walter and the sheriff in hell. Plainly he hated Walter for ending his life . . . but I should like to know why the sheriff was mentioned in the same breath as the man who was killing him. Yes. You are right. We should speak to Will Skinner again and hear what he has to say.'

Chapter Forty-Five

Exeter City

It was only a short walk to Will's house, and once there, they asked Will to accompany them to where he had found the first body again, away from his wife. She appeared distressed to see Will being taken, but Baldwin was not of a mood to take much notice of her.

'I've told you all I can, masters,' Will said when he saw them standing in his doorway.

'We want a little more.'

With a bad grace the watchman jammed a hat upon his head, took up his staff, and joined them.

'Do you go the same route every day?' Baldwin asked.

'Yes.'

'It reminds me of a story. A man who had lost his family in a fire. Every day this man walked past his home. Every day he relieved that nightmare. Simon, how would you live with yourself if you had lost Meg's love and Edith and Perkin in the same night? It is hard to imagine how any man could cope. But he did. Until one night when he snapped. He was walking past his ruined old house, when what should he see but a man pissing in the ruins. It enraged him. Made him mad with anger, and he drew his knife and killed the man.'

'Not pissing. He'd puked. Right there where their bodies had lain.'

He could see that scene again in his mind's eye as though it was only last night. There was the little line of three bodies near the alley itself, all set out neatly, their faces yellow in the glow from the flames as his house burned, and then, as though there were only moments between the two occasions, he saw Mucheton heaving again, vomiting over them. Except no – they weren't there by then. It was some years since they'd died. 'But I thought he was throwing up over them. I

couldn't bear it. It was right where they'd been. And here he was . . .
Well, he fell back against the wall. I went up there, and peered through
the slats in the fence, and I could see where he'd done it. So I turned
to speak to him and almost fell flat on my face. He was right there,
passed out. So I . . . I don't know why, it was just in my head to do it.
I drew my knife and ran it about his throat.'

Simon studied the man. He remained still now, his hands gripping
the slats of the fence as he stared in at the house where he had once
been happy. And now all was lost.

'I have one more question, Will,' Baldwin said. 'The man you
killed in the undercroft. Why was that?'

'You think you know so much, don't you? You know *nothing*.
Michael, his father came from Warwickshire, all right? And Michael
is an old friend. When John tried to kill the king, the Sheriff of
Warwick was one of the conspirators. So when the whole thing went
wrong, he declared that John had died in prison, and freed him. He
told John to come here. He thought Exeter should be safe enough for
him. And then, of course, he arrived only to see the messenger he'd
last seen in Coventry. He assumed the man must be here to warn the
sheriff and others about him.'

'Which was a concern?' Simon questioned, thinking about the
bishop's suspicions about Matthew.

'We didn't want him to learn about John any more than the bishop.'

'So you assisted John in killing the king's messenger?'

'We saw him with that other man,' Will said. His voice had grown
cold, quieter and more distant, as he stared back at the house. 'I hoped
it was his friend. But I didn't know then . . . we knocked him out when
we took the messenger, and John cut off his finger to learn what was
in the purse and what the man had in his head. We knew that there was
something worth knowing – but he wouldn't admit it. So we had to
kill him. John was an expert in that. Throttled him with a little
weighted cord, and then hid the body in the garbage heap.'

'And you found him there,' Simon said. 'Why? That must have
brought attention to you.'

'I was sure he was a friend to that assassin. I wanted him to suffer
loss as I had. And to make him fear. John said to leave him concealed,
but I would not. Why should I?'

'This man, the messenger's friend,' Baldwin said. 'How did you know he was the one who had burned your house?'

'People saw him here about that time.'

'I see. And who told you?'

'Michael. He was trying to help me.'

'Of course he was,' Baldwin said sarcastically. 'He was so keen to help you that he destroyed any vestige of peace you could have found. So – did John kill the man in the undercroft?' Baldwin was listening carefully to each word, Simon saw. He didn't look at Will's face or eyes, he was noting every cadence of his voice instead, his eyes picking up on every twitch of Will's hands and feet.

'Oh, John had nothing to do with that. He left the room for a few moments, and I saw that man going in. I wasn't planning to kill him, I swear, but as soon as he sidled in, it was obvious he knew what John was attempting. So I followed him in. You know what was ironic? He thought I was only there because I was one of the city watchmen. He opened the door and let me in properly when he saw me. So I cut his throat for him.'

'Just so you could silence him,' Simon said, but then he understood. 'No! Because you thought he had set fire to your house!'

'It *was* him . . .'

Baldwin snapped: 'How do you know that?'

Will waved a hand, but then stated firmly, 'The messenger – James. He confirmed it. Said the king sent an assassin to Exeter to destroy someone who was creating trouble – me! The king didn't need that, not when he had just lost battles against the Scots, and had suffered from Bristol's rebellion. He didn't want any more trouble from the west. So he sent a man who killed my children. Well, Keeper, I've repaid him.'

Simon and Baldwin exchanged a look. It was Simon who wondered aloud, 'James the messenger told you that was the man?'

'No! He denied it, the lying snake! But he couldn't deny that the man had been here when my children died. I remembered seeing him just at the time, although then he was wearing the livery of a messenger for the king. It was clear, though. James could deny it was him, but who else could it have been? There was no one else in the city at the time. Didn't matter how much pain John gave him, he wouldn't change his mind, even though we knew the truth. He could deny that messenger's part all he wanted but I knew the truth.'

There was no one else in the city at that time who was so plainly a stranger, Baldwin told himself. That was why Newt was dead. It made him feel a dreadful heaviness of spirit to think that Newt could have been killed for such a reason – because he had been remembered in the area at the time of Will's disaster. And the man who was truly responsible, Walter, had escaped because he was unnoticeable. As a spy and assassin should be. His invisibility was his protection – and caused Newt's murder.

He preferred not to dwell on James's end. The poor fellow had tried to protect his friend, and his ever more desperate defence of Newt had only meant his death had been more painful and slower. At least it showed that James was a man of honour.

'What now, Will?' Simon asked.

He smiled. 'You arrest me and I hang. What else is there?'

Baldwin thought of this man's wife, scarred and maddened. Where was the profit in killing Will too? He shook his head bitterly. 'So you want to die too? What then? No. You go home, Will. There's been enough death already. But there is one thing I do want to know. Where are the other models which John made? Do you know?'

'No. He took them with him when he left the undercroft. I don't know where he went with them.'

Baldwin nodded, and waved dismissively. 'Go. There's nothing to be served by having you punished any further. Go away and try to have a life again. See if you can't cease hating, and try to start forgiving.'

'Forgive?' Will stared at him. 'Would you?'

Simon was intrigued when Baldwin stopped in the street, head down towards the cobbles, and then made off westwards beside the Fleshfold. 'Where now?'

'I want to talk to the man Michael. Let us go and visit him.'

It took little time to walk along the street to Michael's house. There was a beadle standing outside as they arrived, and Baldwin frowned and walked up to him. 'We wanted to talk to Michael Tanner – is he here?'

'No, sir. He's off at the castle. He was wounded by the madman here. Had his fingers cut off, would you believe? The sheriff himself ordered that he ought to be brought to safety.'

Exeter Castle

Matthew puffed out his cheeks. The reports he had received seemed to show that the man was dead at last, and thank Christ, the wench was out of his hair as well. Sweet Jesus, but the last week had been dreadful.

'Husband? Are you well?'

Alice had walked in behind him without his hearing, his mind was so far distracted with other matters. 'My love, of course!'

She evaded his encircling arms, walked to her chair and sat down, watching him cautiously. 'You did it, didn't you?'

'What?' His mind was still on the last issue from which he had been rescued, and he smiled openly. 'The girl? I swear to you on the gospels, dear lady, that I never so much as touched her.'

'You really swear this?'

'Of course I do, Alice. I could not look at a woman such as her when I have you, could I?'

Her relief was so palpable, it made his heart warm to see it.

'Now, my love,' he said. 'I think that when I next travel to London, I should like you to come with me.'

'Will you be going there soon?'

'There is a new parliament being called, and I think that I shall be asked go to it.'

She pulled a wry face. 'It is so very far.'

'And the roads are dreadful in the winter, I know. But it would be good for you to get away from this city for a few weeks, and it would make my journey so much more pleasing.'

'Very well, my husband. Of course I shall come with you.'

'I am glad to hear it.'

His pleasure was so entirely natural and unfeigned that she felt herself flushed with a warmth that rose from her belly and flooded every part of her. It was such a relief to see that he did indeed still love her.

It was ridiculous. She ought to have realised from the outset that her man could not have loved that wench. If anything, Alice should have instantly guessed the child was insane. Her behaviour was entirely demented, after all. Yes, in the future she would always trust her man. If Matthew was at all interested in other women, would he have insisted that she went with him to London? Of course not! He would want her far away so that he could go and visit the stews of Southwark alone and not have to explain why he had been out all night.

He was a lovely man. She adored him. No more nonsense about distrusting him.

There was a clattering of weapons outside, and she saw her man roll his eyes heavenwards. 'That fool! I swear I shall have him thrown into the gaol to rot for a week if he does that once more!'

'Sir Matthew?'

They looked at the doorway.

Sir Matthew groaned inwardly to see Sir Baldwin and that bailiff marching in. 'Yes?' he asked curtly. 'I am busy.'

'Yes. So am I. I would like to speak to you in private for a little,' Baldwin said tersely.

'I am listening.'

Baldwin smiled, but then turned to Alice. 'My lady, if you could leave us a little while.'

She shot a look at her husband. He was fuming, she saw, but there was no point in causing an argument here in the hall. 'Don't worry, husband. I have affairs too. Perhaps almost as urgent!'

Her barb had struck, she saw. The keeper and this bailiff both looked a little ashamed to have been so rude. It was all you could expect from an uncouth rural knight, she reflected as she left the room. Manners and chivalry came from exposure to Court and the fashions which pertained there. Sir Baldwin was too coarse to have spent time with ladies in a court.

With that happy thought, she left the hall and went about her business.

'Well? You have insulted my wife. I hope you have good reason.'

'My problem is whether I ought to arrest you myself, or merely tell the bishop about you and leave all to him,' Baldwin said.

Sir Matthew leaned forward. 'I could have *you* arrested for that. It is a gross slander to say that I deserve arrest! I could call my guard now and have you both taken from here and . . .'

'Call him in by all means,' Baldwin said, baring his teeth. 'But as soon as you do, this affair becomes publicly aired. Do you want your guards to know what you have been up to?'

'I have only ever done my duty. I think you should go now!'

Simon, watching from beside Baldwin, was taken by his demeanour. There was much bluster about him, but it was evident that he spoke more quietly, and that he did not call his guards into the room.

Baldwin nodded as though he was in accord with Simon. He walked to a stool and sat comfortably. 'Naturally some of this is conjecture – I do not know all the details – but I think I have put together the bulk of the story.

'This all began some while ago, didn't it? I do not know when you first became disillusioned with the government of the Despensers and the king, but you and others felt that you ought to hasten the end of a system that had done so much damage to the nation. Your friends found out about a necromancer of power, and they instructed him in what to do. He had to kill seven people. The king, the two Despensers, father and son, and several others from the nearby convent.

'When the attempt failed, because one man grew anxious and blurted the truth to his sheriff, he could hardly have known that the sheriff himself was in agreement with the band of conspirators.

'They were all arrested, and then, soon afterwards, released. Except for two. One of these was the necromancer himself, of course. The other was the man who warned of the attempt. How close am I so far?'

'Please continue. The story is fascinating.'

'John of Nottingham somehow managed to escape from the gaol. Yet – and this is the curious part – the gaol at Warwick is all but impregnable. I know it well enough. Be that as it may, John of Nottingham came here. And as soon as he arrived, he was able to find a man who could give him rooms. Not only that, but in the same house was a man who had the tools necessary for a necromancer to perform his trade. That was most fortunate. What was more, he was introduced to a man who would be happy to help him kill even a king's messenger, if ordered.'

'And I suppose you think all this was my plan?' the sheriff asked.

He had paled, and his hand gripped the armrest of his chair.

'Not all, no. But much of it. You wanted the assassination to succeed, didn't you?'

'I have come to this position because of the goodwill and support of my Lord Despenser. What would I want him harmed for?'

'There are many who fear him. Any man who can accumulate so much power in so short a space of time is to be feared.'

'So what exactly are you accusing me of? Trying to kill the king and his adviser? The man who had me placed in post?'

'Someone had to tell Will that his family had been killed by Walter. Who was it told him that? You don't want to say? Then let me guess. Perhaps it was Michael. I have a feeling that Michael is quite deeply involved in all this.'

'Why?'

'We have heard that he is here with you, Sheriff. Where exactly?'

'He is resting. I would prefer you didn't disturb him.'

'Why is he here?'

'I took pity upon him. Is that a surprise? He had his fingers cut off by that lunatic!'

'You mean the king's man? The man who was trying to catch the necromancer who was determined to kill your king?'

The sheriff nodded. 'So you condone torturing the innocent? Interesting.'

Simon reached forward and placed a hand upon Baldwin's shoulder. He could feel his friend's muscles writhing with eagerness to strike the sheriff, but then they became rigid. After witnessing the destruction of his order, Baldwin had a deep hatred of any forms of torture or injustice.

'How well do you know the Sheriff of Warwick?' Baldwin asked.

'This is all most interesting, Keeper, but I have matters of real importance to occupy me. I think our meeting is at an end.'

Baldwin stood. 'Then I shall leave you, Sheriff. But be aware that I will investigate any fresh murders with vigour. Especially if I hear of any harm coming to Will Skinner or to . . . Robinet. I feel sure I have an interesting story to tell my Lord Despenser. And the king, of course.'

Chapter Forty-Six

Exeter Castle

While they were talking, Alice walked out in the court. She had no friendly maid now, but she was content with her own thoughts. Apart from anything else, there was no confidante whom she could trust with news of her brother.

She had not seen him since Jen's slaughter of poor Sarra. He had appeared as though from nowhere that day, but then he had slipped away as she was taken up to Langatre's house.

It was probably for the best. Sarra had been able to take him food and drink on occasion, and she said that he had been very grateful, but since her death there was no one whom Alice could trust. Perhaps, though, it was better this way. She could not keep on following him, hoping against hope that she might see him in town. Better that they should keep apart, and prevent any additional risk to her husband. She had done enough to worry him already, poor Matthew.

But she would like to see her brother once more. Just to talk. She missed him.

Outside, Baldwin was about to cross the court when he saw Lady Alice with a maidservant. He licked his lips, hesitated, and then crossed to her. 'Lady, I am sorry for my rudeness just now. There were matters which had to be discussed.'

She did not pretend that she liked him. 'Sir Baldwin, you bullied me at Master Langatre's house, and now you have insulted me again. I have enough to worry about, after my maid tried to kill me, without worrying about you.'

'You are quite right. I am deeply sorry, my lady, and only hope that next time we meet, we shall do so in happier circumstances.'

'So do I.'

She watched him turn and walk from the place. All she felt, though, was an overwhelming relief that Baldwin and the bailiff had not realised that her brother was in the city. He – and she – were safe for now. Only her husband knew of Maurice, and he would not do anything to harm her brother while he remained in the city.

Sir Matthew had actually seemed quite relieved to hear that the strange person whom she was seeing was only a traitor and outlaw, and not a lover.

Thursday, Vigil of the Feast of St Andrew[10]

Polsloe Priory

Jen felt the shackles slip off her wrists and stood a moment rubbing her chafed skin. The sun was a thin, weakly reminder of summer, and in her thin tunic and worn cloak she was frozen.

'You are the mad girl from Exeter?'

This was a large, cheery woman with a red face and perpetual smile. Under her nun's wimple, her blue eyes twinkled merrily.

'I am called Jen,' she admitted.

'Good! At least you know your name. Come here, child. The bishop has asked us to look after you and try to make your demons leave you.' She spoke as she led Jen into the convent, under a great stone arch, and into a broad courtyard. 'So that is what we must do, isn't it?'

Jen nodded. Since the day she had been exorcised in the cathedral by the bishop himself, she had felt weary, but a little better. The only strange thing, to her, was that she could not understand why her love would allow her to leave Exeter. Surely he wouldn't wish her to be away from him for very long?

She was led along a pathway to a little chamber. 'This is your home now, child. You are to stay here with us until you are cured or God takes you to His own.'

That was all she knew. Matthew would soon have her out of here. He loved her.

---

[10] 30 November 1324

Wednesday, Vigil of the Feast of St Nicholas[11]

The Bishop's Palace

'Sir Baldwin, I am glad you could visit me one last time.'

The bishop sat at his table, and rose as Baldwin entered, waving to the servant behind him. Soon they were alone.

'You wished to see me?'

'Sir Baldwin, the date of the next parliament has been set. It will be early in the New Year.'

'And you still wish me to go?'

'Of course. Who else would be so able to serve the interests of our country so well? Others may offer their strong right arms in battle, but some, like you and I, must use our brains.'

'I do so already. I perform a useful function here, where I feel comfortable, and where I flatter myself I can do some good.'

'Sir Baldwin, you know already that the country is in turmoil. There are enemies of the king who would have him destroyed. You know this.'

'My Lord Bishop, I know well that I could be thrown into the turmoil. And I would die. I am a lowly rural knight, not some great baron. If I am hurled headlong into politics, it may cost me my life. What then would happen to my wife and children? Would you see them protected? Or would you watch another man take my little manor and deprive my family of their holdings?'

'This need not happen. If you are honourable in your dealings . . .'

'There are honourable men in parliament?' Baldwin asked scathingly.

'If there are too few, you could help! Become a member of the government, and do the good you crave!'

'One man against the rest?' Baldwin smiled. 'How refreshing that one can be so influential.'

'The king needs sensible, level-headed advisers. If you join his parliament you can do much good. Help him make the right decisions.'

---

[11] 5 December 1324

'By advising him to do whatever he wishes, you mean? His friends the Despensers would soon have my head if I recommended any action which they deemed against *their* interests.'

'You must appreciate the danger which surrounds the realm, Sir Baldwin. We are a small nation. The world's greatest army is only a few leagues over the sea. The king of France could attempt to invade us at any time, and can you imagine how well our host would acquit itself against his men? Armoured knights in their thousands. Bowmen from Genoa and Lorraine, men-at-arms from all over France, Lombardy, you name it, all will flock to his banner to take a piece of the profits of stealing our king's inheritance. Do you want to see that?'

'He has the best ambassador he could wish, yet he holds her prisoner.'

'The queen's loyalty is not absolute. Her brother is king of France. Which man should she support?'

'Her king – but he is the very man who has humiliated her recently. He must make amends.'

'And it requires men of standing and character to make sure he realises that.'

Baldwin smiled thinly. 'You think he would listen to a knight from his shires?'

'If enough in parliament said the same, then yes. He might.'

'What of you, Bishop? Would you support the queen?'

Stapledon looked away for a moment, but then said quietly, 'Yes. I would help anyone who could ease our affairs abroad.' He looked across at Baldwin and smiled thinly. 'Does that surprise you?'

To answer a question like that directly was dangerous. 'It was only a short while ago that you told me you had suggested that our queen's household should be dispersed. Then you told me that you thought you were to be asked to administer her estates in Devon and Cornwall. What is next? Her children to be taken from her?'

Bishop Stapledon nodded slowly. 'They are heirs to the English crown. They must be protected.'

'You would have them removed from their mother?'

'For their protection – yes.'

That was the moment when Baldwin changed his mind, he realised later. At the time he simply left the bishop without agreeing or refusing, but later he knew he would have to go. It was while he was sitting in his hall, his daughter Richalda on his knee, listening to her cooing and singing. The thought that the king could accept the advice of others and have his wife deprived of her children was so repugnant, it made him feel physically sickened. If the best advice the king was receiving led him to take his children from their mother, Baldwin could hardly do less good. He could sit back in comfort here in Furnshill and complain, easing his soul with the reflection that it would do little good for him to lose his own life and thereby lose his children. Better to be in at the fight.

'I will go,' he muttered.

'What was that, my love?' his wife asked.

Baldwin looked at her and then he smiled. The decision was made. His fate was sealed. 'Would you like to travel to London, wife?'

The road to Tavistock

Simon endured the ride to Tavistock without listening to much of Busse's talk. So far as he was concerned, the task was complete: Busse had been followed, and he had indeed tried to visit Langatre. It was a shame, especially since Simon was still convinced that Busse would make the better abbot.

It was a thought that remained with him all the way back, and for his part Busse seemed pensive too. Only Rob was his usual self, whistling tunelessly, talking and complaining about the length of the journey. 'Is it far now?'

'Be silent!' Simon snapped after the last plaintive cry. 'Christ in chains, you whine like a child!'

'It is very cold, is it not?' Busse commented, his cloak pulled tight about him.

Simon looked about him wonderingly. There was no snow, no hail, not even a fine mizzle, which was a blessing. 'It's not too bad.'

'You are not talking to me, Bailiff. Are you so concerned about my misdemeanours that you refuse to speak to me any further?'

'I don't know what you mean.'

Busse smiled quietly at that, and was quiet.

On this return journey Simon had acquiesced in the monk's wishes concerning their route, and now they were passing along the great road to Cornwall, passing through Crediton, then south-west along to the northern tip of the moors before turning southwards. As the sun started to sink in the west, they reached the little village of Bow, a place Simon knew quite well, and he was looking forward to stopping for the night. There was a windblown and sad-looking furze bush hanging over the door of the large inn at the centre, and he suggested that they pause for the evening.

Soon they were inside, Simon gripping a large jug of ale, warming it with the poker he had heated in the fire. Busse had a large mazer of wine in his hand, and he smiled with a sort of sad amiability as Simon tested his ale. 'You appear to have lost all confidence in me, Bailiff. Do you think that I will lose the post?'

'Oh, I don't know about that sort of thing,' Simon said uncomfortably.

'But you think that a future abbot should not indulge his whimsy by consulting a man like Langatre?'

Simon set his jaw, but he was no hypocrite. 'I do not suppose to understand the use of a man like him.'

Busse's brows rose. 'What do you mean?'

'A necromancer. A man who . . .' Simon's hand lifted, and he wriggled his fingers as he sought for the correct word. 'Who conjures demons to do his bidding. I'll have nothing to do with such things, and I don't understand why anyone else would. I fear such things too much to . . .'

'Simon . . . oh, Bailif! Do you think I would ask him to produce a black demon to go to Tavistock and carry away my brother de Courtenay?' Busse suddenly chuckled aloud. 'Oh, Bailiff – would that it were that easy! No, all Langatre can do is foretell a little of the future. Not that accurately, I dare say, but he is a useful man to speak to. It seems to clear any confusion. And I had much before I made this journey. I wanted to think more deeply about whether I wanted to be the abbot. I was not sure. In my humility, I wondered whether de Courtenay might not be a better man for the job than me. And that made me fear.'

'And Langatre put your mind at rest?'

Busse nodded, his eyes shining in the firelight. 'He pointed out to me that a man who was anxious about the awesome responsibilities of power would perhaps be better for our community than one who was utterly convinced of his fitness for the duty.'

'So a man who thinks he is right for a job is necessarily the worst man for it, eh?' Simon ventured.

'Unless it is a mason taking on a building, or a herdsman asking to look after the cattle!'

Simon nodded to himself. 'Or,' he added, 'a good stannary bailiff who finds himself promoted to a new post in a different town.'

'As I said on the way to Exeter, my friend, if you wish to leave that post and become a bailiff once more, I should be pleased to confirm it. What did de Courtenay offer you?'

Simon shrugged. 'What does it matter what he suggested?'

'Well, if he had asked you to watch me at every moment, and report back to him, then there could be some trouble for me. If you preferred him to me, that is.'

'You knew?'

'From the first moment after we arrived in Exeter when I turned and noticed that excellent servant of yours behind me. His stern visage is hardly inconspicuous even in a large gathering. So what will you do?'

'I cannot lie to him,' Simon said, aiming an idle kick at his snoring servant.

'No – but if you do not embellish, I will be content.'

Simon eyed him, and gave a slow grin. 'All right.'

Busse raised his mazer. 'A toast, then: to brother de Courtenay, and his patience, for I hope to be in post for many long years to come. And another toast, my friend: to the good stannary bailiff, and long may he endure on the moors with the tinners he administers!'

Chapter Forty-Seven

Monday, Christmas Eve

Exeter City
And as they drank into the long night, Will closed the door on his wife's petulant complaints, hunched his shoulders against the cold, and set off once more on his nightly route, up the great street from the South Gate, and right along the way to the Palace Gate. He passed down the alley, and when he reached the burned remains of his house he stopped for a long time and stood, staring, at the place where his children had lain.

His body was found the next morning, huddled in a corner of the path, not far from where Mucheton had been murdered. There was no sign of pain on his face, and no apparent wound when Coroner Richard had him stripped and rolled over.

'So what in God's name was there for him to smile about when he died, then, eh?' the coroner muttered to himself.

'Peace, Coroner,' Baldwin said. 'Just peace.'

Dartmoor
Maurice found a shelter as he walked down past Scorhill. For a man used to constructing little shelters, it was always easy to find a place. Always look for a fallen tree, look away from the wind, and imagine how someone else would make a refuge. This one was hardly the picture of comfort, and some of the covering had blown away, but it took little time to gather up more fallen leaves from about the place and replenish the roof of the little shelter, and for one man there was space to spread out inside.

This was not the direction the sheriff would have expected him to go, and he was moderately certain that he was safe here for a while if he wanted. After a few days he could leave and make his way to the coast, pick up a ride with a sailor there. There were no fishermen or traders who had much respect for the king. They deprecated his customs and tolls on all their efforts.

Soon he would be able to escape and make his way to France. And once there, he would find Lord Roger Mortimer and join his force.

There was nothing left for this country but war and death. And to the victor there would be a great spoil: England.

Maurice broke twigs and gave a hawkish smile. Yes. He would like to be with Mortimer when the lord returned. The rewards would be great.

But his levity was short-lived. The last weeks in Exeter had been sad. To have to say farewell to his sister had wrenched at his heart – and then there were all the strange events and the murders.

He was glad that the girl had been safe, although it had shocked him to see that the man who went to the hayloft to rescue her had been the same man who had killed the fellow in the undercroft that day. As old Will had lifted the latch on the hay loft, Maurice had grabbed his sword-hilt, ready to go and protect the child, but then he saw how kindly the old fellow had helped her down, and passed her his own old cloak, a dreadful, worn and threadbare one compared with the newer, but bloody one he had discarded in the alley after the killing, and Maurice had felt easier in his mind.

Trailing after the two, he was still bitter that the girl had been left in the loft all night. He'd returned to the place early in the morning to make sure that she had been released, and when he saw that the doors were still locked, he'd almost gone to open them and see whether she had escaped, but Will's appearance had saved him the effort. Typical, he thought, that a priest should leave the poor girl up there all night – but then she was probably warm enough, and safe enough from most dangers.

There would be more danger to come. He hoped she would be safe . . . and that his sister too would be safe from the risks of the war which was surely coming now.

He had taken his leave of her two days ago. At the time she had said that her husband was well enough protected because of his alliances with the king's advisors. And it was that which worried him most, because if she depended on Despenser, Maurice was sure that her husband would be viewed as an enemy by those who would come to seek Despenser's destruction. Like these madmen who proposed to remove him by means of mommets made of wax.

Fools! The only secure way to remove a man like Despenser was with a steel blade in the ribs, not some nonsense with a little lead or horn pin.

Still, provided he could return here to protect his sister before anything went wrong, the coming war should give him a chance to renew his fortune.

War could not come soon enough.

Marshalsea, Easter Term in the nineteenth year of the reign of King Edward II [12]

He shivered uncontrollably now. His unkempt beard was alive with creatures that bit and scuttled, making him scratch and rub until sores formed. After so long in gaols, he had the prisoner's contant cough, the bowed back and anxious, fretful expression, knowing that any day could be his last.

When he first came here, he tried to keep a tally of the days by scratching into the stonework of the walls with a rock, but that had soon failed him when winter arrived and day followed night without light. It was impossible to tell what was happening outside, and soon all seemed irrelevant. What was the point of reflecting on the world outside when all that mattered was in here?

It was four or five years now since Robert le Mareschal had been first arrested. At the time it had seemed to him that he would probably soon be rewarded, but although he had waited long for the news, nothing had happened. In those days, of course, he had still been away at Coventry. That was when he had stood up in court and made his prosecution.

Perhaps it was foolish to expect many of them to break down and confess, but how was he to know? He was unused to the ways of the king's courts. All he knew was, he had to stand and make his

---

[12] 1326

accusation. That was what Croyser had said, anyway, and the sheriff had appeared to be on his side. He'd been almost as nervous as Robert as they waited for the jury to arrive. It seemed that way to Robert, anyway.

And then the men had walked in. All the twenty-five who were still alive. By then, of course, John was long dead. He had died before the Easter term while he was in the sheriff's custody, the lucky bastard.

There was a rattle of chains further down the corridor of the gaol, and Robert le Mareschal's ears pricked. No. Nothing more.

Yes, all the twenty-five had stood there, the bastards, and even as Robert declared their crimes, telling how they had offered him and his master money, how they'd made the first payments, how they'd brought the wax and the linen to make the figures, and how their money had gone into the murder of de Sowe, they'd shaken their heads like saddened uncles called to witness the downfall of a favoured nephew.

So the jury, formed only of local men, had found them all innocent. Not one had been found guilty. Which meant that the man who had accused them must himself be guilty: Robert.

Never before had he appreciated the irony of an innocent man's making a true statement of another man's crime which a jury then found to be wrong. The sheriff had looked and sounded stern as he read out the verdict in the court of Gaol Delivery, and suddenly Robert understood that the reward for making his truthful statement was this: he should suffer the penalty which the men he had accused would have endured had they been found to be guilty. He was to hang.

The chains came closer. He huddled against the wall, too scared to move into the darkness in the corner of the cell.

There was a rattle in the lock, and the door opened. Two men stood outside, the gaoler and the sheriff. 'Come on, you're all right,' Croyser said.

It made him almost fall to the floor with relief, he was so comforted by those few words. 'Oh . . . oh . . . oh, sir . . .'

'Get up, man. Come on!'

He allowed them to lift him. The gaoler put a hand under his armpit and hefted him to his feet, and he was walking, climbing stairs, shuffling along corridors, his ossified joints complaining at every step, his muscles, so long unused to effort, almost giving way.

'Here.'

The gaoler stopped him heading towards the main exit door, and instead he was taken to another door. There was a noise outside, a feral, thumping, pounding noise, and he couldn't place it at first.

Then he knew it. He understood. Turning, he would have fled, but the gaoler held a chain from his shackles, and even as he felt himself soil his clothes as the terror came back, Robert found himself being pulled backwards into the daylight, in front of the large crowd who stood stamping on the ground in their annoyance at the delay; dragged on his belly to the ladder with the rope dangling above it.

And his last thought as the life was choked from him was that the look on the sheriff's face was relief. Because at last he had removed the last witness to the crime in which he had been a conspirator.